KILLING OF A KING

KILLING OF A KING

DEVIN REED

Killing of a King

Published by AuthorSource Media
www.AuthorSourceMedia.com

ISBN: 978-1-947939-42-4
Printed in the United States of America

PROLOGUE

Timmond held his infant daughter against his body as he closed and locked the door to his small home for what he believed to be the last time. He stood where he was for a while, staring up at his house. Memories of his life in this house came flooding back to him. Good ones at first, but then the bad ones crept in. The most recent ones. He shook his head to clear them away, then grabbed his son's small hand and started away from the house. He stopped at a nearby bush, dropping his son's hand, and reached inside, fishing out a small, wooden box. He slipped his key inside, then, dropped the box back into the bushes. Grabbing his son's hand again, Timmond led him away from the house, without looking back.

He was done with this place.

It was dark, but the moon and stars were just bright enough to see by. Very few lights shone in the windows of the houses he passed. That was what he wanted. That was why he left this late. He didn't want anyone to see him go.

Timmond let go of his son's hand and adjusted the pack he had slung over one shoulder. Most of his possessions had been left in his house, but small children required a lot of necessities, so his pack was very heavy. Before he was able to grab his son's hand again, he saw a figure walking toward him. Even though he couldn't see well enough in the dark to identify the man, he immediately knew who it was. He stopped and let the newcomer reach him.

"So, you really are leaving," David said. It was more a statement than a question.

"Yes. I told you I was going to. Didn't you believe me?"

"I did believe you, but I was hoping you would change your mind. You've lived here your entire life. Everyone you know is here. You really want to leave that all behind?"

It took a moment for Timmond to answer. He looked around at the houses that surrounded him. They were well built, simple structures. Squat, with low ceilings. Most of them were perfect squares. Many houses had small trees in the front yard. Timmond had climbed almost all of those trees in his youth. He would never see these houses or trees again.

"Yes. There is nothing for me here anymore."

"But what about the Paladins? What are we going to do without you?"

"You don't need me. Someone better than me will lead them."

"There is no one better than you!" David shouted. Timmond couldn't help but cringe. He was afraid David's shouting would wake people up and that was the last thing he wanted. Timmond glanced around at the nearby houses, but all the windows stayed dark.

"I am going, David, and nothing you can say will stop me."

"Listen," David said, his voice going quiet once more. "I know that what happened was terrible, but you can't allow it to make you lose your faith."

"Too late," was all Timmond said. Then he grabbed his son's hand again and walked passed David.

"Wait!" David called out. Timmond quit walking, but he didn't turn around to face his friend.

"Where are you going?"

"As far away from Zion as possible."

"Think of your children! Can they make such a journey? Are you going to make Aiden walk the whole way to wherever you are going? He's only three!"

Timmond hadn't thought about that. His only thought was to get away from here, but he had begun to second guess his decision to leave this late at night. But not for long. After a few moments, his resolve came back. "I will buy a horse and wagon in the first town I come to."

"But we have horses and wagons you can buy here. Turn around. Go home. Wait until morning. I will help you buy everything you need tomorrow. Just don't leave in the middle of the night."

"No." Timmond knew he was just being stubborn. What David said made sense - it would probably be better for the kids - but despite all that, he knew he wouldn't wait. Timmond couldn't spend one more night in this city. "I don't want anyone to know I left."

"Everyone will find out tomorrow," David insisted.

"By tomorrow I plan on being miles away from here." Timmond started walking again. It seemed that David had finally given up, because he didn't say anything else. He just stood there and watched his friend walk away.

"David," Timmond suddenly said before he had gotten too far. David looked up expectantly. "Don't follow me. I don't want anyone to know where I am going. I want to forget this place. I want to forget my past and start all over. I will start a new life with my kids far away from the memories."

Without another word, without looking back, Timmond left.

1

Dorn was walking down the elaborate palace hall toward his room, planning on going to bed, when he spotted a man slipping into the king's bed chamber, shutting the door behind him. He hadn't really been paying attention to his surroundings as he strolled down the corridor. They were so familiar to him that he needn't look where he was going. He didn't notice the elaborate carpets his feet walked upon, or the beautiful murals on the walls. His thoughts had been on his comfortable bed when they were interrupted by the man.

Dorn halted in surprise. It was nearing midnight, but the hallway was well lit with torches, so he knew he wasn't mistaken. Who was the man dressed all in black sneaking around the castle? He obviously wasn't supposed to be there. Not even thinking to call for the guards, Dorn made his way to the king's room and slowly cracked open the door.

He peeked through the door; the room was pitch black. He opened the door a little wider and crept inside. The light coming in from the open doorway did little to illuminate the room, and he saw nothing but blackness. He listened, but heard nothing. He made his way to the closest torch on the wall, not needing light to show him the way, for he knew the king's chamber well. It was too dark to see the fist coming at his face.

The punch knocked him to the ground, the force taking the breath from his lungs. He sat on the floor, stunned, his back pressed against the wall, and his jaw throbbing.

Suddenly he felt searing pain in his stomach. He reached down and felt something warm and slick. Blood…his blood. He had been stabbed.

He saw the man rush through the door into the hallway. Dorn thought he had to be delirious, for when he caught a glimpse of the man's face in the torchlight, it looked to have a yellowish tint to it. *I must be seeing things*, he thought. *People don't have yellow skin.* If he hadn't been so scared and in pain, he would have laughed at his own foolishness.

The man's steps could be heard clearly on the tiled floor of the palace as he ran down the corridor. Then there was a sound of commotion in the hallway. People were shouting, metal was clanging. More footsteps could be heard rushing down the hallway. The guards must have spotted his attacker.

After a few minutes four soldiers dressed in the palace guard's red uniform burst into the king's chamber. One of them lit a torch on the wall and spotted Dorn. He rushed to him. "What happened? You're injured!"

Dorn struggled to speak. "There was a man… dressed in black. I don't know what he was… doing here. He… stabbed me, then ran away."

"King Michael has been murdered!" cried one of the guards. Everyone looked to the bed and saw the king lying in his own blood. One of the guards turned and pointed at Dorn. "Murderer!"

"No…Not me…It was… the man in black," Dorn asserted. He groaned in pain. In all his years, he had never felt pain like this.

"Where did he go?" the guard who had come to him asked.

"He ran out into the…hall. I…heard commotion outside."

"Let's go!"

They left Dorn bleeding on the floor, their only thought to catch the assassin. One hand clutching his wound, he slowly crawled to the hallway to get some help. Every movement throbbed. He looked down the hallway ahead of him, then to the left and right. The hallway was deserted; there was no one in sight, not even the king's personal guards. *They must be chasing after the assassin*, he thought.

With a sigh, Dorn gave up, collapsing in the doorway to the king's chamber. He knew he was going to die. The pain was so great that he almost welcomed the release of death. He regretted only that he was unable to help his king. Maybe if he had been a little quicker, he could have saved him. Who was he kidding? He was no fighter, he was only one of the king's personal servants. What could he have done to help him? No, it wouldn't have made any difference. His beloved king would have been murdered anyway.

Dorn felt worthless and alone. His vision started to blur, and eventually, he blacked out.

*   *   *

They were arguing again. They didn't realize that seven-year old Dorn was in the other room, listening, just like he did almost every night. They were speaking in loud whispers, trying not to wake up their son who they thought was asleep in his room down the hall, but Dorn could hear every word they said.

"That is the third person you've healed for free this month," his mother complained, and Dorn could picture her face turning red with anger. "How do you expect us to live if you don't receive any payment for your services?"

"They didn't have any money," his father replied gently. He was always gentle, always calm; the complete opposite of his wife. "I'm not going to turn someone in need away because they can't pay. Anyway, they said they would pay me when they could."

"Everyone says that," Dorn's mother snapped. "The entire city knows that they can bring their sick here and all they have to do is tell you they don't have any money and they get your services for free. Is that any way to run a business?"

"I don't know what to tell you honey. I just can't send people away. It is their lives we're talking about here. What kind of man would I be if I just let them die because of money?"

His mother didn't say anything for a second. "You're a good man and that is why I love you. But this can't go on. We're living in poverty as it is. I work as hard as I can at the laundry, but it just isn't enough. I can't take it anymore."

"I know, I know."

*   *   *

Dorn's eyes opened. His vision was blurry. He didn't know where he was. He couldn't make out his surroundings. Suddenly, he saw the face of a woman as she leaned over him, peering into his eyes, silver hair falling around her face. She looked kind. She smiled when she realized he was looking at her.

"How are you feeling Dorn?"

The pain in his abdomen had lessened, but it wasn't totally gone. He felt weak.

Dorn opened his mouth to reply, but no sound came out. His vision dimmed, then darkness overcame him once again.

*   *   *

"I heard you and Momma fighting again last night, Papa," Dorn said as he walked to the market with his father the next day. The sun was bright and warm, and Dorn and his father took their time.

"Did you?" his father asked.

"Yes."

His father didn't say anything and didn't look at his son. He just kept walking.

"Do you really think Momma will leave us?"

His father didn't answer for a moment. He sniffed. "I don't know, son. I hope not."

The boy looked up at his father. Dorn thought that he sounded sad. "Is it because we're poor that she gets mad at you?"

"Partly."

"What's the other part?" Dorn pressed.

His father sighed. "It's because…"

They heard a loud crash ahead of them and a man's voice yelling. "Stay here," Dorn's father ordered and immediately sprinted up the street towards the sound. Little Dorn ignored his father's order and hurried after him. The boy struggled to keep up with his father's long strides.

They entered into a large square. There were numerous people milling about a broken, tipped over carriage. They heard a man hollering, obviously in a lot of pain. Dorn's father made his way through the crowd, gently pushing people aside, explaining he was a healer, with Dorn right on his heels.

When they finally broke through the throng, what they saw shocked them both.

King Miles was trapped under his own tipped over carriage, writhing and screaming in pain. Only the king's upper torso was visible. The horse that was pulling the carriage had also fallen over, and it was squirming on the ground, struggling to get up, since it was still tethered to the carriage. The horse's neighs were frantic with panic.

Despite his shock, Dorn's father didn't hesitate long. "I am a healer," Dorn's father assured one of the guards. "I am here to help."

"Okay, good." Dorn could hear relief in the guard's voice. "So, what do we do?"

"First, we need to get him out from under the carriage. I can't tell how badly he is injured if I can't see his whole body." As usual, Dorn's father was calm under pressure. He had once told Dorn that a healer must keep other people calm, and to do that he had to stay calm himself.

"It's no use," the guard said. "I've already tried lifting it. It's too heavy."

"Of course, it's too heavy for just one man. You're not thinking straight. You need to settle down. There are dozens of people here. Let's get them to help us lift it."

The two men recruited several of the bystanders to help them lift the carriage. The horse got to its feet as they lifted the carriage upright. Dorn could see that the carriage door was open. That must have been how the king had fallen out.

The men set the carriage down and the healer rushed to the king. Dorn's father gasped.

The carriage had pinned the king at his waist. His hip bone was crushed flat, as were his legs, down to the knees. Dorn saw the king's plight and cried out. His father told him to turn away from the sight.

The king looked down at himself. A look of horror crossed his face. "Oh no!"

"Calm down," Dorn's father said soothingly. "Just relax. You're going to be just fine. We're going to fix this. Just lay back."

Despite the horrible shock King Miles must have been going through, Dorn's father's words seemed to sooth him. He laid back and breathed easier, though his face was very pale. "My legs are crushed," the king moaned. "I can't feel my legs."

The guard, suddenly recognizing the healer, knelt down beside the king.

"You're going to be just fine Your Majesty. This is Blake, the famous healer. He has healed hundreds of people in the city, including my wife. I know he can heal you, too. Just hang on Your Majesty. Just please hang on."

*   *   *

And he did heal the king. Although he would never walk again, Dorn's father saved his life that day. Blake had to amputate the king's legs, but with an advanced surgical procedure, he was able to sew the king's lower legs to his hips, creating shorter, yet movable legs. He looked odd and couldn't walk, but the king was comforted to know he regained some movement and still had a semblance of legs.

In payment, King Miles moved Blake, his wife and his son into the castle. He appointed Dorn as his personal servant and hired Blake as the royal healer. Dorn's parents stayed together, living long, happy lives once money was no longer an issue.

Dorn and the king became very close. He went everywhere with the king, always on hand in case His Majesty needed anything. Sometimes they would just talk for hours. Dorn enjoyed those talks most of all. He came to realize that the king was just a normal man with a lot of responsibility who feared that he wouldn't be a good ruler. The king wanted to do what was best for his country, and Dorn respected him for that.

He also became good friends with the king's son, Michael who was a couple years older than the prince. Of course, Dorn had a lesser station in life, but those things didn't matter when your years on the earth were still in the single digits. When Dorn wasn't working, he was with the little prince. He thought of the royal family as his second family, especially since he spent more time with them than his father and mother. His parents didn't seem to mind. They hoped that he would rise higher in life than they did.

Now, Dorn was grown and his parents were gone, along with the king he had served so faithfully for so many years. The man who had been killed that night was his dear friend, the former prince who had become king after his father's death. He had kept Dorn on staff as his personal servant during the regime change.

*   *   *

Dorn opened his eyes again. He was still lying in the same bed as before. He looked around the room and saw several other beds in neat rows. The white walls were bare, nothing adorning them. His abdomen still hurt and he looked down to see a white bandage wrapped around his torso. An older woman with silver hair, dressed in white entered the room carrying a tray. She came up to him, smiling. He recognized her as the same woman he saw when he had woken up before. He recalled that she was the head nurse of the palace, but he couldn't bring her name to mind.

"Awake again I see," she said. Her voice was pleasant. "I hope you plan on staying with us a little longer this time. I brought you food in case you had woken up. Are you hungry?"

Dorn was famished. "Yes. And thirsty too."

The nurse handed him the tray of steaming hot soup and bread. There was a mug of water as well. He hurriedly ate and drank everything. "Where am I?"

"You are in the clinic," the nurse replied. "You were brought here just in time, too. Your stab wound was very serious and if the guards had been a little slower, you wouldn't have made it. You would have bled to death."

"And King Michael? Were you able to save him?"

The nurse looked down. "No." She took a moment before she continued. "He was never brought to me. He was dead by the time he was discovered. I am sorry. I know who you are. I know what great friends you two were."

Dorn felt tears streaming down his face. "I've known him since I was just a child," Dorn said softly. "We grew up together."

"I know." She put a hand on his arm. "I know. I am so sorry."

Dorn had a thought. "Queen Laurel! She must be warned! The killer could come after her! We must send someone to protect her!"

"Calm down," she replied. "She has already been told. As you probably know, she went to the annual Veteran's Banquet in Rindley with the prince and princess to honor all the soldiers in the army. We sent a messenger to her and they have told her the news. She sent word back that she wanted to see you as soon as possible, since you were the one who discovered the king and saw the murderer."

"She has already been informed and sent word back?" The nurse nodded. "How long have I been asleep?"

"Three days."

"Three days!"

"You were severely injured. Your body needed time to heal itself, so it shut down for a while to regain its strength. That is why you were famished when you woke up."

"What has been done with King Michael?"

"He was sent, in secrecy, to her majesty. She wanted the body with her, but she doesn't want the kingdom to know of his murder just yet."

"When do you think I'll be strong enough to make the trip to see her?"

"I don't know. How do you feel?"

"Let me see," Dorn replied as he swung his legs over the side of the bed. He set his feet down on the floor and hesitated. He looked at the nurse. "Where's the latrine?"

The nurse pointed to a door on the far wall. "Through that door over there."

Dorn got to his feet and immediately felt light-headed. He wobbled, and the nurse rushed to steady him. "I'll help you get there, just lean on me."

"I guess I'm not quite strong enough to make the trip yet, huh," Dorn quipped as they made their way through the door and into a small room with a bench that had a hole in the center. She helped him sit on the bench and left the room. In the doorway she paused and said, "Give me a holler when you're finished and I'll help you back to your bed."

As soon as she shut the door, Dorn felt tears streaming down his face. He hadn't had the chance to grieve for his dear friend. The tears weren't only for himself though; they were also for the royal family and the kingdom. King Michael was a fair and just ruler who always put his people first. Everything he had done as king, he did for the benefit of his subjects. The people loved him for it.

Almost all the people loved him. There was one person in the kingdom who despised the king. *Would he have had King Michael murdered? Would he go that far?* Dorn just didn't know.

Two days later, when he was feeling strong enough, Dorn was on his way to Rindley to report to Queen Laurel about what he knew about her beloved husband's murder.

2

Prince Easton met the man dressed in black behind one of the tents that were set up just outside the small village of Rindley. The soldiers who took part in the ceremonies and games stayed in this enormous camp, for the town wasn't big enough to hold them all. Easton often wondered why this celebration was held in this backwater town every year. There were much better places for such an event, like the capitol city, Tosun. At least in Tosun there were decent taverns that catered to the high class. In Tosun he wouldn't be surrounded by lowly soldiers and smelly horses.

Now, the camp was silent and dark, for it was late at night, and even on holidays, the captains of the army still upheld the curfew. The sky was full of clouds, which was fortunate, because it blocked out all moon and starlight, making it easier to avoid being seen. The camp was in a huge, flat, grassy field that provided no cover. If someone saw him meeting with his contact, his plan was finished. He shivered. The night breeze was cool, and it carried with it the smell of horse manure.

Despite the yellow of the man's skin, he didn't see his contact until he was right next to him. Easton scowled as he almost bumped into the strange man.

"You could have said something!"

The yellow-faced man just smiled.

This strange man made Easton feel very uncomfortable and he longed to go back to his room at the inn. But he had to finish this meeting.

"What took you so long to get back here? You killed him four days ago."

"I had to lose the castle guards," the assassin hissed. "They were tracking me, so I had to come a round-about way."

The prince shivered. Even this man's soft whisper was creepy. It reminded him of how a snake would talk. It fit the assassin perfectly. He hoped this conversation wouldn't take very long.

"Well, how did it go?"

"Haven't you heard?"

"I know you killed him," replied Easton. "But how did it go? Did you have to fight the guards on the way out? Did anyone see you? What did my father do when he saw you?" Easton grinned wickedly. "Did he scream? Did he beg for his life?"

"No. He was asleep. He didn't even know it happened." An amused expression crossed the yellow face at the sight of the pitiful prince's angry expression. "Another man came into the sleeping chamber while I was still in there though. A thin, balding man, probably mid-forties."

"Ah. That would be Dorn. He is my father's pathetic personal servant. He was also a great friend to my father. He never liked me. What did you do to him?"

"I gutted him."

Easton laughed at that. "I guess that makes up for your blunder with my father. I wish he'd been awake when he died, though. He should have known what was happening to him."

The assassin held out his empty hand.

Prince Easton pulled a heavy bag of gold out of his cloak and handed it to the mysterious man.

The assassin held the bag of gold out before him as if making sure it weighed enough. Finally deciding it was the correct amount, he put the bag into his cloak. "When do we leave?" he hissed.

"Tomorrow night. I have a few more things to take care of before I go."

"I will be here at midnight."

Easton was about to reply when he realized that the man was no longer there. Easton had been looking right at him and the man simply vanished before his eyes! He shivered again as he turned around and walked back to town. How did the man with yellow skin do that? It wasn't natural.

He didn't see the shadowy figure in the darkness following him.

*   *   *

Queen Laurel looked up and saw Syth, her dark-skinned protector, standing in front of her. She hadn't heard him come in. She never did. For the thousandth time she was glad he was on her side.

She was sitting at the desk, drumming her fingers on the wood as she waited impatiently for Syth to return and give his report. "What did you find out?"

"I followed the prince like you asked me to." Syth had a slow way of speaking, like he was making sure to pronounce every word perfectly. "He didn't know I was there. Neither did his yellow-skinned friend."

The queen sighed. "I knew he had something to do with his father's murder! He has been acting strange ever since we arrived in Rindley. How could he…" She started to sob. This was just too much. She forced herself to stop crying. After a few moments she was finally able to regain her composure. She wiped her tears away from under her blue eyes and pulled her long blonde hair away from her face. "Did you hear what they were saying?"

"A little, My Queen. I dared not get too close to the assassin. I heard Easton asking questions. He wanted details about the murder. You will be happy to know that the king was asleep when it happened. He did not suffer."

Laurel was shocked. "He wanted details? How heartless can someone be? It was his own father!" She paused. "Well, it was a good thing that he didn't suffer. And I'm glad that he died ignorant of his murder being ordered by his own son!"

"What will you do now, My Queen?"

That's a good question, she thought. She didn't answer right away. "I need to confront him about it," she replied finally. "I need to hear it from Easton's own mouth. Please send for him first thing in the morning."

"Aren't you afraid he will kill you too?"

The queen barked a laugh. "Ha! He doesn't have the guts to do it himself. He had to hire someone to murder his father while he slept, because he couldn't do it himself. He wouldn't dare harm me. Especially not with the entire army right outside town. I need to know why my husband is dead. What has driven him to such rage?" She paused, remembering an incident from years ago. When she continued, her voice was breaking. "Then, I will have him arrested and executed for his crime." She buried her face in her hands and started to cry again.

Without a word, Syth turned and left the room.

*   *   *

Dana looked up as her younger brother, Prince Easton, entered her room. There were tears streaming down her face. She had been lying on her bed, crying. She didn't think she had ever cried so much in her life. In fact, she didn't think it possible that a person could have so many tears. Dana had never imagined she would lose a parent when she was only twenty-one years old. She loved her father very much, and she didn't know if she would ever get over his loss.

"It'll be alright, Dana," Easton said gently as he sat on the bed beside her. He wiped her tears away with his hand. He ran a hand through her dark hair. Besides the difference in their hair and eye color, she looked just like her mother. Everyone commented on her beauty.

"I have some information about father's murderer," her brother said. "I plan to track the killer down and avenge father. Then, when I return, I will take the throne and rule this kingdom with you beside me. Together, we can make father proud."

Dana sniffed and sat up. "Track him down? Easton, the assassin got into the palace without being noticed. You know how many guards there are. He fought off the guards and escaped, all by himself. I don't think you could track him. And even if you did find him, do you really think you could *kill* him? No offense Easton, but I don't think you would stand a chance. You would just end up getting killed too." She started sobbing again.

"I've already thought of that," her brother replied gently. "I would like to take Jaden with me. I would feel very confident in my mission if I had him at my side."

Dana sniffed and wiped her tears. "You know he doesn't like you," she said. "I don't think he would agree to go."

Easton gave her a sour look. "Couldn't you just order him to come with me? He does whatever you say, does he not?"

"Yes. But because he wants to. He is not a slave, Easton. He is free to do whatever he chooses. I've told him as much. He chooses to do as I ask him."

"But you're the princess!"

"You know I don't let that go to my head, Easton. I don't take pleasure in ordering people around like you do."

"Fine." Easton said, clearly not pleased with the way the conversation was going. "Can you at least ask him?"

"Okay. I'll ask him. But I already know what he'll say."

At that, her brother stood, turned, and left the room. Dana got up and went to find Jaden.

*   *   *

"Dorn, my friend," the queen said as she embraced the man. Dorn had arrived early that morning and went straight to the queen. She smiled warmly at him. "It is so good to see you. How are you doing? Are you healing well?"

They broke their embrace and looked at each other. "Yes, My Queen. Physically, I feel fine. The pain from the knife wound is gone. It is the emotional wounds that will take a while to heal, I'm afraid."

"Ah yes. He loved you very much. You were his dearest friend. I'm so sorry. I would like to keep you employed as my personal servant if you'd like."

"I would like that," Dorn said. "But how are you doing? I can't imagine how hard this is for you."

"To tell you the truth, I'm surprised I am able to stand right now. All I want to do is lie down on my bed and cry until sleep comes. But, I'm the queen. I have to be strong for my people. Still…I miss my husband terribly. I miss him so much my stomach aches. I need justice to be served, but it will come at a price." She gestured to the chair in front of the small desk against the far wall of the room. "Please, sit down."

Dorn did as the queen asked and watched her as she took a seat at the edge of the large bed. The bed took up most of the room. The innkeeper had given her the best room available, but it was still small and cramped.

Dorn was confused. "A price, My Queen?"

"Tell me what happened that night. I'm told you saw the man who killed him."

Dorn noticed the change of subject, but he didn't press the woman. "Yes, I caught a glimpse of him. I was in the hallway outside the king's chamber when I saw a man sneak into the room. Fearing the worst, I followed him, not waiting to call the guards. I should have. I got there too late. The room was pitch black. The darkness wouldn't have hindered me, for I know the king's chamber well, but it apparently hadn't hindered the assassin either. Before I could take five steps, I was knocked to the floor. He stabbed me in the stomach and left me to die. As he left the room, I could see his face in the torchlight coming from the hallway. His skin was *yellow*. I heard fighting in the hallway, but I heard he got away."

"It's true," the queen said. "The assassin got away. But I know who hired him."

Dorn could see the pain in her eyes. "Who?" he asked hesitantly.

The queen didn't answer right away, and Dorn didn't push her. He could tell she was struggling. She swallowed. "Easton," she finally whispered.

"Oh no." When Dorn was lying in his sickbed, he had wondered who could have ordered the king's murder. Only one name had come to mind. Prince Easton. He didn't tell the queen that though. "How can that be? Are you sure?"

The queen nodded. "Yes. I had Syth follow him last night when he went out to the solders' tents. He saw him meet with someone and over-heard their conversation. The man Easton met with had yellow skin. They discussed the murder and Easton gave him a bag of gold."

"I am so sorry, My Queen. Does Princess Dana know?"

The queen shook her head. "I've tried to get up the courage to tell her, but I can't. She already hurts enough. This news will kill her. She and Easton are very close."

"I know. Princess Dana is the only person I have ever seen him get along with. What will you do?"

Queen Laurel cleared her throat. "I've already decided to send for the best group of mercenaries in the land. You probably know the one I'm talking about. They are led by a man named Tim."

"Ah yes. You couldn't ask for a better group. They will track down the yellow man and dispose of him, no doubt about it. What will you do with Easton?"

"I will have justice." She saw the look on Dorn's face. "It must be done! It kills me to even think of, but I can't let this pass. If it were anyone else, we would have them killed without a second thought. He must pay for his crimes." She took a deep breath. "I will confront him today."

"Is there anything I can do to help, My Queen?"

She forced a smile. "No."

"Then may I ask a favor?" She nodded. "May I be allowed to accompany this band of mercenaries? I don't know what kind of assistance I can provide, but I feel it is my duty to help find this man."

"I understand. I will tell Tim that I wish you to accompany him." She smiled again. "And Dorn, if I were the assassin, I would fear for my life when you caught me."

Dorn smiled and took his leave.

*　　*　　*

Prince Easton saved Queen Laurel the effort of finding him. A guard knocked on her door and announced that the prince wished to speak to her. When he entered her room, the queen was sitting on her bed, thinking. She had been trying to build up the courage to confront her son, and now that he was standing in front of her, she was left with no choice. She didn't know if she was ready.

The room was small and felt a little cramped with both of them inside. Her son opened his mouth to speak, but Laurel interrupted him. "Why did you do it?" she demanded.

Easton hesitated. "Do what? What are you talking about mother?"

"You had your father killed!"

Easton stood there, frozen. He swallowed. "What makes you say that? You honestly think I would have my own father killed?"

"No," she admitted. "I had no idea you would stoop to such a level, but last night I had Syth follow you. He saw you talking to the infamous man with yellow skin. He heard your conversation."

He backed away from her. "He isn't here now, is he?"

"It's just you and I," she assured him. "Why did you do it?"

"You want to know why I did it, mother? You really want to know?" He stepped toward her. He seemed to be gaining confidence. "I loathed that man! I was never good enough for him. Everything I ever did was wrong. He hated me!"

Queen Laurel stood up. "He loved you!"

He took another step toward her. "Did he, mother? Did he?" Laurel was surprised to see tears streaming down her son's face. "If he loved me so much why was he going to give the kingdom to Dana?"

That surprised her. She slowly sat back down. "What?"

"Oh, you didn't know? A couple months ago he came to me and told me. He said I was mean and cruel and selfish and that I would ruin the kingdom if I were king. He told me that even though I am the rightful heir, the people didn't deserve a man like me as their king. He said they deserved *better*. 'Dana is what a ruler should be' he said. That's not how it's done, mother! That's not fair! I'm the prince! I'm the eldest son! I should get the throne!"

"So you killed him? What are you going to do next? Have me killed? How about your sister? Are you going to have her killed now that she is going to get the throne?"

He was sincerely shocked. "Kill Dana? Do you know nothing, mother? Dana is the only person on this earth who cares about me, who accepts me for who I am. She doesn't try to change me. It's not her fault that father chose her. She didn't ask for it. Do you honestly believe that I would harm her?"

The queen didn't answer his question. "How did you expect to get away with it? What is your plan?"

"I guess I can tell you. You cannot stop me now. I am going to leave. I am going across the sea to chase after the man who killed my beloved father. I will catch him and return with an army at my back. I will bring my allies here to hunt down the rest of the people who planned my father's murder. The people will welcome me with open arms for avenging their beloved king. And if they don't, if they decide that they don't want me as their king, I will use that army to take the throne."

Easton began to pace around the tiny room. "I am well aware that the common folk don't like me. I don't want riots erupting once I have the crown. I must protect my people, after all, and so I found an ally to help me keep my kingdom."

"Protect your people? You care nothing for the people! You care only for yourself!"

"The people care nothing for me!" Easton shouted. "Why should I put them first when they wouldn't even blink an eye if I had been the one murdered? They probably would have rejoiced if it had been me!"

"You brought that on yourself," the queen said quietly. "I have watched you grow up into a cruel and selfish person. No matter what your father and I did, you never changed. It broke our hearts to see the man you have become." Easton had stopped pacing, so Queen Laurel stood up to face him. "My only comfort is that he didn't know you were behind his murder. The people hate you because of the way you treat them. They hate you because of the choices you made. It is your own fault."

"Well," Easton said, "my fault or not, I will be the king. I will not let father or the people rob me of the throne."

"And what of your sister? What will you do with her? After you leave I will tell her what you have done and why. She will know that your father chose her over you."

Easton didn't answer right away. The thought of his sister knowing he was the one who had their father killed obviously pained him. When he did speak, he spoke so quietly the queen could barely hear him. "I will give her the same choice that I give you. She can accept me as king and rule with me, or she can reject me and claim the throne for her own. But know this Mother, I will not be denied my birthright." With that, he turned and left.

*   *   *

The queen sat back down on her bed after the conversation with her son. She was shocked, hurt and confused. She couldn't help but remember him as a little boy. They had had so much hope for him. He had the love of his parents, not to mention his older siblings and the palace staff. He had the influence of a wonderful king to teach him how to rule the right way. Although she didn't know where she had gone wrong with Easton, she still blamed herself. It troubled her greatly.

Then, once again the memory of that horrible day from long ago came back to her. The king and queen had known that Easton was responsible, even though he had always denied it. Only Princess Dana had believed him innocent, but Laurel had always known. But she couldn't prove it.

"My Queen?"

She didn't answer.

"My Queen?"

This time, Laurel looked up to see Dorn standing next to her chair. "Yes?" she finally answered.

"Are you alright? How did things go with the prince?"

She looked at Dorn. "The prince?" Suddenly, she awoke from her dazed condition. "The prince!" She stood up and walked out of the room, her strides quick and purposeful.

"Where are you going My Queen?" Dorn asked breathlessly as he struggled to stay beside her.

"Has my son left yet?"

"Yes. He left a few minutes ago."

The queen looked at him. Did you think to stop him? Did you call the guards?"

"My thoughts were of you. As soon as I saw him leaving the inn, I came straight to you. I am sorry."

"Oh, it's not your fault. It's my own. I sat in my room sulking like a child while my murderous son gets away. He couldn't have gotten very far. Does anyone know which direction he went?"

"I will ask around, My Queen."

"Thank you, Dorn." She stopped him before he turned to leave. "And Dorn, could you please have someone send for Tim and his mercenary band?"

"Yes, My Queen," Dorn replied, then took his leave, calling for guards to find prince Easton. The queen continued in search of in the captains of the royal army. They were going to need to prepare for war.

3

Aiden flinched as an ax thudded against the soft wall of the house he was leaning against, embedding itself just inches from his head. He was having trouble fighting his fear. He had lost track how of many times he had almost died since this battle began. The rush, the terror, and the excitement was a feeling unlike any other. He looked over at Layne, with his duel axes slashing through bandits with lightning speed that belied his large stature. He appeared calm and confident. Watching his best friend's calm face, one could almost forget there were over a dozen men trying to cut them down.

He was brought out of his thoughts by the sight of an enemy rushing towards him, an ax raised high. Aiden braced himself, twisting to the left as the man reached him. Aiden turned and stabbed the man in the back with his sword as he flew by. The big bandit didn't make a sound as he hit the ground, dead.

Aiden pulled the sword out of the dead man and turned to face the other bandits, only to realize there were none left standing. Their bodies were lying all over the ground. Not one of them had escaped. Aiden sighed, relief flooding through him at surviving his first real battle. He spotted Brione walking towards the largest house in the village. The mayor of the town, the man who had hired them to rid the town of the bandits, had barricaded himself and his family inside when the battle had started.

"So, what did you think of your first job?" Layne asked as he came up to Aiden. He bent down and wiped his axes clean on the grass. Aiden was panting while his friend's breathing was even and calm. Layne was taller than Aiden by three inches, with a muscular build and dirty blonde hair. He was twenty years old, two years older than Aiden, but the two became fast friends when Aiden's father took Layne and his brother into the mercenary group after their parents died.

Aiden turned around and saw the usual big grin on his friend's face. "It was fine," he answered, his own expression serious. "Just another day on the job."

"Yeah right. I saw the look on your face; you were terrified."

"Don't listen to him Aiden," said Layne's older brother, Dustin. "At least your pants are still dry, which is more than I can say for Layne on his first job."

Dustin looked like an older version of Layne, only his hair was brown instead of dirty blonde, and he had a slighter build, but he had the same handsome facial features as his younger brother. He also had a more serious disposition, yet he could joke around if the situation arose.

Aiden laughed. "Seriously? Why haven't I ever heard this story before?"

"Because it's not true," replied Layne, glaring at his brother. "Dustin, why do you have to make up stories to make me look bad?"

"There are a few reasons," said his brother. "One, because I'm your older brother and it is my job to pester you. Two, I'm trying to encourage Aiden; your first job is a big deal after all. And three, because it's true. You *did* wet yourself on your first job."

"I did not!" Layne's face betrayed him.

"For some reason, I believe Dustin," said Aiden, still laughing at his big friend.

"Of course you do," Brione, the commander of the group, second only to Aiden's father, Tim, said as she approached them. She had a thin, yet shapely body and long brown hair framing her beautiful face. It was easy to underestimate her in battle because of her looks. That was a fatal mistake many men had made. She was strong and quick and a match for any man in battle. "Dustin always tells the truth." She looked at Layne. "Unlike some other people I know. I don't even have to know what you are talking about to know that Dustin is right."

"We're talking about how Layne wet himself during his first job last year," said Dustin with a grin.

"Dustin!" Layne yelled. Aiden laughed even harder.

"Well," replied Brione, "I didn't hear anything about that, but if Dustin says it happened, then it probably did."

"You never heard about it," said Dustin, "because I never told anyone to save Layne from embarrassment." He gave Layne a little shove. "I pushed him into a pond so that no one would know."

"So why are you telling them about it now?" cried Layne. He slugged Dustin in the arm.

"Ouch," said Dustin, but the grin never left his face. He rubbed his arm. "To keep you from getting a bigger head than you already have."

"Like it could get any bigger," Brione muttered to Aiden.

Layne looked exasperated. "Here I am, trying to be a good role model for Aiden, trying to be someone he can look up to, and you go and tell him about that. He just turned eighteen. He's still very impressionable. We have to be careful about what he sees and hears."

The other three laughed.

"Well, what's the count?" Dustin asked Brione.

"We killed seventeen bandits, and the mayor paid us ten gold pieces per bandit."

"Not bad," said Aiden.

Layne gave a snort. "Not bad? We should be getting paid a lot more than that for putting our lives on the line for these people. We could have been killed! Haven't you guys ever thought about doing bigger and better things with our skills?"

"Helping other people is good work Layne," Brione argued.

"I know, and it's not that I'm not glad we're helping, it's just that we could be making so much more money doing something else. Like living in the capitol for example, being a great knight. Having all the ladies shower us with favors as we march off to battle against the country's foes. Returning victorious, our horses weighed down by the spoils of victory, the women basking in our glory!"

Dustin looked at his brother. "Being a knight isn't like that. They really don't get very much glory. Less than most people think."

Aiden's jaw dropped. "You were a knight?"

"Yes," Dustin replied.

"How come you never told me? Does my father know?"

Layne gave Aiden a face. "Of course he knows. You think the great Tim wouldn't know something like that about someone he hired to work for him?"

"Why don't you ever talk about it, Dustin?" Aiden asked. "Brione, did you know about this?"

"Yes," she replied. "I am second in command. I know nearly as much as your father about what goes on around here."

Aiden pressed. "Why don't you talk about it, Dustin? It must have been exciting."

Dustin sighed. He didn't seem like he wanted to discuss the matter. "Not really. It's a lot of ceremony and not much else. It was a steady wage, which was nice, but it wasn't for me. I don't like to talk about the past. I'd rather focus on the here and now." With that, he walked away to chat with some of the townsfolk who had emerged from their homes.

"That's no reason not to talk about something," Aiden said to himself. He turned to Layne. Why'd he leave?"

"I don't know," Layne shrugged. "He doesn't talk about it even with me."

"I'll have to ask my dad when we get back home."

Brione looked at Aiden. "My advice is, don't push it. He obviously doesn't want to talk about it. If he wanted you to know, he'd volunteer the information. Until then, drop it."

Aiden reluctantly agreed with her.

"So," Layne asked, "how many bandits did each of you take down?"

"It's not a competition," Brione replied at the same time as Aiden blurted out, "Three!"

"Only three? I took out six," Layne said with a wide grin.

Brione sighed. "You're a bad influence on Aiden, you know? We shouldn't be proud of the people we kill. It's a difficult task we have and should only be done when absolutely necessary."

"I didn't say anything about killing," Layne argued. "I said 'take down.' There's a difference. And anyway, it isn't really about the bandits, it's about how much we were able to help the townsfolk. It turns out that I helped them twice as much as Aiden."

Brione shook her head. "You're hopeless." Layne just grinned at her. She turned and left them.

Aiden looked at his friend. "You enjoy teasing her, don't you?"

Layne chuckled. "What can I say? It's what I'm good at. It's probably the one thing I am better at than fighting."

"Oh, I can think of others."

"Like what?"

"Lying."

Layne gasped in mock horror. "Me? Lie? I never lie!"

Aiden couldn't help but laugh. "Yeah right."

"There are three things I am very good at and lying is not one of them."

"Oh yeah?" asked Aiden. "What are they?"

"One is fighting, the second one is teasing people and getting under their skin, and I'll tell you about the third thing when you are older."

Aiden couldn't help but laugh at that, too. Layne always made him laugh. That was one reason Aiden liked him so much. The only problem was, sometimes it was hard to tell if he was serious or joking.

"Well," Aiden said with a grin, "at least you got a little of your own medicine. Dustin got you pretty good."

"Yeah," Layne admitted. "I taught him everything he knows. If it wasn't for me, that guy would never even crack a smile. He'd be just like Brione."

Brione and Dustin walked back up to them. "Well," said Brione, "it looks like our business here is almost done. The townsfolk offered to pay us extra if we dispose of the bodies for them, and I agreed."

The people in the country of Blanderly burned the bodies of the dead, so the four friends set up a large pyre, returned what little valuables the bandits had on them to the townsfolk, and burned the seventeen bandits' bodies. After they were finished Brione said, "Let's get back home." She smiled at Aiden. "Tim will be interested to know how his protégé did on his first mission."

They left the town heading west, the townsfolk watching them go, calling out their thanks.

"See how much the people appreciate what we did for them?" Brione asked Layne as they walked.

He nodded.

"And you still say it's not worth our time?"

Layne just grunted, not saying yes or no.

None of them noticed the girl standing in the shadows of one of the houses, watching them go. Her gaze followed one person in particular.

*   *   *

The early spring day was warm and bright as they traveled through a forest, the sun streaming through the branches above their heads. Only Layne spoke as they traveled. The other three mostly kept their thoughts to themselves. Birds were singing and small animals were rustling in the bushes. A squirrel chattered at them from a branch as they traveled underneath. A world at peace, Aiden thought. A world that knew nothing of the confrontation that had just taken place. A confrontation that had cost seventeen men their lives.

They cleared the trees and arrived in the hill country where they had their base of operations an hour later. It was a small stone fort set at the top of the highest, treeless hill, offering a view of the country surrounding it. It had been abandoned when Tim found it a couple years earlier. The structure had one square, squat building made of stone, surrounded by a six-foot high stone wall. The wall had two openings, one on the front and one on the side, neither of which had a gate. There was a lot of space between the building and the wall, so that's where the company trained and spent most of their free time. The building had two doors, one in front and one in back. It had rooms enough for everyone to have their own, although they were small and cramped. There was also a dining area and a main foyer for the group to meet in.

When Aiden walked in the door he saw the new recruit, Zach, standing in the foyer. Zach looked at Aiden but said nothing, his dark face an expressionless mask. Zach very seldom said anything, and he hadn't told Aiden anything about himself, but he was the best fighter Aiden had ever seen. He wielded his two short swords with a quickness unmatched by anyone Aiden knew, including has father. Still, Zach gave him the creeps, with his intense stare and mysterious past. Aiden felt that every time the dark man looked at him, he was judging him, and he didn't necessarily like what he saw. Yet, his father trusted him, so Aiden tried to trust him too, however difficult he found it.

"Where is my father?" Aiden asked Zach.

"In his room," Zach replied in the deep voice and strange accent that the group seldom heard. He spoke slower than anyone he had ever heard before. It was weird to hear someone who moved so fast speak in such a methodic manner.

"Thanks," Aiden said over his shoulder as he hurried to talk to his father. Brione and the brothers stayed in the foyer.

As he passed his little sister's room, the blonde-haired girl rushed out of it and crashed into him, almost knocking him to the floor. "Aiden!" she cried as she threw her arms around him. "You're back! I was so worried about you. Are you hurt?" She ran her hands over him, searching for wounds. Aiden grabbed her hands.

"I'm fine, Veronna. Don't worry," he said as she hugged him again.

"How was your first job?" she asked as she backed away from him. "Were you excited? Were you terrified? I know I was worried about you."

"It was good. And yes, if you must know, I was a little scared. But I was with Brione and the brothers, so I was safe enough. You were probably in more danger than me anyway. You had to be here with Zach."

He grinned at his joke, but could tell by the look on his sister's face that she was not amused. "He is just down the hall you know," she scolded. "He could have heard you."

"It was just a joke," Aiden said.

"I don't think he has much of a sense of humor."

"Then he won't fit in here very well I'm afraid," Layne put in as he came up to them.

"Oh Layne," Veronna replied and smacked him in the chest. "Listening in on other peoples' conversations again?"

"Hey. I can't help it if you two are blabbing loud enough for the entire fort to hear. If you don't want people listening, then speak quieter." He looked at his friend. "Oh, and by the way, Zach did hear your little comment, Aiden. I was in the room with him at the time and I heard it clearly."

Veronna paled a bit at that and looked down the hallway. She couldn't see Zach. "You should go see father," she advised Aiden. "I know he's anxious to talk to you."

Her older brother grinned. "That's where I was going when you tackled me."

"Oh! Sorry." She brushed at his clothes that she had wrinkled when she hugged him. "There, now you look more presentable."

Aiden laughed and continued down the hallway to his father's room. He stopped in front of the door and glanced back down the hallway. Veronna and Layne were watching him. He was strangely nervous to talk to his father about his first job. He mustered up his courage and knocked. He waited for his father to answer before he opened the door.

The room was sparsely decorated. There was a small bed against the far wall, a desk with a chair in front of it, a wash basin and a small dresser. The only other thing in the room was a picture of Aiden and

Veronna that Tim had a master painter make for him sitting on the desk. There was nothing on the wall, no rug on the floor. Aiden had asked his father one time why he didn't decorate his room more. He was a commander of a fighting force, Aiden had pointed out, albeit a small one. He should have more in his personal quarters. He had told Aiden that the band had too little money to waste on such things. He was perfectly content without them anyway.

He looked at his father. The big man was standing by the small window. In his late thirties, Tim was still strong and fit. His hair was light brown. His brown eyes - looking at Aiden at that moment with pride - were sometimes gentle, sometimes hard, depending on the situation. Now, they were full of love and…what? Sadness? Looking at his father's face was like looking at a mirror through time for Aiden. He resembled his father strongly.

"Aiden my boy, come inside. Shut the door." Aiden did so and his father beckoned him to sit on the chair. Tim stood in front of him. "How did it go?"

Aiden smiled. "It went well, father. I was scared silly, but I made it."

Tim looked deep into his son's eyes. "Now I want you to tell me the truth. Did you kill anyone today?"

Aiden looked confused. "Yes," he said hesitantly.

Tim nodded. "I see. Tell me how you felt when you killed them."

Aiden thought about it for a moment.

"It's okay," his father said. "Take your time."

"Well," Aiden said after a moment of thought, "at first I didn't feel anything. The bandits were trying to kill me. I simply fought in self-defense. I couldn't think of anything but staying alive."

"I understand," his father said. "But how did you feel after the fighting was done?"

"Well, I was glad to be alive." His father chuckled at that. "But then, on the way back here, it hit me. These people were human beings, just like me. They probably had families and friends that cared for them just like I do. It was a devastating revelation.

"But then I dismissed that thought. Those men were dangerous. They hurt other people for their own selfish reasons. I realized that society would be helped if these people weren't around to cause havoc."

"Did any of them surrender?"

"No."

"Bandits usually don't. They know they are headed for jail if they are captured. And then, if their crimes were bad enough, they will be executed. They think it better to die fighting, no matter if the odds are stacked against them. But I am glad to hear that you felt that way, Aiden. Killing is serious business. It can be devastating because they are human beings, but at the same time, they are bad people who hurt the innocent, and we can't allow that. That's why it is so important to be very careful who we kill. We only kill in self-defense or in defense of innocent people. If justice is served in killing, then we do it. But it can still be hard sometimes."

"What if those bandits would have surrendered?" the younger man asked.

"Then I would have let them live and taken them to jail."

"I think I would have too," Aiden said.

Tim smiled, pulled Aiden to his feet and hugged him. "That's what I wanted to hear. You are a good man, son. You will be a fine leader of this group one day."

"Not anytime soon I hope," Aiden said.

Tim smiled at that. "I hope so, too. Not for a long, long time."

Aiden and his father broke their hug and walked to the door. Tim opened it, then stood aside, letting his son go out first. Tim patted Aiden on the back before they walked out to the foyer to find everyone there, waiting on them.

"How do you guys think he did?" Tim asked the group.

"Who?" asked Layne.

Brione rolled her eyes and Veronna sighed.

"Aiden, of course" the blonde-haired girl said.

"Aiden?" Layne continued. "Why are we talking about Aiden? What did he do? It's not like he went on his first job today or something."

Tim laughed at that. "I guess that means he did well Layne. Otherwise, you wouldn't be joking about it."

"He did okay I guess," Layne answered.

"He did great, Tim," Brione assured, smiling. "You would have been proud. I was impressed at how composed he was. I knew deep down he was frightened, but he didn't show it."

Tim looked at his son. "Good man. Everyone gets scared, you just have to overcome your fear."

Zach, who was keeping watch at the open door came up to Tim. "Someone is coming."

"Who?"

"He looks like a soldier of the Royal Army. He's riding in fast."

Tim went to the door and saw the lone man riding hard for the little fort. The man was wearing light armor for riding, with the royal crest emblazoned on the front: two fists, each holding a lit torch, crossing one behind the other to form an X. The horse hadn't come to a complete stop yet when the man leapt off and ran to the door of the fort, almost stumbling into Tim.

"Are you Tim?" he asked, panting.

"Yes. You're in quite a rush. What can I do for you?"

"Her Majesty the Queen requests your presence in the town of Rindley immediately. It is most urgent."

"What is this about? I can't just go without any information."

"I am just a messenger, sir. I do not know why. I was told only that it was urgent that you come as soon as possible."

Veronna came up to them, looking excited. "Oh Daddy, can we go? I've never met a queen before!"

"Shush Veronna," Tim replied. She obeyed, but didn't lose her excitement, hopping from foot to foot in anticipation of her father's answer. He thought for a moment, then answered, "Okay. I'll go. But I go alone."

"Daddy!"

Tim turned to his daughter. "Listen Veronna. I must hurry and I can travel much faster by myself. I'm sorry, honey."

"But Dad, you said yourself that I am a great rider. You said just the other day how surprised you were at how good I am getting. I'll keep up."

"You did say that, dad," Aiden put in.

Tim shot his son a frustrated look." Then he turned his attention back to his daughter.

She was looking at him hopefully. He looked back at her, smiled and said, "Alright." Veronna squealed in delight and hugged her father. "Go now, get your riding cloak. We have no time to take anything else. Hurry."

He smiled fondly after his daughter as she rushed out of the room and down the hall to her quarters. The royal messenger cleared his throat to remind the mercenary leader that he was still there. Tim turned to him.

"Sir," the man said. "Do you need me to escort you or do you know the way?"

"I know where Rindley is."

"Good. Then I shall go ahead and report to the queen that you're on your way. She is staying at The Fool's Errand. She will be pleased to hear you agreed to come." With that, he bowed respectfully to Tim, got back on his exhausted horse, and left the fort. He kept his pace much slower now, trying to give his horse a chance to regain its strength.

Tim turned back to the group. "It's not a long ride to Rindley. If Veronna and I hurry, we can make it in a day. We should return tomorrow, or the day after at the latest." He looked around the room. His eyes stopped on Aiden. "While I'm gone, I leave Aiden in command." There was shocked silence in the room. "Brione, you aid him any way you can." Still silence. "Well?"

"Yes sir," Brione finally replied.

"Why?" Layne and Aiden blurted at the same time.

"Because Aiden will take over as leader of the group one day," Tim replied. "This will be good practice for him. It'll be fine."

"Alright sir," Layne said. "I didn't mean to question your judgment."

"I know Layne."

"It just took me by surprise is all."

"I know Layne," Tim said patiently.

Veronna came running into the room, her riding cloak trailing behind her. She held a bundle of dried meat and a canteen of water. "I'm ready!"

Tim smiled. "Alright, we're off. Be safe. Do your chores. Don't slack on your training. And remember, Aiden is in charge."

"Aiden?" Veronna asked as she went out the door with her father. "Why is Aiden in charge?"

When the door shut Aiden looked around the room at all the people he was suddenly responsible for. "Okay…"

4

The cloaked woman walked into the tavern, hood up to conceal her face. It was hot and stuffy in the room with all the bodies that filled it, and the fact that she was wearing a cloak didn't help. The tavern was bursting with the usual evening crowd and there were very few unused chairs at the tables. Hard working men finished with a full day's labor were trying to relax before heading home. Serving women carrying trays of drinks struggled to make their way through the crowd. The room was bright, loud, and highly uncomfortable for the woman.

She scanned the crowd, looking for one man in particular. She had come here because she knew he was a heavy drinker. She made her way through the crowd to the bar, getting jolted every few feet. Ignoring the curses of the people she had to shoulder her way past, she reached her destination. She hadn't realized that her hood had fallen back a little, revealing more of her face, and more importantly, her hair.

She stood at one end and looked down the bar. The bar top was very clean. The owner obviously took pride in his establishment. She could see her reflection in the polished wood. Her eyes met those of a drunk man. He was ugly, with small, beady eyes and a scar running down the left side of his face. He was staring at her. She glared back at him. "Can I help you?" She asked.

"Do I know you?"

She became nervous. "No, of course not," she answered, trying to calm her nerves. "I'm not from around here."

The man ignored her glare and kept staring. "I'm sure I know you." His words were slurred. "Ah, yes. Those eyes. A man can never forget eyes like that. Or that hair. You're the wife of…oof!"

She punched him in the stomach and he slid off his bar stool onto the ground, clutching at his midsection and groaning in pain. She quickly adjusted her hood. "Pervert!" she said loudly. "I am a lady and I will not stand for that kind of behavior. Now apologize!"

The men nearby glanced at her, then at the man on the ground and roared with laughter. That was a common event at the tavern. A man says something vulgar to a woman and gets injured because of it. The owner of the tavern didn't allow the men to strike back. If a man did strike back, the owner would call for the guards and have the man arrested. Then the man would be banished from his establishment for life, in addition to spending the night in jail.

She went back to scanning the room and at last she found him, sitting by himself at the far end of the bar. She cursed herself. She had gone to the wrong end. She readjusted her hood and, stepping over the injured man on the floor, approached the lone man.

The big man turned to her. Recognition registered on his face and his eyes narrowed. "You! What do you want, slut?"

"Excuse me?"

"I know who you are," he growled. "I recognize you. Your eyes are dark green, and your red hair isn't totally hidden by that hood. You're Amanda, my late son's whore of a wife. Answer me quickly before I have the owner remove you forcibly. What do you want?"

"Listen Platte. I've found him. I found the man who killed your son."

Platte took another drink from the mug he was holding and grunted. "You have, have you? And why would you come all this way to tell me where he is? I thought you ran away with him."

She looked shocked. "Ran away with him? No! You have it all wrong. He kidnapped me. He forced me to go with him. I didn't want to. I hated him for killing Reinhold. I escaped one night when he was asleep and I've been in hiding ever since. I'm so afraid that he will come looking for me."

"You didn't hate him," Platte spat. "If you did, why were you with him behind my son's back?"

"He manipulated me. I was young and innocent and he was older and devious. I didn't know what I was doing. I'm so sorry about what happened."

Platte looked at her. A change fell over him. He didn't look at her with hatred anymore. He now looked at her with longing. She had seen that look in his eyes numerous times when she was married to his son. "You're sorry are you? You know what? I should kill you right now and be done with you. But if you're sorry," he smiled, grabbed her hand and pulled her closer, "then maybe we can come to some sort of an agreement."

Amanda was repulsed, and it was all she could do not to pull away from him. This man disgusted her. She had hated him when she was married to his son, and she hated him still. Yet, she believed he would follow through with his threat to kill her. She had known how devastated he was about his son's death before she had decided to approach him, and she was willing to do just about anything to get back at the man who had shunned her. The *only* man who had ever shunned her. "Let's talk about that later," she said seductively. "Let's find your son's killer first."

Platte thought about it for a second. "Alright. Where is he?"

"He is with Tim's mercenaries."

Platte's eyes widened. "Are you crazy? We can't attack him at his fort! We would be slaughtered! It's suicide!"

"Calm down," Amanda said, glancing quickly around the room to see if anyone was looking at them. A few of the patrons were. She continued in a hushed tone. "Do you want to avenge your son or not?"

"I have already taken my revenge," he decided. "Anyway, I would love to kill Dustin, but not at the expense of my own life."

"What do you mean you have already taken your revenge?"

"Never you mind about that." He changed the subject. "I really don't think it is a good idea to mess with someone in Tim's mercenary group."

"You are well known. You can hire a lot of men to accompany you. Tim is a good man, by all accounts. If we explain the situation to him, maybe he will just hand the murderer over. For justice, or something like that. He is famous for his sense of justice."

Platte looked nervous. He rubbed his bald, sweating head. "I don't know about this Amanda."

Amanda sat on the fat man's lap and put her hands around his neck, suppressing a grimace. "Ah, come on. Do it for me." She smiled at him and stroked the back of his head.

In the end, he agreed. They would hire men and go to the mercenary's fort the next day.

*   *   *

Queen Laurel stood as her servant announced the arrival of Tim. When the man walked into the room, she stared. He was a magnificent specimen of a man. Tall, broad shouldered, well-built, and handsome. He was finely dressed, but not in fancy clothes. The fact that his hair was beginning to thin did not take away from his attractiveness. This was the first time Laurel had met the famous Tim, and she was impressed. She found herself brushing at her dress and trying to straighten her hair.

"Ah, Tim. Welcome. And thank you for coming on such short notice." She looked at Veronna. "And this beautiful young lady must be your daughter."

Veronna blushed. She took the hand offered by the queen and bowed the way her father had told her she must on their journey there. "Thank you, Your Majesty. I am Veronna. It is a pleasure to meet you." When she raised her head, her face was beaming.

"Veronna is a beautiful name," the queen said. At that comment, Veronna's smile widened ever further.

"Thank you again, Your Majesty," she said.

The queen gave her hand to Tim. He took it and bowed. "I am also pleased to meet you and I hope I am able to aid you anyway I can."

"I am sorry to have you come so quickly, but this is an emergency. Please, sit down." She gestured to a group of soft chairs set in a semi-circle. They waited for her to sit down, then followed suit. "I have some bad news. We haven't been telling anyone this, but my husband, King Michael, has been killed."

Veronna gasped. "The king is dead? That's horrible!"

Tim raised his eyes in surprise. "That is terrible, Your Majesty. I am sorry for your loss. He was a good man."

The queen continued, "I have discovered who hired the assassin and I want to hire your band to catch the criminal and kill him."

Tim, again, looked surprised. "No trial? You want us to just kill him and be done with it?"

"No need for a trial. This man admitted to me that he hired the assassin. You see, my son, Prince Easton, is the one who hired the killer." They heard a gasp come from a doorway at the side of the room. The queen motioned for one of her guards to investigate.

"Oh no," Veronna said, covering her mouth with her hands and shaking her head.

"Why?" asked Tim.

"Because he was bitter that his father was going to give the throne to his sister. Easton and my husband never got along. They always fought about the way Easton lived his life. The king didn't think Easton would be a good king, so he was going to make sure that he never would be."

Just then the guard who had investigated the noise escorted Princess Dana into the room. She was crying. Tim and Veronna both stood when she entered.

"Why didn't you tell me mother?" she wailed. "Were you going to keep this from me forever?"

The queen turned to her daughter, a concerned expression on her face. "No, Dana. I was going to tell you after Tim left. I wanted to get this business over with and then we could mourn your brother together."

"Must you kill him?" Dana asked.

"Tim," Queen Laurel said. "Please excuse us for a moment."

"Of course, Your Majesty." The guard escorted Tim and Veronna through the door and into the hallway. He left the door open.

The queen spread her arms out before herself. "What would you have me do, Dana? If this was anyone else, you would agree with me that they needed to be put to death."

"But it's not anyone else, mother. It is your son! My brother! How could you do this?"

The queen raised her voice. "How could I do this? Me? He did this by betraying your father and having him murdered for his own petty pride!" The queen took a deep breath, trying to calm herself down. "That has to be punished, Dana. Do not blame me. You know who deserves the blame. When you are queen you will find that you often have to make very difficult decisions."

Dana bowed her head. "But he is my brother," she said quietly.

"This decision pains me Dana, but it has to be this way. Some day you will see that."

"Can't you just put him in prison? Perhaps he was manipulated. Or he was tricked and he is also a victim. He doesn't have to die!"

"Oh Dana," her mother whispered. She walked over to her weeping daughter and put her arms around her and held her close. Dana returned the embrace. "His trial was held within these walls when he visited me. It was premeditated. It was not manipulation, nor was he tricked. This was his idea. I am so sorry."

Veronna rushed into the room and, to the dismay of her father, threw her arms around the queen and princess. The queen didn't seem to mind though. Neither did Princess Dana. "I want you to track him," she said to Tim as he followed his daughter into the room. "He has already left. That is why I needed you to come immediately; he already had a head start. After he told me of his plans I sent guards to apprehend him, but somehow he slipped through their fingers and got away. He informed me he was going across the sea and that he plans on returning with an army. He said he has allies."

Tim thought about that. "Allies across the sea? There is only one possible place he could sail to. Everywhere else is just too far away."

"The continent of Parken," said the queen.

"Yes," replied Tim. "There are a few people there I know who could provide this army for Prince Easton, but I think I might know who is helping him."

"Who?" asked the queen.

"King Korlas. I know the man. We used to be comrades. He is an evil man who I could easily see conspiring with your son for control of the country. I am sure this is where Easton is heading." He paused. "If it is King Korlas, we may be in serious trouble. He is not the kind of man who would pass up the opportunity to snatch this country from your son's grasp."

The queen swallowed. "Will you accept the job?"

"Yes. I will accept the job. Are you sure you want us to kill him instead of bringing him back here?"

"Yes," the queen said. Dana wailed.

"Alright, that's what we'll do then.

Veronna let go of the queen and hugged Princess Dana close. She stroked the back of Dana's long, dark hair as the princess cried on her shoulder. That was just like Veronna, Tim thought as he watched his daughter try to console the princess. She didn't care who the person was. If someone was sad or injured, be they royalty or pauper, Veronna was there to raise their spirits if she could.

"My servant Dorn was a witness to the murder," the queen said. "He was also stabbed, but he survived. He was my husband's closest friend. He would like to accompany you on your journey. Would that be alright with you?"

"Of course," Tim said. "You are my employer. We will do things the way you want them done."

"Thank you," said the queen. "He will meet you in the port city of Blanden. Meet him at the Starlight Inn."

"As you wish, Your Majesty."

Tim had one more request. "Your Majesty?"

"Yes?"

"I was wondering if I could ask a favor of you."

"Go ahead," she replied.

"I have a man in my employ," Tim explained. "He was a knight in service to your husband, King Michael. Four years ago he left the knighthood. I don't know the reason and I never asked. But I know the man. I know he must have had a good reason for deserting and I also know in most places that desertion is an offense punishable by death. I ask you to drop the desertion charge against this man. He will be helping me track down your son, and in turn, he will be helping the country."

"What is this man's name?"

"Dustin, your majesty. He is from the village of Marbur. I will be willing to take less money for the job to pay for his charges being dropped."

The queen pondered for a moment. "I will grant your request. It was unlike my husband to punish deserters by death. I believe he usually had them imprisoned but I will pardon your man. And I will not hear of giving you less money. I will happily do this for a man that you obviously think highly of."

"Thank you very much, Your Majesty."

The queen had one of her guards pay Tim in advance, a substantial sum of money, and father and daughter left with heavy hearts. When they left the room, Queen Laurel and Princess Dana returned to holding each other.

*   *   *

At mid-afternoon the day after Tim had met with the queen, Aiden and the mercenaries were out in the yard, training. The day was warm and bright, and the friends were enjoying the fresh air as they trained. Brione sparred with Dustin, the fiery woman getting the better of the ex-knight most of the time. Aiden and Layne sparred with each other, as usual. Aiden was amazed at his friend's natural fighting ability, how easily and precisely he swung his duel axes. Even when he put aside his twin axes and used his monstrous battle ax, he was too quick for the younger and less experienced Aiden. Aiden wondered how a man who was as large as Layne was could move so swiftly. Zach was nowhere to be seen, and that was just fine with the group. Zach never trained with them, unless Tim requested it.

They were about to change sparring partners when Zach appeared from the back of the fort. "Riders are coming," he announced. The others stopped and looked at him.

"Riders?" Aiden asked.

Brione walked up to the dark man. "How many?"

"Many," he replied, although he looked at Aiden and not Brione. "Probably fifty or so. They are coming fast."

Dustin approached them. He turned to Aiden. "What should we do?"

"Why are you asking me?"

"Because," answered Brione, "your father put you in charge. You have to lead us."

"Okay," said Aiden. "Well, just because I'm leader doesn't mean I'm going to make a decision on my own, so I'm going to ask for everyone's council. Brione?"

"Well, we don't know who they are and what they want. Although, if they were friendly, they probably wouldn't have so many men with them. When the queen's messenger came, he was alone. I would guess that they are not here as friends."

"I agree," said Dustin. "I believe they are hostile."

"Me too," said Layne, although no one could tell if he was serious or just playing along, because he had a smile on his face.

Aiden thought for a second. "We don't want to seem weak. That would just make them bolder. I say we should stay in a group by the door to the fort and confront them there until we figure out who they are and what they want. I think one of us should watch the back entrance in case they try to sneak in that way. Zach, I would like you to do that. Sound good everyone?" Zach nodded.

"Wow," said Layne. "A leader for only a day and already getting the hang of it. You boss others around like a natural!"

Brione gave Layne a sour look, then turned to Aiden. "Yes, that is a good plan." Dustin nodded his agreement.

They moved to their positions and waited.

The first rider appeared a few minutes later. He was a fat, bald man, probably in his fifties. Another rider came right behind him, this one much smaller. Aiden thought it was a woman, but it was hard to tell, for she was wearing a cloak with the hood drawn up. Fifty or so men came riding in behind the pair and took up positions just outside the entrance in the wall.

"I'm here to speak with Tim," the balding man announced. "Where is he?"

Aiden stepped forward. "Tim isn't here. I am his son, and I lead the group in his absence. How can I help you?"

The man scanned the little group until his eyes fell on Dustin. His eyes narrowed at the sight of him. "We are here for that man." He pointed. "We have come for Sir Dustin."

The others looked at the ex-knight. He didn't return their looks, he was looking at the speaker. Recognition registered on his face. "Platte," he whispered.

"You know this man?" asked Layne.

"Yes."

Aiden looked back to the riders. "What do you want with him?"

"Four years ago he murdered my son. We have come for his life."

"You lie!" cried Layne, taking a step towards the man. Dustin had to hold him back.

The fat man smiled. "Do I? Why don't you ask him yourself?"

"Well," said Layne to his brother. He had stopped struggling and looked at Dustin. "It can't be true, can it?"

To everyone's shock he answered, "It's true."

The big man's grin widened. "See, he admits it. Hand him over to us so that justice may be served. That is what your group is all about, isn't it? Seeing that justice is served to criminals? Hand him over!"

"No," Aiden replied. "I know Dustin. He is one of the best men I know. If he did kill your son, I'm positive he had a good reason. I will not hand him over to the likes of you, so I suggest you be on your way."

The man laughed at that. "Listen, *boy*." He spat the last word. "I have fifty riders with me. You are only four. If you don't hand him over peacefully, we will kill every single one of you."

Aiden was terrified, but he forced himself to smile wickedly. "We would like nothing more than to see you try."

The fat man was taken aback by that comment. "What did you say?" There was a nervousness in his voice now that wasn't there before. Aiden's bluff had its intended effect. The big man thought for a moment. The cloaked figure whispered something in his ear. The man shook his head and said something back. They argued for a moment, then the fat man turned back to the group.

"It seems to me that you are not thinking clearly. I will give you a chance to mull it over, to clear your heads and see what the obvious answer is. It would be a shame for my men to kill all of you when only Dustin is guilty. We will give you two hours to think it over. But, if after two hours you still refuse, we will be forced to kill each one of you. My men will be watching both entrances to your fort, so don't even try to escape." The man looked at Dustin. "I suggest you comply to our wishes Dustin, if you want your friends to survive. Do the right thing. Isn't that what Tim would want you to do?"

"You have no idea what my father would want," Aiden said.

With that, the group went inside, locking the door behind them.

5

"Wow Aiden," Layne said as the group sat in the common room of the fort. "That was some convincing acting. Did you see the look on that fat guy's face when you told him we wanted him to attack? He was terrified!"

"Yes," said Brione as she stepped away from the window where she was keeping an eye on the men outside. "You did very well. You said that you didn't want to seem weak to our enemies, and you didn't. Your father will proud of you. We all are."

Layne gave his friend an encouraging slap on the back. "I think that cloaked person wanted them to attack right away, but you scared the leader so bad that he didn't want to. Now we have two hours to figure out what to do."

Aiden looked at Dustin, who hadn't looked at the others or said anything since they entered the fort. "What is going on Dustin?"

Everyone's attention turned to the ex-knight. Dustin glanced at all the others in turn, his anguish showing plainly on his face. He sat down on the couch. "It's true. I did kill that man's son. He has every right to take me away and bring me to justice. Just let him do it."

"But why did you do it?" asked Brione as she sat next to Dustin. "What happened?"

"Does it matter?"

"Yes, it does," answered Tim from the entrance to the hallway.

Everyone turned to look at Tim as he came into the room. Veronna, looking pale, walked in behind him, followed by Zach.

Aiden went to his sister. "Veronna, what's wrong? Are you injured?"

She looked at her brother. He had never seen such a worried expression on Veronna's face before. "No, I am fine. It's just that my trip to see the queen wasn't what I had expected."

Layne laughed. "Not as exciting as you had hoped, huh?"

"No," she replied. "Too exciting." She sat down, and Aiden sat next to her. "First, we find out that Prince Easton murdered King Michael a few days ago and is now heading for Parken to get an army and come back and take the throne."

"Wow," Layne said.

"My thoughts exactly," replied Tim. "The queen hired us to go after him. We are all going to go across the sea, catch him, and put him to death."

"Then," continued Veronna, "when we returned to the base, we find it surrounded by strange men who are watching the place. We had to leave our horses a ways away and sneak into our own home through the back. Dad had to take down three men for us to get through, and Zach had to help by taking down another one." Veronna sniffed. "I saw four men die today." Aiden put his arm around her.

She turned to her brother. "What is going on Aiden? Who are these people? Why are they here?"

"I don't know who they are, but they came to take Dustin away. The leader said that Dustin murdered his son." Veronna gasped.

"Then Aiden scared him so badly," added Layne, "that he didn't attack. He gave us two hours to turn him over." He turned to Tim, a broad grin on his face. "You should have seen it, Tim. It was great!"

"Once again, I am impressed," the mercenary leader said. "I am proud of you, son. You were in a difficult situation and bought your group time to try and get out of it like a good leader should. I just wish I was here to see it." Aiden grinned at the compliment.

He turned to his daughter. "And Veronna, those four men aren't dead. We just knocked them unconscious. I don't kill people if I don't have to. Don't worry, you didn't see anyone die." Veronna's face relaxed.

"Now," Tim continued, turning back to the group, "returning to the situation at hand. Dustin, you say you killed this man's son. Tell us the circumstances."

Dustin looked at his leader, at the man who had become like a father to him after his own parents had died. He took a deep breath and began his story.

"I was seeing a married woman," Dustin began.

"Seriously?" Layne asked. "You courted a married woman? That goes against your code!"

Brione glared at him. "Hush, Layne. Let him tell the story."

"I didn't know she was married. She never told me. Although now that I look back on it, I should have known. She was married to one of the most influential men in the city. He was an advisor to King Michael himself. I had seen him in public with his wife before, but never up close, so I didn't recognize her."

Dustin paused. No one said anything, not even Layne. He took a few moments to gather his thoughts, then began his story with all eyes upon him.

"Her name was Amanda. One night I was at her house. She had made me dinner…"

*   *   *

"Do you want some wine?" Amanda asked Dustin.

They were sitting in the living room of Amanda's small but tidy house. It had a comfortable feel to it. The couch that Dustin was sitting on was soft and inviting. The only other pieces of furniture in the room were a small table in the center and two padded chairs. It was after dark, and the two had just come back from a long walk in the moonlight. They had just finished a dinner of roasted pork and steamed vegetables. He was studying the walls, which had a few paintings of nature scenes or flowers, when she asked him the question.

The knight looked at her and smiled. "I would love some."

She went to the kitchen and pulled two mugs from a cupboard and poured the wine, never taking her forest green eyes off Dustin as she returned to the couch and handed him one of the goblets. Dustin looked into those eyes and thought they were the most beautiful shade of green he had ever seen. He ran his hand through her dark red hair. He had never felt this way about anyone before. He thought he was falling in love with her.

He was about to tell her that when the front door burst open.

"Amanda!" shouted the man who had come through the doorway. Dustin could also see a large, older man behind the newcomer.

"Reinhold!" Amanda cried as she jumped to her feet. Dustin stood up beside her.

The man looked at Dustin. "Who are you? What are you doing in my house with my wife?"

"Your wife?" Dustin turned to Amanda. "You never told me you were married."

"It didn't seem that important," she replied in a weak voice. She looked down at her feet.

"Not important!" both men exclaimed simultaneously.

Suddenly, Dustin recognized Amanda's husband.

"Reinhold! The king's advisor! I had no idea this was your wife!"

"Do you take me for a fool?" the man asked with a sneer. "Everyone knows this is my wife. I am one of the most famous and influential people in this city. Everyone knows who I am and in turn everyone knows who she is. You are lying!"

The older man behind Reinhold spoke for the first time. "Kill him, son!"

Reinhold drew a knife from his belt and grinned wickedly at the unarmed Dustin.

Dustin cursed himself for leaving his sword by the door. He hadn't thought he would have need of it. He put his hands up in front of himself, stepping protectively in front of Amanda. "Now, Advisor Reinhold, *just calm down. This was a mistake. I will leave and you'll never see me again."*

Reinhold sneered. "A mistake? Have you slept with her? Have you?" He shouted the last part.

"No, of course not!"

"Why not?" Reinhold pressed. "If you thought she was available, why haven't you slept with her?

"Because I'm not like that."

"What do you mean, not like that? She is a beautiful woman and you're a young, healthy man. What is there to stop you? Especially if you thought she was available."

Dustin and Reinhold had been circling each other during the conversation. Suddenly, Reinhold lunged forward, swinging the knife wildly. Dustin easily jumped back and avoided the blade. "Answer the question!" Reinhold shouted. "Why didn't you sleep with her? Is she not beautiful enough for you? Are you saying that my wife isn't beautiful?" It sounded to Dustin as if Reinhold was angrier about the fact that he hadn't slept with his wife than the fact that he had found them together. It was like he was insulting the man.

Dustin grunted as he dodged another wild swing, this one closer than the first. "I haven't slept with her because I don't believe in being intimate before marriage."

"What kind of rubbish is that?" This remark came from the big man still standing in the doorway. "What a joke!"

Dustin glanced his way, but didn't answer.

"He is obviously lying," Reinhold's father continued. "Just kill him and be done with it."

With a growl, Reinhold went for Dustin. He leaped and stabbed towards Dustin's chest, but the younger man stepped aside with ease. Dustin grabbed a chair and held it out in front of himself. That didn't deter Reinhold. The crazed man kept up the attack, his slashes knocked harmlessly aside by the makeshift shield.

"Stop Reinhold!" Amanda screamed. "Don't kill him!" Reinhold's father cheered his son on.

Dustin, having had enough of the battle, swung the chair, hitting Reinhold's hand and knocking the knife away. Dustin dropped the chair and rushed in, tackling the man and pinning him to the ground. Reinhold had another knife stuck in his boot, and he went for that now. Dustin saw the movement and grabbed his arm, preventing him from getting the blade. Dustin had both of Reinhold's hands pinned to the floor now, trying to think of how to calm the man down. Reinhold was squirming violently, trying to get the younger man off of him.

Suddenly, Dustin was roughly yanked off the man and pulled to his feet. Reinhold's large father had him from behind, his arms wrapped around Dustin's torso, pinning his hands to his chest.

The large man grunted when Amanda threw herself onto him, holding on with one arm around his neck and hitting him with the other. A bystander would have been amused at the sight of three people locked together, one a woman screaming at the top of her lungs and flailing at a man with all her strength.

The large man twisted back and forth, trying to get the crazed woman off of him. She hung on for a few moments, but eventually her grip gave out and she went flying. She hit a wall and fell to the floor, landing in a heap. She didn't move after that.

Reinhold stood up and drew the knife from his boot. His grin returned. "Now you die. And after I kill you, I'll kill my beautiful wife for her unfaithfulness. How does that sound?"

Dustin glanced over at Amanda. She wasn't moving, but he heard her groan.

As Reinhold reached him and lunged forward, Dustin cried "No!" and spun around with all his might. Around came the large man hanging on Dustin's back. The knife slid into Reinhold's father's side. Dustin's momentum kept the big man moving, so the knife was torn out of Reinhold's hand before it went in very far. The large man cried out in pain and let go, stumbling to the floor. Reinhold stood there, shocked that he had accidentally stabbed his own father.

Dustin was enraged. He had never felt such great anger in his life. "I was going to let you live. I was just going to disarm you and walk out of here, but not after you have threatened Amanda's life. I won't let you hurt her."

Dustin was standing by the door. He leaned down and picked his sword up. He looked around and found another sword leaning against the wall a few feet away. He grabbed it and tossed it at Reinhold's feet. "Pick it up," he ordered.

Reinhold glanced down at the sword, then looked back at Dustin. "What game are you playing?"

"Pick it up," Dustin repeated. "I'm playing your way now. This is what you wanted."

Reinhold swallowed. "No."

"I do not want to kill an unarmed man. In fact, I didn't want to kill you at all. But I cannot allow you to live and give you the chance to murder your wife. Now pick up your sword. I am going to kill you either way. You can either die fighting or die helplessly. It's your choice."

Reinhold quickly picked up his sword. "Alright. I'll just kill you and then kill her. I cannot tolerate an unfaithful wife. I am an important man. She should feel privileged to be married to me." He had a white-knuckle grip on his sword. Dustin could see the fear in his eyes. It wasn't the look that a trained fighter would have. "Come on then!" Reinhold cried.

With a yell he charged at Dustin, his sword held over his head in both hands. He swung his sword down mightily, hitting nothing but the wood floor, for Dustin had dodged to the side. The knight swung his sword, slicing his enemy's right arm, giving him a deep gash. Reinhold cried out and stumbled back, clutching at his wound with his left arm.

"You're not much of a fighter, are you?" Dustin mocked.

Reinhold howled and rushed in again, this time with a horizontal swing. It was awkward because he was unable to use his dominant hand. Once again, Dustin easily dodged and counter-attacked, giving the man another gash, this time across his abdomen.

"I'm getting tired of this," said Dustin, and he went on the attack. The clang of metal against metal rang out as Reinhold desperately blocked Dustin's attacks. Dustin was driving him back towards the wall when he

fell. Reinhold's father had crawled over and grabbed Dustin by the ankle, tripping him. Dustin went down, but twisted as he fell so that he landed on his back. He kicked at the big man, connecting with his head. The big man let go of Dustin's ankle and curled up, groaning in pain and cradling his injured head in his arms.

Reinhold came at Dustin before he had a chance to get up, sword raised once again over his head. Dustin raised his own sword, and before Reinhold could slow his momentum, he impaled himself on it. He stopped, dropped his sword, and fell over.

Dustin got to his feet and pulled the sword from the dead man's chest, wiping it clean on Reinhold's shirt.

"You killed my son!"

Dustin looked over at the big man. He was struggling to get to his feet. "You killed my son!" he repeated. He stumbled out the front door. Dustin could hear him crying out as he ran down the street. "He killed my son!"

"Dustin." He looked over as Amanda got to her feet. She had to use the wall for support. "Dustin, are you alright?"

"Yes," he replied. "I'm not injured." He looked at the dead body on the floor beside him, and the enormity of what he had just done finally hit him. He had just taken a man's life.

"No!" He cried as his knees grew week next to Reinhold. "No, no, no."

"What's wrong?" Amanda asked as she knelt beside him.

"I killed him. I killed a man."

"What does it matter? He would have killed you. And me too."

"I've never killed a man before."

"Dustin." Amanda looked into his eyes. "You had to."

"No, I didn't. I didn't have to kill him. I could have disarmed him or knocked him out if I had to. He wasn't a very good fighter. I went too far. When he threatened you, I snapped. I didn't have to kill him, but I did because he made me so angry. I murdered him!"

"No. You were defending me. I would be dead if it wasn't for you. You're my hero." She tried to kiss him.

Dustin pulled back and got to his feet. She got up with him, clinging to him as if she were afraid to let go. "No. I have to get out of here. I'm sure that man will call the guards. I can't go to jail. I have a family. Parents and a little brother. They need me." He untangled himself from her. "They need me. I have to go."

"Wait! I'll come with you. There is nothing for me here now."

"No." Dustin turned to her, his pain showing plainly on his face. "You lied to me. I thought I loved you, but…" He sniffed. "No. You can't come with me."

"But what about Reinhold's father? He'll bring the guards. He'll have me arrested and for cheating on his son. I have to go with you. Please." That last word was barely a whisper.

Dustin thought about it. He was torn. He saw the fear in her eyes. They reflected his own fear. "Alright." They ran out of the house, not bothering to close the door behind them.

*   *   *

"I took her with me but left her in a safe place when she was sleeping. I couldn't look at her without remembering her deception. Reinhold would still be alive today if she hadn't lied to me. I never would have gotten involved if I had only known." Dustin paused for a moment. He wiped at his eyes with the back of his hand. "I never heard what became of her."

The room was silent. No one was looking directly at Dustin.

"Come on Dustin," Layne said after a moment, looking up at his brother. He gave Dustin a weak grin and slugged him on the shoulder. "Buck up. You know had to kill him. He made you do it. Besides, you've killed many people, and every one of them deserved it. This Reinhold guy did too. I know you wouldn't have done it otherwise."

"I had never killed anyone before that night. Your first time taking a life is devastating. At least it was for me. And no, I didn't have to kill him. I could have gotten away without killing him. I let my anger take over."

"What about Amanda?" asked Aiden. "He would have killed her if you had let him live."

Dustin rubbed his face with his hands. "She could have also escaped. Reinhold didn't have to die."

Tim put a hand on Dustin's shoulder. "Thank you for telling us. I know it must have been hard for you. But remember, you acted honorably. You not only saved your own life, but Amanda's life as well. I condone what you did."

Dustin sniffed. "Thank you." Dustin and Tim shared a smile.

Everyone was silent for a while. "Now," said Tim, "we need to figure out what to do with all these men outside that are determined to harm a member of our family."

6

Tim stepped out of the fort and stood in front of the men alone, his hand on the hilt of his great broadsword. He addressed the leader.

"I am Tim. I am told that you wish to speak with me, but first I want you to listen. You will not take Dustin. He has explained to me the situation of your son's death and I have concluded that he has done nothing worthy of your vengeance. Your son didn't give Dustin much of a choice, so he isn't going anywhere with you and your thugs. Now, you have come uninvited to my home, and I must insist that you leave."

The fat man turned in his saddle and addressed the figure next to him quietly. She replied sharply. He turned back to Tim. The big man gulped, trying to fight his fear. "I don't care who you are. I am taking Dustin with me. He killed my son and must pay for his crimes! We outnumber you fifty to five. You have no chance." He grew more confidant after he said this.

"You are wrong," Tim answered. "We are seven and you only have forty-six men with you now."

There was a commotion among the men and the leader paled. "How?"

Tim interrupted him. "I am going to let you leave here right now, and I will forget this ever happened. If you do not leave my fort in five minutes, my men and I will kill every last one of you. It's your choice."

"You're bluffing," said one man.

Tim smiled. "Am I?"

"You can't possibly expect to defeat nearly fifty men," the leader said, though he didn't sound as if he fully believed his own words. "You have no chance. Just hand the murderer over and we'll be on our way. You will never see us again."

"If you don't think we stand a chance, then by all means, attack us." Still the man hesitated.

"You have four minutes," Tim said.

The cloaked figure leaned over and whispered something to the big man. He argued, but the figure seemed adamant. Finally, defeated, the leader turned back to the mercenary.

"Three minutes," Tim said before the man had a chance to speak.

"Alright!" yelled the leader. "You have just made a big mistake, Tim. I offered you the chance to stay alive, but you have refused. We will kill your group and take Dustin by force. Then I will be known as the man who killed the great Tim."

"Very well then," Tim said and without another word entered the fort, shutting and locking the door behind him. The men surrounding the fort came inside the wall and into the courtyard, some pulling out swords, others drawing bows. They waited for the mercenaries to show themselves. Their nerves were beginning to show. Some shifted in their saddles, others coughed nervously. No one seemed comfortable waiting out in the hot sun.

Suddenly, a window in the front of the building shattered. The archers instantly let loose toward the window, some arrows flying inside, others bouncing harmlessly off the outer wall. The twangs of bowstrings could be heard, and four men fell off their horses. But the arrows didn't come from inside the fort. Two came from behind and two came from the right of the attackers.

The riders looked around, franticly searching for the bowmen, but they were nowhere in sight. Platte sent five men back outside the wall to search for their attackers. They dismounted and did as they were told. Brione and Layne were waiting for them just outside the opening in the wall. While Tim was talking to the leader they had climbed over the back wall and came around the outside to the front of the fort.

The first man came into view and Brione dispatched him immediately with a sword thrust in the chest. Layne confronted the next two with his duel axes. He sent one ax high, the other low, his enemies positioning their swords to block accordingly. But Layne stopped in mid-swing and reversed his axes, sending them the opposite directions. He was too fast for his enemies to block. One man was taken down with an ax in the gut, the other was slashed across his throat. Both crumpled to the ground.

Brione was facing the other two men. She had her sword in one hand and her bow in the other. She struck at one man with her sword, then blocked the other man's swing with her bow. Suddenly, Brione spun in a circle, striking an enemy with her sword and then immediately with the bow. The man blocked her sword, but the bow strike took him by surprise as it struck him across the face, breaking his nose and knocking him backwards. The fierce woman completed her circle with a block of the second attacker's sword with her own.

Layne joined the fray and suddenly the man was fighting two foes at once. He cried out, threw his weapon to the ground, and tried to escape, running away from the fort. Layne chased him down and tackled him to the ground. "I yield, I yield!" the man cried.

"So do I!" said the man that Brione had knocked to the ground, holding his broken nose.

"Alright," said Brione. "But we can't have you attacking us from behind." With that, she hit the broken-nosed man over the head with the hilt of her sword, knocking him unconscious. Layne did the same to the man he had tackled. They left both men lying where they fell and made for the opening in the wall.

*   *   *

Dustin and Zach were on the right side of the building, each notching another arrow. They heard the group of men trying to break down the front door. They weren't concerned though, because Tim and Aiden were positioned just inside the door to intercept anyone who came through.

They lifted their bows and fired, two more men falling from their saddles. They dropped their bows to the ground and drew their swords as men approached on foot. Dustin had a long sword, Zach wielded dual short swords.

Zach immediately disarmed two enemies with a quick spin that hit both fighters' swords and sent them flying. He stabbed one in the chest, then threw one of his swords into the other man's back as he turned to flee. It hit him square between the shoulders and he fell to the ground, dead. The dark-skinned fighter quickly drew a long dagger from his boot to replace his lost sword and engaged two more foes.

Dustin was also fighting two men, his back to the building so they couldn't get behind him. He didn't have a shield, but he wore steel gauntlets, so he was able to block his enemies' attacks. At first, he was unable to put up any offense, for his enemies relentlessly bore into him; it was all he could do to keep from getting hit. He knew he had to do something fast if he was going to survive. He took a chance.

Ignoring one foe, he blocked the other's swing with his gauntlet, then counter attacked with his sword. The move surprised the man and he stepped back, losing ground. Dustin was in a hurry, he knew the other man would try to stab him in the back, so he pushed forward, attacking the man with his sword, then punching at him with his gauntlets, then attacking with his sword again. He felt a sharp pain in his back and knew that the other man had slashed him. Warm blood started streaming out of the wound and ran down his back. Still, he ignored it and focused on the man in front of him.

Luckily, Dustin was the better fighter, and soon he overpowered his enemy, disarming him and knocking him to the ground with a gauntlet to his enemy's face. He then spun around and blocked the other man's swing with his sword. The man hadn't expected Dustin to face him, so the block surprised him. He lost his grip on his sword and it fell to the ground. When he bent to pick the weapon up, Dustin hit him over the head with the pommel of his sword, knocking the man unconscious. He turned and checked on the man he had punched in the face. He was out cold.

Dustin's back stung, but the pain was bearable. He looked up to see Zach standing among the bodies of six men. They looked at each other, nodded, and together turned the corner to the front of the fort.

*   *   *

Aiden crouched underneath the broken window, arrows flying over his head. Most flew harmlessly to the side after bouncing off the wall in the back of the room, but others came perilously close to bouncing back and hitting him. He still held the hammer he had used to break the window. The front door was being pounded on by men outside. His father was waiting beside the door, broadsword in hand. His sister was hiding in her room with the door locked. Aiden hoped the other four were alright.

Suddenly, the volley of arrows stopped. Aiden looked up to see a man coming through the window. He stood up and hit the man right between the eyes with his hammer. The man's eyes rolled back and he fell backwards. The window didn't stay clear for long however, as another man quickly took his place.

Aiden swung through the window at the newcomer, but his enemy ducked under the blow and grabbed Aiden's arm before he could bring it back inside. The man pulled on Aiden's arm, trying to drag him out the window. Aiden pulled back, but the man was too strong for him. "Dad, help!" Aiden cried.

Tim was there in an instant. He grabbed Aiden's torso and pulled with all his might. He gritted his teeth, his muscles bulged, and down to the floor went father and son, pulling the other man through the window and into the room. Tim immediately stood up and seized the intruder. He easily picked up the man and threw him back outside, knocking back two men trying to get in the window. He helped his son up, made sure he was alright, and went back to the door. It sounded to Aiden like the door would burst any minute.

Aiden ducked under another volley of arrows. The door finally splintered and two men forced their way into the fort. Tim was there to meet them with his broad sword. At the same time the men came through the doorway, more tried to come through the window again. Aiden dropped his hammer and drew his sword. He swung at the first man, who dodged backwards, his momentum taking him back out the window. A second man shoved the first out of the way and tried to make his way in.

The man swung at Aiden with is sword, trying to push the young man away from the window. Aiden didn't back away, though. He stood his ground and blocked the attack, countering with a forward thrust. The enemy hadn't expected this, so he didn't have time to avoid the stab, and Aiden's sword plunged into his chest. The man cried out, clutched his chest, and fell to the ground. Through the window Aiden saw more archers lifting their bows and aiming for him. He ducked just as they loosed. As the arrows flew overhead, he looked over towards the door to see how his father was doing.

*   *   *

Tim was doing just fine. The two men who had rushed into the room were finding no holes in his defense. He was using his broadsword to keep both from moving away from the door, hemming them in with horizontal swings and preventing any more men from coming inside.

Tim took a mighty horizontal swing, right to left. The first man blocked, but the swipe was too powerful, knocking his enemy's weapon out of the way while the force of his swing kept his own sword going. It hit the man in his midsection, stopping when it hit his spine. But Tim kept up his swing, the sword sweeping the man off his feet and into his comrade, knocking them both to the floor, the dead man pinning the live one underneath him.

"I surrender!" cried the pinned man as Tim walked towards him. The mercenary leader wasn't concerned about anyone coming in through the broken door. He had seen a few men watch as he dispatched his enemy, and they had run the other way in fear.

Tim looked down at the man. "You surrender?" Tim laughed. "Didn't you hear me tell your boss that I was going to kill every single one of you?" Seeing the look of terror on the man's face, Tim laughed again.

"Alright," Tim said. "I will spare your life." He hit the man over the head with the broadside of his sword, knocking him out cold.

Tim looked at his son, who was still crouched beneath the window. The arrows had stopped coming, and they could hear no more sounds of battle coming from outside. "Let's go outside and see what's going on," Tim suggested.

Father and son exited the building to find Zach and Dustin holding the leader, the cloaked figure, and seventeen men at sword point. They had all dismounted and had dropped their weapons in surrender. Layne and Brione were each hauling an unconscious body from outside of the wall.

Tim walked up to the leader of the group. The big man looked terrified, sweat dripping down his face. He cringed as Tim came up to him. He quickly looked in all directions, frantically trying to find a way to escape. There wasn't one.

"It has been four years," Tim began. "Have you been searching for Dustin this whole time? Is your hatred that strong? You were there the night your son was killed. How can you believe your son's death was Dustin's fault when you know the truth of what happened?" The man didn't answer. "Answer me!" Tim yelled.

The fat man was breathing hard and struggling to speak. "Yes…I was there. He shouldn't have been with my son's wife in…the first place. My son was within…his rights when he attacked Dustin. So yes…it was Dustin's fault."

"You have been searching for him these past four years?"

"No. I quickly found out where he lived. I…went to his house, but he wasn't… there." He paused. "His parents were, though."

"No!" cried Layne. He lurched toward the man, but Tim held him back. "You killed my parents! You killed my parents!"

Tim, still holding Layne back asked in a grim voice, "Is this true?"

Layne's grief seemed to give the man strength. "I found them at the house. I demanded they tell me where Dustin was, but they refused. I threatened them, but they still wouldn't tell me where he was. I got angry and killed them both. I waited at their house until nightfall for Dustin to come home, but he never did."

Dustin came up to them. He put a hand on his grieving brother's shoulder. Layne had stopped struggling and had his head buried in Tim's shoulder, his body racked with sobs.

"I had taken my vengeance," Platte said. "He killed my son, so I killed his parents."

"Why come attack us now?"

"I was minding my own business one night at my favorite tavern, when my son's widow, Amanda, came up to me with a proposition. She said that she had found Dustin and she wanted him dead." He smiled at Dustin. "You see, she never got her revenge against him. He seems to be very good at making people angry."

Dustin looked closer at the cloaked figure. "Amanda?"

She raised her head, pulled back her hood and looked him in the eye. "Dustin," she said, venom in her voice.

The sight of her hit him like a punch in the gut, and for a moment, he couldn't breathe. Feelings he thought he had put aside came rushing back. This was the woman he had once loved, the woman who he believed had loved him back. This was the woman who had lied to him, the woman who now wanted him dead.

Dustin struggled to speak past the lump in his throat. "Why? I saved your life that night."

"You abandoned me in the woods!" she screamed. "For all you knew I died that night! You just left me there to fend for myself. I didn't know how to survive on my own. You shunned me!"

"We were two miles from the closest town, Amanda. I knew you would be alright." Dustin didn't yell back. He spoke calmly, but there was great sadness in his voice.

"Why did you leave me?" Her voice was quieter now. "Why did you shun me? No one has ever done that to me before."

"Because you lied to me. You should have told me that you were married. I loved you Amanda, and you hurt me. I just couldn't be with you anymore. I couldn't even look at you anymore. But I never meant to hurt you."

"I will never forgive you for what you did, Dustin" she said through gritted teeth.

"So," said Dustin, "where does that leave us?"

Without saying another word, she mounted her horse and started to ride away.

Aiden looked concerned. "Should we stop her?"

Tim looked at Dustin. "It's up to you."

"No," Dustin replied after a moment's thought. "Let her go. If she can't move on, that's her problem."

"But she wants you dead," said Brione. "What if she talks another fool into trying to kill you? She could cause problems later."

"I won't be here, remember? She doesn't know that we are sailing across the sea."

"The question now is," said Tim as he turned back to their attackers, "what do we do with you?"

The remaining seventeen men hadn't said a word during the entire conversation. Even though for much of the time only one man, Zach, had a sword drawn on them, they had seen the prowess of the mercenary group. They realized that the reputation of Tim and his mercenaries was true. They were especially terrified of this dark-skinned warrior. They just sat hunched together against the wall of the building.

"Well," said Layne, tears streaming down his face, "I know what we should do with this scumbag." He pulled out his large battle ax and walked towards Platte. "I would like to do the honors."

"Tell you guys what," Tim said to the other men. "If each one of you swear to me that you will never do anything like this again, that you will never try to kill anyone again, we will let you leave with your lives. If not, we will finish what we started."

Platte spoke up first. "I swear!"

"I wasn't talking to you," replied Tim sharply.

Platte gulped and his face grew pale.

All seventeen men vowed to Tim that they would never try to kill anyone again. Tim made them take their comrades' dead bodies with them. After they rode away, the mercenaries turned their attention back to Platte.

"For the crime of murdering these boys' parents, I sentence you to death," Tim declared.

"You can't do that!" the big man cried. "You don't have the authority to sentence someone to death. You're just a sword for hire."

"You came onto my property and tried to kill me and my family." Tim was angry now. "Believe me, I have the right to kill you. But I won't." He turned to Layne and Dustin. "I will let them do it. It was their parents you murdered after all."

"Thank you," Layne said. "Dustin, please hold him down."

Dustin nodded, and the brothers approached the terrified man.

*   *   *

After the deed was done and the brothers had washed up, they met everyone else in the main foyer for a group meeting. Dustin looked grim, and Layne still looked upset. Dustin had discovered that his wound wasn't deep, and with Veronna's help, had bandaged it up. Normally, Tim would have replaced the broken window by now, but since they were leaving, he didn't worry about it. Though he had swept the pieces of glass out the broken front door.

"Are you two alright?" Tim asked the brothers.

They both nodded. "It is good to get some closure," Dustin said. "And to finally get some justice for our parents."

Layne rubbed his hands together. "We did well," he said. "Those guys didn't stand a chance."

Brione gave him a disgusted look. "Where is your humility? Your arrogance will get you in trouble someday."

"I'm not arrogant, I'm just telling the truth."

"We got lucky," said Tim.

That comment silenced everyone. They all looked at Tim.

"Lucky?" Veronna asked after a moment.

"We were lucky," Tim answered, "that they were not trained soldiers."

"Did you know that before they attacked?" asked Aiden.

"Yes," his father replied. "I could tell by the way they sat on their horses, by the way they glanced around nervously, and by the way they fidgeted. I could tell right away that they were just thugs hired by a bully."

"So," said Layne, "what now?"

Tim looked at each member of the group. "Now we must focus on getting to Blanden where we will set sail for Parken."

"I can't wait!" exclaimed Veronna. "I have never seen the sea before!"

"It can't be as big as they say," said Aiden. "A body of water so big you can't see land for days at a time? I doubt it."

"Weeks," corrected their father. "You can't see land for weeks at a time."

Aiden's eyes were big. "Really?"

7

Queen Laurel knocked on her daughter's door. "Dana?" No answer. She tried again. "Dana?"

She waited for a moment and when her daughter still did not answer, she entered the room. "Dana? Are you awake? We're leaving today. We're going…" Her breath caught in her throat. Dana wasn't there. Most of her belongings were still in the room. The bed was unmade and the washstand was dry. It appeared that she had packed and left quickly. She looked around the room, wondering where her daughter could be when she saw a piece of paper sitting on the small table by the bed.

She went over to the table and picked up the paper. It was Dana's handwriting:

Mother,

I know how you feel about Easton, but I cannot just sit here and let him get killed.

I believe that deep down he is a good person.

I believe that he should be punished for his crime, but not by death. I am going to follow the group you hired to kill my only brother and do whatever it takes to make sure they don't kill him. Don't worry about me. I am taking Jaden with me, so I will be safe.

I love you so much. I'll see you when Easton and I return home.

Love,
Dana

Queen Laurel sat on the bed and cried.

*   *   *

Tim and his group spotted the sign for The Starlight Inn just down the street. They picked up their pace as they made their way through the crowd. The trip had taken a long time. The group only owned two horses, but someone had either stolen them or drove them away from the fort. So they had made the journey on foot. They walked into the inn and stopped at the doorway to look around. It was just after midday, so there weren't many customers in the common room. The large room was well lit by sunlight coming in through the windows. The room was clean and well kept. The floor was swept clean, the polished tables reflected the sunlight. A serving girl came out of the back room, and as the door opened the group could smell the aroma of cooking meat.

A thin, middle-aged man with thinning brown hair sat at the bar. He was wearing simple traveling clothes. A burley man with a full brown beard sat next to him. He was telling his companion a story and laughing loudly. He was wearing very nice clothes and looked to be a noble or a lord. Only one table was occupied. Two people sat in the far corner drinking out of mugs. Both were wearing cloaks with the hoods up, so the group couldn't see their faces. The strangers glanced at the mercenaries as they entered, then turned their attention back to each other.

Tim had everyone take a seat at a large table and went to the bar alone. He stopped next to the smaller man. "Are you Dorn?"

Both men looked at the newcomer. "Yes, I am," the skinny man said. "You must be Tim."

Tim nodded. The two men shook hands. Tim's gaze moved to the bigger man. "And who is this?"

"I am Gunfer, the captain of the ship that is to take yin to Parken," the man said with a deep voice and a thick accent, reaching past Dorn to shake Tim's hand. "Ah, the great Tim. It is truly a pleasure to meet ye. Ye are well known e'rywhere I sail. In e'ry port city, people speak yer name with respect."

"And I am glad to meet you as well Captain Gunfer," Tim replied. "When do we set sail?"

"Eager to leave, huh? Well, this is a large city with a large seaport. We are not scheduled to leave until midday tomorrow."

Tim nodded. "Then we will have time to rest. That is good. Most of my men aren't used to sleeping on the ground. They will appreciate getting a good night's rest in a real bed."

Dorn spoke up. "I thank you for allowing me to accompany you on your mission. I want to see my friend's killer brought to justice."

"Think nothing of it," Tim replied. "Now, how can you help us? What can you do?"

Dorn looked confused. "Do?"

"Yes, do. Can you wield a sword? Are you a good shot with a bow? Can you track? What can you do?"

Dorn looked down. "I can't do any of that. I am merely a servant. I know how government works. I know how things work in castles and palaces. I have a little knowledge of healing. My father was the greatest healer in the kingdom, and he passed a little of that knowledge onto me before he died."

Dorn looked Tim in the eyes. "The truth is, I don't know if I can be of any help to you and your group. All I know is, I want nothing more than to help you bring the king's killer to justice. I will do whatever you ask of me. I am very good at following instructions." Dorn looked very determined.

Tim smiled at the man and put a comforting hand on his shoulder. "We are glad to have you with us Dorn. I am sure you will be a great help to us in our efforts. Come, both of you, meet the rest of the group."

He led the men to the large table where everyone else was seated. After he had introduced everyone and explained to the group that they would be able to rest that night, to the great relief of everyone, Layne asked Gunfer a question.

"How did you get that scar on your arm?"

"Layne!" scolded Brione. "You can't just ask questions like that to people you don't know! It's none of your business."

The big captain looked at the long scar that ran the length of his arm. It looked like a three-clawed creature had sliced the arm open. He smiled at the group. "It's alright I don't mind. I love telling stories of me adventures."

"It's true," Dorn whispered to Tim. "I've been forced to listen to his stories for hours while I waited for you to arrive."

Gunfer sat down heavily between Aiden and Brione, directly across from Layne, and began his tale.

"I am not only a ship captain, I am also a hunter. A very good one at that. I have hunted every single animal on Parken that isn't a carnivore. A couple of years ago, I decided I was getting bored with hunting these kinds of animals. I wanted a true challenge. I wanted danger and excitement. Much to me wife's chagrin, I decided to hunt bears. I…"

"Bears?" interrupted Aiden. Gunfer looked at him. "Are you trying to tell me that a bear gave you that scar?"

"Yes," he answered.

"You mean to tell me that an animal that is covered in hair, stands taller than a man on its hind legs, and can kill a man with one paw swipe did that to you?"

"Yes." Gunfer raised an eyebrow.

Aiden let out a laugh. "Please! Bears don't exist! They're just make believe."

Gunfer looked surprised. "What? Ye don't have bears here?" Everyone shook their heads. "Hmm. Interesting…" He was smiling now. "Well, if ye don't think that bears exist, ye are in for quite a surprise. And not only bears. Ye will be shocked at the creatures that live on Parken.

Giants, ogres, goblins. There are wizards there with magical powers that will render ye speechless if ye witness them. Ye have never been to a place like this before, boy. Get ready."

Aiden's eyes were wide. Brione leaned around the large ship captain. "Don't worry," she said. "He's probably just trying to scare you."

"No, I'm not," said Gunfer. "I'm telling the truth."

Veronna leaned forward. "Does magic really exist?"

"Yes." The reply didn't come from the ship captain, but from Tim. He was looking off in the distance. "Yes, magic does exist. As do bears and all of the other creatures he mentioned. And that's only a few." His gaze went back to the group. "You have never experienced anything like what you are going to experience when we get to Parken. I don't mean to scare you, but we need to be prepared. I will have roughly two months to try to teach you about Parken, and I'll do my best. But it is a place you have to experience firsthand."

Aiden looked at his father. "Have you been there before dad?"

It took a while for Tim to answer. "Yes, I have. And so have you and Veronna." He looked down. "You two were born there."

The siblings gasped and looked at each other. "Really?" asked Veronna. "We were born in a land of magic? Can we do magic?"

Tim smiled at his beloved daughter's excitement. "Not that I know of."

"Oh," she said quietly. But then she brightened up and turned to her brother. "But it will be exciting to go to a land of magic, won't it, Aiden? Maybe we can learn!"

Aiden didn't answer her immediately. He was staring at table, a vacant expression on his face. Suddenly, he seemed to realize that his sister was talking to him. "What was that?"

Veronna looked concerned. "What's on your mind?"

"I just found out that I have a past that I know nothing about." He turned to his father. "Why didn't you ever tell us? Don't you think it is important for a person to know where they are from?"

Tim looked surprised at his son's comment. "I'm sorry. I didn't think we'd ever go back there again. I have a lot of bad memories of Parken. I moved here, to the country of Blanderly, to start a new life, to get away from the past. I wanted to forget everything about my past life. Everything except your mother."

"Did it work?" Veronna asked. "Did you forget?"

"Sometimes it seemed to work. When I am spending time with you two, I forget all the bad times. Veronna, you look just like your mother. I see her in you. But the past haunts a person. I can't ever totally forget, no matter how much I want to."

Veronna got up and gave her father a hug. "I had no idea," she said.

"Now," said Tim as he rubbed his daughter's back, holding her tightly, "let's go talk to the innkeeper about some rooms for the night."

*   *   *

Princess Dana and Jaden watched the group from underneath their hoods. They pretended to be deep in conversation with each other, but in actuality they were keeping a close eye on the mercenaries. They were trying to hear what was being said, so they sat silently. It was very hard to hear, and Dana cursed herself for taking a table in the back corner, but she didn't dare sit anywhere else for fear of being recognized

After Tim's group left, the two companions sat at their table for a few minutes, wanting to make sure that no one from the mercenary group came back into the common room. When they were certain it was safe, they left their table and approached the innkeeper, who was standing behind the bar.

"Innkeeper," Dana said, "when is that group of people who were just here sailing out?"

The man looked at her like she was an idiot. "What kind of question is that? I can't divulge that information." He turned his back to her.

Dana wished she could just reveal to him who she was and command him to tell her what she wanted to know, but that was too dangerous. She had to take a different tactic.

"Do you even know?"

The man snorted and turned back to her. "Of course, I know. Captain Gunfer stays here whenever he sails to Blanderly. He is a regular, and a good friend." He seemed to be proud of the fact that he knew the captain. "He tells me about his plans, so yes, I do know when he will sail out. But I can't give that information to anyone. Sorry."

Dana knew she needed to change tactics if she wanted to be on the same ship as Tim and his company. She decided the best way was to bribe the innkeeper. She took out a bag of gold from underneath her cloak and set it between her and the innkeeper on the bar.

He glanced down at the bag, then looked up at her with disdain. "You're going to try and bribe me?"

"Listen, I will give you this money if you just tell me the name of his ship." He just stared at her. She sighed. "His ship's name isn't a secret, is it?"

The innkeeper studied them, trying to see underneath their hoods. "Why do you want to know? Your persistence is very suspicious. Who are you?"

"Don't worry, we mean Captain Gunfer no harm. We want to sail with him to Parken."

"Why didn't you approach him yourself?"

"It's complicated. But believe me when I say he is in no danger from us. Please, the name of his ship?"

The innkeeper thought about it for a moment, then took the money bag and placed it behind the bar. "I'll give you the name of his ship, but nothing more. Actually, the captain's safety isn't in question. Do you know who his passengers are? Tim and his band of mercenaries. They are well known around the country for their prowess. Only a crazy person would try to harm anyone on that ship with them onboard.

"And the man they met here," he continued, "is the personal servant of Queen Laurel herself. The captain has the backing of the throne. You just keep that in mind."

"We will, I assure you. Now, the name?"

"Portia's Choice. He named it after his daughter." He glared at them. "That is all I'm going to tell you! Now, if you're not going to buy anything, please leave my inn."

*　　*　　*

The funeral of King Michael was an extravagant affair. Much more extravagant than he would have liked. Every citizen in the kingdom was welcome to come and give their respects. Thousands arrived to pay their respects.

The procession started in the courtyard, where the path leading to the palace was lined with thousands of white roses. The king's personal guards wore their gold ceremonial armor. Twenty men marched in front of the casket, which was made of wood but painted gold, and twenty marched behind. Real gold would have been too heavy to carry. Queen Laurel walked alone beside it. Her children should have been there with her. But one had killed the man in the casket and fled, the other had gone on a dangerous and foolhardy quest to save him. She was surrounded by thousands of people, and yet she had never felt so alone in her life.

The casket was carried by the king's personal advisors. That was their own idea. They had each volunteered for the position. They each loved the king dearly.

They walked up the steps leading to the palace. The staff, dressed in white, lined either side of the stairs. As they entered, the halls were lined with the majority of the knights of the realm, wearing the colors of the kingdom: several shades of red ranging from a light red, almost pink, to a dark crimson. They each had one hand on the hilts of their swords, the other in a fist placed over their hearts, their heads bowed as the casket passed.

They laid the casket to rest at the foot of the great red and gold throne. There, they opened it so all the mourners could see his peaceful face. She sat on the throne all day as an endless stream of people came into the throne room to get one last look at the king. They showered her with kind words, words of hope and strength. She appreciated their concern for her. Her heart swelled as she saw the love these people had had for her husband. Yet, all she wanted to do was be alone in her time of grief. Grief not only for her deceased husband, but also for her lost children. To her, they were both lost.

After what seemed like an eternity, she stood up and gave the most difficult speech she had ever given in her life.

"I want you all to know that King Michael loved you. His first thoughts when he woke up in the morning, and his last thoughts before falling asleep, were of you. He wanted to do what was best for his country and its people. I cannot tell you how many sleepless nights he spent worrying about a decision he made or a law he passed, wondering if it was the right thing to do. He loved you more than you will ever know. And I know you loved him as well. I will be eternally grateful for the love you had for my husband."

Queen Laurel paused, gathering her thoughts. "I hope you can love me as well as I take over the monarchy of this country. I never thought I would have to do this, I never wanted to do this, but I will. You can take comfort in knowing that I too will do everything I can for the benefit of this country, just like my husband did. I see bright days in our future if you will support me like you did my husband.

"Not only was he a good king, but he was a loving husband and father. Unfortunately, not everyone loved him as much as he loved them. I am going to tell you something that is very difficult for me to say, but you have a right to know." Laurel wiped a tear running down her cheek. "My son, Prince Aiden, hired an assassin from across the sea to murder his own father!"

She could hear gasps from the crowd, followed by exclamations of shock and dismay. She waited for it to die down before she continued.

"My son has allied himself with King Korlas of Parken. After my husband's murder, he fled across the sea to Parken. He plans on returning with King Korlas' army at his back, to take over the country and rule. He did this because King Michael refused to give the throne to him.

"Good people. Our country has been blessed to be able to avoid the horrors of war for over one hundred years. We have known peace and prosperity. But that peace is about to be shattered. My son comes with a foreign army at his back, intent on destroying anyone who stands in his way. Well, I intend to stand in his way. I sent a group of mercenaries to track my son down and bring him to justice. But if they should fail, we need to be prepared.

"I told you that I believe bright days are in store for us in the future, but we must get past these dark ones first. I will be here for you always. Will you be here for me?"

Despite the terrible news, the crowd gave a deafening cheer in support of their queen. She managed to give the people a warm smile, then turned and walked away.

This terrible day wasn't over yet. It had started with a somber mood, it ended with a worse one.

Tears streamed down her cheeks as she watched the open casket burn, the flames eating the body of her husband. Now Queen Laurel had no more tears to shed. She was all cried out. It was time to look forward. She had to do what was best for the people. She had to take into consideration the idea that maybe Tim might fail and her son might survive. She had to be prepared for war.

8

Everyone was gathered in a large room with two beds, a clothing chest, a table, chair, and water basin. The room was cared for just like the common room. It was clean and smelled fresh. Zach was seated on the chair at the table, with everyone else sitting on a bed. Tim was standing in front of them, addressing the group. Gunfer had retired to his room to attend to his daughter, who had been sick lately, so he did not attend the meeting.

"The man that killed the king is a Zantan Robber," Tim was explaining. "The Zantan Robbers, who are named after the group's founder, are people who misguidedly longed for power; so much so that they sold their souls to the Dark God for it. Their yellow skin is the Dark God's mark."

"What powers did they receive?" asked Dustin.

"They were given speed, agility, quickness, fighting ability. You name it, they have it. They are the perfect fighters. And the perfect assassins."

"That doesn't sound like enough to me for such a high price," said Brione. "You would think they would get magical abilities at least."

"No," Tim replied. "The Dark God gave those to a different group of people. A worse group."

"What could be worse than the Robbers?" asked Dorn, who recalled his almost fatal encounter.

"Dark Paladins," Tim replied. "Paladins are God's righteous champions. They have his protection and power, yet have to follow his rules.

Dark Paladins longed for a power they could use anyway they wished. They have been seduced by the Dark God."

"Is their skin yellow as well?" asked Aiden.

"No. They also gave their souls to the Dark God, mistakenly thinking that he will back them up when in need. They were wrong. He won't. He will drag them down to Hell"

"Well," said Layne, "at least the Robbers will be easy to spot. You know, yellow skin and all." He looked around the room, grinning at his joke, but no one else seemed to think it funny.

"I don't think so," said Dorn. "The one that killed the king snuck into the *palace*. No one should have been able to do that."

"It is because of the power they have received from their Dark God," said Tim.

"How do we defeat these Robbers if we face them in battle?" asked Dustin.

"I don't think it will come to that. They are not a fighting force, they are thieves and assassins. I don't ever remember seeing more than one or two together at a time. We'll be alright if we just stick together. I believe our group is more than a match for them."

"Tell us about magic!" Veronna exclaimed. "I bet it's exciting to live in a land where there are wizards and magic!"

Tim smiled. He could always count on his Veronnna to lighten up a conversation. "Yes honey, it is exciting. But it can also be terrifying. You'll understand when you see magic at work."

Veronna looked more excited at that, if that was possible. "Do you think I'll get to see magic? Oh, I hope so!"

"How does magic work?" asked Dorn.

"Well, I am by no means an expert on the subject, but I do know a little." Tim thought for a moment on how to proceed. "Magic is the power of the mind. There are no magic words or hand movements like you hear about in stories. You think something, and it happens."

"Just like that?" asked Layne doubtfully. "It's that simple?"

"Actually no," Tim answered. "It's not simple at all. You aren't born with the knowledge of how to manipulate things with your mind. You have to be taught. It takes years to learn it. It takes great skill and concentration. So much so that a wizard can only do one kind of magic. It is too complicated to learn more than one."

"How many different kinds of magic are there?" Veronna asked. Her attention was riveted on her father's every word.

"There are many different kinds. Mages use elemental magic. Fire, earth, water, and air. Some people can learn two different types of elemental magic. These people are called sages.

"Then there are necromancers, who can raise the dead and curse their enemies. There are illusionists, who make you see things that aren't there. There are druids who can control earth and plant life. They have great relationships with the animals and can call them to their aid. There are telekinetic people who move things without touching them, and telepaths who can read and control other peoples' minds.

"Some wizards can imbue items with magic powers. There are wizards who can summon beasts from this world and others to attack their enemies. Some can polymorph themselves and others into different creatures, some can shape shift. And then there is the power of God, light magic that he gives to his Paladins. And, as you can probably guess, The Dark God gives dark magic to his Paladins, too.

Veronna was bouncing up and down on the edge of the bed. "Did you know any wizards, Dad?"

"Yes, I did. They are some of the best people I've ever met."

"I would love to be a druid!" Veronna said. "To have animals come whenever you call them would be amazing!"

Tim laughed at that. "Yes, I guess it would." His face turned serious again. "We have to be very careful. Wizards can be great allies, but very powerful and dangerous enemies. It would be best if we finish this job as quickly as possible and stay out of the affairs of Parken as much as we can. Understood?"

"Yes," everyone replied, Veronna more solemn than the rest.

"Now," Tim continued. "Everyone, go to your rooms and get some sleep. You have earned a night in a comfortable bed. Tomorrow we start on a long and difficult journey, and we'll need our strength. Good night everyone."

*   *   *

The party woke up early the next morning; Dorn, because he was used to early mornings, and the rest because they were all excited about the journey they were going to embark on that day.

Captain Gunfer and his daughter had returned to his ship early to get it ready for the two-month trip, so the rest of the group made their own way to the docks. Blanden was a large port town, though not as large as Tosun, the Capitol of Blanderly. It was built in the hills that bordered the coast. Almost anywhere in the city you could look east and see the bay beneath, with its hundreds of ships docked at harbor and hundreds more farther out, all leaving, or waiting for their turn to dock. It looked like a huge mess to the untrained eye, but to the close observer, it was a well-organized operation.

When the group first caught a glimpse of the sea, they stopped and stared. None of them had ever seen the sea before, except Tim and Zach, and they all marveled at how enormous it was. Beyond the ships in the bay they could see…water. And more water after that. Nothing but water. No hint of land beyond the city was in sight. The sunlight reflecting off the water made the sea shine. Aiden had never seen anything like it before.

Aiden turned to his father. "We're going to spend two months in that?"

Tim laughed. "Preferably on it, not in it. But yes, we are."

Layne shot Tim a look and shook his head at the man's attempt at humor, but didn't say anything.

'It's beautiful," Veronna whispered.

"Yes," agreed Brione. "It is. It kind of makes you feel small and insignificant, doesn't it?"

"Brione," Layne said, "I'm sure a lot of things make you feel small and insignificant. Like me, for example."

Brione glared at him. "You sure know how to ruin a beautiful moment Layne."

The man put his hands up in defense. "I am only kidding."

"That's all you ever do," Brione snapped and stocked down the street, the others having to hurry to catch up to her.

"Why do you always do that to her?" Aiden asked as he hurried beside Layne.

"It's a gift, Aiden," the bigger man replied. "We shouldn't hide our gifts from the world. We should use them."

Aiden smiled. "If I didn't know any better, I'd say you had a crush on her."

Layne stumbled and fell to the ground. "What!" Aiden didn't stop and wait for him. Instead, he spun around, trotting backwards so he could look at Layne, laughing at his friend. Layne got to his feet and ran to catch up.

"What did you say?" Layne demanded.

"I said that if I didn't know any better, you have a crush on Brione because of the way you tease her."

"Well," Layne replied, brushing himself off as he walked, "You don't know any better. She's way too serious for me. Anyway, she's like my sister! And I tease everyone, not just her. She's just an easier target than everyone else because she takes it so seriously. I get a reaction out of her. I…"

"You're talking pretty fast, trying really hard to defend yourself."

Layne stopped talking and looked at his friend. "Shut up."

That made Aiden laugh even harder.

They spent the rest of the morning slowly making their way towards the docks, taking in the sights and sounds of the city as they went. Except for Dorn and Tim, they were all from small towns. Dustin had spent some time in Tosun as a knight of the realm, and Brione had been to the capitol city a couple of times, but they still weren't used to the hustle and bustle of big cities.

The streets were a lot like their smaller home towns, with people going from place to place. Hawkers were calling out their wares in loud voices, shop owners were standing in doorways, grinning and trying to coax customers into their store, promising them the best products at the most reasonable prices. Carts were traveling on either side of the road, hauling everything from dirty laundry to hay. The mix of strange and familiar sights and sounds was enticing to the small group.

They saw large churches made of huge blocks of rough stone. Ancient gargoyles clutched the sides of the buildings, and spires soared hundreds of feet into the air. Each church had a man in robes standing on the massive staircases that led to each building, preaching to small gatherings of people. They saw numerous inns, massive wooden structures that sometimes were up to three stories high. Aiden imagined they held hundreds of rooms, with people from all over the world converging in one place, sharing stories of exotic places and harrowing adventures.

The girls were running from shop to shop, looking in windows and exclaiming when they saw something they liked. Aiden smiled as he watched the usually serious Brione run hand in hand with the much younger Veronna, excited faces peering into windows. Shop owners beamed at them and pulled them inside, only to have Tim go in after them and retrieve them.

Tim smiled as he watched them. "Your sister has a way with people," he told Aiden. "Your mother did too. They both have the ability to bring out the best in people."

Tim bought supplies that the group would need for the journey, then they finally reached the docks.

The smells had changed the closer group got to the docks. The aroma of fish was heavy in the air, and the breeze coming from the ocean brought the smell of salt to their noses. The group passed well-built, shirtless men hauling everything from barrels to rolled up fishing nets on their shoulders. The docks were so big that it took them almost an hour to find Captain Gunfer's ship. It was a huge vessel, with several decks and four masts. The words *Portia's Choice* were painted in large black letters on both sides of the hull. The captain's quarters was a large, square building in the middle of the top deck. Captain Gunfer was just stepping out of it as the group walked up the ramp and boarded the ship.

He waved the group over. "Welcome," he said cheerfully. "What do ye think of her?"

"Well," replied Tim, "I'm no expert on ships, but she's beautiful. I'm very impressed." Captain Gunfer was beaming.

Everyone was looking around wide-eyed and open-mouthed. Only Tim and Zach had ever been on a ship before, and this was one large enough to impress even experienced sailors. There were dozens of crewmen going about their business. Several massive sails were being unfurled above them.

Layne was looking up at the sails, and when he looked down, he saw a girl. She looked to be a few years younger than him. She was petite, with long, jet black hair. His blue eyes met her green ones, and they couldn't look away. She was walking towards them, smiling warmly. "Wow," he whispered.

She stopped in front of the group, standing next to Gunfer.

"This is my daughter Portia," Gunfer said, beaming. "Portia, this is the famous Tim and his mercenary company."

"Hello," she said. "It's nice to meet you. I've heard so much about you."

"It's nice to meet you too," replied Tim. "This is my son Aiden, and my daughter Veronna…" He continued to introduce the rest of the group, but she had stopped paying attention. She was staring at Aiden. When he noticed, he quickly looked away. He looked at Layne, who's eyes were fixed on Portia.

When the introductions were complete, Gunfer asked Portia to take the group below and show them their cabins.

"Alright," she said. "Please come with me everyone." Her gaze lingered on Aiden before she turned away.

*   *   *

"So," Portia said as she watched Aiden unpack after bringing everyone to their cabins. She sat on one of the beds. "You're a mercenary?"

"Yes," Aiden replied without looking at her.

'That's got to be pretty exciting."

"I guess so."

"I wish I could have an exciting life like you. Don't get me wrong, I love sailing." She paused as she watched him. "I'm my father's navigator you know."

"Hmm," he replied, only half listening to her.

"Well, anyway. I would love to get off the ship for a while. Nothing ever happens on this boat. Pirates are too scared of us. We have a reputation as a ship you don't want to mess with. It gets pretty boring sometimes. I want *adventure*. I want to *do* something with my life. I know I would miss my father and the crew, but…"

Aiden didn't say anything.

"What is your broge?"

"My what?"

"Your broge?"

"Your ancestors," she reiterated after he didn't say anything. "Who were they?"

"I don't know." He still hadn't looked at her.

"What do you mean you don't know?"

"My dad has never told me about it."

"Oh." She frowned. "That's too bad. I love learning about peoples' ancestors. My ancestors were royalty."

"Hmm."

"How old are you?"

Aiden stopped what he was doing and finally looked at her. "Why do you want to know that?"

"Because I'm pretty sure we are about the same age. Everyone is older than me on this ship and most of them treat me like a little kid. It will be good to have someone my own age to talk to for once."

He went back to his unpacking. "I'm eighteen."

Portia beamed. "I knew it! I knew we were about the same age. I'm seventeen. This is going to be great!" In her excitement she moved closer to him. She was now sitting on the bed where he was unpacking his stuff.

He looked at her again. "Why do you speak differently than your dad?"

"What?"

"Your dad has a different accent than you do. His is thick, while yours is fainter. Why?"

"He has been sailing his entire life. He has been to a lot of ports all over the world. I guess he just picked up bits and pieces everywhere he has been. My accent isn't as thick because I have only been sailing with him on this ship for a few years. When I was younger, I stayed at home with my mom when my dad sailed on his long journies. I only went on the shorter ones, closer to home." Her face turned somber. "After she got sick and died, my dad started taking me with him on Portia's choice. That's when he discovered my talent for navigating."

Aiden regretted asking the question. "I'm sorry about your mom."

Before she could say anything there was a knock on the door and Layne popped his head in. He smiled when he saw that Portia was in the room.

"What are you guys doing?"

"Nothing," said Portia quickly.

"She's talking and I'm unpacking," replied Aiden.

"Then, I'm not interrupting?"

"Well…" Portia started to say, but Aiden interrupted her.

"No, not at all. Come in."

Portia frowned, but Aiden ignored her.

"How do you like your cabin?" Aiden asked his friend.

"It's just like this one," said Layne, "except the company is better in here." He winked at Portia as he said this. She didn't seem amused. "I'm glad that we only have to have two people to a cabin. It would be pretty cramped if we had to have more."

"You should be happy," Portia snapped. She sounded irritated. "These cabins are much bigger than most. You don't know how lucky you are to be on my father's ship."

"I'm sorry," Layne said, putting up his hands. "I didn't mean to offend you. I think this ship is amazing."

"It is." She gave a firm nod, the matter closed in her mind. "Aiden, if you would like a tour of the ship, I would be happy to give you one. I think you would really enjoy it. Come find me later." With that, she turned and left.

"Wow," Layne whispered as he watched her leave the cabin. "She sure is something. I love the way she talks." A confused expression crossed his face. He looked at Aiden. "Wait a minute. Why didn't *I* get an invite for a tour?"

"Maybe she doesn't like you."

"Doesn't like me?" He looked at the doorway to the cabin. "She doesn't even know me." He looked back at his friend. "Anyway, what's not to like?"

"I don't know," Aiden said with a grin. "I like you."

*　　*　　*

They had been out to sea for four days before the crew started noticing the disappearances. Crew members were going down into the storage cellars and not coming back up. It seemed to be happening at random. Three different people would go down and come right back up, then one man would go down and wouldn't be seen again. It was scaring the crew. Captain Gunfer called Tim and his mercenaries together to address the problem.

"We're not used to this kind of thing," he explained. "Give us a ship full of pirates to fight and we'll take them on without blinking, but this is different. Anything could be down there. I would like ye to take yer group down below and find out what is taking my men. I will pay ye if need be."

Tim looked at each of them in turn. They all gave him a slight nod or a smile. "Okay," he said to the captain. "We will go down and discover what is doing this. No extra payment is necessary. It's what we do." He looked around the group again. "I'll go down first, with Zach right behind me and Brione taking up rear guard. Everyone else will be in single file between us. Let's go."

As they headed towards the door that would take them below, Aiden heard a voice call out. "Be careful Aiden!" He turned and saw Portia watching him, a concerned look on her face. During the last four days, when she wasn't navigating for her father, she had been following Aiden everywhere. She would talk nonstop about her life, her past, and her ideal future. Aiden only half listened to her and very seldom said much in return. He found her childish and annoying. Why couldn't she tell he wasn't interested in her? It got to the point that when he saw her coming, he would start up a conversation with anyone who was close by. He even inadvertently started chatting with Zach, although that swiftly ended when the dark-skinned man simply stood up and walked away, giving Portia freedom to talk to Aiden.

Layne didn't help the situation any. When he tried avoiding Portia by talking to Layne, his friend would include her in the conversation. Layne couldn't fathom why Aiden didn't like the attention Portia was giving him. Layne told him more than once that he would love the attention from her. True, Aiden thought, she was beautiful, but looks weren't everything. He told Layne that he could have her.

But for some reason Portia wasn't interested in Layne. She only had eyes for Aiden and neither of the friends knew why.

Aiden's thoughts were brought back to the task at hand when his father opened the door and started down the ladder. Zach followed him, then Dustin, then it was Aiden's turn. He slowly went down the ladder, looking up as Layne started down after him. Then he looked down and discovered he was three rungs from the floor.

He stepped off the ladder and looked down the corridor. The group was bunched a little farther on, waiting for everyone to come down. The hall was dimly lit by lanterns hanging on the wall on either side.

They were spaced close enough to each other so that there were no dark spots in the corridor. They slowly moved down the hallway, stopping to search each room they came to. They stayed as a group, not daring to split up. The captain was right, anything could be down here. Although the rest of the group couldn't understand what kinds of things could be threatening them, Tim did. He was from Parken. He had seen the things that lived there.

They had found nothing when they finally reached the last door in the hall. Tim slowly opened the door and led the way inside. It was a storeroom. There were food stuffs, extra sails, and other sailing supplies covering the floor and walls. The group could see three doors besides the one they entered. They went to the first one, opened it, and found a small closet with more supplies. They moved to the next door and opened it. Tim gave a small exclamation of surprise and opened the door all the way. There, tied up on the floor and unconscious, were the missing sailors. Tim walked into the small room to make sure they were alright. The rest of the group turned towards the last door as they heard it creek open. Suddenly, a black clad figure burst out of the room, twin short swords held in front of him. Behind him came another figure, this one cloaked and its face concealed.

Everyone drew their weapons and prepared for a fight. They were surprised when Zach exclaimed "No!"

Tim came out of the room with the unconscious sailors and looked from Zach to the newcomers. There was a definite resemblance between Zach and the man wielding the short swords. They were both black skinned and had the same build and fighting stance. Tim could see recognition in both men's eyes as they looked at each other.

"Do you know this man?" asked Tim.

"Yes," replied Zach. "We trained together in our home country."

Layne was holding his huge battle ax that he kept strapped across his back and looked as though he were about to advance on the dark man when Zach spoke again. "Do not attack. If I weren't here, Jaden could kill every single one of you."

Suddenly the smaller figure stepped forward and pulled back the hood of its cloak. Tim gave another exclamation of surprise as he looked at the beautiful woman.

"Princess Dana!"

"That's the princess?" asked Layne.

"Yes," Dana replied.

Tim seemed to have quickly recovered from his surprise. "What are you doing here? Did you attack those sailors we found in that room?"

"Yes," she answered. She was speaking in her princess voice, the one she used when she expected to be obeyed. "They discovered us, so we had to knock them out. We couldn't afford to be caught too quickly. We didn't want the captain turning around and taking us back to Blanden. How long have we been at sea? It's not easy to keep track of the passing of time down here."

"Four days," Tim replied. "And you haven't answered my first question."

"Jaden and I are going with you to find my brother. I will not let you kill him. Arrest him if you must, but he can't be killed without a trial first."

Tim was speechless. He didn't know how to respond. The idea of the princess going on this dangerous journey with them was unheard of. Yet he couldn't seem to find the words. Finally, he managed a brisk, "No."

"No? I am your princess. I command you to take me with you."

Tim stood his ground. "My answer is no, Princess. It is too dangerous."

Dana snorted a laugh. "Do you think me defenseless? Jaden and I hid on a ship full of people for four days without being discovered. When your man said that Jaden could kill every one of you, he wasn't lying. Do not worry about me, Tim. We're going."

"It is up to the captain to decide if you even make it to Parken," Tim said. "Remember Princess, you do not rule over Captain Gunfer. He does not live in Blanderly. Let's go talk to him."

*   *   *

Aiden was leaning against the ship's railing with Layne and, unfortunately, Portia, watching Tim, Princess Dana, and Captain Gunfer talking in the captain's quarters. As they watched, wondering what was being said, Brione walked by, deep in conversation with Dustin. Portia watched them go and then turned to Aiden.

"What's Brione's story anyway?"

Aiden looked at her, unable to answer for a moment. He hadn't heard her talk about anything but him and herself since he had met her.

"Her…her story?"

"Yeah, her story. I mean, how did a woman become second-in-command of the most famous mercenary group on two continents?"

Aiden hesitated, thinking. "I…actually don't know. I've never realized before now that I know almost nothing about her past."

Layne spoke up. "I know her story."

Aiden looked surprised. "You do? How?"

"One night a while back I accidentally overheard her talking about her childhood with your dad."

Aiden raised an eyebrow. "Accidentally?"

"Well…" Layne said. "Anyway, I overheard them talking. She said that her parents had five kids. She was the middle child, and the only girl. Brione adored her father, but he preferred to spend his time with her brothers. Oh, she knew that he loved her, but he didn't like to include her in 'boy activities.' He thought her place was in the home with her mother.

"Brione didn't take this sitting down, however. Her father was an adventurer, an explorer. He took his sons with him wherever he went, not intending to take her along, but she would sneak out and follow them. She became very good at tracking them and not being discovered. She went without fear, not realizing how dangerous it is for a little girl out in the wilderness.

"When she would finally be caught, her brothers would be furious. Her father was not happy with her, but she could see pride in his eyes when he looked at her. If they were far enough away from home when they discovered her, her father would allow her to stay with them for the rest of the trip if she promised him to be careful and stay out of their way. If they were only a day or two away from the house, he would send her back with one of her brothers as escort.

"Her brothers were always angry with her if they were the one selected to escort her home. Brione said that they would usually beat her on the journey back to the house. They were severely punished afterwards, first by their mother, then by their father when he arrived home. But they continued to do it. They hoped to stop her from following them. It didn't work. She became so good at tracking them without being seen that after a little while, she was never caught in time to be sent home."

"That's awful," said Portia.

"Yeah," Layne agreed. "When her father would teach them sword play, she would try to learn too. At first, her father refused to teach her. She would watch them practice, then later, when she was alone, she would take a stick and copy what they did. One day, her brothers found her practicing with her stick. They laughed at her, calling her names and asking if she wanted them to teach her. When she eagerly said yes, they took sticks and beat her with them. They beat her senseless. Her father caught them doing it. He punished them like he had never punished them before. He stopped teaching them sword play and started teaching her."

Portia laughed at that.

Layne grinned at her, then continued.

"She was a quick learner. He taught her everything he had taught his sons. They would watch, but weren't allowed to participate. They were angrier with her than ever, but her father warned them not to touch her again. So they left her alone.

"He trained her for two years. At the end of the second year, he allowed her to fight her brothers. It was four against one, and she not only beat them, she humiliated them. Her father just watched her do it. She said that after that her brothers never bothered her again.

"I think that is why she is so serious. For two years she did nothing but train with her father. She worked very hard. She didn't have time for goofing off with friends. I think she has carried that over to her adult life. It's kind of sad, actually."

"Yeah," both Portia and Aiden agreed.

After a moment of silence, Portia spoke up again. "But how did she become second-in-command? How did she meet Tim?"

Before Layne could answer her, Tim came out of the captain's quarters, Dana following close behind. Tim looked furious.

"Do you realize how much harder you just made my job?" he yelled. Aiden was surprised. He could count the number of times in his life he had heard his father yell on one hand. "Not only do we have to find your brother, but now I have to protect you in the process! Do you know what your mother will do to me if you are killed under my protection? Do you?" Dana looked taken aback. She hadn't expected Tim to yell at her. She just looked at the mercenary leader for a moment, then turned around and went to her cabin. Aiden thought he saw a tear or two running down her cheeks.

Tim approached Aiden and the others. "Well," he announced as he reached the group. "She is staying on the ship with us. Captain Gunfer says we're too far out to sea to turn back now. We would lose too much time in our search for the prince."

Aiden was pleased. The three of them were watching the princess speak with the captain and Tim, but Aiden only had eyes for Dana. She was the most amazing woman he had ever seen. Beautiful and strong, willing to do what she believed to be right. She had proven that by following them all the way from the palace and hiding from everyone on the ship for four days. That couldn't have been easy. Yes, life could be a lot worse than spending two months at sea with Princess Dana.

Suddenly, Aiden was very excited about this journey.

9

The voyage across the sea had been a swift one. One of the crewmen of the ship that had carried Prince Easton was a wizard who studied wind magic. He kept the sails full with wind at all times, except when he was sleeping. With his help, they made it to Parken in only one month, half the time it would have normally taken. Almost too quickly, Easton thought.

His plan was going smoothly, but now came the dangerous part, and he was nervous. He had never met King Korlas and he didn't know what kind of man he was. Easton had had a lot of time to think on the voyage across the sea, and unpleasant thoughts started coming to him. Why was King Korlas so keen on helping him? What was in it for him? King Korlas had risked much. Blanderly was a powerful nation. Although they hadn't had a war in decades, they had a large standing army and a very good economy. Korlas was either desperate or very confident in his power to risk assassinating King Michael.

When the ship had docked at Kingston, the yellow-skinned man, hidden under the hood of his cloak, led Easton to the King's River, where they boarded the king's personal riverboat after the man gave the password to the captain. Easton had the impression that the captain had no idea who Easton's escort was.

Easton studied the assassin for the hundredth time. He was intimidated by the yellow-skinned foreigner, but he had to admit the man was useful. Easton was fleeing the guards when the man appeared at his side, telling the prince to follow him. The man was able to slip the guards and Easton found himself heading to Blanden hours earlier than he had planned.

The trip to Parkos from Kingston usually took about two weeks to complete, but it only took a few days by river. Even though they traveled upstream, against the current, the rowers were large and strong men who knew where the current was the strongest. They rowed to the side of the strong currents and were able to make good time. They also had a wind mage to help.

Easton stepped off the riverboat that had brought him up from Kingston, and he was furious to find such a pathetic escort waiting for him. Only two men awaited him as he disembarked from the boat. He now ruled Blanderly and deserved more than two men as an escort. He demanded that someone run to the king and tell him to send a proper escort, but the two men neither budged nor spoke a word. They just stood steady, waiting to leave.

They paid no attention to Easton, just looked straight ahead as they walked. Easton glanced from side to side, trying to get a glimpse of the yellow-skinned man that he had made the trip across the sea with. As soon as the boat docked the man disappeared and Easton met his escort. He hadn't seen his father's killer since. He studied the two men walking on either side of him. They both wore dark blue armor with King Korlas' crest, a red horned beast standing on two legs like a man, a tail ending in a spike curling up on its left, emblazoned on their chests. They each had swords at their hips and a pair of long knives in their belts.

Easton and his escort reached the guards at the palace gate and stopped. The guards were dressed the same as the escorts. After a quick description of who their charge was, the guards let the three men inside. The huge gates slowly opened with a loud squeal, and Easton was able to see the courtyard and the palace behind it.

The prince had lived in a palace his entire life, but he had never seen such beauty before. The courtyard was a huge garden with several walkways winding their way through the flowers, fountains, and fruit trees. People strolled leisurely down the paths, some stopping to pick fruit from the trees, others pausing to smell the flowers. Still others lounged around the fountains, sticking their hands or feet in the cool, refreshing water. The fragrances of the different types of flowers blended into an intoxicating aroma. Easton was sure that the flowers weren't just thrown together haphazardly. It was with careful planning that the gardeners had chosen which flowers to plant. Otherwise, the smell would have been overwhelming, unpleasant.

His escort walked quickly through the beautiful garden, not noticing the scene around them.

They passed through the gardens onto a stone walkway that lead to a large door into the palace. Easton craned his neck to look up at the massive building. It was easily three times as large as his home, and that was the biggest building in the entire country. He thought of the hundreds of people who worked for his family in the palace, and guessed that King Korlas had to employ thousands of servants to run this place.

They walked up the great stone steps where they met two more men at the door and once again stopped. These men were both big, muscular, and wearing armor black as midnight. The same emblem was on their chests, but the beast on their armor had a red crown over its head, and it was holding a red spear. His escort handed him over to the two men in black armor, then took position at the doors as Easton and the two guards went into the palace.

There was a different feeling to these guards than the ones prior. The other men were big, but they just seemed like normal men. These men had a power to them; Easton could feel it. It emanated from them as they moved down the corridors.

Inside the palace was just as beautiful as outside. Tall windows let in ample sunlight, so the torches on the walls were unlit. The floor was white marble that gleamed in the sunlight. As Easton looked down at it, he could almost see himself reflected back. All along the walls were tapestries of every color, all embroidered in gold. The tapestries depicted scenes of war, peace, love and nature. Carpets with beautiful, intricate designs were laid out on the floor. Flowers from the gardens were in vases everywhere; small ones on windowsills, large ones on the floor. The palace had a pleasant aroma of flowers, making Easton feel like he was still outside.

The three men passed several doors lining the hallway, but continued straight ahead. Numerous servants wearing blue uniforms with the horned-creature on the front hustled by, pausing only to give a quick bow to his two guards, then continued on their way. Easton thought it odd that servants would bow to guards, which meant these men must be more than just simple soldiers.

The further into the palace they went, the more black-clad guards they encountered. Soon, they saw no one, except black-armored soldiers in the corridor. Not long after that, they came to an open doorway. From this side of the door he could tell that the room was a large audience chamber. A red carpet embroidered with gold ran from the entrance to a large, black and blue throne sitting on a raised section of floor, with three wide steps leading up to it. A man was standing next to the throne.

He was an impressive figure. Middle-aged with graying black hair, he was tall, muscular, and handsome with dark brown eyes and a square jaw. He wore black and blue robes which were open in the front, revealing the same armor his guards wore, but somehow, his armor was a deeper black, darker and grimmer, like a deep cave where no light entered. Easton thought it odd that a king - for this surely was King Korlas - would need to wear armor in his own audience chamber. A wide smile was on the king's face as he opened his arms wide.

"Welcome Prince Easton," he said. He extended his large hand in greeting when the guards brought Easton to him. Easton took it, wincing a little in his firm grip. "I am so glad that you made it. I am King Korlas. It is so nice to finally meet you."

"I feel the same way," Easton assured him. "I hope our alliance will be beneficial for both our kingdoms."

Korlas laughed. "You rehearsed that on the trip here, didn't you?"

When Easton looked embarrassed, he laughed again. "Don't worry about it. It is natural that you would be nervous. To tell you the truth, I am a little nervous myself."

"Really?" Easton couldn't help but sneer at that. "And what do you have to be nervous about? I am here in your country, at your home, surrounded by your men. You have nothing to lose in this. If I fail to gain the throne, you are out nothing."

The smile faded from Korlas' face. "You are correct," he said in a cold voice. "You would do well to remember that fact. I have nothing to lose and you have everything."

"So why do you offer to help me gain the throne?" Easton asked, his temper rising.

"You can rule your little country…as long as I rule you. You will serve as a figurehead. I will hold all the *real* power."

"I decline. I want to go home." Easton started to turn away, but the two guards stepped in front of him. "Out of my way!" Easton ordered.

The men didn't budge. "I would calm down if I were you," Korlas said. He sounded amused. "These two men are my personal guards. Do you know what that means?"

"No," answered Easton through gritted teeth.

"That means that they are Dark Paladins, the champions of the Dark God."

Easton turned back to the king. "What do you propose we do now?"

"I have a wizard in my employ," Korlas replied. "He has great powers. He is the one that informed me of your plight. Now he has given me new information. Your mother has hired a band of mercenaries to follow you here and kill you."

Easton couldn't believe it. "My mother wants me killed? How does your wizard know this?"

"He has powers beyond the understanding of normal men. He uses these powers to gain information, which makes him even more powerful. Just be content that he knows. Now, there is something else. Your sister and her bodyguard are following them."

Easton was shocked. "What? Dana is coming here? Why?"

"Why, to stop them from killing you of course. Princess Dana thinks that there is some good in you, that you are worth saving. Personally, I agree with your mother. A man who has his own father killed doesn't deserve to live."

Easton was furious. "Then what are you waiting for? Why not just kill me now and get it over with?"

"You should be happy. You get to live and be king of your country. You will bow only to me. Doesn't that please you?"

When Easton didn't answer, the king continued. "We are not going to do anything but wait for now. The man that leads the group that is coming for you is very powerful. You will stay here until he and his group arrive. I will take care of them and then we will see what we can do about putting you on your throne."

"And what of Dana? What will you do with her?"

Korlas smiled. "I think that a marriage will bring our two countries closer together. Don't you agree?"

"Marriage!" Easton roared. "You want to marry my sister? No! You're out of your mind. She'll never agree to it."

"She won't have a choice in the matter."

Easton was speechless but seething with fury. He wouldn't just sit here and let this happen to her. Without thinking of the consequences, he pulled a knife and attacked the king. The two guards didn't budge, not viewing Easton as a threat to their king.

Korlas also didn't budge. He simply continued to stand in place with a bored look on his face. Just before Easton reached him, the prince cried out in pain, dropped his knife, and fell to the ground. Korlas laughed as he watched Easton convulse on the floor.

Easton had never felt such pain. His insides felt as if they had ignited on fire. He tried to scream, but he couldn't breathe. His body shook uncontrollably and there was nothing he could do to stop it. Blackness was closing in, he thought he was going to pass out. Before the darkness totally enveloped him, the pain suddenly stopped. He lay on his side, coughing and gasping for breath.

He was finally able to roll to his back and look up. Korlas was standing over him, a scowl on his face. He slammed his boot onto Easton's chest, taking his breath away again. "I told you to calm down, Little Prince. My guards are not the only ones who have the power of the Dark God at their disposal. Dana has no choice, she will be my bride, and there is nothing you can do about it. To tell you the truth, I am glad that you just did what you did. It allowed me to properly demonstrate to you the situation you are in. Now, I suggest you cooperate, so I don't have to do so again. I promise you, it will be worse next time."

Easton couldn't answer. He grunted something that Korlas took as agreement. Korlas spat on him and turned away. "Get him out of my sight," he ordered as he walked back to his throne. "Take him to the dungeons." One of the guards picked up the prince and flung him over his shoulder. Korlas didn't watch as they left the throne room.

Korlas sat on his throne, thinking. This Prince Easton was pathetic. If this was what all rulers of Blanderly were like, he would have no problem taking control of the country. He smiled to himself. This was going to be easier than he had thought.

"Ricardo, I know you are there. Just come out."

The dark-skinned wizard came out of the shadows and stood before King Korlas. He didn't kneel. He never knelt. He was wearing dark purple robes, with gold around the neck and sleeves. His black hair was cut short. He was clean shaven and looked younger than he was. His dark eyes stared unblinking at the king. Korlas glared at him for a moment before speaking.

"Did you hear that?"

"Yes." Korlas glared again. He irked him that the wizard never addressed him properly.

"All of it?"

"Yes."

"What do you think?"

"I think he is a weak fool and you are wasting your time on him. I have told you that before."

Korlas threw up his hands. "What would you have me do?"

"You are the king," Ricardo sneered. "Who am I to tell the king what to do?"

"You are my advisor!" Korlas yelled. "That is your position: to advise me! Do your job!"

"Kill him and be done with it. You are wasting your time. You don't need

him. You can easily take over his country on your own. Kill him. That is my advice

to you."

"I spent too much effort bringing him over here just to kill him. No, I intend to use him. I will not kill him. Not now anyway."

Ricardo sneered again. "Why do you demand my advice and then ignore it? Why do you even keep me around if you are just going to disregard what I say? It is pointless for me to be here."

"Just because you advise me doesn't mean I always have to do what you say. My word is final, not yours."

"I see. Well, enjoy it while it lasts."

Korlas was surprised by the remark. "What is that supposed to mean? Are you threatening me?"

Ricardo smiled, there was no warmth in it. "No. Just an observation."

"Someday Wizard, I will kill you. I don't know what kind of powers you have, but they are nothing compared to the power that my god gives me."

"Exactly," said Ricardo. "He gives you your power. He can take it away. Without him, you are nothing. My power is my own. No one gave it to me, no one can take it away. I know your god. He is full of promises, but he doesn't back you up. He seduces you with power, then he snatches your soul and drags you down to hell with him. I do not fear you, Your Majesty." The wizard made the king's title sound like an insult. "You, or your god."

"Get out of my sight," the king whispered.

Without another word the wizard turned and left.

King Korlas sat in his throne, brooding for a long time.

*   *   *

Prince Easton didn't know how long he had been hanging over the large guard's shoulder, but it seemed like an eternity. Every step was agony. His insides were jolted every time the guard put his foot down. He almost wished that he would just die so the pain would end. Almost.

It was hard to see the layout of the castle. His head was down, so all he could see was the repeated floor patterns and the guard's feet. The further they walked, the darker the corridors became, until he could barely see. He started to shiver, for it was getting colder. The guards laughed at his discomfort.

After what felt like hours, they arrived at a thick wooden door. The guard that was not carrying him pulled out a large key ring with numerous large keys. He fumbled with them in the dim light for a moment until he found the one he was looking for. He unlocked the door and pushed it open. It opened with an earsplitting creak. "We can hear that all the way upstairs in the palace proper," said the guard carrying him. "If you somehow get out of your cell, the whole palace will know about it. You wouldn't make it a hundred steps before we caught you."

The man walked into the cell and roughly dumped Easton in a heap on the floor. The ground was hard and cold, but it was a relief to get away from the jolting of the journey down there. Without another word the two guards left, shutting the door behind them. In the darkness, he heard the door being locked from the other side. Then, silence.

The tears came, unbidden. Easton could not believe what a fool he had been. He couldn't believe he had trusted a total stranger. He was happy his father was gone, but he wished he had done it himself. He was such a fool.

He sat for a while in self-pity and loathing. He didn't know how long he had been in that cell. It could have been hours or days or weeks. No one came for him. He received no food or water. He was cold, hungry and thirsty, and angry at himself.

Suddenly, he remembered that Dana was on her way there. If he trusted what the king had said, that is. Anger flared up at the thought of this tyrant taking advantage of his beloved sister. She was the only one who had ever cared to understand him. She was there for him when no one else was, including their parents. He couldn't let this happen to her. He had to save her.

*   *   *

Korlas entered his private meeting room in a bad mood. His discussion with Ricardo had both angered and concerned him. He had no reason to doubt the Dark God, but the things the wizard had said had hit him hard. He couldn't help but wonder if what he had said was true. He thought it best to get rid of the wizard once and for all. He would show the ignorant fool his god's true power. He sat in the only chair in the room behind a large wooden desk and waited for his regular meeting to begin.

The secret door on the far side of the room slid open and a black clad figure silently stepped through. He looked up at the king and pulled his hood back. Korlas looked into the yellow face. The yellow-skinned man knelt on one knee. He got back up to his feet and asked, "Orders, Master?"

"There is a group of mercenaries on their way here, right now. I have acquired the King of Blanderly and they intend to take him back. My wizard tells me that they are still at sea, but they will arrive in Kingston in a little less than a month. I want you to take some men and wait for them outside of town to be sure you aren't discovered. You will have plenty of time to prepare and get yourselves over there. I want you to lead the group and choose the men. Take as many as you feel necessary."

"Yes, Master." The Robber turned to leave.

"One more thing," Korlas added, causing the man to stop and turn back to the king. "I know the man who leads the mercenary group. He is very strong. Be careful when you confront him. Do not underestimate him. I don't care what you do with the others, but I want the leader, Tim, brought to me alive."

"Yes, Zantan," the man said, turned, and left. The secret door closed behind him, leaving the leader of the Zantan Robbers alone with his thoughts.

10

Amanda sat up on her bed and wiped tears from her eyes, forcing herself to stop crying. She looked at her blankets, they were soaked with her tears. She had been crying non-stop ever since she had seen Dustin that day at the fort. She hated him. At least, she thought she did. But seeing him that day, seeing the shock and hurt in his eyes, she had to force herself to stay on her horse and not throw herself on him and shower him with kisses. She had harbored her hatred for him for so long that she had forgotten how strong her feelings for him had been.

She never wanted to see him again, and yet she missed him terribly. In her mind she could picture throwing her arms around him and holding him close, then doing one of two things. Sometimes she pictured herself jabbing a knife in his back and smiling at him as he died. Other times she pictured herself kissing him like she used to. She felt so confused.

She walked to the water basin and washed her face. Eyes still closed, she groped for a towel to dry off. When she lowered the towel, she was looking into a pair of dark brown eyes. She screamed.

She turned and tried to run, but the man was lightning quick. He grabbed her from behind and held her close to him. She struggled to get away, but his grip was iron. She couldn't move. She tried to kick his shin, but she was positioned badly and couldn't make solid contact. She tried to bite him, but his arms were too low for her mouth to reach. Her arms were pinned against her torso, so they were useless. She was helpless.

She did the only thing she could do. She screamed again, only louder this time, in hopes that her neighbor would hear her. "Help!" she cried as loud as she could. "Help!"

"Be quiet!" the man ordered. "I am not here to hurt you." But she didn't hear a word he said. She continued screaming at the top of her lungs.

Then her attacker made a mistake. He put his hand over her mouth, giving her the opportunity to bite him. Hard. He cursed and released her, clutching his injured hand. She bolted for the front door.

Once again, the man was too quick. He was on her once more before she took two steps.

Amanda struggled harder than ever. The man couldn't get a good grip on her. Her elbow connected with the man's face. Blood began pouring from his nose. Amanda wiggled free and tried to bolt again, but the man threw his leg out, tripping her. She hit the floor face first, but immediately rolled to her back so she could see her attacker.

He was on her in an instant. She was shocked that the man could continue to move so fast. She was winded already. He tried to sit on her, to keep her in place, but she kicked at him, keeping him back.

He caught her leg and held it to the side, allowing him to sit on her torso. She pummeled him with her fists, but he caught those as well, pinning them to the ground. She tried to bring her legs up over his head and wrap them around his neck, but she couldn't get them high enough. She started to panic.

He moved his body up so that his legs were holding her arms down, freeing his hands.

"I didn't want to have to do this," said the man, surprisingly slowly, "but you give me no choice." Suddenly, a knife was in his hand. Amanda screamed in terror, realizing that she was about to die. The man raised the knife over his head and held it there for a split second. Time seemed to slow as Amanda watched the knife descending towards her.

*   *   *

Her vision slowly came back to her as she awoke. She looked around the room she was in, but she couldn't see any details because her vision was blurry. She realized that she was on a comfortable bed, lying under the blankets. Her head hurt. She raised her hand and felt a large bump on her forehead where the hilt of the man's knife had made contact.

Her vision slowly cleared and she realized that she was still in her own house, in her own bed. She looked out the window. It was still dark. The lamp on her desk was burning brightly, lighting the room. She looked around, but didn't see any trace of the man.

Looking around her little room she couldn't help but compare it to her old house, the one she lived in with Reinhold. It wasn't the one he had caught her with Dustin in. That was one of his several, smaller homes that he used occasionally to get away from the pressures of his position. The fact that he had decided to go to the exact house that she and Dustin were in was an amazing coincidence. Or perhaps, it wasn't. Maybe her husband was having her watched and he knew about Dustin and chose that night to confront them.

No, she was comparing her small home to the large, almost palace-like house that she lived in when she was wife to the king's personal advisor. It was a massive structure, with dozens of rooms and a garden with a fountain that held exotic fish. She loved to sit at the edge of the fountain and soak her feet in the cool water and just think as she watched the fish swim by.

She had maids and servants and attendants. She had women who bathed her and helped her dress. She had been doing these things on her own now for so long that she now thought that lifestyle seemed a little ridiculous. It was nice at the time, though. It had made her feel special. Important.

She especially remembered the bed. It had been huge. It could easily fit ten people her size comfortably. It had a canopy with the most beautiful curtains. The mattress was soft and there were dozens of fluffy pillows to rest her head on. Sometimes she wouldn't get out of bed all day. She had her servants bring her meals to her while she read.

She had been married to one of the most powerful men in the entire kingdom, yet she had thrown it all away for a lowly knight. Reinhold hadn't even been a bad man. True, he had never been a very attentive husband and he never did pay much attention to her, but he had never been cruel. At least not until the day Dustin was forced to kill him to save both of their lives. She didn't understand why her husband had gotten so mad when he discovered them together. He didn't seem to care much about her. She thought that he had married her for her looks. Amanda felt that he had only wanted her when she was on his arm and in his bed.

She remembered the first time she saw Dustin. She was running up the stairs to the palace when she tripped and twisted her ankle. She fell to the ground and couldn't get back up because of the pain. Suddenly, a man crouched down beside her and asked if she was alright. She looked into his brown eyes and saw his genuine concern for her.

When she told him she couldn't walk, he picked her up and carried her into the palace. It felt good to be cradled in his arms, a feeling she wasn't used to. She asked him to tell her a little bit about himself. He answered by saying he was from a small town in the country. He lived with his parents and younger brother. His parents farmed, but they didn't have much. He had decided to come and try to be a knight for a little extra money to send home.

She thought he was the most selfless man she had ever met. He was handsome, too. And gentle. She liked that. Reinhold had not been gentle when they were together.

She thought about telling him who she was, but she couldn't bring herself to do it. She wanted to spend more time with this man and she knew she wouldn't be able to if he knew the truth. Instead, she told him she was a worker in the kitchens and that was where she was headed. She had him drop her off at the hospital wing and told him that when her ankle was better she could make her own way to the kitchens. After he left, she longed to see him again.

She discovered when he got off duty every day and waited for him at the stairs to the palace. They would spend the rest each day together. He would tell her more of his family and his life on the farm, and she would tell him of her childhood, so she didn't have to lie. Her mother was a dress maker and her father ran the shop where they sold the dresses. The dress shop was, in fact, where she had met Reinhold, but she didn't mention that.

The more time she spent with Dustin, the more she liked him. He made her feel good about herself without having to do things for her, like her servants did. He complimented her without innuendos. She was comfortable with him. She found herself falling in love with this knight.

Then they got caught. Then he abandoned her. When she thought of the time she had spent with him, her heart swelled with love, until she remembered that part. Then she would feel nothing but hate.

She was brought out of her thoughts by the door to the room opening. The man who had attacked her came in, shut the door, and then leaned against it. She sat up in the bed. For the first time she saw that he had dark skin.

"I'm glad to see that you are awake. I was afraid that I had hit you too hard. I didn't want to hurt you, you know. But you forced me to. You wouldn't quit fighting." He spoke very slowly.

"What do you expect?" she asked. "You come into my house unannounced and uninvited. You attack me without a word and you expect me to believe you mean me no harm?" Her courage surprised her. This stranger was terrifying, and she knew that he could kill her very easily if he wanted to. "What do you want with me?" she asked.

"It is my master that wants you. The man you hate has left his home, but my master knows where he is going. He wants me to take you to him so that you will have a second chance at killing him."

She sat in stunned silence. She couldn't believe what she had just heard. She had the chance to see Dustin again! But what would she do once she did? Finally, her voice came back.

"Who is your master? Why would he want to help me? And how does he know that I tried to have Dustin killed?"

"My master has great magical powers. He *knows* things. He knows you hired your ex-father-in-law to kill Dustin. He knows you failed. He knows where Dustin is going. I can get you there. That is all you need to know."

"Where will I be going?"

"That is all you need to know."

"You sure aren't very persuasive," she said, getting even braver now that she knew he wasn't planning on killing her. "You attack me instead of talking first, and now when you do talk, you don't give me enough information. I think your master should have sent someone more competent."

The look on the man's face didn't change, but she could see the anger in his eyes. Her fear returned as she thought that she may have just crossed the line.

"If I didn't have orders to take you to my master safely, I would cut out your tongue."

"We are going to your master? I thought you were supposed to take me to Dustin."

"Dustin is also going to my master. He just doesn't know it yet. So, what is your answer?"

She was conflicted inside. She wanted to see Dustin again more than anything, but she didn't know if she wanted to kiss him or stab him. She hoped she would have enough time on the journey to figure it out.

"Okay. I agree. I'll go with you."

The dark-skinned man smiled.

*　　*　　*

Queen Laurel was standing in her war room with the officers of her army. They were making plans for the defense of Blanderly, in case

Easton did come with an army at his back. Most people would shudder at the thought of killing their own countrymen, but not her son. Not if his countrymen were standing in the way of him getting what he wanted. Ideas were thrown out, but it was difficult to plan when you knew nothing of the enemy. Who was this King Korlas? She had heard his name before, but did not know much about him. He had suddenly come into power and no one knew how.

She didn't know how big his army was or what kind of tactics they intended to use. How many footmen did they have? What percentage of the army was cavalry? How many pike men and swordsmen? They just couldn't make a good plan without information.

For that matter, why did King Korlas want to help her son? She suspected that he would take advantage of Easton. Despite everything, she couldn't help but feel a little sorry for the prince. He would be a victim of his own making.

Her immediate concern was how Easton had managed to make contact with King Korlas. The only explanation that she could think of was that Korlas had spies woven into the kingdom. Then another thought crossed her mind. Were the spies still there? The thought terrified her.

*   *   *

Syth was standing in the shadows, listening to what the queen and her officers were saying. They didn't know he was there. He wouldn't be caught unless he wanted to be. They ended the meeting and went their separate ways, promising to meet again in a few days. He stayed hidden until he was alone in the room.

After everyone else had gone he left his hiding place and went to the table. There were maps and diagrams spread out, showing where all the troops in the army were stationed. He looked at all of them very carefully. His master was in his head, looking through his eyes, seeing what Syth was seeing.

Very good, Syth, his master's voice said. *I want you to attend all their war meetings so that I will know their plans.*

Yes Master, Syth replied mentally.

I have other things to deal with now. But we will speak again later. I will be with you when they have their next meeting. With that, the presence in his head was gone. He was alone again.

He left the war room and headed to his personal chambers. The servants and palace staff didn't give him a second look as he passed them by. At first, they would stare at him and his brother when they would walk through the halls. The people in this country had never seen men like them before. Syth and Jaden simply ignored the stares. Now, the people who worked at the palace were used to the dark-skinned protectors of the royal family. Some even tried to strike up friendly conversation with them, but Syth and Jaden just ignored them.

When he arrived at his chambers, he found the queen waiting for him. He stopped in the doorway, surprised to see her here. She had never come here looking for him before. He bowed his head slightly. "My Queen."

"I have a job for you Syth," she said. There was a strange excitement in her voice. "I believe there is a spy in the palace."

"Really, My Queen?"

"Yes. I was thinking about my husband's murder and I decided that there must have been a spy in the palace, someone close to my family, who knew my son's situation. That is the only way Easton could have had contact with assassins from across the sea."

"I believe you may be correct, My Queen," Syth replied. Where was she going with this?

"I would like you to investigate everyone in the palace. The staff, my late husband's advisors, everyone. I know it sounds like a big job, but I am confident in your ability to do it. Question everyone. This spy must be found before they can cause more havoc. You're the only one capable of doing this for me."

"My Queen, you are correct, this will be a big job. A huge job. I will probably need some help."

"Use whatever resources you need. Everything I have is at your disposal."

"Alright. Do not worry My Queen. I will find this spy, if he is still here."

"Thank you, Syth. I knew I could count on you. I don't know what I would do without you."

11

Aiden was standing at the ship's railing, watching the city of Kingston as it drew nearer. It was good to see land again, after not seeing any sign of it for two months. It was daunting to get up every day and go to the top deck and see nothing but water. Aiden couldn't believe how large the sea was. He had commented on this to Captain Gunfer, and the captain had laughed and told him that this was just a tiny part of the sea. Aiden's jaw had dropped in surprise.

His pleasure at traveling with Princess Dana had died quickly. She had no eyes for him. She was pleasant enough to him, but certainly not interested. Anytime he had built up the courage to talk to her, she only ever asked him about Layne, dashing his hopes. He wanted to say something untrue, to make Layne look bad, but he couldn't bring himself to do it.

He told her that Layne was a man that was good at everything he did. Whenever he learned something new, he was an expert at it in just a few hours. Even if Aiden taught his friend something, Layne would be better at it in no time. Aiden had to admit to her that he was somewhat jealous of this.

As Aiden had thought, that conversation made her even more attracted to Layne. She went to find him immediately. He stayed where he was for a long time, looking at the endless water and feeling sorry for himself. When he heard someone coming towards him, he looked up.

"Did Princess Dana find you?" Aiden asked.

"Yes," Layne replied without looking at him.

Aiden swallowed. He looked down. "How did it go?"

"It didn't."

Aiden looked up again. "What?"

"She came to me and told me she thought I was the most interesting man on the ship. She said that she had a talk with you and that you had only good things to say about me." He turned to his friend. "What did you tell her?"

"I told her that you are the kind of person that makes me sick," Aiden replied with a smile.

Layne laughed. "Oh, that's real good."

"I told her that you are good at everything you do. You can pick up a skill or trait in no time, while it takes normal men months or longer to master it." Aiden's gaze went back to the water lapping at the ship. "I really look up to you, you know."

Layne didn't reply. He just grinned and slugged his smaller friend in the shoulder.

"I'm serious, Layne."

Layne looked uncomfortable. "Come on now," he said. "We are mercenaries. We don't talk like that." They both laughed.

"So," Aiden said, "what did you say to the princess when she said those things?"

"I told her that I was honored by her praise, but that my heart belonged to someone else."

"Are you crazy?" Aiden was shocked. He would give anything for Princess Dana to show interest in him. "Have you seen her?"

"Of course. But I told her the truth. My heart does belong to another."

Aiden snorted. "Another who doesn't share your affection." He immediately regretted the words. "Layne, I'm…"

"It is true," the big man said, a look of sadness crossing his face. He sighed. "Portia does not share my feelings. But that doesn't mean that I should ignore them or toss them away. I can't help the way I feel about her. Now you know how I feel when I see Portia following you everywhere and you not caring. I just can't see how you can't be thrilled by the fact that someone like her wants to be with you." Layne's grin returned. "Besides, why would I want to be with royalty? What could I give her that she doesn't already have? And have you heard the way she talks? She has to perfectly enunciate every word she says." Layne leaned in close, lowering his voice. "I think she thinks that she is better than us because she speaks so properly."

Aiden's thoughts came back to the present as he gazed at all the ships around them in the harbor. The city wasn't nearly as large as Blanden, and neither was the harbor. There were much fewer ships here, although they still came in every size imaginable. They ranged from small to long, two-person vessels to massive ships with multiple masts. Aiden spotted one that was even larger than Portia's Choice.

They had to wait for almost an hour before it was their turn to dock. While they waited, Tim called everyone together for a quick meeting.

"Okay," he said when they were all crammed into his cabin. "When we disembark from the ship, we are going to follow Captain Gunfer to a tavern. He has a friend there that he says should be willing to help us. He will guide us to the city of Parkos, where King Korlas lives." He looked at his daughter and smiled. "His friend is a wizard."

Veronna beamed. "I really get to meet a wizard?"

"Yes."

"How exciting! Isn't that exciting Aiden?"

Her brother replied with a smile.

Tim looked back to the rest of the group. "If I remember correctly, it is about a two-week journey to Parkos from here. We will try to keep as low a profile as we can. We don't want to get involved in anything that does not concern us. We just want to retrieve Easton and get home. Understood?"

Everyone responded affirmatively. As they left the cabin, Dana pulled Tim aside. Jaden waited by the door, keeping the princess in sight. She waited until everyone else had left the cabin before she spoke.

"When you say 'retrieve Easton'," she asked, "what do you mean?"

"I mean get to him, and get home, taking him with us."

"So you're not going to kill him?" She asked hopefully.

"I haven't decided yet. Your mother hired me to kill him, so I am obligated to do so. However, your presence here changes things. First we at least have to get him away from Korlas. We can figure out what to do with Prince Easton after that."

"Alright," Dana said. "Don't kill him before then."

When they reached the top deck, the rest of the group had already gathered their belongings and were waiting on deck. Tim noticed that Portia was standing close to his son. He smiled to himself at Portia's persistence and Aiden's disinterest. He had noticed the girl hanging around Aiden the entire trip. Tim thought she was a nice girl, and very pretty. For some reason though, Aiden just wasn't interested.

He had also noticed Layne's infatuation with the girl. He felt bad for the large young man. But it would all end today. They would leave the good captain and his daughter behind, maybe never to see them again.

As the ship hit the dock with a loud thump, the crew scrambled to tie the ship to the dock and put the ramp into place. After the ramp was down, Tim and his group followed Captain Gunfer and his daughter down onto the dock. They made their way through the crowd, weaving around sailors and workers running to their respective ships, or hauling gear on their shoulders. The smell of fish, salt water and sweat encompassed them, overwhelming their senses. They covered their noses with their hands or shirts until they left the docks and entered the road. The wind was blowing from the east, so it took the stench away from them, back out onto the water.

As they walked along the broad street, Aiden saw a young man running towards them. "Portia!" he cried as he hurried to them. "Portia, wait up!"

"Oh no," he heard Portia say under her breath.

"Who is that?" Aiden asked her.

"Just a boy who is infatuated with me. His name is Cory. He can get pretty annoying."

Aiden watched the young man as he approached. His dirty-blonde hair was long and flowing out behind him as he ran. He was tall and lanky, with skinny legs and arms that seemed too long for him. His face was splotched with acne, making him look a few years younger than Aiden. His clothes were plain and loose fitting, like they were a couple sizes too big. He looked like he was wearing an older sibling's hand-me-downs. He was smiling broadly as he ran.

He stopped as he came up to the group, panting and bending over, trying to catch his breath. "Hey… Portia."

She rolled her eyes. "Hi Cory."

He looked at her dad. "Hello Captain Gunfer."

Gunfer nodded. "Cory."

He looked back at Portia. "So, where are you going?" He spoke with a strange accent.

"We are going to meet a friend at a tavern," she answered.

"Oh," Cory replied. "Which one?"

"I don't know."

"The Maiden's Kiss," Captain Gunfer said.

Portia glared at her father. He simply smiled back at her.

"Oh," the young man replied. "What do you know? I was just on my way there too. I was…just running some errands for the owner of the tavern. He hired me the other day. I run errands and stuff for him. I just finished the errand and now I'm on my way back. I can walk with you."

"Great," Portia said under her breath.

"What?" Cory asked.

"I said great. That's great that you can walk with us."

"Oh," he said and grinned. Aiden noticed that his teeth weren't straight. Cory forced his way between Portia and Aiden as they continued walking up the street.

Aiden couldn't help himself. "Look at that," he whispered to Layne. "Portia has put you on the same level as that guy."

Layne just looked at his friend, then punched him.

"Ow!" Aiden said, rubbing his wounded shoulder.

Cory looked at the group as they walked. "You're not from around here, are you?" he asked Tim.

"No," Tim replied. "We just came from across the sea."

"Well, welcome to Many Names."

"Many Names?" Brione asked. "I thought this city was called Kingston."

"Yes, it is," said Cory. "But the people in this city like to make up nicknames for things."

"Really?" Veronna asked. "Like what?"

"Well, people call this street Fisherman's Row or Sailor's Way because it is by the docks. But the real street name is King's Way. A little further up the street there are a lot of inns. People call that area Sleepy Street. But it is still King's Way."

"That is odd," Brione commented.

"Yeah," Cory continued. "But it doesn't stop there. People call the men who patrol the streets at night the Dark Watch, or the Midnight Guards. They are really the Night watch. Different people call them different things. You just have to know what they are talking about when having a conversation. Otherwise, you could get completely lost."

"Are all cities in this country like this?" Dustin asked.

"Oh no," Cory said. "Just this one."

"This place is weird," Layne whispered to Aiden, who wholeheartedly agreed.

Down by the docks the streets were wide and lined with bait shops and large warehouses where they built and repaired boats. Further along the street the buildings changed to inns and taverns, serving the crewmen and passengers coming off the ships. These streets weren't very crowded, causing Aiden to feel much more comfortable walking in this city.

He heard snippets of conversation as people walked by. They all spoke with the same, strange accent Portia had. He turned to his father. "Dad? Why don't you speak the same way these people do?"

"I used to, when I first came over to Blanderly," Tim Replied. "But after a few years of living there, my accent changed. People talk like the people around them, after a time."

After walking for a while, they found themselves in front of a large building with a sign over the door. The sign had a young woman kissing a man in armor on the cheek. Aiden noticed his sister was beaming with excitement at the thought of meeting a real wizard in this building.

Cory led the way in, the rest of the group entering one after the other.

Portia turned to Cory. "Well Cory, if you know the owner, then why don't you introduce us to him?"

The young man's face was red. "Well…um…he's probably not here. He probably went home early…to…er… spend some time with his family. He does that quite often."

"I'm sure he does," Portia said.

Cory smiled and fidgeted, as Portia's eyes narrowed.

Gunfer located his friend in the far corner of the room and led the party over to him. Cory stayed behind. The man stood up. He looked to be in his late twenties, with long dark hair that framed his face. He wore a dark goatee that he kept neatly trimmed. His dark eyes appeared intelligent. He wore comfortable looking brown robes without adornment. He smiled at the captain and shook his hand.

"Gunfer," he said in a friendly voice. "It is good to see you again. You are right on time, as usual."

"Yes, my friend," Gunfer replied. "The wind was good to us."

The wizard around the captain. "Who are all these people?"

Gunfer turned to the group. "Tylersen, this is Tim and his mercenary group." He continued to introduce the mercenaries. Tylersen shook hands with each of them in turn. As a precaution, when he introduced Dana, he didn't give her title. "Everyone, this is my good friend, Tylersen."

"Please, call me Tyler." He turned to the captain. "You travel with interesting company my friend. What is going on?"

Before Gunfer had the chance to answer, Veronna stepped up to Tyler. "Are you really a wizard?" she asked, wide-eyed.

Tyler smiled. "Yes, I am. I usually don't get this kind of reaction when people hear of what I am."

"Why?" Veronna asked, confused by the remark. She couldn't imagine anyone not wanting to meet a wizard.

It was Gunfer who answered. "Because most people who can't do magic don't trust people who can. People fear what they don't understand. Especially something as powerful as magic."

"But not you though," said Portia. "Huh, Dad?"

"No," the captain grinned. "Not me. But I do admit that I, too, used to fear it. Why don't we all have a seat and I will tell ye what changed."

The group took seats around the table, anxious to hear the captain's tale.

"One day," Captain Gunfer began, "I was sailing north up the coast to the next port. It was a ways away, in Order lands, but they don't take kindly outsiders."

"What do you mean, Order lands?" asked Dustin. "What is Order?"

"Order is a religion," Gunfer answered. "As their name states, they believe in Order. Everything has a place. There is no time for revelry or merrymaking. They work hard, and their army is one of the best trained in the world. They consider anyone who does not belong to the faith of Order to be followers of Chaos. Since they are continuously at war with Chaos, they have no qualms about attacking their neighbors or not allowing outsiders into their lands.

"Anyway, I was sailing up the coast, keeping close to the shore, because the waters farther out are dangerous. Pirates roam those waters. For some reason, on this day, a fleet of pirate ships decided to come closer to the cliffs that made up the shoreline. They spotted us and attacked. I think there were six of them. We didn't have the ability to fight six pirate ships at once, so we fled. But they were fast and gained on us quickly.

"No matter how fast we were able to go, they were faster. That is why pirates are so dangerous, ye see. They use speed instead of muscle to get what they want. They have the fastest ships on the sea. Luckily for us, a kind stranger was on the cliffs that day and saw our plight."

"I have no love for pirates," Tyler said.

"Well, we were running for our lives" the captain continued. "We were losing hope, when suddenly the cliff seemed to come alive. Large boulders tore off the face of the cliff and flew at the pirate ships. Three were hit and sunk immediately. The next thing I saw blew my mind. Giant arms made of rock came out of the cliff and reached for the remaining ships. Each hand grabbed a ship and pulled it toward the cliff. The ships smashed to pieces when they hit. The remaining ship fled.

"I was terrified that we were going to be next, but after the final pirate ship left, the cliff returned to normal. We were stunned. We had no idea what had just happened. We looked around and finally saw a figure standing on the cliff, waving to us. I watched as he collapsed to the ground.

"We went to shore on a longboat once we passed the cliffs and a beach appeared. We searched for the one who had helped us, and finally found him, collapsed on the edge of the cliff. He was barely conscious, so we took him back to the ship and waited for him to recover. That man was Tylersen."

"You really have the power to make the cliff do that?" Layne asked. He couldn't hide the awe in his voice.

"Yes, I do," Tyler replied. "I am an Earth Mage. I can control rocks and stones, the earth itself if I need to."

"Wow," Veronna said.

"Why did you collapse?" asked Dorn.

"Magic is mentally taxing," the wizard replied. "Especially magic of the magnitude I used that day. Use it too much, and your mind can't take it anymore. It starts to get hard to think, then you finally pass out, or even die if you're not careful. But with rest, we recover."

"That's amazing!" Veronna exclaimed. Tyler smiled at the high praise.

Tyler turned to Gunfer. "We got off topic, Gunfer. What have you gotten yourself involved in?"

"These people are here searching for a man that murdered someone of very high standing in their country. We have reason to believe that the murderer is in Parkos. So I came to ask ye a favor. I told Tim here that ye might be willing to help them get to Parkos. Ye know, as a guide 'n protector."

"Did you now?"

"Yes," Tim answered. "We need your help. I will pay you for your troubles, of course."

Tyler thought for a moment. "I will need more information than I have so far received before I make a decision. Who is the man of high standing that was murdered?"

"Why does that matter?" Dana snapped.

"It matters because I need to know how important this man was. What are you willing to do to apprehend this murderer? That is important information."

Tim was the one who answered. "The man who was murdered was King Michael. Prince Easton hired a man with yellow skin to murder him after the king told him he was going to give the kingdom to another. After the murder, the prince and the assassin fled here. Queen Laurel, hired us to follow Prince Easton here and apprehend him." Tim reached out and placed a hand on Tyle's shoulder. "I am afraid that if we don't get to the prince in time, war will be inevitable between Parken and Blanderly."

The wizard thought for a while without saying anything. Finally, he looked up at the group. "Well, the cause is a good one. Plus, the money doesn't hurt either, I could really use it." He thought a moment more and nodded. "Yes, I will accompany you to Parkos."

"Thank you, Tyler," Tim said, shaking his hand. "We must leave as soon as possible. Easton had a good head start on us, and we want to get to him before he can fulfill his plan to go back to Blanderly with an army at his back and take the throne by force."

Tyler snorted. "An army? Where is he going to get an army from?"

"King Korlas."

Tyler seemed surprised. "Well, things just got a lot more dangerous," he said. "Korlas is giving the prince an army?" He shook his head. "But I have given you my word, and I intend to keep it." He glanced out the window. "It is getting late. Why don't we find an inn for the night and leave for Parkos tomorrow?"

12

They walked down King's Way (or Sleepy Road, or Inn's Street, or any number of names, depending on who you talked to) arriving at a nice, three story inn called The Traveler's Stop. It was painted white while the door and window panes were a dark green. The common room was clean and smelled faintly of flowers. There was no dirt on the floor or dust on the counters. The patrons were clean and polite. There were no sailors or dockworkers at this inn. These people looked to be merchants or people of wealth. Some even had the bearing of nobility. There looked to be a few officers in the army as well.

The group made their way to the counter, where the innkeeper watched them approach. He was a large man, middle-aged, his hair was combed straight back, his mustache neatly trimmed. His white apron was spotless. He wiped his already clean hands with a rag. "How can I help you folks?

As Tim was getting rooms for the night, Aiden noticed that Portia was sulking. On their way over here, Aiden had overheard Portia and her father arguing about something, although he could not hear what they were saying. By the look on Portia's face, her father seemed to have won the argument.

He watched Veronna take a seat between Layne and another man who looked to be in the army. The man looked over at Veronna and he grinned a grin that Aiden didn't like at all.

"Well hello," the man said as he looked her up and down. "What is your name?"

Veronna was about to answer, but Layne beat her to it. "Her name is not interested."

The man looked angry. "I wasn't talking to you, boy. I was talking to the young lady."

"Exactly," Layne replied. "She is a young lady. Too young for you."

"I think we should let her decide." He looked at Veronna again. "Well?"

Veronna was nervous. "Um…sorry. I think I am too young for you. I'm only fifteen."

"That's okay. I like them young. I have a room here at the inn that they keep empty for me. I can use it whenever I want. Would you like to come up?" By the slur in the man's voice, Aiden could tell that the officer had been drinking for a while before the group had arrived.

"No. I don't think so," Veronna replied.

"Aw, come on." He put his hand on her shoulder.

Layne stood up. "She said no."

The man stood up too. Layne dwarfed him. "Well I say yes." He put both hands on her shoulders.

"Take your hands off her," Layne said threateningly. Aiden walked over and stood beside Veronna. The rest of the group turned to see what was going on.

"Do you know who I am?" The officer sounded furious. His hands were still on Veronna's shoulders. She was too scared to move.

"No," replied Layne. "And I don't care. She doesn't want anything to do with you, so take your hands off her."

The man pulled Veronna against him. The entire group went for the man. Layne got there first.

Layne's fist connected solidly with the man's chin, sending him flying. He crashed onto a table where a couple sat eating their dinner. The table split in two under the man. The couple screamed, their dinner flying into the air and splattering on the walls.

"Guards!" the man cried from the floor.

Half a dozen men stood up from the table they were sitting at and rushed Layne, none of them drawing their weapons. The first one to reach him was thrown back by a punch to the face. The next one ran into Aiden and Dustin, and together they forced him to the ground and held him there. The man struggled and swore, but the two mercenaries were too much for him.

The third man slammed into Layne, knocking him back against the counter. The man wrapped his arms around Layne's torso and squeezed, trying to take his breath away. Layne put both his fists together and slammed them onto his assailants back. Again and again he hit the man until he finally let go and backed away. Layne dropped him with a punch to the jaw.

Another man was fighting with Tim. Tim punched him in the stomach, doubling him over. A knee to the face sent the man flying back. He hit the floor hard and didn't move again.

The rest of the group converged on the two remaining men. Everyone except Gunfer, Portia, and Tyler. They lived and worked in Kingston. The last thing they needed was trouble with the law.

Together, Brione, Jaden, Dana, and Zach dropped the two soldiers, leaving both unconscious. The fight was over almost before it began. No one in the group was injured.

Aiden, still holding the man on the floor with Dustin, looked to the doorway. The original man was standing in the doorway, calling for more guards. They came almost immediately. A dozen men or so came into the inn. The man pointed at Layne. "That man attacked me. Arrest him!" These men did draw their swords.

Brione, Dustin, and Layne all started to draw their own weapons, but Tim stopped them. "No. We are already in enough trouble as it is. No more fighting. Dustin, Aiden, let that man up." Reluctantly, they did so. He got up and joined his fellow guards.

The men surrounded them, swords and spears pointed at their faces. The original man slowly walked up to Layne and punched him in the face. Layne started for the man, but Tim held him back.

"Do you know who I am!" the man screamed in Layne's face. "Do you? No? I am the captain of the town guard. I command every soldier in this city. You attacked the wrong man. You fool!"

"I wouldn't have hit you if you hadn't been trying to force a young girl to go to your room with you. You're despicable." He spit in the man's face.

Then man turned red. "You'll pay for that! Guards, arrest him. Take him to Criminal's Hole. Let's see how tough you are in a cell." Two men tried to grab Layne, but he pushed them off. "Let go of me! I didn't do anything wrong!" It finally took five men to control him. Dustin took a step forward, as if he was going to interfere. But Tim put a hand on his shoulder and stopped him.

"You!" the man pointed at Veronna. "You're coming with me. Take her!" As two men went to grab Veronna, Tim stepped in front of them. "Out of the way!" one man said.

"Touch my daughter," Tim said quietly, putting a hand to the hilt of his sword, "and every single one of you will die." There was such menace in his voice that every man stepped back.

"Fine," said the Captain of the Guard. "She's too ugly for me anyway. But I am taking that boy to jail. The rest of you, get out of my town. Right now. I will have a dozen armed men escort you out. They will have orders to kill you if you give them any trouble. If I ever see you in my city again, I'll kill you." He looked at the men holding Layne. "Let's go." They walked out of the inn. Layne looked back at his family as the soldiers forced him out of the building.

*   *   *

"We're just going to let them arrest Layne?" Dustin demanded. He was furious. "He didn't do anything wrong! He was just protecting Veronna!" They didn't have much fear of the soldiers overhearing. They stayed in the doorway, not wanting to get too close to the furious group.

"I'm sorry!" Veronna cried. "Okay? I know it's my fault. I'm sorry." She broke down, crying.

Dustin calmed down immediately. He put a comforting hand on her shoulder. "It was not your fault, Veronna. It was that captain's fault. Please don't blame yourself."

"He is right," Tim added. "You did nothing wrong. The fault lies entirely with that man."

"What do we do now?" asked Brione. "Are we just going to leave Layne?"

"What else can we do? If we don't leave the city, they will kill us. Then we will be no good to Layne. Let's leave the city, then we'll figure out what to do." He turned to Dustin and put a hand on his shoulder. "Don't worry. We'll get your brother back. I don't think they realize what they have on their hands." Tim smiled. "Layne is not going to be an easy man to keep in prison."

Dustin nodded.

Tyler came up to Tim. "Listen. It would be too risky for you and your group to come back into town and try to save your friend. You will be killed on sight. But I won't."

"What are you saying?" asked Tim.

"I'm saying that I will get Layne out of jail. You guys leave the city, but camp nearby. Stay hidden though. You don't want to be caught by a patrol. You'll be out of the city, but the captain is so angry, he might have his men kill you if they see you. I will break Layne out of jail, then we will meet you."

"Why would you do that for us?" asked Tim. "You would be putting yourself at great risk."

"I gave you my word that I would help you on your quest. Besides, I am already at great risk if I am to help you go against King Korlas. Don't worry. I will be very careful. It might take a few days. I have to make a plan and wait for the right time. But I will get your friend out of prison. I promise. Just head north out of town and you will find a clearing surrounded by large boulders. You can see the road from there, but people on the road can't see you if you are in the ring of boulders. It is a good place to camp. We will meet you there."

Tim looked around at his group, then back to the wizard. "Well, that is as good a plan as any. We will trust you Tyler. Our friend's life is in your hands. We will camp just north of town and wait for you there. Does that sound good to everyone?"

"Maybe someone should stay and help him," Dustin said. The rest of the group agreed.

"No," Tim said. "Tyler is right. It is too dangerous for us to stay here. We will do as he says. We will all leave the city."

Gunfer walked up to Dustin. "I realize that you are concerned for the welfare of your brother. I understand. But believe me, you can put your trust in Tyler. He is very capable. He will succeed in freeing your brother. Do not worry."

Dustin swallowed, then nodded. "Okay."

"Let's get going," Tim said.

The innkeeper tried to give Tim his money back because they weren't going to spend the night, but Tim refused. He told the man to keep it, for all the trouble they had caused and the table they had broken. The innkeeper wished them well, then started cleaning up. Tim led his group out the front door. The soldiers led the mercenaries east, then north out of town, the wizard, Gunfer, and Portia headed in the other direction. Tyler went home and father and daughter searched for another place to spend the night.

*   *   *

As she walked behind Tyler and her father, Portia hung back a little, simmering in anger. She had asked her father to let her go with Tim's group. She said that she wanted to help, that it was for a good cause. He denied her. She said that she wanted to go off on her own and see the world, to get away from the sea for a while. Once again, his answer was no. She argued with him, but to no avail. He told her it would be much too dangerous for her.

She stayed back from them, glaring at her father's back as she slowly walked down the street. They were walking west, towards the setting sun.

The sunlight got in her eyes, so she turned her head away from it and saw Cory trying to stay unseen in the shadows as he kept pace with her. He realized that she had seen him and tried to slip away, but she stopped him.

"Cory!" she called softly, not wanting her father to hear. "Cory! Come here!"

He hurried over to her, looking slightly nervous.

"What are you doing?"

"Nothing," he replied, looking at his feet as he walked.

"You're following me, aren't you?"

"Well…"

"Why are you following me?"

He finally looked at her. "I always follow you, Portia."

"What! Why?"

"To protect you. To keep you safe. The streets can be dangerous, you know. Especially in this part of town. I would die if anything happened to you."

Portia didn't speak for a moment. The two walked in silence. Finally, Portia looked over at him. "You really like me, don't you?"

"Yes," Cory replied.

"Why? I haven't been very kind to you. Why do you still watch over me? Why don't you go find another girl to be with? One who is more deserving of your affections?"

Cory smiled. "Because no one is more deserving of my affections than you."

"You really think so?"

"Yes."

Portia thought a moment. "Would you be willing to help me?"

"Of course!" he replied immediately. "Anything!"

"Well, my father has given me permission to go with Tim and his group on their journey to Parkos. But they needed to leave the city very quickly, so I have to catch up with them later. The only problem is, I don't know if I will be able to find them on my own. Do you think you could help me?"

"Yes!" Cory exclaimed, excitedly. Portia looked ahead at her father, afraid he had heard Cory, but he didn't seem to have heard. "I can find them. I know I can. You'll see. I'll take you right to them."

"Okay," Portia said. "Then meet me tonight. Follow us to the inn where we are staying, then wait for me by the entrance. I'll meet you there as soon as I can." He agreed and fell behind, although he continued to follow them like Portia had asked.

When Tyler left them to go to his house, Portia rushed to catch up with her father. She thought it best to walk beside him now; she didn't want him looking back for her and seeing Cory following them. He looked at her when she came up beside him, smiled, and put a hand on her shoulder. He had told her that he understood her desire to go out on her own and do something more with her life, and he had seemed sincere, but he didn't think she was ready yet.

After a while they found an inn and went inside. Portia didn't bother to look at the sign that displayed the inn's name. She stood silently as her father paid for a room. She followed her father up the stairs, then entered their small room which consisted of two beds, a table in the corner, a lamp that was already lit on the table, and a chest for their belongings at the foot of one of the beds. Moonlight shined through a small window in one of the walls.

She flopped onto her bed and watched her father set their gear in the corner. He sat on the edge of his bed, taking off his boots. He didn't look up at her or utter a word.

She endured the uncomfortable silence. They hadn't fought very much throughout her life. She had always been content with her duties as navigator. She had been sailing with her father for as long as she could remember. Not on the ship he had now, and not on his long journies, but he would take her on shorter treks. When she was little she would sit in the captain's box and watch her father and the crew go about their duties on the ship. She was fascinated with sailing from a very early age and wanted to learn everything about it. Her father introduced her to every job on the ship, and she took to navigating immediately.

She was a natural. She had an incredible sense of direction that no one could explain. Talented navigators used the sun and stars to tell their position. Not Portia. She knew exactly where they were and where they needed to go on a cloudy day. She didn't have to even glance at the sky to guide her ship true. Her father was amazed at her ability and quickly appointed her as the ship's navigator.

She had been happy that she and her father had shared a common interest. It wasn't until recently that she had desired something new in her life. Something more. She didn't think her father knew how to take it. It was strange for Portia to see her large, strong father look so uncomfortable.

Finally, her father looked up at her. He had a sad look on his face. "How are ye feeling?"

"Okay, I guess," she replied.

"Listen. I know yer not happy with me right now, but I have my reasons for not letting ye go with Tim and his mercenaries."

"Like what?"

The question seemed to take him by surprise. Apparently, he hadn't thought she would ask for specifics. He cleared his throat. "Well, first of all, it's too dangerous."

"But I would be with Tim!" she exclaimed. "I have heard all the stories about him. I know how strong he is, and so do you! I would be safe with him and his group."

"Safe?" her father said. "Ye think ye would be safe? Look at what happened tonight! They were just minding their own business, trying to get some rooms for the night, and look what happened. One of them got arrested!"

"But it wasn't his fault."

"It doesn't matter! Do ye think that the enemies they are going to encounter care about fault? There are so many stories about Tim because danger follows him wherever he goes. He is a mercenary, Portia. Danger is his life, and I don't think that he has ever done anything as danger-ous as what he is planning on doing now. He is going to take on a king.

Have you heard the stories about King Korlas? He was just a cousin to the king when he left to be trained as a Paladin. One day he returns, then the king dies and everyone in line for the throne just starts dropping dead. Suddenly, he is the next in line.

"Now I don't know about ye Portia, but that seems odd to me. What happened to everyone? How did they die? Why didn't Korlas die as well? He is a very dangerous man, Portia. Not to mention the fact that he has the resources of an entire kingdom at his disposal. That is why it is so dangerous."

"You can't keep me away from danger forever, dad. I'm not a little girl anymore. I'm a woman now. I have to live my own life." When her father didn't answer she said, "What other reasons do you have?"

"What?"

"You said reasons. More than one. What other reasons are there?"

"Oh, yeah. Well…Who will be my navigator? Ye are the best navigator I have ever seen. My business will suffer without ye." He gave her a pained look. "I will suffer without ye. I have never been away from ye since ye were born. When I lost yer mother, it hurt. But I knew I would be alright because I still had ye.

"I must admit that part of the reason I don't want ye going with Tim is a selfish one. I would miss ye too much. I know that one day I will have to let ye go off on yer own, but I'm just not ready to do that yet."

She gave him a smile and put a hand on his arm. "I know Dad. I will miss you too. I have loved spending everyday with you. A lot of girls don't get the opportunity to do that. I've been lucky. But even the lucky girls have to move on with their lives. I'll come back and be your navigator again. I would miss the sea too much if I didn't. I just want to go for a little while."

"I understand. But now is not the time. Later though. I promise. Can ye just wait a little while longer?"

She nodded. "Yes Dad. I can wait."

She excused herself and went to the community latrine. She really didn't have to go, but she couldn't stand being in her father's presence anymore. She was still set on her plan, but somehow, guilt still ate away at her.

Someone was in the latrine when she got there, so she waited. After a while a woman came out. Portia rushed through the door and locked it behind her. She went over the plan in her mind and hoped that everything went smoothly tonight.

*   *   *

Gunfer was snoring loudly, his back to Portia as he laid on the bed furthest away from the door. She waited a long time, making sure he was deep asleep. Then she got up out of her own bed, dressed in the dark, quietly opened the door to their room, and slipped out. She silently closed the door behind her and crept down the stairs to the common room. She carried her shoes in her hands. She didn't want them to make noise on the wooden stairs and wake her father.

She didn't know how late it was, but the common room was empty. She heard the sound of people cleaning in the kitchen, which was through a door back behind the counter. She called out as loudly as she dared and a large woman in a stained white apron came through the door.

"Yes?"

"I was wondering if you had paper and a quill I could use. I would like to leave a note for my father."

"Yes dear," the woman replied. "Hold on just one moment." She started rummaging behind the counter, finally finding paper and a quill. She set them on the counter, along with a container if ink. "That will be one silver piece."

"What? I don't want to buy them. I just want to use them to leave a note for my father."

"I realize that," the woman said. "But ink is hard to come by. It is expensive. If you wanted to buy these things, it would cost two gold pieces. Just using them once is one silver."

"Really?"

The woman sighed. "Do you want to use them or not? I am busy right now. We have to clean up dinner and get ready for breakfast, so I don't have time to wait on you. Well?"

"Yes. I will use them." She fished out a piece of silver from her pack and handed it to the woman. The woman pushed the writing utensils closer to Portia, then turned back to the door leading to the kitchen. She promised she would be back in a few moments and she had better not steal the ink. Portia promised that she wouldn't and the woman disappeared from view.

Portia had talked to Princess Dana on the voyage over here about her journey. She had said that she left a note for her mother to let her know why she left. Portia thought that sounded like a good idea. No matter what, Portia had decided that she was going to go after Aiden, and this way, she would avoid any unpleasantness with her father that her decision would bring. She would tell him in the letter what she would have told him face to face. It would be much better this way.

She ran through in her mind again what she planned on saying. She spent the entire time as she waited for her father to fall asleep thinking about what she would write.

Finally, she put the quill to the paper.

Dad,

First, I want you to know that I love you very much. I listened to what you had to say and I thought about it. I truly did. But I came to the conclusion that I have to do something more with my life. I think that helping the mercenary group is a good cause. I befriended Princess Dana on the journey here and I want to help her and her brother. Everything is going to be alright. Please don't worry about me. I will be fine. I have Tim to look after me. And Tyler will be with me as well.

You know how capable he is. I am sorry that I am telling you this way and not face to face, but I think this will be easier for both of us. Don't be sad. I will come back when their quest is finished. I will be your Navigator again.

But most importantly, I will always be your daughter.

I love you.
Portia

She read and reread the letter multiple times. Was she doing the right thing? Did she really want to go? Her father was right, it would be dangerous. But she would be well protected. And she would be with Aiden.

That was the real reason she wanted to go. She would never admit that to her father though. She had fallen in love with Aiden on the trip over here, and even though she knew he didn't return that love, she needed to be with him. She felt good when she was around him. They didn't have to speak, they just had to be close. Being without him for the few hours she had been was agony. She had to get back to him.

She sat at the counter, drumming her fingers on the wood. She was impatient for the woman to return. She said she would be back soon. What was taking her so long?

After what seemed like an eternity, the large woman came back into the common room.

"Still here are you?" she asked. She looked to make sure that the ink was still on the counter. "Is there anything else I can do for you?"

"Yes. Could you please make sure that my father gets this letter when he comes down in the morning? He is a large man, with a full beard. His name is Gunfer. He will probably ask about me. My name is Portia."

"Okay," replied the woman. "I'll make sure he gets the letter."

Now that she was done with the hard part, Portia rushed out of the inn. She found Cory waiting by the front door.

"Thank goodness!" he said. "I was beginning to think you had changed your mind. Dawn can't be more than a few hours away."

"We'd better get going then," said Portia. They headed north.

*   *   *

A sudden light filled the darkness of the cell as the door opened. Easton had to squint his eyes to keep the sudden brightness from hurting them. He had no idea how long he had been in this cell, but it seemed like forever. It had been so long since he had seen light for more than a few minutes at a time that he felt himself a creature of the dark now. Light was an intruder. Darkness was a comfort. A friend.

Someone had come to give him food and water periodically. He thought perhaps once a day, but he wasn't sure. Light would flood the room and he would see the chamber pot over in a corner. The person who brought him the food would hold the door open while Easton relieved himself. As soon as he was finished and he had hold of the food and water, the person would leave, leaving Easton in total darkness once more. Easton couldn't find the pot very easily when it was pitch black, so he did his best to hold it until his food came.

His eyes finally adjusted to the light and he saw a large guard standing in the doorway. "Get up," the man said. "King Korlas wants to speak with you."

"Is he here?" Easton asked. His voice sounded strange to his ears. It had been a long time since he had spoken to anyone.

The guard laughed at him. "No! You think the king would enter such a place as this? This place is for scum like you." He laughed again. "Fool!"

Easton slowly got to his feet. This was the first time the king had summoned him since he was sent down here. He had gone through what he was going to say in his mind over and over again. Now that the moment was almost here, he was suddenly very nervous. He could admit to himself that Korlas terrified him. Especially after their last meeting.

As they made their way to the upper levels of the castle, Easton looked at his surroundings and wondered why he didn't recognize anything. Then he remembered that last time he'd come through here, he had been on the shoulder of a massive guard. All he could see was the floor. He had been too injured by what Korlas had done to him to walk on his own. He shivered at the memory of the pain and helplessness he had felt.

It took them a long time to reach the throne room. Easton's muscles were stiff and aching from not moving for so long. He hadn't moved around his cell for fear of hitting a wall. Now he wished he had, just to keep his muscles loose.

As they approached the open doorway to the massive room he saw Korlas sitting on his throne, watching him. The king was smiling.

"Ah Easton." The king rose as Easton and his escort entered the room. "How good to see you again. How are you holding up? Are you enjoying your stay here? How do your accommodations suite you?"

"How do you think?" Easton snapped. He couldn't stop himself.

"Now now, Little Prince. That is the kind of attitude that got you sent to the dungeon in the first place."

Easton made himself calm down. He was the King of Blanderly. He was an important man. He deserved respect. Even from this horrible man. It angered him when people disrespected him. But he couldn't let his anger get away from him this time. He didn't want to go back down to his cell again. He took a deep breath before responding.

"You are right, Your majesty." He bowed. "I sometimes find it hard to control my tongue. I beg your forgiveness."

"Freely given, Little Prince." He turned to the guard who had brought Easton up from his cell. He smiled. "It's not every day that the future king of a country snivels before you." The guard laughed.

It was even harder this time for Easton to keep his cool. He wanted nothing more than to punch King Korlas in the face. But he knew that would probably be the death of him. He ignored the comment.

"I have been thinking ever since you put me in that cell," Easton said. "I have decided to agree to your terms. Living as the king of Blanderly is definitely more appealing than being in that cell, even if I do have to rule under you."

"And what about me wishing to marry your sister? Have you changed your mind about that too?"

Easton could not keep the glare from his face as he thought about his beloved sister marrying this tyrant. Korlas laughed. "I guess not," he observed.

"I will learn to deal with it," said Easton. "Who knows? Maybe she will even come to love you someday." Not likely though, Easton thought. He planned on killing Korlas long before he had the chance to marry Dana. He just needed to wait for the right opportunity.

Korlas smiled at that. "Good. That's good. I see that a week in the cell has done wonders for your attitude."

Easton was stunned. "Has it only been a week?"

Korlas and the guard both laughed. "Yes," said the king. "The darkness takes away the sense of time. The loneliness does too. We want to disorient our prisoners. It robs them of their spirit…their inner fire, their hope. It seems to have worked like a charm on you, Little Prince."

"Can I ask you one favor?" asked Easton. The king nodded. "Could you please quit calling me Little Prince? It is disrespectful. Please call me King Easton. I am King of Blanderly now."

"You need to earn my respect, Little Prince. I do not give it freely. Only when you have earned my respect will I call you by your name and title." He turned to the guard. "Since our guest has decided to cooperate, take him to one of the guest rooms up stairs. Make sure it's a nice one. We don't want him changing his mind again."

The guard laughed as he left the room, Easton following close behind.

13

Layne had immediately been taken to a cell in a large, stone building a few blocks down from the inn. He went in silence. The soldiers didn't speak either. He had looked back at the inn numerous times as he had been led away, one man holding each of his arms, one man in front leading the procession, and numerous other soldiers walking alongside or behind with weapons drawn. He was looking to see if anyone would come after him. No one did.

They walked him down streets with dark, empty buildings. All the shops were closed. There were few people out on the streets this close to dusk, but those that were stared at him as he passed. He could see the looks on their faces, see them judging him. They didn't know who he was, but if he was being taken away by the City Watch, he must be a criminal. And, based on the number of soldiers, a dangerous criminal. He tried to ignore their stares, but found it difficult to do.

When they reached the building, one of the men had to unlock the front door. It was after hours, and no one was there. They pushed him into a large room full of chairs and a big wooden desk. Behind the desk were three more chairs, probably where important people sat, Layne thought. They led him across the room, through another locked door and into a narrow hallway. The hallway was very long, and they passed many closed doors. The only sound was of the soldiers' boots pounding on the stone floor.

At last, they reached the end of the hallway. They stopped in front of a large door that looked exactly like all the other doors they had just passed. A guard opened the door and the two men holding his arms roughly pushed him inside without a word. They quickly slammed the door and locked it. Layne heard their footsteps fading as they walked away.

Layne looked around at his surroundings. His room was very small, with only a small stone bed and a chamber pot. "Well, this is just great," he said aloud.

*   *   *

The group found a good campsite about half a mile north of the city in the cluster of boulders that Tyler had told them about. The boulders hid them from view of anyone passing by on the road. It was dark by the time they set up camp, so they dared light a fire. No one would be able to see the smoke in the darkness, and the boulders should block the light of the fire from anyone who might be traveling by on the road.

They decided they were probably safe from anyone passing by, so they didn't bother to set a watch. No one said anything as they lay in their bedrolls. Everyone had a lot on their minds. The only sound was the night insects chirping. So far, this journey wasn't going very well, Tim thought. They had a couple stow-aways on the ship that they hadn't planned on. Then, the first day in Parken, they lose one of their number. Tim almost regretted taking the job. Almost. He knew it was for a good cause, and that was the way he tried to live his life: doing good. That was the way he was raised. Plus, the life of a mercenary was not an easy one and the money that the queen had paid them would help a lot.

Although he did not think he could bear it if they didn't get Layne back. True, it was the nature of their profession, but it just didn't seem right that Layne was being punished for doing the right thing. Tim wasn't very surprised though. That was the way life was. Unfair.

Layne's was a presence the group needed. Not only was he an incredible fighter, given time he would probably become the best in the group, his natural cheer and ability to joke brought a much needed good mood to an otherwise hard lifestyle. You saw a lot of battle and death when you were a mercenary. It could be hard on a person's soul if they didn't know how to cope. Layne brought a point of view that was fresh. He kept the mood light, making others feel good in the process.

Tim felt very bad for what had happened in the inn. It was an injustice. Layne had only been protecting Veronna. It never should have happened at all. Tim was the leader, he should have prevented it from happening. At the very least, he should have been the one to be arrested. As the leader it was his duty to protect his group. He hadn't done that. He had wanted to avoid confrontations like that. He hadn't done that either.

He sat up and glanced around. Dustin was sitting up, staring out into the night. All the others were lying down, but Tim didn't think anyone was sleeping. He stood up and walked toward Dustin.

"Get some sleep," he said to everyone as he walked. "We don't know what will happen in the next few days and we need our strength." No one answered.

He sat down next to Dustin. Dustin didn't look at him. He was fiddling with a piece of grass. "How you are holding up?"

Dustin looked down, then tossed the grass aside. "Not very well."

Tim rubbed Dustin's back. "We'll get him back. Don't worry."

"It should have been me that got arrested."

Tim looked at the younger man. "Why?"

"I am the eldest. I am supposed to watch out for him, protect him. If anything goes wrong it should be me who gets in trouble, not Layne."

"You need to stop thinking like that Dustin. If anyone should be in a cell, it should be me."

Dustin finally looked at Tim. "You? Why?"

"Because I am the leader. It is my job to protect you guys. If anyone gets in trouble, it should be me. I feel terrible about what happened to your brother. I feel terrible that I couldn't prevent it from happening. In a way, I feel responsible. But I also know that it wasn't our fault. Layne did what he did because it was right. The captain was in the wrong. It's not your fault or my fault. It just happened. We need to move on and not be too hard on ourselves. We'll get Layne back. You'll see."

"Yeah," said Dustin. "But what are they going to do to him until Tyler can free him?"

"I don't know," Tim admitted after a long pause.

"That's the hard part. I hope they will just leave him in a cell and that's all. But I doubt it. I don't think they will be so nice to him. That's what I'm afraid of."

"Me too. But Layne is strong. He'll be okay."

Dustin smiled. "I know," he said softly.

"Now," said Tim as he got back to his feet. "Try to get some sleep. We're going to need our strength for the journey to Parkos."

"Okay."

Suddenly, a man in a black cloak stepped into the firelight. Tim couldn't see his face because his cowl was up, but he was pretty sure he knew what this man was.

The man pulled back the cowl, revealing a yellow face. Everyone jumped out of their bedrolls and grabbed their weapons. "Are you Tim?" the yellow man hissed.

"What do you want?"

"Are you Tim?"

"Yes. What do you want?"

"You have to come with us. Our master wants to see you."

"Us? I see only you."

Three more men stepped out of the darkness, one on each side of the fire. Now the group was surrounded. The first man smiled.

Tim had known there were more men out there. He wanted to make them come out. "There are nine of us, and only four of you," Tim said. "I'm not going anywhere."

"Oh, I think you'll change your mind." He glanced over his shoulder and two more Zantan Robbers stepped up beside him. Each one had a person in their arms, a knife to their throats.

"Portia! Cory!" Tim exclaimed. Cory looked terrified. Portia was crying. Neither dared move a muscle nor make a sound.

"You will come with us Tim, or these two will die."

"Now calm down," Tim said. "Just let the kids go, and we can talk." He needed time to think. He needed to keep them talking while he figured out what to do. He didn't believe for a minute that the men would just let Portia and Cory go, even if he agreed to go with them.

"I told you the terms. Come with us, and we'll let them go. We will leave your group alone to do as they wish. Our master only wants you."

"Can we all go?"

"My master only wants you."

"Well," said Tim. "I don't believe that you will let everyone else go after I give myself up to you. It's not in your nature to do that." He took a small step to the side, just to see what the yellow men would do. The man holding Portia immediately pushed the knife harder to her throat. A drop of blood ran down her neck. She whimpered. The man holding Cory didn't react. Tim glanced quickly over his shoulder at Zach. The dark-skinned man gave a slight nod. He had noticed as well. They would need to kill the man holding Portia first, because he was paying more attention.

Quicker than thought, Zach drew a knife from his belt and threw it at the man holding Portia. It hit him between the eyes, imbedding itself up to the hilt. The man's grip fell away as he hit the ground. Portia ran as fast as she could to Tim, trying to reach the safety of the group. Tim ignored her and lunged toward the man holding Cory, drawing his sword as he did so. He wasn't fast enough. The man slit Cory's throat and dropped him to the ground. Cory lay there, eyes wide as his life blood spilled out of him.

"No!" Tim cried as his sword met the killer's blade. Tim saw the first man rush past him towards the rest of the group. He heard the clash of metal behind him as battle was engaged. Then he concentrated on the man before him.

The man was quick, lunging in towards Tim, then back out again, looking for an opening. Tim's large sword kept the knife at a safe distance.

If the Zantan Robber thought to find an opening, he was sorely mistaken. There wasn't one. Then Tim went on the offensive.

His sword went high, then low, then high again. The man ducked under the first swing, stepped away from the second, and ducked under the third. Tim was hoping that the man would try to block his swing. The sword would have easily knocked the knife aside, but the yellow-skinned man was too smart for that.

The Zantan Robber went on the offensive again, his quick strikes difficult to block. He was confident in his speed and ability. Tim couldn't keep up with his speed, and the man knew it. A smile appeared on the Robber's face.

The Zantan Robber stabbed straight forward with his knife. Tim stepped aside and grabbed the man's arm. He spun, putting his back to the man. He pulled the man in close, leaned forward, and flipped his enemy over his shoulder. The man hit the ground hard. Still holding onto his enemy's arm, Tim stabbed down with his sword. The man jerked to the side as best he could, but the sword sunk into his right shoulder. Tim pulled his sword out, intending to stab him again, but the man's foot came up and hit Tim in the chest, knocking him backwards. The yellow-skinned man was up in an instant.

He faced Tim, his injured arm hanging limp at his side. He switched the knife to the good hand and came forward. Tim was surprised at the relentlessness of the man. Even injured, he fought on. The man was still good with his other hand, but not as quick. Tim had the advantage now.

The man swung his knife at Tim, but he blocked it, knocking it to the side. Tim thrust his sword forward, stabbing the yellow-skinned man in the heart. The man dropped his knife and clutched at the sword. There was a strange grin on his face. Tim pulled the sword out and the man's body slumped lifelessly to the ground. He was still grinning.

*   *   *

Zach had intercepted the first Robber as he rushed past Tim and towards the group. He drew two swords and slashed at the man. The man blocked with his own two swords. Back and forth they went, trading blow for blow. Their strikes were so quick that a bystander couldn't differentiate the sound of one blow from another. It was one continuous clang.

The sparing went on for many moments, with neither combatant gaining an advantage. Suddenly, Zach thrust his foot out, kicking the man in the midsection. The Zantan Robber was so focused on Zach's swords that the kick took him by surprise. He doubled over, and Zach was on him. Before the man had time to straighten up, Zach lopped off his head. There was only one type of person that was more than a match for a Zantan Robber in hand-to-hand combat, and that was the dark-skinned warriors from the far away country of Abberdon.

Jaden also didn't have much trouble with the Zantan Robber he was facing. He had told Dana to stay behind him and out of harm's way. She watched wide eyed as her body guard dispatched the yellow-skinned man intent on killing them. She had never seen her family's dark-skinned protectors in a real battle. She couldn't help but be fascinated by the fluid way Jaden moved.

There wasn't an opponent that the warriors from Abberdon hated more than Zantan Robbers. Their master told them to give no quarter when fighting them. They were to kill any Zantan Robber they saw on sight.

*   *   *

Dustin and Aiden were taking on one of the Robbers together. They were each standing on one side of him, striking at him at the same time. The man had two long daggers, one in each hand, and was having no trouble parrying the attacks. The mercenaries knew that they would have to change tactics if they were going to defeat the man.

Suddenly, Aiden stepped back. He stopped attacking the man. The Robber went to block a blow that didn't come. He stumbled slightly but caught himself. The slight stumble gave Dustin the chance to score a hit. His sword slashed the Zantan Robber's right side, drawing blood.

The Robber continued his attack on Dustin, periodically looking over his shoulder to see if Aiden would rejoin the fight. He didn't.

When the Robber was satisfied that Aiden was out of the fight, he turned his full attention to Dustin. He pressed Dustin hard. Dustin gave up a lot of ground very quickly. He was barely able to block the man's attacks. The wound in the man's side didn't seem to slow him down at all. Blood was dripping freely to the ground, but the man didn't seem to notice. He kept coming.

Dustin was starting to wonder what had happened to Aiden, when he saw him rush at the yellow-skinned man's back. The man must have heard Aiden's footsteps, because he turned in time to parry Aiden's sword thrust.

Well, that didn't work, Dustin thought as he desperately defended himself. But Aiden had the right idea. They couldn't defeat this foe on ability alone. They needed to turn the tables, to throw him off his guard. Tim had taught them that there was always a way to be victorious in any confrontation. They just had to find it. He always said that no enemy was unbeatable. If you truly believed that an enemy was unbeatable, he had already defeated you.

They were back to attacking him from either side. They had run through this scenario several times in training. Two of them would each attack Tim from either side, and they would have to figure out how to defeat him. They decided to use a tactic they had practiced. They nodded to each other, then Dustin went left and Aiden, following suit, also moved to his left. Suddenly Dustin was in front of the Robber, and Aiden was behind him. The Robber quickly adjusted his stance so that the two men were on either side of him again.

The Zantan Robber didn't like having opponents in front and behind him, so they tried the move again. This time, he moved with them, so they stayed to his sides. They had also practiced this, so they knew what to do. They switched direction. Aiden went right and then Dustin went right as well. They were in front of and behind him again.

Unfortunately, this man was quicker than Aiden's father. He was able to quickly adjust and put the two men at his sides again. They changed directions again, each going the same way, and immediately attacked. They didn't want to give their enemy time to adjust again. Once again, then man was too quick for them. He parried their attacks and countered.

Dustin was running out of ideas. He was about to label the situation as hopeless when a fourth fighter joined the fray. All Dustin saw was a black whirl, the flash of steel, and the yellow-skinned Zantan Robber falling lifeless to the ground. Zach stood over the dead man, looking at Dustin and Aiden.

"You did well," the dark-skinned man said. A rare compliment. "Not many men would have survived long enough for me to come help them." Dustin and Aiden shared a small smile. They were relieved to be alive.

*   *   *

Brione was unfortunate to face the final man alone. She stood protectively in front of Veronna and Dorn. She knew they would be of no help in this battle. Veronna screamed as the yellow-skinned man rushed Brione.

Brione was instantly on the defensive. It was all she could do to block the man's strikes. She had no chance to counter-attack. Her only advantage was that she had a long sword. Her enemy had only two daggers. Then, her advantage disappeared.

The man pushed a button on the bottom of each of the daggers' hilts, and they instantly grew to twice their previous length. Now he had two weapons that were almost as long as Brione's sword. He came at her again.

He was too quick for her and she cried out in pain as his sword sliced her leg. She quickly glanced down. There was a bloody gash in her pants. She cried out again as his other sword slashed across her arm. Suddenly his boot flew up and connected solidly with her chest. She went down to the ground with a grunt. She lay on her back, gasping for breath.

She heard Veronna scream and looked over. The yellow-skinned man was striding towards Veronna and Dorn. Veronna was cringing behind the healer. Dorn held a small knife in his hand. He stood bravely before the man, but Brione could see the terror in his eyes. They all knew that Dorn had no chance against the Robber.

"No!" she screamed as she got to her knees. She stumbled to her feet and ran towards the man. She lunged, landing just at his feet. She threw both arms around his legs and pulled them together. He fell.

He looked over his shoulder at her as he lay on his stomach. She could see the hatred in his eyes. He started to turn his body towards her.

Suddenly he stopped and flopped to the ground. Brione saw a knife sticking out of the back of the man's head. Dorn, the terrified look still on his face, was standing over him. He was breathing hard. "I've never killed a man before," he said.

Brione got to her feet and threw her arms around Dorn. "Thank you," she said. "You saved my life." Veronna came up from behind him and hugged him as well.

"Is everyone alright?" asked Tim. "Is anyone hurt?"

Everyone confirmed that they were alright. "I'm injured in a couple places," said Brione.

Dorn examined her wounds. They were painful, but not very deep. He bandaged them up and told her they would heal with a little time. It would be painful for her to walk for a little while though.

Tim walked up to the healer. "I want to thank you for saving my daughter and Brione. They would probably be dead if not for you."

"I've never killed anyone before," Dorn replied.

"I know it's hard. But you did it out of need."

"I'm just glad that I was able to finally contribute to the group."

Tim patted him on the back. "You picked a good time to do it."

"I've never fought against anyone like that before," Brione said to Tim.

"We are lucky that we have Zach and Jaden in the group, and that there were only six of them. If there were more, we would have been in trouble."

"Do you think they found us by accident," asked Dustin, "or do you think they knew we were here?"

"The man who spoke for them said that his master wanted me. It was no accident that they found us. They knew where we were. Somehow. That means that they will probably send more men after us. We need to get out of here."

"But what about Layne?" said Dustin. "He will expect us to be here waiting for him. We can't just leave!"

"If we stay here, we will die," Tim said. "We cannot defeat a large group of Zantan Robbers. We must leave. We will meet up with Layne and Tyler later. They know where we are headed. We will meet them in Parkos if we have to. But we can't stay here."

Dustin realized that his leader was right. If they stayed where they were, they would die. Then they would be no good to Layne. But he wasn't happy about leaving.

"Don't worry, Dustin," Veronna said. "Tyler is a powerful wizard. He can protect Layne."

"Yeah," Aiden agreed. "And Layne isn't exactly helpless himself."

Their attempts to comfort Dustin didn't have the desired effect, but he smiled and nodded anyway.

Tim walked up to Portia. "Now, what to do with you?"

Portia was laying over Cory's body, weeping. See looked at Tim, then stood up and wiped her eyes with the back of her hand. She stood tall, with her shoulders back, as if defying him to tell her to go back to her father.

"Why are you here?" he asked quietly.

"I want to help you," she replied just as quietly. She sniffed and wiped her nose.

"Why?"

"Because…I am not going back to my father. I have to go with you!"

"Why?"

"I can't tell you. Just please let me come. I'm not going back."

"You want to come with us, but you are already hiding things from us," Tim said. "Not the best way to start."

"Dad," Veronna said from behind him. "She doesn't want to go back to Kingston. If we don't allow her to come with us, she would be in danger. Please let her come."

"She will be in danger if she is with us," her father replied. "Portia, you saw what we face. You saw how deadly our enemies are. And these aren't the worst of them. Do you still want to come?"

She didn't hesitate. "Yes."

"If I say no, what will you do?"

"I will follow you. I am coming with you whether you like it or not."

"Then I won't stop you. We can't take you back to your father because we will be killed if we return to the city. Just keep in mind that I will do my best to protect you, but I can't promise that I will succeed." He looked around the campsite. "Let's get away from here."

"Wait!" Portia cried. "What about Cory's body? We can't just leave him like this!"

"You just joined our group and you are already slowing us down," Tim replied.

Brione limped up to Tim. "She has a point, Tim. He was not an enemy. He was a friend of Portia's. Gunfer told me they bury their dead in Parken. That's what we should do. He deserves to be buried."

"Alright. But we are not going to bury the Robbers." Everyone else agreed.

Jaden and Zach dug a grave and Tim and Dustin gently laid the body in it. Aiden, knowing the pain that Portia was going through, placed his arm around her shoulders and pulled her close. She wept into his shoulder. No one in the group said a word over the grave. No one knew him. Just before they began filling the hole with dirt, Portia stepped forward.

"Cory was my friend. He liked me and did everything for me. I took him for granted. I asked him to help me find you, knowing that he would never say no to me. He agreed. He found your campsite and we were captured. It is my fault he was killed. He was a good man. A kind man. A true friend." She broke into tears. "I'm so sorry Cory. I hope that someday you will be able to forgive me."

"Does he have any family?" Tim asked. "Any next of kin? Anyone we need to notify?"

Portia shook her head. "No. He was an orphan. He lived on the street. He had no family. He was alone."

"Alright. We have no one to notify of his death. That will make things easier."

Tim, Dustin, Zach, and Jaden filled in the grave. Portia went back to Aiden to be comforted. She buried her head in his shoulder and started weeping again.

After everything was finished, they quickly packed up their gear and headed north. Tim glanced at the body of the Zantan Robber he had killed as he passed by. The grin was no longer on his face. Now, there was a look of sheer terror.

14

Layne had been kept in the cold cell all night. He had seen or heard no one. They brought him no food or water. He was hungry, thirsty and he could admit to himself, frightened. He didn't know what they were going to do to him. Nothing good, he knew. The fact that he was here, even though he did nothing wrong, made him realize the kind of people he was dealing with.

It seemed to him that he stayed in that cell for days, although he knew it had to have been just one night. He found that he couldn't sleep. There was too much on his mind. There was too much uncertainty as to what was going to happen to him when someone came for him.

Finally, with a loud creek, the door swung inward, letting in the light from the hallway. It blinded him. He was used to the pitch blackness of his cell. He shielded his eyes with both arms.

"Get up," said a deep voice.

Because of the glare coming from the open doorway, Layne couldn't see the man, but he had a deep voice and sounded large. His muscles were stiff from lying on the ground all night, so he moved slowly. The man kicked him in the gut. Layne grunted in pain and clutched at his stomach. "Move faster!"

"Injuring me isn't going to make me move faster!" Layne snapped. He couldn't help himself. It probably would be smart to keep his mouth shut, but he was angry. He expected another kick, but it never came.

"Just hurry up!" came the deep voice. "They are waiting for you. They don't like to be kept waiting."

"Who doesn't like to be kept waiting?"

The man didn't answer. Layne's eyes were getting adjusted to the light. He could finally make out the man. He was indeed large. He stood with his big hands on his hips as he waited impatiently for Layne to get moving. He had long brown hair and a full beard. Brown eyes stared at Layne from underneath bushy eyebrows. He wore only boots, pants and a vest. The vest displayed his massive arms and big chest. There was a sword strapped to his waist, and Layne was sure he knew how to use it.

"Oh, now you're silent? You wouldn't stop talking when you first came in here."

"Don't make me kick you again."

Layne slowly got to his feet. "You're not going to tell me who is waiting for me?"

The big man waited to speak until after he chained Layne's wrists. He grinned. He only had a few teeth. "No. You'll find out when you get there."

"Ooh," said Layne. "It must be someone scary."

The man's grin faded. It turned into a glare. "Come on."

The man stepped aside to let Layne go out first, then followed close behind. He was right on Layne's heels. Layne could feel the man's breath on his neck. He was surprised their feet didn't get tangled up.

He was able to study the hall as they walked down it. It was very long and bare of any decorations. All the doors looked identical, thick wood with no bars or windows. Just a handle and a key hole.

The two men entered the main room. They passed two more guards standing on either side of the doorway. Neither of them looked at Layne or his escort as they passed. They kept their eyes straight ahead. They were both as large as the man who had come to retrieve him. Both were dressed and armed the same as well.

Layne took a quick survey of the room. Three men were sitting behind a large wooden table, facing a large crowd who were seated on either side of the room. Almost every seat was occupied. There was a hum of conversation as the crowd chatted with each other. He scanned the crowd, trying to locate someone from the group, but found no one. He hadn't expected them to be there.

He looked at the three men who, he expected, were in charge of his fate. Two of them were in their later years. One was bald, the other had thinning gray hair. The third man, sitting between his two associates, was younger, probably in his mid-thirties. He had a full head of blonde hair, and blue eyes that were watching Layne at the moment.

All three were wearing purple robes of office. Layne guessed them to be judges. There was a stack of paper in front of each of them. A lone man stood before the judges, his wrists and ankles in chains. He was speaking to them, but only the two older judges were paying attention. The younger man was still staring at Layne. Another man was standing a little to the side, looking at his own feet.

The two older men conferred with each other, bringing the younger into the conversation. They discussed quietly for a few minutes, then turned back to the prisoner. It was the younger man who spoke.

"We have heard your defense Fisher, and have taken it into consideration. We have also taken into consideration the testimony of this witness." He gestured to the man looking at the ground. "The two stories differ greatly. So, who are we to believe? You, a man who has a great deal to lose if he is found guilty? Or the witness, who has nothing invested in this case? Who is more likely to tell the truth?"

The prisoner shifted nervously. "I wasn't there. I was at home that night."

"This man says you were there. He saw you."

"He's lying!"

"Why would he do that? He would gain nothing by lying. But you would. Wouldn't you?"

"But..."

"Silence!" The prisoner shut his mouth. The younger judge stood up. "The testimony of this witness proves you are the one who murdered the innkeeper of the Drunken Wench. You are sentenced to death!"

"No!" cried the prisoner.

The judge had to raise his voice to be heard over the yelling man.

"You will be hanged tomorrow at noon." He turned to the two guards at the doorway. "Take him back to his cell."

The men seized the prisoner and dragged him out of the room. "No!" the man cried as he struggled against the guards. "I didn't do it! I was at home with my family! Speak with my wife! She will tell you! I swear! You have the wrong man! This is a mistake! No!"

The door slammed shut behind the trio. The man's cries could only be faintly heard now. Two more large men took their places by the door.

Layne saw the younger judge gesture for the witness to come forward. The man approached the desk and leaned forward. The middle judge said something to him, then handed him a small purse. Layne was positive the purse held coins. The man accepted the purse and hurried out of the building. When he passed by Layne, he could see the look on the man's face. He looked haunted.

"Next please," said the middle judge.

There wasn't anyone in front of Layne, so he stepped forward.

"Will the accuser please step forward," said the younger judge.

Layne turned back to the crowd. The captain from last night stood up and slowly came forward. Layne hadn't seen him sitting there. He limped up to the table, nodded to the three judges, then took his place in front of the table to Layne's left side. He looked at Layne and sneered. Layne knew that he faked the limp. Layne injured him, but not that bad. Not as bad as Layne had wanted to. Not as bad as the captain deserved. He had only punched him once.

He knew the black eye, broken lip, and swollen face was real though. His one punch was a good one. He smiled back.

The middle judge looked through some papers before he spoke. "Layne, is it?"

Layne nodded.

"I said, Layne, is it?"

"Yes."

The judge nodded. "That's better. It says here you attacked the captain of the city guard last night. I can see by looking at him that this is true. Do you deny it?"

"No," Layne answered. "But let me explain."

The judge held up his hand. "There will be time for explanations later." He glanced back down at the report. "It also says here that the attack was unprovoked."

"What! That's a lie!"

"No need to raise your voice," the younger judge replied. "I am just reading what the report says. I didn't write it and I'm not saying you are guilty. I am just stating what the people who were there said."

He motioned to the captain. "We have a witness. But first let us hear from the victim. Captain, will you please tell us what happened?"

"Yes, Judge." He sneered again at Layne. "I was sitting at the bar in The Traveler's Stop, when this man and his group of friends came in. I was minding my own business when they come up to the bar. A young girl sits next to me. I believe in being polite, so I strike up a conversation with her. I guess this man here must have feelings for her and became jealous and got angry with me.

"I told him to calm down, that everything was alright. He wouldn't. Suddenly, he punched me in the face. Well, you can see he is a big man, and I went flying. I crashed onto a table and broke it. I got up and fought back. I was holding my own against this much bigger, younger man when his friends entered the fray and overwhelmed me. I managed to call the guards and we finally brought the situation under control.

"Then we arrested this man because he was the cause of everything and banished his friends. They are never to come back to this town on pain of death."

"He is lying," said Layne.

"Oh, is he?" asked the judge. "Why should I believe you? Do you have someone who can back up your claim that he is lying?"

"No," Layne replied. "The captain here conveniently banished the people who would speak up for me from the city."

"I had to!" the captain exclaimed. "They were dangerous people!"

"Why didn't you just arrest them?" asked Layne.

"Because you are the one who started it. You attacked me!"

"Because you were trying to take advantage of an innocent young girl!"

"How dare you...!"

"Silence!"

Both men fell silent and turned towards the judges. The younger judge was on his feet, anger clearly displayed on his face. He looked at Layne.

"You will have your chance to defend yourself. It just so happens that we have a witness to this crime. Will the innkeeper of The Traveler's Stop please step forward?"

Layne recognized the man who stood up and came toward the table. It was the innkeeper. The man stood to the side where the witness of the previous case had stood.

"Will you please tell us what happened last night in your inn?" asked the young judge.

"Yes," the man replied. "The incident happened exactly the way the good captain said it did. I was paying close attention. He is a very important man and I give important people extra good service.

"He was minding his own business when a large group of people entered my inn. They came up to the bar where the captain was sitting, and the young lady sat next to him. He did strike up a conversation with the girl, and I was close enough to hear every word they said. It was totally innocent."

"What did he say to her?"

"He asked her name and where she was from. Just the normal things when you introduce yourself to someone."

"I see," said the judge. "Go on."

"Well, they were just chatting, then the defendant started yelling at the captain. The captain tried to calm him down, but it didn't work."

"What did the defendant do?"

"He stood up and tried to get between the captain and the girl. The captain stood up too. I'm guessing he did this to show the defendant that he was not intimidated by him."

The judge turned to the captain. "Is this true? Is that why you stood up as well?"

"Yes, Judge. People like the defendant here try to use their size to push people around. I wanted him to know that he wouldn't be able to do that with me. I thought that maybe if he saw that I wasn't afraid of him, he would step back and calm down. It didn't work."

"Continue," the judge said to the innkeeper.

He nodded and went on. "Well, as the captain said, he couldn't get the man to stand down. They argued for a moment, then the defendant punched the captain in the face. He went down, breaking one of my tables in the process. I do expect compensation, if you don't mind."

The judge waived his hand. "Yes, yes. Go on."

"There was a struggle, then this man's friends ganged up on the captain. He called to his guards, who, up until then, hadn't joined the fray. Then..."

"Why not?"

The man stopped his story. "Why not what, Judge?"

"Why hadn't his men joined the fight?"

"Well, I don't know," the innkeeper replied.

The captain spoke up. "They trust me to call them when I need them, Judge. I like to take care of situations myself when I can. And I usually can. I have given them orders that when they are with me, they are to wait for my signal before acting. I know when I have a situation under control better than they do."

"I understand," said the young judge. "I am the same. I would rather take care of things myself." He turned back to the innkeeper. "Then what happened?"

"Well, then the guards came and stopped the fight. They detained the defendant and took him away. The captain banished this man's friends from the city. They were not happy about it, but they left soon after the incident."

"Okay. Thank you." The judge turned to Layne. "You see, we have two people who have told us identical stories. It seems to me that the report is true. But we will allow you to tell us your side of the story before we make our judgment. You may begin."

"Well, I doubt you'll believe a word I say, but okay. The part about him already being at the bar is true. And it's true that Veronna, the young lady, sat beside him. He did turn to her and ask her name. I immediately stepped in and told him to back off."

"And why did you do that?" asked the judge. "It sounds to me like he was just being polite."

"Well, he wasn't."

"What makes you so sure?"

"I saw the look in his eyes. I saw how his gaze roamed over her when she sat down. She is just a young lady, and I saw the lust in his eyes."

"Are you an expert at reading other people just by looking at them?"

"Well, no. But it was obvious."

"Alright. Go on with your story."

"Well, then he suggested they go to his room."

"That is a lie!" the captain roared.

"No, it's not!" said Layne. "It's true!"

The two men argued at the top of their lungs, forcing the young judge to slam his hands on the table again. "Enough!"

They both shut their mouths and turned to the judges. The young judge's face was reddened and he was breathing hard. Layne could see the fury on his face.

"You are both adults, yet you act like children. You will speak calmly when in this court room. Do you understand?"

"Yes," they both answered at once.

"Now, since you each differ on what happened, I will ask the witness." He turned to the innkeeper again. "Did he ask the young lady to escort him to his room?"

The innkeeper didn't answer for a minute. He seemed to be debating with himself. Finally, he put his head down and said, "No."

The answer didn't surprise Layne. He realized that either the judges or the captain had paid this man off or threatened him.

"Okay," said the judge. He turned to Layne. "Well, now that that is settled, please continue. But this time, please do not lie to us."

"What's the point?" asked Layne. He was furious now. "You are not going to believe anything I say. I will tell you what happened, then the captain will deny it. Then you will ask this so-called witness that you either paid off or threatened, and he will back the captain's story.

"I can tell you that he grabbed Veronna and pulled her against him, against her will, but you won't listen to me. I could tell you that I punched this man defending the honor of an innocent young girl, but you won't care. I don't know what you are looking for, but it's not justice."

Layne turned to the crowd. "This is not a court of law. This is a farce. Your judges are corrupt. Your captain of the city watch is corrupt. I feel sorry for you."

The room was dead silent. No one could believe that this man would dare say such things to these respected judges. Layne glared at the people for a moment, then turned back to the table.

The two older judges looked furious. The younger judge had a blank look on his face. Suddenly he grinned. Then he started laughing. He threw his head back and roared. He beat his fist on the table as he laughed. It took him a long time before he finally stopped. "No one has ever dared speak like that in this room. I like you. You're a man of conviction. You lie, but I believe you actually believe what you say."

"I do not lie," replied Layne, though he knew it was pointless. The judges had decided his fate before he came before them. He had just wasted his breath.

"Oh yes, you do. And you do it with conviction. I like that. I will enjoy sentencing you." He paused for effect. "And punishing you." Layne didn't react.

The three judges put their heads together. They spoke softly so no one could hear. After a few minutes, they all turned back to Layne.

"We find the defendant, Layne, to be guilty of attacking a respected city official without provocation. I have not made my decision yet on what your sentence or punishment will be," said the young judge, "so I hereby send you back to your cell until I can come up with a suitable punishment. Your crime was a serious one. The punishment should fit the crime." He paused again, waiting to see how Layne would react. He was disappointed. Layne didn't react at all.

The young judge shook his head and grinned. "Take him away." The two guards by the door immediately moved to escort Layne back to his cell.

*   *   *

Tyler watched Layne and the two large guards go through the doorway from under the cowl of his cloak. He hadn't wanted Layne to recognize him. He didn't want Layne to do something foolish out of desperation.

After the door closed behind the three men and two more guards took up positions beside it, Tyler turned his attention to the three judges. The two older judges were named Oscar and Kargen and were of little note. They were there to appease tradition. There had always been three judges in Kingston. Before, they were all on equal footing. Now, although three people sat behind the table, there was really only one judge. The judge's name was Riktor, and no one knew anything about him. He had just shown up one day as a new judge and had been controlling things ever since. The two older judges had been there before him, but he had quickly taken over. Now, the other two were there just for looks. Whatever Riktor wanted, happened.

Everyone was afraid of Riktor. He didn't seem to want to find justice. He just wanted people punished. Tyler couldn't remember a trial where a defendant was found not guilty. Sometimes it was obvious that the defendant was innocent, but Riktor would either pay a witness to lie or bully them. Either way, there was always a witness to prove the defendant's guilt.

Tyler didn't know what Riktor received in return for pronouncing everyone guilty. Maybe he had a boss who told him what to do. Maybe he got some kind of sick pleasure from making people suffer. Either way, he knew Layne was in a lot of trouble. He had to figure out a way to rescue him. He had to do it soon.

He waited until the next trial was over then left.

15

The first thing Tyler had to do was figure out where Layne's cell was. It would be almost impossible to try to rescue him from anywhere except inside his cell. If he was out of his cell for any reason, he would be heavily guarded. He would probably be the only person in his cell. The custom was to keep the violent criminals separate from everyone else. The best time to free him would be when he was alone.

He was standing across the street from the courthouse in an alley between a bakery and hat store. As he was watching the people going in and out of the courthouse, his stomach rumbled. He realized he hadn't eaten at all that day in his rush to get to the courthouse before the trials had started. The aroma wafting from the bakery almost made him leave his post. Almost.

He needed to scout out the courthouse. He needed to know who came and when and how often they did so. Anything he learned would be of great help.

It was nearing sundown when the two older judges came out of the courthouse and made their way down the street. There was no sign of Riktor. This was the only thing of note that had happened all day. There had been guards getting off duty and others starting their shifts, but nothing else of note had happened. Tyler was getting desperate, so he acted.

He left the spot he had occupied all day, his stomach still grumbling, and followed the two elderly men at a distance. He took the opportunity to make a quick stop at a street vendor selling fruit. He grabbed an apple and a bunch of grapes. It wasn't the freshest produce by any means, but after not eating a thing all day, it was delicious.

The streets were starting to clear out as people began heading home for the night, so it wasn't difficult to keep track of the two judges. Tyler walked and ate his meal as he considered his next move.

The sounds of the city enveloped him. He could hear music playing from inns and taverns as he passed. From one of the more expensive inns he heard the voice of a bard telling an extravagant tale. He only heard a few moments of the tale, but he could hear that it was about the great dragon slayer, Humphrey. Tyler didn't understand why he was called a great dragon slayer. Everyone knew it was impossible to kill a dragon. Humphrey had certainly never killed one, although it wasn't for lack of trying. He was lucky he had lived as long as he did. The story said that he had encountered the black and white dragons and survived before he was finally killed by the blue. Tyler guessed he was called a great dragon slayer because he had tried more than anyone else ever had.

He went further down the street and the bard's voice faded. It was getting darker and he could hear mothers down the side streets calling their children in for the night. Blacksmiths, working late into the evening, were still pounding away at some type of armor or weapon. Laughter came out of inns and taverns as their doors opened to let patrons in or out.

The streets were almost totally deserted now except for Tyler and the two judges. Tyler was glad for all these city sounds because it drowned out the sound of him biting his apple, and the sound of his boots on the road. Sometimes on the cobblestone streets sound would travel further than one would think. He didn't want Oscar and Kargen to know they were being followed. They might try to make a break for it. True, Tyler was much younger than they were and he could probably catch them, but he didn't want to risk it. It would be easy to lose them on the city streets.

The two men stopped and conversed for a moment, then one continued walking down the street and the other turned down a side road.

Tyler hesitated. He hadn't had much time to plan this out, and he didn't know what he should do now. Which one should he follow? Was one of them more likely to know the information he needed than the other one? He finally decided to follow the one that continued down the street he was on. He was too far away to tell if it was Oscar or Kargen. They both had the same thin build. He guessed it didn't matter either way. One was probably as good as the other. At least, he hoped that was the case.

He tailed the judge for a long time. The judge never turned down another street. Tyler was surprised at the energy of the man. He looked quite old, yet he never stopped for a rest. His pace was quick, but it was steady. The man seemed strong.

Tyler quickened his pace just a bit to make sure he wouldn't lose the old judge. He started to wonder how far away the man lived. He couldn't imagine having to walk this far every day for work. Especially at this man's age.

Suddenly, the man quickened his pace. He was walking faster. Tyler was forced to speed up as well. Then, the man started running. Once again, Tyler was forced to speed up. He had to run to keep from losing the judge.

Why was he running? Did he realize Tyler was following him? The judge turned down a side street and disappeared from view. Tyler forgot about caution and sped up, not wanting to give the man a chance to disappear.

He turned the corner and saw that the street was a dead end. He saw the judge standing against the far wall. Tyler slowed down to a walk again. The judge watched as Tyler approached, his face expressionless. Tyler couldn't tell if he was afraid or not. The wizard looked at the old man's hands to make sure he didn't have a weapon. He didn't. His hands were empty.

"You might want to look behind you," the Judge said. Now Tyler was close enough to see that it was Oscar he had been chasing. Tyler stopped but didn't turn around.

"Why?"

"Just do it."

Tyler slowly turned around. There was a group of at least a dozen men standing in the entrance of the alley. It was hard to tell exactly who they were in the fading light, but he thought Kargen was standing in front of the group. He must have gone down the side street and found a Dark Watch squad.

"Why were you following us?" Oscar inquired.

"How did you know?" Tyler asked.

"We suspected you were following us for a while. That is why Kargen went another way. He was gathering some of the Dark Watch to follow you. When I picked up my pace, I noticed you did too. When you started running after I did, I knew for sure. Now I'll ask you again. Why were you following us?"

"I don't want to hurt you," Tyler said instead of answering. "Have your men stand down. I don't want to be forced to hurt them."

Kargen laughed. "What could you possibly do to a dozen armed soldiers?" The soldiers laughed as well.

"I am a mage," Tyler answered. "I have the power of the earth at my command. Don't make me use it."

The soldiers stopped laughing.

Tyler continued. "I was merely following you because I need information. I didn't plan on hurting you. I only wanted to ask you some questions."

"About what? What information do you need?"

"I know that Layne, the man who was convicted of attacking the Captain of the City Guard is innocent."

"How do you know this?"

"I was there. I was with his group of friends. The captain did try to take the young girl to his room against her will. I saw him grab her. I saw her struggle. Yes, the man did punch the captain, but he was just defending the girl." He turned to the soldiers. "He did what anyone of you would have done if you had seen a lady in distress. Just because it was the captain doing it, doesn't make it alright. The man does not deserve to be punished for doing the right thing."

Oscar took a step toward Tyler. He surprised Tyler by saying, "We believe you." He spoke quietly so the soldiers wouldn't hear.

"You believe me?"

"Yes. We know many of the people who are brought to court are innocent. But there is nothing we can do about it."

"Why not? Why do you just sit back and let innocent people suffer for something they didn't do?"

"Riktor." It was Kargen that spoke. Tyler turned to him.

"Why don't you stand up to him? Is he truly so powerful?"

Oscar didn't speak for a few moments. Finally, he said, "Riktor has a sort of power about him. You can feel it when he is around. I don't know what it is, but I do know that it is evil.

"He just showed up one day with a letter from King Korlas himself saying that he is to be the new judge in Kingston. I told him that we already have three judges and that there is no room for him. He just smiled and walked away.

"The next morning the previous judge, Rilo, was found dead in his bed. The doctors examined him and concluded that his heart had stopped while he slept. It was odd because Rilo was only in his late twenties. He was young and healthy. He shouldn't have just died in his sleep like that. Kargen and I suspected foul play. We didn't think it was a coincidence that Riktor would show up claiming to be the new judge, then the current judge dies, making room for him. But we couldn't get anyone to listen to us. We talked to people in secret of course. We didn't want Riktor to know we suspected him."

Kargen continued the story. "Everything changed after Riktor became a judge. He proclaimed himself Head Judge. We had never had a Head Judge before. When it was us and Rilo on the judgment seat, we were all equal. We discussed cases together before we came to a verdict. Riktor ended that. Whatever he decided, that is the way it would be.

"At first we fought against it. But he quickly ended that."

"What did he do?" asked Tyler.

"He demonstrated his power. Not on us, but on a man convicted of murder. He led us to his cell, dismissed all the guards and tortured the man. The thing is, he never touched him. He just stared at the man and he started screaming in pain and writhing on the floor. It went on for a long time. The man begged him to stop. But he wouldn't. He didn't say a word. He just kept staring. The man on the floor kept screaming.

"Then, blood started pouring out of his ears and nose. We begged Riktor to stop, but he ignored us. Finally, the man stopped screaming and went still. He was dead. Riktor turned to us and said he was the Head Judge. He told us that he could do the same thing to us or anyone else if he wanted to. He warned us to always remember that day."

Oscar spoke up again. "After that day, Kargen and I didn't dare speak up against him. The sight of that man in so much agony is etched into our minds. We will never be able to forget it. Now, we don't say a word in court. Our presence there is just for show. Our opinion doesn't matter. Every criminal brought before us is found guilty. Almost every so-called witness is lying. Riktor either threatens them or pays them to lie."

"Why does Riktor find everyone guilty?" Tyler asked.

"We don't know," said Kargen.

"I was at court today. I saw you two discussing the fate of the prisoners with Riktor. What were you talking about if your opinion means nothing?"

"Oh, we talk about the defendant," said Oscar. "He asks us what we think. We tell him that we think the defendant is guilty. Sometimes he smiles and calls us liars. Other times he just agrees. He knows what we will say, but he asks us anyway. It's a reminder of the power he holds over us." The old man snorted. "Like we could forget."

"What information do you need?" asked Kargen.

"I think that we should go somewhere else, or at least send the soldiers away," said Tyler.

Kargen turned to the soldiers. "It is alright. This man means us no harm. You may go back to your duties."

The soldiers turned and left.

Kargen went to stand beside Oscar and gave Tyler a questioning look.

"Well," said Tyler. "I promised Layne's friends that I would break him out of his cell. I need to know where his cell is. I need to know when the guards change shifts. I need to know the times he will be taken out of his cell for any reason. Things like that."

"I don't know about this," said Kargen. "Riktor is very powerful. You could get killed trying to rescue Layne."

"I promised his friends. I have to try. I need your help."

"If we do help you, and Riktor finds out, he will torture us," said Oscar.

"Don't you think it's time to end Riktor's reign? He has corrupted the prestigious position of judge. People look up to judges. He is tainting the name of Judge. People do not expect a fair trial anymore. They know they will not get one. This has to change."

"Are you thinking of saving Layne," asked Oscar, "or getting rid of Riktor?"

It finally hit Tyler that he had just proposed to get rid of Riktor. He hadn't planned on that, it just came out that way. But now he thought about it. This was his city. This was where he lived. The people of the city were being unjustly put to death for crimes most of them didn't commit. He had to help them, didn't he?

"Yes."

"Yes?" Oscar asked. "Yes to which one?"

"Both," Tyler replied. "If I can. I will save Layne from death, and in the process, if the opportunity becomes available, try to kill Riktor."

"You would be wise to try to avoid Riktor altogether," said Kargen. "I don't think you would survive the encounter."

"Neither would Riktor, I think," said Tyler. "I believe him to be overconfident in his power. Someone could take him by surprise. But, like I said, only if the opportunity presents itself. I will not go looking for him. Rescuing Layne is more important at the moment.

"But, if I don't get a chance to get rid of Riktor, when I am finished with the obligation I have to Layne and his friends, I will come back and kill him. That I promise you."

Oscar and Kargen shared a long look, even though they had a hard time seeing each other's faces in the fading light. It was almost as if they knew what each other was thinking. They both nodded.

"Okay," said Oscar. "We will help you. Let us go to my home so we can plan."

*   *   *

Ricardo watched from the shadows as King Korlas met with several people from the realm. He met with people like this every day, for a good few hours. Ricardo would watch him, grateful he himself wasn't the king. He didn't think he could take talking to all these fools every day.

The people who came to speak with the king ranged from farmers to judges to officers in the army. Their problems were as varied as they were. Most of them could have been taken to someone else to solve. He was surprised that Korlas allowed these people to enter his throne room.

Although he disliked these meetings, he felt it necessary to be there. Korlas wanted him to listen to everything that was said and then advise him. Ricardo was there for his own reasons. He thought it very important to know everything that goes on in the realm, although most of what he learned in these meetings was useless. Knowledge was power, and he had more knowledge than anyone. Only he knew how he acquired that knowledge.

Sometimes, like today, it got to the point where he found it hard to pay attention to what people were saying. A lot of the topics were very boring and of little use to him. But there was also another reason he had a hard time focusing. He had other things on his mind. He needed to inform the king of his Robbers' failure, then get back to more important matters.

After what seemed like many hours the meetings finally ended. Korlas' personal guards escorted the people out of the throne room and closed the door behind them. The King stood there for a moment looking at the massive door, apparently deep in thought.

"Come, Ricardo"

Finally, the wizard thought. He left the shadows and stood in front of the king, who was sitting on the throne.

"Well, what do you think?"

"I think you waste your time with these meetings. Couldn't all these people go complain to someone else?"

Korlas smiled, still seeming lost in thought. "This is what it is like to be a king, Ricardo. If you find it boring, stay away from rule."

"I know you," Korlas said. "You don't care about these peoples' problems. You don't even care about these people!"

Korlas finally turned to him. "You're right. I don't care. But the people need to think that I do. They love me. They support me. That is very important when you are a king. I pretend to be a loving king who cares for the welfare of his people, and they in turn give me total devotion. It is a small price to pay."

Ricardo decided not to let the matter wait any longer. "Your Robbers have failed."

Korlas looked surprised. "What?"

"The Robbers you sent to capture Tim. They failed."

"How do you know about that?"

"Must you really ask me that? You know I know things. Did you honestly believe that I didn't know you are Zantan?"

"Well, no. I didn't think anyone, but my Robbers knew. No one is supposed to know. How long have you known?"

"Almost from the very first. You can't hide anything from me, Your Majesty." He added the title as an afterthought.

"How do you do it?" Korlas asked. "How do you get your information?"

Ricardo didn't answer. He just stared at the king. He should know better than to ask Ricardo that.

Korlas waited for an answer. When he finally realized that no answer was coming, he asked, "Well, what happened?"

"They were slaughtered. They didn't kill a single member of Tim's group."

Korlas looked angry. "Impossible! How many of my Robbers were there?"

"Six."

"Six!"

"Yes. Six."

"I told that idiot Tim was powerful! I told him to make sure he took enough men!"

"Sounds like overconfidence to me," Ricardo observed.

"Do you know where they are headed?"

"To Hell I would assume."

"Not my men! Tim's group!"

"Oh. Tim's group." Ricardo enjoying enraging the king. "Yes. They are headed north. They are on their way here."

Korlas started pacing. He began talking to himself. "They are coming here. What should I do? Should I send more men after them? Should I just sit and wait for them to come to me?"

"May I interject?"

Korlas stopped pacing and turned his glare at Ricardo. "What?"

"If you allow them to come here unhindered, they will be able to attack you on their terms. But, if you send more of your Robbers after them, and they are able to capture Tim, then you have the upper hand. Then you are in control."

Korlas thought about that. "Yes. That is a good idea. Thank you."

Ricardo spread his hands. "That is what I am here for."

"But this time I will make sure they take more men. Twenty-five should be enough."

"I agree."

Korlas waved his hand. "You are dismissed, Wizard. I have some things to do."

Without bowing, Ricardo turned and walked out of the room.

He made his way down the corridor to his quarters. The inside of the castle was almost as beautiful as the outside. Huge windows lined the hallways, letting in sunlight. Each window had drapes.

The drapes ranged from every color imaginable. Intricately worked carpets in the middle of the floor muffled his footsteps. Most of the carpets were blue or red, trimmed in gold. Pedestals holding expensive vases or other artifacts were placed periodically in the corridor. The items in this one hallway probably cost more than a small village.

Ricardo knew the beauty of the palace was all for show. There was nothing beautiful about Korlas. He served a god of death. A god of hate. A god of chaos. No one knew of course. No one except Ricardo, his men, and the king's guards. The king's personal guards served the same god. They were Dark Paladins, just like Korlas, but not as powerful. Korlas was the Dark God's chosen one.

He came up to the door to his chambers and stopped. The door was magical. It allowed only him and the people he allowed into the rooms beyond. He placed both his hands on the door in just the right place. But that was only half of it. If someone did figure out the correct place to put their hands, they still had to think of the correct word. If they didn't, they would die a very painful death.

Ricardo thought of the word and the door swung inward. After he was inside, the door closed silently behind him.

His chambers were sparsely decorated compared to the rest of the palace. There was an outer chamber with a couch and a couple of chairs. Nothing adorned the white walls. A doorway led to another room with his small bed, a round table with a single chair, a large dresser for his clothes, and a small bookcase full of books.

There was a third room with a magical chamber pot that made the waste vanish by itself. It amazed his men when he held meetings in his chambers and they had to relieve themselves. It also had a large tub in it.

He went straight to the table and sat in the chair. He closed his eyes, slowed his breathing, and placed his hands on the table. He put all thoughts out of his mind except one, the man whose thoughts he wanted to occupy. He sent his mind into Syth's thoughts.

16

Syth was walking down the corridor toward the war room when he felt the presence of his master in his mind. He missed a step and almost fell, but he braced himself against a wall and was able to stay upright. When his master entered his mind, it came suddenly and with no warning. It was a disorienting experience. He always had to stop what he was doing for a moment until the feeling passed. One positive aspect of it was that Syth always knew when his master was occupying his mind.

Syth.

Yes Master?

Have you done what I commanded you?

Yes, Master.

And what affect has your actions had?

It has put fear into the hearts of everyone in the castle, Master. No one trusts anyone. They are losing their military leaders, so the army is less formidable. It is going just as you had planned, Master.

Good. Keep it up. I want the country as weak as possible when we attack.

Yes, Master.

Are you headed for a meeting now?

Yes, Master.

Good. I will stay in your mind for a while. I want to see for myself what affect you are having on the country's leaders.

Syth didn't want his master to stay in his head, but tried to keep the thought to himself. He knew he had no choice in the matter. He couldn't force his master out. His master wanted to look over his shoulder, so to speak, and make sure he was doing what he was supposed to. Syth resented that his master thought he had to keep an eye on him. Syth was the best man his master had. He should have more faith in him.

Syth hoped that his master couldn't hear his thoughts while he was in his head. He had never asked, and his master had never volunteered the information, but Syth had never gotten the impression that his master could do such a thing. If he could, Syth would have been in trouble on more than one occasion. Syth was a loyal man, but sometimes he didn't like or agree with what his master ordered him to do. Now was one of those times.

His master had ordered him to start killing the high-ranking officers in the army while they slept. He had already framed someone for being a spy, and that man had been quickly executed. But his master wanted to sow more fear, and in the process cripple the army. It had had the desired effect. Now the people in the palace lived in fear. They thought their enemies had been taken care of with the spy, and they had relaxed, but now there was an assassin in the palace and no one knew who it was.

No one thought that it could be Syth. Although he was an outsider and probably the most logical possibility, he made a show of working very hard to find the assassin. It couldn't be him, they thought.

Syth was a ruthless killer in battle, but he also had honor. There was honor in dispatching an enemy that was fighting you face to face. There was no honor in killing a man while he slept. Syth hated killing this way.

When he killed the first man, he had woken him up first. His master had become enraged. He hurt Syth for a long time. He could do that when he was in your head. Syth tried explaining to him the dishonor of killing a sleeping man, and that he was confident in his ability to win if the man was awake, but his master wouldn't listen.

His master told him that the man might have been able to cry out and raise an alarm. There were guards all over the palace. Someone could have heard and caught Syth in the act. He forbade Syth to ever take a risk like that again. Syth hadn't.

So even though he didn't like it, he killed four more officers and aides in a three -week period. All the while he pretended to be investigating the situation, to try and find who was doing it. He played the part well. No one suspected him.

He continued walking down the corridor. The war meeting was going to start soon. The queen would expect a report on how his investigation is going. He couldn't keep saying he didn't have any leads. People might start to get suspicious. Or worse, the queen might assign someone else to help him. That was the last thing he wanted. He didn't need someone getting in the way of his plans. He had to think of something to tell her.

As he got closer to the meeting room, a plan formed. That was one reason he was his Master's most capable man. Not only was he an unparalleled fighter, he had a quick mind. By the time he reached the meeting, he was confident in his decision.

The war room was much less crowded now. Five spots around the large table in the center of the room were empty. Besides the queen and himself, only five men were there. Five very nervous looking men, Syth noticed. The five men gave him a greeting and the queen motioned him over to her.

These five were the lucky ones who hadn't been chosen for death. These five had been the least influential of the queen's war advisors.

Four of the five were normal looking, easily forgettable men. Syth didn't even know their names. But one, the next in line to be killed, was different. He was young, which was the only reason he hadn't been in the top five, and very capable. He was the one who held the meetings together while all the others panicked. He was smart and very good with a sword. Syth thought him more capable than any of the others and had wanted to kill him first. But his master had refused him. He wanted to kill them according to rank. Syth didn't want them to know what to expect. His master did. He said it would make them even more afraid, knowing they were next.

The ones who had expected to be next had taken measures. They had posted guards, but it didn't make any difference. One had posted many guards, but once again, it didn't help. Syth killed them all.

Syth looked at the young man, Sam by name. He was tall, broad shouldered, and muscular. Smiles came easily to his handsome face, even while the murders were happening. He had a positive outlook that rubbed off onto people around him. He was giving the queen a comforting smile now.

Syth stood at the queen's left and faced the others. She asked him quietly if he had anything to report. He nodded. Did he have any leads? He nodded again. She looked relieved.

She turned to the others. "I thank you all for coming. We live in hard times and we need to stick together. All of us fear for our lives, but I finally have good news for you. Syth has a lead on these murders. I will give the floor to him."

"I have discovered something very troubling," Syth began. "The one who is committing these murders does not live in the palace. Although just like with the murder of King Michael, someone in this palace is behind them. I have learned that someone in the palace has hired the services of another yellow-skinned assassin."

Everyone in the room gasped.

"Yes. It is true. That is what my investigation has turned up."

Very good, came his master's voice. *They all fear the Zantan Robbers.*

"How do you know this?" asked one of the men.

"And who is the one who is behind it?" asked another.

"You don't need to worry," said Queen Laurel. "I have complete confidence in Syth. If he says that a yellow-skinned man is killing all our friends, then I believe him."

"I have seen the man in the palace," Syth said.

"Well, why didn't you dispose of him?" a man yelled.

"Why did you let him get away?" asked another man.

"He saw me and ran. I pursued, but as everyone here knows, they are very hard to catch. I lost him. I haven't seen him since, although I have searched everywhere."

"And how do you know that he was hired by someone who lives at the palace?" asked Sam. The smile was gone from his lips.

"I saw the assassin speaking with a man dressed in the livery of the palace."

"Well, who was it? And why didn't you capture him?"

"I'm sorry, but I didn't see his face. I was more concerned about the assassin. I thought he was the bigger threat. But I did catch a glimpse of the man the assassin was talking to as I ran by. He was tall, thin, with long brown hair past his shoulders. That is all I was able to see. After I lost the assassin, I returned to the spot where I had seen them speaking, but the liveried man was gone."

"Very good Syth," said the queen, putting a friendly hand on his arm. She turned her attention to the five men watching her. "This is the first real lead we have had. I knew Syth would find out who was killing these men. Now we can have the guards search the palace for all the men that fit this description."

She turned back to Syth. "Please have the guards stationed outside the room see about this immediately. And please bring the men that are standing in the hallway inside."

Syth gave her a nod. "Yes, My Queen."

He turned and walked to the door. The queen began discussing something with the other men, but he didn't listen to what they were saying. His master was speaking to him again.

That was very good, came his master's voice. *Give them a phantom to chase, one they already fear. If they have their sights on something else, they will not look in your direction.*

Thank you, Master, Syth thought.

He reached the door and opened it. A guard turned to him. Syth also saw four other men standing in the corridor. He addressed the guard.

"The queen wishes you to set up a search of the palace. Gather all the men who are tall, thin, and have long brown hair. They need to be questioned."

"Where shall I keep them detained until they are ready to be questioned?"

"Take them to the throne room. I don't think Her Majesty is holding audience today. She can question them there. Make sure they are well guarded."

The guard saluted. "Yes, Syth." The dark-skinned man was treated with great respect by the palace staff. Everyone knew he was the queen's personal guard. He was with her the majority of the time.

After the guard left, Syth turned to the four men who were looking at him expectantly. Syth noticed that one of them fit the description of the non-existent man he sent the guard to find. "The queen wishes you to enter the war room now," Syth told them. He held the door open for them as they entered the room, then entered as well, shutting the door behind him.

The men lined up in a straight line in front of the massive table, facing the queen. Syth took his place beside her. The queen addressed the five men on the council.

"My friends," she began. "I have chosen these four men to replace our fallen brothers on this council. I believe them to be qualified and capable to fulfill the duty. Please welcome them."

The five men nodded at the newcomers. It was then that everyone in the room noticed that one of the men was tall, thin, and had brown hair past his shoulders. The queen looked at Syth. The five other men shared glances.

"What would you like me to do, My Queen?" asked Syth.

Before she could answer, one of newcomers stepped forward and spoke.

"We thank Your Majesty for choosing us for this important task. We are grateful for your faith in our abilities. We know that defending the country is of utmost importance, and we promise to make you proud."

When he finished, he bowed and stepped back in line. The queen smiled at them, then turned to the other five men.

"Gentlemen, may I introduce Gyles, Trigg, Jaxon, and Crew."

Gyles was the large, blond man who had spoken. Trigg was the smallest man of the group, with short black hair and a goatee. Jaxon was a little older, bald, and had a scarred face. Crew was the man that everyone in the room was looking at. He was tall, thin, and had brown hair past his shoulders. He didn't seem to notice that everyone was staring at him.

The queen continued. "I called you in here late for a reason. We have already talked about the murders and we have a lead. I didn't want you to know that. I wanted to know how you felt with the situation as it has been the past couple weeks. It gladdens my heart to know you are willing to accept the positions with the knowledge that your lives will be in danger. It shows me what kind of men you are."

She turned her attention to Crew. "Unfortunately, the lead we have is that a tall man with long brown hair living here at the palace had hired the assassin who is committing all these murders. I have commanded the palace guards to gather all the men in the palace who fit this description and detain them until they can be questioned. I am afraid that I will have to ask you, Crew, to turn yourself into the palace guard immediately and be questioned with everyone else."

Crew looked surprised, but not nervous. "Oh…okay, Your Majesty. I have nothing to hide. I will gladly submit myself to questioning."

"Good," Queen Laurel said. "Thank you for your cooperation. I do not believe that you are involved, but we must question everyone."

Crew bowed. "I understand Your Majesty."

"Syth, will you please escort this man to wherever you told the guard outside to take everyone?"

"Yes, My Queen. Since you are not holding audience today, I told the guard to gather everyone in the throne room."

"That will be fine, Syth."

Syth turned to Crew. "Come Crew, follow me."

*   *   *

After Syth and Crew left the room Queen Laurel turned to the remaining eight

men. She looked each one in the eye, trying to gauge their feelings about the situation. She already knew she could trust the five original war council members to do what was necessary. They had proven themselves time and again over the years while they served her husband. It was the three new men standing in the room she had concerns about.

She had handpicked the four newcomers herself. She had picked them because she thought them the best men for the job. Yet they hadn't proven themselves in situations like the ones they were about to face. They were the targets of a dangerous and seemingly unstoppable assassin. They were expecting an invasion from a country they knew almost nothing about. And now they were being thrust into military leadership, green and unproven. It was a daunting task for anyone. It boosted her faith in them that they had so gladly taken on the positions.

"Now, if the killer stays true to form, the next one he will attack is Sam. I want to post guards at his chambers every night until he attacks."

"But Your Majesty," said one of the men. "We already tried that before and it didn't work. The assassin simply killed all the guards and then the man inside the room."

"Yes," agreed the queen. "That is true. But this time, I want to post Syth there as well. If anyone has a chance to stop this yellow-skinned devil, it is him. The assassin won't expect to find him there. He will be in for a nasty surprise."

"I agree," said Sam. "But I would also like to help. I think that if Syth and I work together, we have a better chance of catching the guy."

"Well, do you have a plan in mind?"

"Yes," Sam grinned.

After Sam told everyone his plan, they talked about the defense of the country. Little did Queen Laurel know that sending Syth away prevented the assassin from ever learning the plan they implemented to stop him.

*   *   *

Sam waited in his room that night for the attack to come. He sat on his bed with no light, his sword lying across his knees. The assassin was supposed to believe that he was asleep. It was a simple plan really, waiting for the assassin to come while pretending to be asleep. Then he and Syth could fight him together and hopefully kill him. The only problem was that they had no idea what night the assassin would attack. Sam couldn't go without sleep for too many nights.

He hadn't told Syth about his plan. He thought it better that the dark-skinned man not know. He should be left to do his own thing. He would be more effective that way. He didn't want to bother the queen's protector with too many details.

Plus, he didn't fully trust the man. No one knew anything about him. He was a stranger.

While waiting in the dark for the man who was intent on killing him, all he could do was think.

He had been excited when he was selected to be on the war council. The council consisted of the top ten generals in the army. He was the youngest man ever to be selected to the council. It was a great honor.

He hadn't seen any real fighting since he joined the army. Not many people had. Blanderly had enjoyed a period of peace that had lasted years. The army still trained and played war games, but very few men died. The ones who had died had been killed accidentally.

Although Sam had never been in a real battle, he was well trained in battle tactics. He quickly rose in the ranks. The men came to look at him with respect and admiration. They came to him with any questions they had concerning warfare.

He was also a master swordsman. He had practiced swordplay since he was a young boy, and he found he was a natural. He had the ability to study his opponent and discover the way they liked to fight. He had excellent balance and coordination. He was quick to react and change his fighting style when the need arose. He was the perfect man for the council.

But being on the council turned out to be a lot different than he had imagined. Instead of working towards keeping the country safe, the council members were just trying to survive. It didn't start out this way of course. He had been a member on the council for almost two years now. He had greatly admired King Michael and enjoyed working with him. Now he greatly admired his widow. At first it had been wonderful, being on the council. Now, it was terrifying.

But it will end tonight, he vowed. The assassin will attack tonight, and it will end. Then things could go back to normal.

The longer Sam waited, the more convinced he was that the attack would not take place tonight. He didn't dare sleep though. He needed to be awake and ready, in case the assassin did come.

*   *   *

Syth waited in the shadows down the hall from Sam's chambers. He watched as the guards outside the room slowly grew sleepier. He would wait until they were almost dead on their feet before he attacked. He was confident that he could defeat all of them even if they were alert, but he decided it best not to take that chance.

The guards couldn't see him, but they knew he was there. No one was supposed to know exactly where he was. That was part of the plan.

He began to grow impatient. He had waited to get rid of Sam for too long. He would be the most troublesome of the members of the council, and Syth was glad the time had finally arrived. If it had been up to him, he would have killed Sam first. Happy that the time had finally arrived, he drew his swords.

But then he got a troubling feeling. Something was wrong. He couldn't tell what it was, but he could feel that something wasn't right. Something was different. It vexed him not to be able to put a finger on it.

Should he attack tonight as he had planned? Should he wait? He longed to put an end to the queen's top military commander, but he had survived a long time because he always followed his instincts. His instincts told him that he shouldn't attack Sam tonight.

He quickly formed a new plan and hurried away. He had to be quick.

*   *   *

Sam suddenly heard commotion outside his room. He didn't hear any metal clanging, but he heard men shouting. He thrust open the door, sword in hand.

"What is going on? Is it the assassin?"

One of the guards turned to him. "No, sir. At least, not here, sir."

"What do you mean?"

"Well, sir, the assassin killed someone else."

"Someone else? Who?"

"Costuck, sir. He was found murdered in his bed just a few minutes ago."

Costuck was the man on the council just below Sam. The assassin had changed his tactics. He had stopped killing the council members in order. Sam spotted Syth speaking with some of the guards a little ways down the hall. He went over to him.

"And where were you, Syth, when Costuck was being murdered?" Sam demanded of the dark-skinned man.

Syth turned to him, his face expressionless. "Where do you think? I was watching your door, like I was ordered to. I can't be in two places at once."

"You're right. I'm sorry. I wonder why he didn't attack me tonight. Why did he change his tactics?"

"Maybe he spotted me," Syth said. "He might have seen me hiding in the corridor and decided to go for an unguarded victim."

"Possible," Sam said, thinking. "But whatever the reason, now that we don't know what the assassin will do next, we are in a lot of trouble."

17

Aiden watched Dustin examine his new weapon as they rode their mounts northeast along the wide road toward Parkos. He held the blade out in front of him, not paying attention to the road, trusting his mount to stay with the group. He pushed the button on the bottom of the hilt and watched the blade extend to twice its previous length. He gave a small smile, and then pushed the button again. The blade immediately retracted. Aiden thought he looked pleased with his new weapon.

Brione, on the other hand, who had the other sword, wasn't paying any attention to hers. It was strapped to her waist beside her other knife. She had examined it for a few minutes, then put it in her belt and seemed to forget about it.

Tim had offered the weapons to Zach and Jaden first. They seemed insulted by the offer. They said they would never use a weapon that was previously used by a Zantan Robber. When they refused, Tim offered the weapons to the two people who had been in the group the longest, Brione and Dustin.

Aiden saw that Brione looked troubled. He urged his mount next to hers so he could speak with her.

"What's on your mind?" he asked.

She glanced at him, then looked away. He had never seen her like this. It took a while for her to answer his question. "I have never been totally dominated like that in a fight before. I feel ashamed. If it wasn't for Dorn, a man with no fighting ability, I would be dead right now. Portia would probably be dead too."

"Don't worry about it," Aiden replied lightly, trying to boost her spirits. "Dustin and I fought together against one and we couldn't defeat him. We had to have Zach's help. If he wasn't there, we probably would have died too. It's not your fault."

"Yeah, but I still feel like it was. I feel like I'm not good enough."

"Brione, you are one of the best fighters I have ever seen. I don't even come close to you. Don't worry about it. We all had trouble with them."

"Zach and Jaden didn't. Your father didn't."

"Now you are trying to compare yourself to my father? Brione, he is the best fighter I have ever seen. And there is no comparing anyone to Jaden and Zach. I think they were swinging a sword when they came out of their mother's womb."

Brione couldn't help but laugh at that. "Thanks Aiden. You made me feel better."

"I'm glad," he replied. "Besides, you can use the fight that night as a goal to improve."

"What?"

"Your new goal can be to be able to defeat a Zantan Robber in combat. I'm sure you'll get another chance to face one before our job is done."

"Yeah," Brione said. "I'll do that. I'll train harder with the goal of beating a Zantan Robber one-on-one. Who knows, the battle that night might make me a better fighter. Thanks again Aiden." She smiled at him. He returned the smile.

"But to be honest with you Aiden," Brione continued, "that isn't the only reason I was feeling sad."

"Oh yeah?"

She nodded. "Yeah. I don't know how you do it."

Aiden was confused. "Do what?"

"I don't know how you can have such a positive outlook when your best friend is missing and in danger."

Now Aiden understood. Brione missed Layne. She was worried about him.

"You miss him, don't you?"

She didn't say anything. She just nodded. Aiden saw a tear running down her cheek. "I miss him too," he said.

"You know," she said, looking off at something to the side, "that boy gets on my nerves more than anyone I have ever met." Aiden laughed at that. He knew it was true. "He is lazy, he doesn't take anything seriously, and he is always joking around. I think he enjoys making me angry." Aiden knew that he did, in fact, enjoy making her mad. It was one of his favorite things to do. But he didn't tell her so. She was already upset enough as it was. She looked at him now. "He does, doesn't he?" Aiden just shrugged.

"But you know what? The funny thing is that I miss him terribly. I miss his laughter, his jokes, and yes, his teasing. I would endure his teasing for the rest of my life if he would just come back to us safely. The group needs him. He would do anything for anyone in the group without hesitating. He proved it in that inn."

She reached over and took his arm. "But why am I telling you this? He is your best friend. I'm sure you feel the same way." Aiden nodded. "How are you holding up? Really?"

Aiden thought about it. How was he holding up? "I'm alright, I guess. I am terrified for him. But I also know that he is very resourceful. I'm sure he will be okay and that he will be back with us safely again. He must be eager to tell us all about his ordeal. And half of what he says will probably be true."

They both laughed at that.

"Brione?" She turned to him. "Can I ask you a question?"

"Yes."

"Well, on the ship, Layne, Portia, and I were talking about how you became such a good fighter."

"What?"

"Well, Portia asked about it, and Layne told her."

"And how does he know? I've never talked to him about it."

"Well…he overheard you talking about it with my dad."

Brione snorted. "Overheard, huh? He was probably hiding close by and intentionally listening in."

"Probably," Aiden agreed.

"That's just like him." Brione seemed disgusted. Aiden was amazed at how quickly Brione's attitude towards Layne could change. Just a few seconds ago she had nothing but kind things to say about him.

"Well, anyway," Aiden continued, "now that we know how you became a great fighter, Portia and I were wondering how you met my father and became second-in-command of the group." When he said that, Portia brought her horse closer so she could listen.

Portia wasn't skilled on a horse. She was used to the unpredictable movements of a ship, yet was uncomfortable on the animal. She had difficulty climbing up onto the horse, then had trouble bringing it under control. They only had time to give her a quick lesson. They had bought the horses at a town a few miles north of Kingston the day after the fight at the camp sight. They were in a hurry and didn't have time to properly teach her how to ride. Luckily, everyone else had at least some experience with horses. They had been riding for two days now, and she had improved slightly, but not much.

"You don't remember how I met your dad?" Brione asked. "You were there when I joined the group. You were old enough to remember."

"Well, I was used to new recruits just periodically showing up. I never asked questions about them."

Brione thought for a moment before turning to Aiden. "I have never told my story to anyone. Your dad knows because he was there, but no one else does. It may be good to tell someone my story. It's about time I get it off my chest.

"As you know, I was trained to fight by my father. My brothers didn't like me at all, but after my father stopped training them and started training me, their hatred of me only grew. When I was a young woman, my parents passed away. They both died of the same illness. My father first, my mother a couple days after. It was a miracle that my brothers and I didn't get sick, too.

"After my parents died, our home belonged to my oldest brother. Of course, he allowed my other brothers to live there. And, against my brothers' wishes, he let me stay there too. He said it was not right that someone send a family member away, and that our parents would want him to allow me to continue to live there."

She paused in her story to take a long drink from her water skin. Portia and Aiden glanced at each other, but didn't say anything. Finally, she continued.

"My brothers let me live at the house, but they had nothing to do with me. They hardly ever talked to me, and I had to fend for myself. They never shared food or drink with me. If I didn't earn my own money to buy my own food, I would go hungry. I went to sleep hungry many nights at first.

"But then I got lucky and was hired as a guard at a local tavern. The owner was a friend of my father's and he knew how good I was at handling a sword. He let me carry one while I was at work because I was a woman. He didn't let anyone in the tavern if they were armed.

"The only problem was that since I was a woman, many men wanted to prove themselves against me. They thought that it was ridiculous that a woman was hired to keep the peace at a tavern. They wanted to prove that I didn't belong there. It didn't matter to them that I was armed, and they were not. They fought me anyway. I never killed any of the men, but they never beat me either. Then one day…

*   *   *

Brione was leaning against the bar at the tavern, keeping an eye on the crowd. She had been lucky today. Today was the first day that no one had come in looking for a fight. She never had any problem taking care of troublemakers, but it got on her nerves that men would come in just to fight her. But not today. Not yet anyway.

She sipped on a glass of ale as she watched. The ale in this tavern was the best in town. The food wasn't too shabby either. She had just finished a meal of meat and potatoes and felt satisfied and content. This was a good job and she was grateful to the shop owner for giving it to her.

It was early evening and a large group of men arrived at the tavern. The day's work was finished, and they sought a drink and the companionship of peers before heading home for the night. Brione kept a close eye on them, but no one seemed to want to cause trouble.

Since the tavern was pretty quiet at the moment, she looked up at the walls. She loved the way the owner decorated the place. He knew a couple talented painters in town and hired them to paint pictures for the walls. They ranged from pictures of mountain ranges to local people. He changed the pictures often, and part of the appeal of the place was to come in and see what new paintings he had put up. She was slightly embarrassed to see that the painting she had agreed to pose for was up on the walls this night.

It had taken a lot of persuading by the owner before she had agreed to it. He said that she was an important part of the tavern and she deserved to have her picture on the wall. It was of her face, from the neck up. Her brown eyes were big, her dark hair framed her face. She was smiling. She didn't think that the beautiful woman in the picture looked like her, but other people said it did.

She had been very uncomfortable posing for the picture. It was so far out of her element that she had never imagined she would do anything like that. But she was grateful to the owner of the tavern for the opportunity he had given her, so she had agreed.

That was months ago. It had taken him a long time to hang it up. It was too soon for Brione's liking though.

After a little while Brione saw a group of three men enter the tavern. They found an empty table and sat down. A very good looking man, probably in his mid-thirties, sat facing her. He sat straight in his chair. They made eye contact. She looked into his brown eyes and saw intelligence there. She saw kindness as well.

Her attention was drawn away from the man by some commotion on the other side of the room. She had to go investigate.

The evening deepened and Brione continued her work. She would glance over at the man sitting with his two companions whenever she could. Every once in a while she would make eye contact with the man again. Whenever she did, he would smile at her. She smiled back.

Then, late into evening, a large man entered the tavern. He stood in the doorway and scanned the room. When he spotted Brione leaning against the bar, he started forward.

"There you are," he said as he walked, dodging tables and serving girls alike. "The great tavern wench who thinks she can defeat any man in a fight. Ha!" It took him awhile to make his way across the room because the tavern was very crowded that evening.

Brione straightened. She squared her shoulders and put her hand on the hilt of her sword. "I don't want any trouble, sir."

The man snorted. "You called me sir? Are you speaking to me respectfully because you are trying to get out of this? Are you scared? I expected more from you. You are not what the stories say you are. I am disappointed."

"Well," Brione said. "If I am such a disappointment, then we don't need to take this any further. Just be on your way, sir."

The man laughed. "I never said that I didn't want to fight you. It is just going to be easier than I had thought."

"Alright. But just remember, I tried to stop this." Brione began pulling her sword from its sheath at her waist.

"Oh no," said the man. "If I don't get a weapon, then you don't either."

"Now you sound like the one who is scared," said Brione. "Is the big strong man afraid of the little woman with a sword?"

The men in the tavern laughed. Even the newcomer with the kind eyes smiled. The man looked furious.

"No," he replied. "But that is the only reason you have never lost a fight, I bet. Without your sword, you are just another weak woman. It is an unfair advantage. You can't use it."

"You want to fight an unarmed woman, is that it?"

The man's face went red as the customers in the tavern laughed again. "No! But I don't want you to have such an unfair advantage. Now, if you had a knife, that would be different. I would allow that. But since it doesn't look like you have one, I guess it will have to be a fair fight."

Brione thought it over for a moment. "Alright," she said. "I guess there will be no talking you out of this." She dropped her sword back in her sheath, then unbuckled her sword belt and placed it on the bar. "Watch over this for me, will you?" she asked the owner, then turned back to her opponent. With a cry, the man rushed her.

Brione stood her ground and waited for the man to get close. As he reached her, arms spread wide to grab her, she hit him with the palm of her hand right between the eyes. The punch was so quick he hadn't seen it coming. It stopped him dead in his tracks. He stood up straight for a moment, stunned, eyes blinking, then fell to the floor.

He recovered quickly though and got back up to his feet.

"I dropped you without the aid of a sword," Brione said. "Are you sure you want to continue this?"

In answer, he bellowed again and rushed her once more. She quickly crouched down and drew a knife from each boot that the man hadn't noticed before. When he reached her again, she spun out of the way, jabbing him in the side as he went past with her knife. Not deep enough to do too much damage, but enough to be noticed. He grunted and stumbled into the bar. It groaned with the weight of the large man.

Once again, he struggled to his feet, putting a hand to his side. He looked at the hand. It had blood on it. "A knife?"

"You said that if I had one, you would allow me to use it," Brione said. "Well, I have one. Two actually." She held them up for him to see.

The man was enraged. He cried out again and picked up a stool from the bar and threw it at her. She dodged, but it hit a customer in the face. Blood spraying from his broken nose, the man who got hit went down. He cried out in pain.

"That's enough!" the owner cried. He reached for the man as he picked up another chair, but he shoved him aside. He threw the second chair at her.

She knew she wouldn't be able to dodge this one, so she threw up her arms to protect herself as much as possible. It hurt a lot when the chair hit her arms.

She lowered her arms again and her attacker was on top of her. He punched her in the face, sending her sprawling on the floor. He was on her in an instant, picking her up and holding her over his head. She still had her knives, so before he had a chance to throw her, she stabbed him in his right shoulder. With a cry of pain, he dropped her. She hit the floor hard. The breath was knocked out of her.

When she recovered a little and finally looked up, she saw the man trying to pull the knife out of his shoulder. He was still screaming in pain. She hadn't realized that she had driven the knife in all the way to the hilt. The man couldn't pull it out. When he tried, it hurt much worse. He finally gave up. "You win," he said.

Suddenly the man that Brione had been glancing at all night long stood up and went to the injured man. "Here, let me get that for you," he said. He gripped the hilt of the knife.

"No!" the man cried. But before he could do anything about it, the man yanked the knife out. Brione's attacker cried out again as the knife came out, the blade dripping with blood.

"Did that hurt?"

"Of course it did, you idiot!"

"Good," said the man with the kind eyes. They weren't kind at the moment. "It serves you right."

The man looked confused. "What?"

"You come in here and challenge a woman who is just doing her job to a fight. Then you injure an innocent bystander. You knock the owner of the establishment to the floor, and damage his place of business. So yes, it serves you right."

"Who are you to judge me? You're no better than me!"

"You're right. I am no better than you. But I have never tried to beat up a woman who did nothing to me. And I certainly have never hurt an innocent bystander before." He turned to the owner. "What do you want done with him? Should we call the city guard?"

The owner didn't answer. He just stared at the man with the kind eyes. Finally, his eyes got bigger. "I know who you are! I didn't recognize you before, but now I do. You're Tim, aren't you? You're the famous mercenary Tim!"

"I am."

"I knew it! I knew it!" He grabbed Tim's hand and shook it vigorously. "It is an honor to have you in my tavern. Excuse the mess. I keep it a lot cleaner than this. But as you know, there was an incident. I am so sorry. It is the girl's fault. She is good with a sword, but ever since I hired her, men have been coming in to challenge her. She has brought nothing but trouble to this establishment. I will let her go if you wish it."

Tim didn't look pleased with what he had just heard. "Of course not. The girl did nothing wrong. She just did her job. You wouldn't send her away for doing her job would you?"

"Well, no, but…"

"The man is at fault. Every man who has ever come into this tavern looking for trouble is to blame. You seem like a smart man. I am sure you knew what the consequences would be if you hired a woman guard. Didn't you?"

"Well, yes, but…"

"And yet you hired her anyway. Why?"

"Well, because I needed a new guard and I knew her father and I knew she was good in a fight."

"And has any of that changed tonight?"

"Well, no. But I told you the truth when I said that she has been nothing but trouble since she got here."

Tim was silent for a moment. He just stood there, looking at the man. Finally he asked, "Do you want to call the city guard or not?"

"No," said the owner of the tavern. "Let him be on his way. I don't think he'll come back to cause any more trouble."

Tim turned to the other man. "Get out of here."

"You'll pay for this!" said the man.

Tim turned his back to the man. "I doubt it."

The man glared at Tim's back. Brione, who had been watching the entire exchange, expected the man to attack the mercenary leader. But he didn't. At last, he turned away and left the tavern.

Brione couldn't believe that Tim was standing in front of her. He was famous. Everyone had heard of Tim. She knew of his sense of justice. The only thing more famous was his fighting ability. It was said that no one had ever bested him. Being a fighter herself, she could tell that the stories were probably true. She could tell by the way he carried himself, by the way he stood. He was always balanced. Without thinking he would adjust his weight so he could react to any situation. Although she had never seen him in battle, she was sure he was a master.

Suddenly she felt very embarrassed that this great man had stood up for her in front of her employer. She didn't think she deserved his praise. She began to feel uncomfortable and wished he would just leave. He granted her wish.

"Well," said Tim. "We shall be on our way. He turned to Brione and gave her a bow. "I'm sorry that had to happen, lady, but you were magnificent. I would count myself a lucky man if I had you working with me." He gave the tavern owner a look when he said that, then turned and left. The other two men followed him out. The owner looked pale.

The owner waited until they had exited the bar and then rounded on Brione. "Do you realize what you just did?" He was furious.

Brione was confused and shocked. She had never seen her employer yell like this before. She had no idea what she had done wrong. "No."

"You made me look bad in front of Tim! Did you see the look he gave me just before he left? He was disgusted. He was disgusted because of you."

Brione was angry now. "I don't see how I did anything wrong," she yelled back.

"Don't use that tone of voice with me! I am your employer! You will treat me with respect!"

Brione threw up her hands. "Then tell me what I did!" she exclaimed.

"I pointed out that you bring trouble to the tavern, and he takes your side like it's my fault. He will probably never come in here again. Do you

know the prestige I would have if that great man was a regular in my estab-lishment? Do you?" She shook her head. "Well," he continued, "it doesn't matter now, because it is not going to happen!"

"I still don't see..."

"Get out," he said quietly.

"What?"

"Get out. I want you out. You're fired."

"But..."

"You're fired!"

Brione stared at the man for a few moments. She couldn't believe this was happening. What was she going to do? How was she going to eat? She looked around the room. Every face was staring back at her. "Alright," she said and turned away from him. She went behind the bar and grabbed her light cloak. Her sword belt was still lying on the bar. She grabbed it and put it back around her waist.

"Listen," the owner said gently as he came up to the bar. "I am sorry for this. I don't usually get carried away like that." Brione just nodded, not looking at him. "But what I said was true. There has been a lot of trouble since you started working here. The amount of fights in the place has tripled because men want to fight you. And now tonight, one of the customers was injured. I will be lucky if he ever comes back. I know it isn't entirely your fault, and I know you don't enjoy fighting, but that is just the way it is. I feel like I have to let you go." She nodded again.

When she tried to leave, he stopped her. "Wait a minute."

She stopped and turned to him.

He reached under the bar and produced a small bag of coins. He held it out in front of her. "Here, take it. It is your pay for the rest of the week." She didn't budge. She just looked at the bag. "Please take it. I know you will need it. And once again, I am sorry about this. But I have to do what I feel is best for my business."

She grabbed the bag and, without a word, turned and left the building.

18

Brione was about to continue her narrative when she heard a scream. It was from Veronna, who was up at the front of the group riding next to Tim. Brione looked for her, but since she was riding at the rear of the group almost everyone was between her and the girl. Her view was blocked.

"Stay here," she said to Aiden and Portia and urged her horse to the front of the group.

"Should we go after her?" Portia asked Aiden.

Portia and Aiden had gotten a lot closer since the night Cory was murdered. She felt responsible for the young man's death, and Aiden was there for her while she grieved, a shoulder for her to cry on. It had felt good to be able to help someone. The mercenary group helped people all the time, but this was different. They helped people in need with swords and axes. Aiden had helped Portia with compassion. It was a nice feeling.

Now he felt comfortable in her presence. He no longer considered her childish and immature. She had lost something when Cory died, and he thought that she had grown stronger because of it. They had been riding side-by-side since they had first bought the horses.

Aiden looked after Brione as she made her way up to his sister. "I don't know," he replied. "She told us to stay here."

"That was your sister that screamed! Let's go make sure she is alright."

"Okay," Aiden said and they both urged their horses on. Everyone had gathered around the young girl, who wasn't screaming now, but was pointing at something on the side of the road.

"What is everyone looking at?" asked Aiden to no one in particular. When he looked in the direction his sister was pointing, he had his answer.

Standing maybe twenty feet from the road was the largest animal Aiden had ever seen. It stood on all fours, yet Aiden still thought that its head would touch his chest. It was covered in black fur. Its head was huge, its dark eyes small as it looked at the group.

It gave a great bellow that made the horses nervous.

"What is that thing?" Aiden asked.

"That is a bear, Aiden," his father answered.

"Bears are real?" Aiden asked in disbelief.

Tim smiled, although Aiden didn't see it because his attention was focused on the huge animal. "Yes son, they are real."

"Isn't it beautiful?" said Veronna.

"Yes," whispered Dana, who was sitting on her horse next to the younger girl.

Suddenly, the beast stood upon its hind legs and bellowed again. It was even more massive now. Aiden couldn't believe how big it was. It easily towered over everyone in the group. Aiden could see its paws for the first time. They dwarfed his hands. He knew this beast could kill him with just one swipe of its great paw.

Behind the bear, out of the trees, came a small bundle of black fur. It was a baby bear, a miniature version of its mother.

"Aw," said Veronna. "How cute!"

The little creature stopped by its mother and gave a small cry. The mother bear bellowed again. It sounded more threatening this time.

"It is now time to go," said Tim. "That mother bear would kill every one of us if she could to protect her baby. There aren't many things in the forest more dangerous than a bear protecting her cubs. Let's get moving."

They hurried their horses away, most of the group looking back over their shoulders, not in fear, but in fascination. Aiden had never seen anything like it. He was stunned that creatures he had thought were just stories actually existed. If bears existed, who knew what else they might see in this strange land. He couldn't help but be excited at the thought.

Veronna maneuvered over to him. She was practically glowing. "Amazing!" she cried. "Did you see that, Aiden?"

Aiden couldn't help but smile. "Of course, I saw it. Everyone did."

"Oh, I wish I were a druid. Dad says that druids can speak with the animals and are friends with them."

"That would be nice."

"Princess Dana! Did you see that?" She hurried off toward the smiling princess. Aiden grinned after her.

Portia came closer. "She is fifteen, right?"

"Yeah."

"Don't you think she is a little immature for a fifteen-year old?"

Aiden didn't tell her that he had considered Portia immature when he had first met her. "I don't know," he said slowly.

"Well, I think she is. Don't get me wrong, I really like her. But it just seems to me that she is a bit childish. That's all."

"Well," Aiden said. "It's not like she has had the strong influence of a woman in her life. My mother died when she was an infant, and my father has been raising us both. She hasn't had a woman around to teach her how to be a woman. My father does the best he can, but he can only do so much for a young girl."

"What about Brione?"

"True, Brione has been around the last few years. But for one, she isn't a typical woman. She is a fighter. And two, because she is a fighter, she is gone a lot. She is always either training or on a job. She doesn't have much time to spend with Veronna and teach her girl things."

"That is a good point. Well, maybe I will be able to influence her while I am with you guys. Maybe I can help her."

"Maybe," Aiden agreed, although he liked his little sister just the way she was. He couldn't imagine her being any different. She was wonderfully innocent and full of life. She was a light in the dark times they were facing at the moment. The thought of her brought a smile to his lips.

They continued to travel, leaving the trees behind and roaming through rolling, green hills. The road was easy. It skirted around the hills instead of over them, which was good for the horses. There were not many trees in sight. Here and there they would see a single, tall tree. It was odd to see country like this. Aiden was used to the forests surrounding the little fort that had been his home for the past few years.

Every so often they would spot a farm in the distance, but no people working the fields. They passed no other travelers on the road. It was a beautiful, warm day, and the absence of other people was strange to Aiden. He didn't know anything about farming, but today seemed a perfect day for farm work. He thought it odd that no one was out working.

Aiden didn't get the chance to hear the rest of Brione's story, because she now traveled at the front of the group with Tim. That left Aiden and Portia to pass the time telling stories of their lives. Before long they were laughing and enjoying each other's company. He liked her loud, joyful laugh.

Aiden glanced over at her during a rare silent moment and for the first time saw what Layne had seen on the ship. She truly was beautiful. He never had a preference when it came to the color of girls' hair, but now he decided he preferred dark hair. Dark hair and green eyes. And small. He liked girls that were small.

Aiden's glance turned into a stare. Portia caught him looking and smiled at him. Aiden quickly looked away, his face going red. Portia laughed.

The group rounded a large hill and saw smoke in the distance. It seemed like it was far away, but they could smell the smoke as well. It must have been a large fire.

All conversation stopped as everyone watched the smoke. Aiden couldn't look away from it. The sight of it gave him a bad feeling. A feeling of danger. He had a strange sense that the fire was unnatural.

The closer to the smoke they got, the stronger the smell became. Soon, the group could smell a new aroma. It smelled like someone was cooking meat. But at the same time, Aiden thought that he had never eaten meet that smelled like that before. Suddenly Tim called a halt and had everyone gather around.

"That is the smell of burning flesh," he informed everyone. "But that is not animal flesh. It is human."

Veronna and Dana gasped as one. "How do you know?" the princess asked.

"I've smelled it before," Tim replied. "I lived in this land almost my entire life. There are many creatures here that will cook and eat humans if they can. I have encountered numerous of them. Believe me, I know the smell."

Veronna suddenly looked very frightened. Her father noticed and put a comforting hand on her shoulder.

"You think that there are things in that village that eat humans?" Dustin asked.

"Possibly. It smells like it. But I think we should go check it out. There might be prisoners. If anyone is alive, we cannot let them suffer such a gruesome fate."

"But we don't have any idea what we are up against!" Dorn cried. "We have no idea what killed those people, or how many of the enemy there are. We could be walking into a death trap!"

"That is true," Tim said. "But we are going anyway. We can't leave any people who might have survived to such a horrible fate. Believe me, we are not unprepared. We will be fine. It is the survivors, if there are any, that we need to be worried about. Let's go."

Once Tim had made up his mind, there was no changing it. No one else tried to persuade him to change his plan. They all turned their horses to follow him toward the smoke, none of them knowing what to expect.

It took them another hour to reach the smoke. It was a lot further than the group had thought. The smell had carried for miles.

They discovered that the smoke was coming from a village. Someone or something had set fire to most of the buildings. They were still a good distance away, so they couldn't see any people or creatures in the village. It looked totally abandoned. Maybe they would be lucky and whatever did this was already gone.

As they approached, they could see that items had been thrown out the front doors of the buildings and left to lie in the street. There was everything from clothing to beds to kids' toys. Most of the items had been broken.

Finally, they came up to the first set of buildings. They were made of both brick and wood. The doors were torn off the hinges, all the windows were broken. Most of the buildings were blackened husks, the fires already gone out after gutting the dwellings. It looked to Aiden that the fires were first started on this end of the village. He could see fires still consuming buildings at the other end of the small village.

As they got deeper into town, the sites were just the same. All the buildings had been looted, the items destroyed and tossed like garbage onto the street. The destruction seemed pointless. It seemed like the attackers had done it just for fun.

Aiden almost bumped into his father when Tim stopped dead in his tracks. There was a large pile of something burning in the center of town. They hadn't noticed it before because they had been focused on the buildings to either side of them.

"Is that what I think it is?" asked Aiden.

"Yes," his father replied.

The girls gasped. Someone behind Aiden vomited. He couldn't tell who.

Aiden saw limbs, human limbs, all tangled together in the pile. The skin was black from the flames. In amongst the limbs were human heads, the expressions of terror and pain frozen on their faces forever. It was impossible to tell male from female. They all looked the same, black and burnt and their hair burned away.

Suddenly, a new smell emerged. One that was so strong that it banished the smell of smoke and burning flesh. It was a foul odor, one that made their noses itch and made it hard for them to breath. Several people in the group began to cough.

"What is that smell?" asked Brione.

"Goblins," Tim answered. The way he said that one word told the rest of the group how he felt about the creatures.

"Do goblins eat humans?" asked Veronna.

"No," her father replied. "But they do enjoy killing us. There must have been a large group for them to attack a village. Goblins are cowards. They won't attack if they think the odds might even be close to fair. They probably outnumbered the people in the village by a large margin."

"What do we do now?"

Tim looked at Brione, who had asked the question. "Well, first you are going to give me your weapons. At least, all the ones that are visible."

"What? Why?"

"We don't want the goblins to know you are a fighter."

"But if we have less fighters, they will be more likely to attack us, won't they?"

"Yes. They will. Normally, I would want to intimidate them and keep them from attacking, but these goblins murdered an entire village of humans. We can't let them get away with it. "

Portia smiled and looked at Aiden. "There is your father's famous sense of justice." Aiden nodded.

"I think if we continue to go through town, the goblins will show themselves and we can see exactly what we're up against," said Tim. "Does anyone have a problem with my plan? If so, say so now."

No one said a word. "Okay. I'll take the lead. Dustin, you're on the right. Aiden, take the left. Zach and Jaden will take rear guard. I want everyone else in the center. Including you Brione. I want the goblins to think we are only five fighters, four women, and one older man. No offense, Dorn. Now, give me your weapons Brione."

She reluctantly did so and they formed into the ranks that Tim had ordered. When everyone was ready, they slowly started forward.

It was a tense group that made their way through the small, empty village. Aiden looked around and imagined what the village must have been like when the people still lived. He could imagine children playing in the streets. Women chatting with each other as they kept an eye on their kids. Men working in the fields just outside of town. He imagined adults laughing and children squealing in delight. Thinking of these things made him feel a little bit better. It made the town feel less dead. But it also made him angrier at the goblins for taking away the lives of all the townsfolk.

After a few moments, he felt a tug on his sleeve. He looked over at Portia, who was riding next to him and she pointed to his left. He looked in that direction and saw what had to have been a goblin.

It was standing in the doorway of a building, just watching the group as they passed. It was short, no more than five feet tall, with green skin. Its face was scrunched up tight. It had long ears that shot straight out to the sides of its head. Its nose was long and narrow. It stood up on two legs like a human, but all its joints were too large. Its knees, elbows, and knuckles were large balls of bone. It wore mismatched clothes that were too big for it, and carried a short sword.

"Dad," Aiden said.

"I see it," his father replied.

Suddenly, more of the creatures appeared all around them. They were on the roofs, in doorways, and in alleys. They had obviously been hiding. There were more than a dozen of them. They were all dressed in mismatched clothing that was either too big or too small for them. They had obviously looted the clothes from the dead townsfolk. Aiden saw one that was wearing a dress.

"Don't draw your weapons yet," Tim said to the group. "Do anyone of you speak our tongue?" Tim called out to the goblins.

The goblins glanced at each other, obviously not understanding what Tim had just asked.

"Does anyone of you speak our language?" Tim asked the question louder this time.

"I do," came a voice. It was shrill and hi-pitched. Everyone looked to where they had heard the voice come from and saw a large goblin coming out of the doorway of a building that looked to have once been an inn. "I speak your tongue. What do you want?"

"We want to know what happened here."

"Why do you care?"

"We saw the smoke and came to investigate, to see if we could help. We want to know what happened then be on our way. We are not looking for a fight. We are just passing through."

"I will tell you what happened! We came and killed every single one of these humans in this town. They trembled before our might and cried for mercy! But we gave them none. Now, leave this place, or we will kill you as well!"

"Okay. We will leave. There is nothing we can do here." He turned to the group. "Come, let us be on our way."

They left the city in silence, keeping in their formation. Aiden glanced behind them and saw all of the goblins watching them leave. He looked back at his father when he addressed the group.

"Now, I will give Brione her weapons back and she will go to wherever the most goblins attack from. Stay in your formations. Try to dodge their swings instead of blocking them. They are small, but much stronger than humans. You're likely to lose your weapons if you parry their blows."

"Do you really think they will attack?" asked Aiden.

"Yes," his father replied. "They would not have shown themselves if they didn't plan on attacking us. They would have stayed hidden and hoped we didn't see them. They wanted to intimidate us first, then trick us and make us feel secure by pretending to let us go on our way.

"Besides, we have horses. Goblins don't eat humans, but they love the taste of horse. They will not pass up on the chance for so much food.

It might be easier to fight them if you dismount. You have an advantage on a horse, but if you're not used to it, it might be hard."

The attack came quicker than Aiden thought it would. Almost the instant his father stopped talking the group heard cries from behind them. They all turned toward the threat, Tim quickly giving Brione her sword. The sight was frightening.

There were at least fifteen of the little green creatures running at them full speed and swinging their weapons in the air. Their battle cries were high-pitched and blood curdling. "Stay in your formations!" Aiden heard his father yell.

Two goblins immediately went down, the hilt of knives thrown by Jaden and Zach sticking out of their chests. Then the rest were upon the group.

Brione moved to the rear of the group to help Jaden and Zach. The center of the attacking force attacked in the rear, the wings swinging around to the sides. Aiden found himself facing two of the creatures. He was on top of his horse, so he had a height advantage. He had leverage because the goblins had to swing up to hit him. He used it to his benefit.

The first goblin swung wildly and missed, and Aiden brought his sword down on top of the creature's head. It split its skull and the creature fell to the ground.

Aiden's horse was not trained for battle, so it panicked and bucked. Aiden had to use both hands to hold on and keep from being thrown off. The second goblin took this opportunity to attack but misjudged where the horse was kicking and caught a hoof to the face. The goblin went down in a heap. Aiden could hold on no longer and was thrown. He hit the ground hard, the breath knocked out of him. He looked up and watched his horse bolt away. He lay on the ground, groaning in pain, and saw a figure come up to him.

*   *   *

Dustin had dismounted and was facing three of the creatures, but saw Tim come up on his left. Tim had also dismounted. The mercenary leader rushed two of the goblins, leaving Dustin to face one. The creature came at him, swinging on old, rusty sword.

Dustin remembered Tim's warning about trying not to parry the attacks and dodged backwards. The sword missed, and Dustin countered. His sword sliced the goblin in the arm. The creature screamed in pain and swung again. This time, all Dustin could do was bring his sword up in front of himself to block the blow. Pain shot up his sword arm as the goblin's weapon hit his, and Dustin dropped his sword. He staggered back as the goblin kept up the attack, swinging wildly. All Dustin could do was give ground while he tried to figure out what to do.

Dustin ducked under one swing and surged forward, wrapping his arms around the smaller creature and trying to wrestle it to the ground. The goblin didn't budge. It took both hands and slammed them down on Dustin's back. Dustin hit the ground and lay there on his stomach, helpless and in pain. The goblin raised its sword high above its head.

*　　*　　*

Tim saw that Dustin was facing three goblins and knew that the young fighter couldn't prevail against such odds. He rushed two of them to give Dustin a better chance. He was the only one of the group, besides maybe Zach and Jaden, who had ever fought goblins. He knew how to fight them, so he needed to take on as many as he could.

He swung his broadsword high then low at one of the goblins. After the creature blocked his blows he spun and swung at the other creature. When that creature parried, he ducked under a swing from the first goblin, and blocked a blow from the second. The pain jolted his arm, but he kept his grip on his sword. He had forgotten just how much it hurt to do that.

The pain slowed him down a bit and the goblins were able to get on either side of him. Instead of waiting for them to attack, he went after the one on his left. He attacked with abandon, trying to make quick work of his opponent before the other could engage him again. But the goblin parried every blow. He had to dodge an attack by the second goblin, which halted his momentum. Then both goblins attacked him at the same time.

He tried his best to avoid their weapons, but he was forced to use his sword to block. Every blow hurt. Somehow, he never dropped his sword and was able to counter all the attacks.

As he backed up, he suddenly hit into someone else. He glanced back to see who it was and discovered that he had run into another goblin, knocking it aside. He saw that it had been standing over Dustin, who was lying on his stomach. He had probably just saved his friend's life.

Dustin quickly got to his feet and rushed to his sword, which was lying a few feet away. Dustin faced the goblin once more, only to see that it was about to attack Tim from behind. He rushed forward and stabbed the goblin in the back before it could thrust its sword into Tim's back.

Then he saw Aiden on the ground and another goblin stalking towards him. The creature didn't seem to be in any hurry. It obviously thought Aiden to be helpless. Dustin rushed to his aid.

*   *   *

The bulk of the enemy force charged at Brione and her two dark-skinned companions. All three of them had dismounted and she stood between them. She saw Zach and Jaden rush into the group and scatter them. With their speed and agility, the two fighters had no problem avoiding the strikes of the goblins. They quickly followed and goblins started falling.

Brione was left with only one foe to face, but she recognized it as the large goblin who had spoken to them earlier. This was most likely the leader of the band. She doubted that this would be an easy fight. The goblin was holding a large ax. It came for her.

She dodged its downward swing and sliced it in the back. Blood appeared, but the goblin didn't even grunt. He came at her again, this time with a horizontal swing. She jumped out of the way, but didn't have a chance to counter.

This goblin was almost as tall as she was and much more muscular. She knew that she would never be able to overpower the creature. She would have to use her agility and wits to defeat it.

The two combatants circled each other, the goblin feigning attacks, but Brione didn't fall for it. She didn't react. Finally, the goblin tired of the game and attacked her again. She waited for the strike to come, for the ax to swing in her direction. It never did. The goblin didn't attack her with its ax this time, it just ran right into her. The move caught her by surprise, leaving her unable to dodge the attack. The goblin's body hit her hard, the weight forcing her to the ground. It fell on top of her and her breath left her lungs with a grunt.

The goblin was in no position to bring its ax to bear, so it started punching her in the side. The stench of the thing was nauseating. The heavy blows throbbed and she knew she had to escape the creature quickly or she was doomed.

She was able to bring her knee up hard into the goblin's groin. He grunted in pain and the blows stopped. It reached down with its free hand to comfort the area, and Brione was able to shove the creature off. It curled up in a ball and whimpered pathetically.

She was able to struggle to her feet and stand over the creature. She looked down at it and almost pitied the thing, it looked so weak and pitiful. But then she remembered what Tim had said about needing to destroy the things, and she quickly lopped off the goblin's head.

*   *   *

Aiden was able to get to his feet when Dustin engaged the creature stalking towards him. He was surprised to discover that he had been able to keep hold of his sword when he fell from his horse. He was still in a lot of pain, but he knew that he had to help his friend. He staggered forward to the combatants and swiftly attacked the goblin.

Both men rained blows down on the creature, and it quickly gave ground. It was able to avoid being struck for the first few moments, but finally strikes started to land on its green body. It eventually went down under the weight of the two fighters' fury. Dustin cut off its head just to be sure it was dead, then they turned to the final battle being fought between Tim and the last two goblins.

His father was holding his own against his foes, although he was on the defensive. He would have overwhelmed one goblin easily, but since he was fighting two at once he had to worry about being attacked from behind. Blow after blow hit his sword, but Tim didn't lose his grip on it. Suddenly, the goblins seemed to realize that they were the only ones left and that now they were hopelessly outnumbered. They turned and ran back towards the village.

Zach and Jaden were on them instantly and had no problems catching up to them. The goblins turned to face them, but they didn't stand a chance against the dark-skinned warriors.

*   *   *

It took them a while to find Aiden's lost horse. It had run about half a mile down the road. They found it grazing on the side of the road. It was now calm enough to let Aiden mount it, and they started towards Parkos once again.

Tim's arm was injured and weak. It hung weakly at his side as he rode. "How were you able to keep a hold of your sword?" Dustin asked him. "I was forced to block one blow and I immediately dropped mine."

Tim smiled at him. "Sheer force of will. I knew that if I dropped my sword, I was probably going to die. I am paying the price for it now though. My arm hurts so badly that it is almost useless. It will heal though. It just needs time."

They made camp that night in a small thicket of trees a few hundred feet off the road. They thought it safe enough to build a fire, but still kept watch. When it was Aiden's turn Portia stayed up with him to keep him company. They didn't speak much, not wanting to wake anyone up. They just sat next to each other, enjoying their closeness.

Aiden glanced over at the sleeping form of Princess Dana and thought it weird how his feelings for her had changed. When he had met her on the ship, she was all he could think about. But he guessed her indifference had cooled his feelings for her. Now he liked a girl that liked him back, and that made all the difference. Although he couldn't help but think of Layne and feel a little guilty. He knew how much his friend liked Portia and wondered what he was going to say when he finally rejoined the group.

The next day they started traveling at dawn. They traveled until midday without incident. But when the sun was directly above them, they saw a man standing in the middle of the road. His features were impossible to make out, but they could tell that he had seen the group and was waiting for them.

Aiden was traveling at the front of the group with his father when they got close enough to see the stranger's face. His father suddenly stopped his horse, a look of surprise on his face. "You have got to be kidding me," he whispered.

"What?" asked Aiden.

But before his father could answer, the stranger hailed them. "Hello! We need to talk."

19

Layne braced himself for the next blow. Although he was waiting for it, it took his breath away. He lay on the floor, naked from the waist up, trying desperately to take in a breath. The man who was beating him had used a whip for what seemed like hours, and now his back was slashed and bloodied. But he had changed to a heavy rod that gave a different kind of pain altogether.

Layne was in a small, square room with no windows and one door. The floor sloped down toward the wall opposite the door and had a drain. The drain let the blood out of the room. The punishers didn't want their victims to drown in their own blood. It also let the water out when they cleaned up afterwards. The only thing adorning the walls were weapons of torture. Heavy clubs, whips with metal pieces woven into them, and several sharp instruments that Layne had never seen before.

Layne heard laughter. It was Riktor. They had brought Layne into this room four times over the last two days. At least, he thought it had been two days. He couldn't be totally sure. Riktor was there to watch and laugh every time. He enjoyed seeing other people in pain. Layne couldn't help but imagine doing these things to him and seeing if he laughed then.

"You are a tough guy I see," Riktor mocked. "You refuse to cry out in pain. Do not be embarrassed, I've heard you cry out before…many times, actually. Go ahead. Let it out."

The judge didn't realize that Layne had no breath to cry out with. Every heavy blow made it harder and harder to breath. He almost wished the man would go back to using the whip with sharp pieces of metal tied into its length. At least he could breathe when the man used that.

Layne didn't reply, and Riktor laughed at him again. When the beatings had first started, the laughter was even worse than the physical pain. Layne was big and strong and had a high tolerance for pain. But the mocking was something he couldn't combat with his size or muscles. It was an emotional pain that cut deep. In that laughter Riktor was telling him that although he was innocent, it didn't matter. Riktor had the power to do whatever he wanted with Layne, and there was nothing he could do about it. Riktor was showing Layne that he was better than him, and at first Layne had believed him.

But the more physical pain he went through, the more he was able to concentrate on it and not Riktor. He almost welcomed the blows, because they dimmed the laughter. *Give me something I know about*, he thought. *I can deal with pain.*

It didn't diminish his anger though. He had done nothing wrong, and yet here he was, being punished while the guilty man was free with only a few less coins to his name. It wasn't right. It wasn't justice.

Suddenly Layne began to doubt everything that Tim had taught him. Tim preached choosing the right and protecting the innocent. Good will prevail, he always said. What world was he living in? Layne always did as Tim had instructed but look at him now! Where had it gotten him? He was being tortured for doing the right thing.

Veronna was like a sister to him and he told himself if he had to do it all over again, he would. He would protect her. But what if it was someone else next time? Some stranger he didn't know? What would he do then? Was it worth doing the right thing in a world like this?

He had no answers, but he had learned that thinking about things like this was a good distraction from what was being done to him. Plus, it angered Riktor when he noticed Layne not giving a reaction to his punishment. The rage he saw on the judge's face when he took the weapon into his own hands was almost worth the extra pain of the enraged blows that Riktor rained down on Layne. When Riktor became tired, he would send Layne back to his cell for a while.

Layne would sit in his cell and brood over what was being done to him. Before now, Layne didn't get angry very often, but now it seemed as if his anger never left. But even though it was almost a foreign feeling to him, he didn't try to cast it aside. He reveled in it. He let it overwhelm him until he felt nothing else. No pain, no sadness, no regret. Just rage. It was a sweet release.

Layne was tired of his torture for today. He decided it was time to end it. He would make Riktor angry so he would send him back to his cell. He searched deep within himself to find the strength to not react to the blows of his tormentors. He even made himself smile at Riktor.

It had the desired effect.

Layne had never done that before, and it enraged the judge. He grabbed the whip from the peg it was hanging on and turned to Layne.

"Don't pretend you aren't in pain! You are no better than anyone else! Quit lying! Cry out! Yell! Scream!"

He slashed Layne across the back. Layne felt skin rip and warm blood flow. Layne was sweating profusely, and the drops got onto the open wound, making the dozens of cuts burn even worse.

Again and again, he slashed Layne's body, moving from his back to his legs. He hadn't had his legs worked on yet, so every strike brought fresh wounds to bear. The pain was excruciating.

Layne found strength that he didn't know he had. Before the next strike came, he forced himself to his feet and turned to face the judge. When the whip came at him, he stuck out his arm. The whip wrapped around his arm and the metal pieces stuck into his flesh. It hurt, but it was what he needed. The metal was stuck fast.

Before Riktor could do anything about it, Layne jerked on the whip. Riktor, who foolishly kept his grip on the handle, was forced toward Layne. Layne met him with a mighty punch to the face. Riktor went down instantly. Layne didn't think he had ever hit anyone so hard in his life.

He was on him instantly. Riktor hadn't moved since he hit the floor, and Layne didn't know if he was even still alive. But he didn't care. He straddled the body of the judge and went crazy. He hit him in the face, breaking his nose and jaw. Riktor's head jerked from side to side as the blows rained down on him.

Strong hands grabbed Layne under the shoulders and heaved him up off the prone man. The hands flung him aside, and he hit the floor hard. He looked up and saw the man who had been torturing him crouching down over Riktor's body. Layne tried to get up, but now that his adrenalin was depleted, he had no strength. The torture had taken its toll.

The man rushed to the door, unlocked it, and thrust it open. "Guards!" He cried. "Get in here now!" Then he knelt beside Riktor and put his ear close to the judge's open mouth.

Four guards rushed into the room. They surrounded the torturer and the judge. "What happened?" one asked.

"The prisoner attacked Judge Riktor! I was able to stop him, but Riktor is unconscious. He is still alive, but just barely."

Layne cursed. *Almost*, he thought. *I almost killed him.*

"What do you want us to do?"

"You, go get a healer. Go as quick as you can. You! Go find the other two judges and tell them what has happened. You two, help me with the prisoner."

The two guards left to the duties they had been assigned. The torturer and the remaining two guards came up to Layne, who was still lying on the floor.

Layne looked up at them as they towered over him, glaring. Against his better judgment he managed another smiled. The next thing he saw was a boot coming at his head. Then, blackness.

*   *   *

Tyler was sitting with Oscar in the judge's small, three room home when Kargen came through the front door in a rush. His face was bright red and he was breathing hard. It looked to Tyler like he had run all the way from the courthouse.

"What is going on?" Oscar asked.

"I have wonderful news!" Kargen exclaimed. He was grinning broadly.

Now Oscar and Tyler were excited as well. They had spent the last two days trying to come up with a plan to free Layne, but everything they had thought of had major flaws and they disregarded the ideas. They had nothing in mind at the moment, and they both could use a little good news.

"What happened?" asked Tyler.

"Well, Layne was being tortured today, and Riktor was in the room watching. Suddenly, Layne just goes crazy and attacks Riktor. He beat him senseless! Right now, Riktor is unconscious and close to death. The healers don't know if he will survive. We can only hope he doesn't!"

Oscar got to his feet. "This changes everything!"

"How?" Tyler asked.

"Don't you see? Layne has just removed the biggest obstacle in setting him free. With Riktor out of the picture, it should be easy to get him released."

"Well..." said Kargen.

Oscar turned to his friend. "What?"

"Since he attacked Riktor and maybe even killed him, a lot of people are calling for his execution."

"Really?" asked Tyler. "Why? Do the people like Riktor?"

"Yes," replied Kargen. "He is very charismatic and likeable. Only a few people know what he is really like."

"Plus, he is a high ranking official," Oscar added. "He represents the people of the city, and they take that seriously. An attack on a city official is almost like an attack on the city itself. No one knows that Layne just did the city a big favor."

"So now we have that problem to deal with," said Kargen.

"How are we going to release him when the townsfolk want him executed?" Oscar asked, almost to himself. The old judge started pacing the small room and muttering to himself too quietly for the other two to hear.

Suddenly he stopped and snapped his fingers. "I've got it!" he exclaimed. He grinned and turned to the other two.

"We will give the people what they want. We will summon Layne to court and try him for his attack on Riktor. Then we will sentence him to death."

"Are you crazy?" Kargen asked.

"No, you don't understand. We are not really going to execute him. We are just going to sentence him to death, to buy us some time." He turned to Tyler. "You need to know where his cell is, correct?"

"Yes," the wizard replied.

"Okay. So here is what we are going to do…"

*   *   *

The next day a battered and bruised Layne stood once again in front of the judges. There were only two this time.

All Layne wanted to do was lay down and sleep, but he forced himself to stand up, straight and tall, not wanting to show any weakness to his enemies. For he considered everyone in this room, from the judges to the townsfolk to the guards, his enemies. Even the guard that looked strangely familiar for some reason. He knew he had seen him before, but he could not think of where. Probably just here in the courthouse, he thought, and dismissed the guard from his mind.

One of the judges stood up and the crowd immediately calmed. All eyes were on the judge as he addressed the room. "My good people! We have heard your outcries about what has happened to our brother Riktor. We are also enraged! Therefore, we have brought the perpetrator here before us again to decide what shall be done with him."

"Kill him!" Came a cry from the crowd.

"Execute him!" Another man said.

"Chop of his head!" This time it was a woman who had shouted.

The judge tried to calm the people by waving his hands in the air and calling for them to be quiet, but to no avail. Layne didn't see the alarmed look the judge gave to the guard he thought he recognized, because he was staring at the people in shock. Layne couldn't believe their reactions.

The judge finally was able to calm the room down. "Let my fellow judge and I discuss the matter. We will take your wishes into consideration."

The two judges put their heads together and spoke quietly to each other. The buzz of quiet conversation began again behind him. Layne strained to hear what he judges were saying, but he couldn't. After a few moments, the judges finished their conversation and the one who had spoken before stood up again. The room was once again quiet.

"My colleague and I have discussed the situation and we both believe that this man deserves death for his actions against our beloved judge." The roar of the crowd was deafening. Layne was once again shocked. He wasn't surprised to hear the sentence. He had been expecting it. He was, however, surprised about the reaction of the people in the room. It disturbed him that these people would be so hungry for a human being to be put to death. True, Layne himself had killed men, but he never relished it. It had needed to be done. He didn't enjoy it. But these people were excited to see him put to death. Tim's teachings began to ring hollow once again in the young fighter's mind.

"The beheading will take place at noon two days from now in the square," the old judge continued.

Many of the people in the room were angry that they would have to wait two days for the execution. They wanted Layne beheaded immediately. The two judges shot each other nervous looks, but in the end, nothing happened. The townsfolk started filing out of the courthouse, talking excitedly to each other. The judges called the two guards at the door to take the prisoner back to his cell.

*   *   *

Tyler stood at the door leading back to the cells, listening to Kargen address the crowd. He scratched his shoulder. The guard uniform he was wearing itched terribly. Oscar had come to Tyler earlier that morning with the garment, telling him to put it on. When Tyler asked where he had gotten it from, Oscar had told him it belonged to a guard who was meant to be on duty at the courthouse that day, but had been unable to make it to his shift. When Tyler asked why, the judge grimaced and told him it wasn't important.

The uniform was a little too big for him. He was tall, but skinny. The guards were mostly larger men, much bigger than the wizard. But it would have to do. He tucked it in where he could and folded parts of it over. He did a good enough job so that anyone looking at him would think the uniform belonged to him.

When he had taken his place at the door beside the other guard, the man looked at him suspiciously and asked who he was. Oscar had told him the missing guard's name was Ned. "Ned couldn't make it today," Tyler replied. "I am a new recruit and was told by the commander to take his place."

That kept the man from asking anymore questions. They waited by the door, neither one speaking. People slowly began to file into the room. When all the chairs were taken, people took places standing in front of the walls. Soon the room was overflowing with people. It became hot and stuffy very quickly.

Finally, after what seemed like hours, Kargen and Oscar entered the courthouse and told them to go get the prisoner.

I am at last going to find out where this accursed cell is, Tyler thought. They went through the door and into a long, dark corridor. The only light was from a few torches placed periodically on the walls. As they walked, they passed several closed doors on either side. Every door looked the same. There were no markings on any of them to distinguish one door from another. Tyler had no idea how he was going to remember the correct door to Layne's cell. He started to worry.

They continued walking down the hallway, passing every door. *I'm glad this guy has been in here before*, Tyler thought. *Otherwise, we would be totally lost.*

They finally came to a stop at a door on their left. Tyler realized that this was the very last door in the hallway. *Well, that makes it a lot easier*, Tyler thought with relief. *I'll be able to find it easily again.*

The guard unlocked the cell with his key and pushed the door open. He pushed hard, probably hoping the prisoner was too close and that the door would hit him. No luck though. Layne was at the far end of the little room, huddled in a corner. When the door opened and light came into the room, the prisoner stood up and looked at the new comers. Tyler realized that Layne couldn't tell who they were because the light was behind them. *Good*, Tyler thought. *He won't recognize me.*

Layne was in sorry shape. His face was swollen and he was hunched over. For the first time Tyler noticed the other guard had a shirt in his hands. Layne wasn't wearing one, and Tyler could guess what his back looked like. The guard threw the shirt at Layne and told him to put it on. Layne let it fall to the floor at his feet and didn't move to pick it up.

"Pick it up and put it on," the guard said. When Layne didn't move, the guard came forward and stopped right in front of Layne. He put his face an inch away from the prisoner's. "Pick it up."

Layne stared the guard in the eyes for a minute, then slowly bent down and picked up the shirt. He must have realized that defying the guard would have been pointless.

"Now," said the guard, "put it on."

Layne hesitated, not wanting to put it on. "Why?" he asked quietly.

"Because," the guard said with a grin. "You are going in front of the judges and you must look your best. You can't go out there with no shirt on."

Layne sighed, but didn't say anything. Ever so slowly, he put his arms through the holes. He grimaced in pain, but no sound came out. Tyler was impressed. When his arms were in and he put the shirt over his head, Layne took in a sharp breath, pain evident on his face. But again, no groan or cry escaped from his lips.

When Layne was finally ready, he walked out the door with his head held high. He didn't look at Tyler or the other guard. Layne waited for the other guard to step in front of him, then they made their way back to the courtroom, Tyler trailing. Tyler watched Layne's back as they walked wondering what horrors the man had endured over the past couple days. He felt terrible that he hadn't been able to free him before now, but now that he knew where his cell was, it shouldn't be much longer. Layne just had to hold on a bit longer.

They reached the courtroom and they took their positions beside the door as Layne made his way to stand in front of the judges' table.

Tyler listened as Kargen stood up and made the speech they had planned. He did it well. He was very convincing. He had the crowd on his side immediately. It was important that the crowd believed what he said. That was the best way to avoid conflict.

Tyler stopped listening after a while, because he already knew what Kargen was going to say. But then the reaction of the crowd put him on his guard. He was afraid that the crowd might not wait for Layne to be beheaded, that they might swarm him right then and there and kill him. He tensed, getting ready to call up his magic if need be. He looked over at the two judges, and when they looked back he could see that they were nervous as well. But the crowd didn't swarm Layne. They behaved themselves, even though they weren't happy about having to wait for two days to see the prisoner die.

Tyler finally let out a sigh of relief when the people started filing out of the courtroom. Everything was going to be alright. He looked at Oscar and Kargen again and saw the relief on their faces as well. Their well thought out plan had almost turned into disaster.

Soon after the last person went out the door the judges had Tyler and the other guard escort Layne back to his cell. The other guard insulted Layne as they walked, telling him that he was lucky he hadn't died right there. He said that he would run him through with his sword right there in the hallway if he could get away with it. Tyler said nothing. He wanted to tell the guard to shut up, but he couldn't without blowing his cover, so he remained silent.

They finally made it to Layne's cell at the end of the hallway and Tyler realized that his job had been made much easier now that he discovered where Layne's cell was. He had thought that he was going to have to come in through the building and walk down the hallway to get to Layne, but now he realized that he could get into Layne's cell from the outside.

The guard opened the door and shoved Layne inside the room roughly. More roughly than was needed, Tyler thought. Then the guard said another snide comment and slammed the door. They walked back down the hallway in silence, which suited Tyler. He had nothing to say to his companion.

Now came the hard part. Waiting. For Tyler to not bring suspicion on himself, he had to finish out his shift. The waiting was torture. He just wanted night to come so he could go about freeing Layne.

*   *   *

A few hours after dusk, Tyler found himself walking alone down the back streets toward the courthouse. He was still dressed in the soldier's uniform. Most people wouldn't think twice about seeing a soldier walking the streets at night. He carried a torch, but it was unlit. The sword strapped at his waist felt uncomfortable. He wasn't used to carrying one. But no city guard would be without one, especially at night, so he had to have it to look authentic. The sky was free of clouds and the moon and stars gave him plenty of light to see by. He ran through the plan in his mind repeatedly as he walked.

As soon as his shift had ended, he headed straight for Oscar's house. The two judges were there waiting for him. They made preparations for the final phase of their plan, and waited until they thought the streets would be almost empty of people. He had eaten a quick dinner and tried to get a little sleep because he didn't know when he would have a chance to again. But he found that he couldn't sleep. This was going to be the most dangerous part of the plan and numerous things could go wrong. If something went wrong now, it would most likely cost both Layne and Tyler their lives. He had to be very careful.

Before he knew it, before he was fully ready, he found himself standing before the courthouse. It was dark inside. No lights were on in the windows. He knew there were guards on duty. They must be in a room that had no windows.

He stared at the dark building for a long time. He was getting nervous and he tried to calm himself down. He had to put aside his fears and just go through with it. Layne was depending on him. So were Layne's friends. He had to do this.

Instead of going to the front door, he walked around to the back of the building. If his calculations were correct, Layne's cell was at the northeast corner of the building. There was no window in Layne's cell, so Tyler wasn't able to look out at the street beyond when he got Layne and then returned him earlier that day, so he was forced to figure it out with his sense of direction. He was almost sure he was correct.

He looked both ways down the deserted street to make sure no one was about. It would be bad if he was seen. As far as he could tell he was alone. He saw no one else. He shut his eyes, lowered his head, and concentrated on what he wanted.

If a passer-by came upon him, they would think that he was doing nothing but standing there. They would be wrong. He was actually calling forth tremendous power. He concentrated solely on what he wanted. He cast everything else out of his mind. His fear was gone, replace by his need. If an enemy were to come upon Tyler at this moment, the wizard would be a helpless victim. He wouldn't even know the enemy was there. He was focused only on the task at hand.

He could feel the power well up in him. It still shocked him to realize how much power the human mind contained. You just had to learn how to use it correctly. True, it was mentally exhausting to use magic, but it was exhilarating at the same time.

When Tyler first started learning the art of magic, the sheer power of it had terrified him. It overwhelmed and intimidated him. The more he learned, the more comfortable he became. But he still felt humbled by the awesome power of it.

Suddenly, the wall that Tyler was standing in front of exploded outward in a spray of stone and debris. Tyler had planned on this happening, so he was standing a safe distance away. He hadn't accounted for the noise though. True, he had expected the explosion to be loud, but the sound was deafening. He knew that half the city had probably heard it. He was going to have to be quick if he didn't want city guards flooding the area while he and Layne were still around. He quickly lit his torch and walked forward.

20

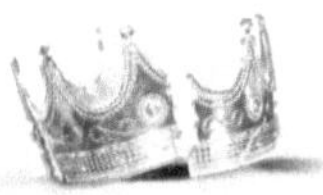

Tyler stepped through the debris-ridden hole and into Layne's cell. He saw Layne at the far end of the room. He was just standing up, a look of disbelief on his face. They were lucky that Layne had been far away from the wall when it exploded. He hadn't been able to warn Layne about what was going to happen, so he had taken a chance. If Layne had been any closer to the wall, he could have been seriously injured. Or worse.

The light coming from the torch gave off enough light so that Layne could see Tyler clearly. "Who are you?" Layne asked. Tyler thought it an odd question since they had met before, but then he remembered that he was still wearing a soldier's uniform.

"I am Tyler," he said. "I was with your party at the tavern. I agreed to help your group make it Parkos."

"Ah, yes," the other replied. "I remember. I saw you at my trial. I thought I recognized you."

"Now, we don't have much time. The Dark Watch will be here any moment, so we must move now. Do you think you have the strength to run?"

"I don't know," Layne replied. "I guess we'll find out."

Layne slowly made his way to the hole in the wall and followed Tyler out. They looked down each street but saw only darkness. "Let's go," Tyler said and headed down one of the streets. They would have to take a round-a-bout way to Oscar's house. If they took the direct route, they might lead the Dark Watch to the house and get the two judges in trouble. It would take longer to escape this way, but they would just have to be careful.

Tyler was immediately alarmed by their slow progress. Layne found it difficult to move quickly, and the wizard was concerned that they would be immediately overtaken if they were seen.

"Can you move any faster?' he asked.

The torch was still lit, so Tyler could see Layne clearly. A look of anger flashed across the big man's face for a moment, then it was gone. It happened so fast that Tyler wondered if his mind wasn't just playing tricks on him. "I will try," Layne said.

They did go a little faster, if only slightly. Tyler could tell that Layne was struggling, but the big man didn't complain. They did their best to stay in the shadows of the buildings where they wouldn't be seen. He tried to shield the torch with his body to make it as hard as possible for someone walking down the street to see it.

Suddenly, when they were only a couple blocks away from the court-house, Tyler heard shouts behind them. The Dark Watch had discovered the hole in the wall and the prisoner gone. Tyler had to fight the urge to go faster. The last thing he wanted to do was get ahead of Layne. He was suddenly glad of the sword at his hip. He wouldn't have much use for it, but he could give it to Layne if the need arose. Layne would need one if the Dark Watch caught up to them.

"Looks like it is time to put out the torch," Tyler said. "The stars and the moon should give us plenty of light though." *And at the same time expose us to the Dark Watch*, he thought. Layne gave a quick nod and Tyler doused the flame.

They stood where they were a moment, waiting for their eyes to adjust to the sudden darkness. It didn't take long, and they were soon on the move again, going as fast as Layne's injuries would allow.

The more they walked, the stronger Layne seemed to get. His pace picked up slightly, and he was walking taller. Tyler was astounded at the strength of his companion. Tyler new that if he had suffered the same injuries, he wouldn't be able to move. Layne made rescuing him easy.

They walked for a few more minutes, turning down random streets to throw off any potential pursuit, when Layne said, "Tyler, I see torchlight coming our way. Behind us."

Tyler looked over his shoulder and saw two torches. It looked like at least five or six men surrounded the torch bearers. While the two men watched, the group of soldiers came to an intersection. One torch bearer turned down a side street, three men following him. The remaining soldiers continued down the street toward Layne and Tyler.

"Quickly," Tyler called as he hurried down the street. They continued to turn down random streets, trying to put as many buildings between them and the soldiers as possible. The only negative thing about that was that Tyler was quickly getting lost. He grew up in the city and knew it well, but he was starting to get a little confused by the darkness and the rush to get away. But he dared not stop to try to get his bearings.

Suddenly, as they were nearing an intersection, several soldiers stepped into the street in front of them, one holding a lit torch. The two groups just stared at each other in the torch light for a moment, then the torch bearer cried. "There they are! Get them!"

Before the men could move however, the ground beneath them started to shake violently. Tyler had not just been staring, he had been concentrating. A wizard learned early in his training to think quickly in dangerous situations, such as the one Tyler and Layne were in right now. Hesitation could mean death.

Cobblestones began rising from the ground underneath the soldiers, and they couldn't keep their feet. They began falling over each other. The ground was only moving beneath the soldiers however, so Tyler and Layne were able to move freely. Tyler knew that the tiny quake would dissipate just moments after he stopped concentrating on it, so he quickened his pace.

As the two men ran through the intersection and turned left down a side street, Tyler suddenly recognized where they were. He grabbed

Layne's arm and pulled him to the left down an alley. Tyler could already here the footsteps of the men chasing them again, so he was relieved that his destination was close. He saw the building he was looking for just ahead. He hoped the door was unlocked.

It was. The pair slammed through the door with such force that they stumbled and almost fell. Tyler quickly regained his balance and shut the door behind them. He locked it, then leaned wearily against it. "I need to rest for a moment," he said. "We should be safe in here for now."

"Okay," Layne said. By looking at the man, Tyler could tell that Layne needed to rest too. He looked pale and out of breath. He leaned against the door next to the wizard. Tyler still thought it was amazing that the mercenary had run all the way in the condition he was in without uttering a word of complaint.

"The City Watch is efficient," Layne quipped.

Tyler nodded. "Yeah, they are. I'm sure that moments after the Dark Watch discovered you were missing, they had one hundred soldiers scouring the streets looking for you."

They heard several boots trudging on the cobblestones outside as soldiers ran past their hideout.

"And you, too," Layne said.

"Yeah," Tyler said. "And me too." *Why am I doing this?* he thought. *This is suicide! How did I get into this situation?*

In echo to Tyler's thoughts, Layne asked, "Why are you helping me? You could have just left me and not put yourself into this situation."

Tyler thought about it for a moment. "I gave Tim my word that I would get you out. I don't think I could live with myself if I just left you to die. I had to help you."

"Well, thank you."

"Don't thank me yet. We are still in danger."

He stood up straight and walked to a staircase at the back of the room. It led up to a second floor. Layne followed on his heels. They slowly ascended.

"When I was a boy," Tyler explained, "my friends and I used to play in this building. Back then it was a shop owned by a friend of my father's. I think he sold hats or something. It has been abandoned for a couple years now. My father's friend used to let my friends and I come here and play. In the ceiling of the second floor, where he kept his extra stock, there is a trap door with a ladder that you can pull down. We used that ladder to get on the roof.

"In this area of the city the buildings are very close together. You can jump from rooftop to rooftop. We would do that all the time. We would chase each other all over the tops of the buildings. I used to know these roofs well. Let's see if I still do."

Their footprints made tracks in the thick dust as they walked down the hall. They passed rooms that had windows, so they dared not relight the torch, for fear of alerting the soldiers. This left them to feel for the trapdoor in the dark. They had a difficult time finding the thin outline of the door, but eventually they managed it.

There was no string to pull, but the door needed to be pushed from a specific spot in order to lower. As the door opened, a ladder slid down to the ground. Moonlight bathed the two companions. Tyler gave Layne a grin and started up the ladder. Layne waited until the wizard was on the roof before following. Tyler pulled the ladder up and shut the door so if the soldiers came into the building, they wouldn't know that Tyler and Layne had gotten onto the roof.

Tyler got on his hands and knees and crawled to the edge of the roof. There were men on the streets below, calling to each other. They checked the opposite side of the roof too. It was the same there. They saw soldiers everywhere. There had to be dozens of groups. Tyler estimated well over one hundred soldiers were prowling the streets, searching for them.

"Let's go," Tyler whispered to Layne.

They headed south on the roof until they got to the edge. Below them was a narrow alley, and across from them was a building about the same size as the one they were on. It was an easy leap for Tyler and would have been for Layne if he wasn't injured. Tyler looked at Layne.

"What do you think?"

"We don't have a choice," Layne replied. "Our only hope is the rooftops. If we go back to the streets, we'll be caught in no time. You go first. I'll come after."

"Okay," Tyler said and jumped the alley. He landed lightly on the roof of the building and turned to look at Layne. "Okay," he whispered. "Your turn." Tyler hoped Layne was up to it.

With a mighty leap, Layne soared over the alley, easily clearing the edge of the roof and landing hard. He went down and laid there on his stomach for a few moments.

Tyler came up to him. "Are you alright?"

"Yes," Layne replied. "But that jump took a lot out of me. I just need to rest for a minute."

Tyler crouched down beside Layne and waited for the other man to be ready. Finally, Layne slowly got to his feet and announced he was ready to continue. Tyler stood up. "I don't think there are any more jumps for a while. We should be able to step from roof to roof now."

"Good," Layne said.

They continued their way over the rooftops. Tyler was correct, there were no more spaces to jump. They were able to step from rooftop to rooftop. Sometimes they had to step up or down when one of the buildings was taller or shorter than the one they were already on, but their journey on the rooftops was an easy one.

Then they came to a space where the next building was too far to jump to. They looked at their surroundings, trying to find another roof to go to. But they soon realized that it was no use. They were going to have to go back to the ground.

They looked for soldiers but saw none in the area. The coast clear, they crept towards the edge of the roof. It wasn't very far to the ground, so they both dangled over the edge by their arms, dropping the last few feet to the street below.

They crouched where they were for a moment, scanning the surrounding streets for any movement. After a few moments of seeing nothing, they got to their feet and started out again. Tyler had a pretty good idea where they were, so he headed west. They weren't very far from Oscar's house. With a little luck, they would make it there without further incident. They stepped out into the street.

And came face to face with a group of Dark Watch soldiers. They were down the street about one hundred feet away. Tyler and Layne immediately changed direction and headed south, away from their destination, running as fast as their exhausted legs could carry them. They could hear booted feet hurrying after them.

When they came up to the next intersection, they saw another force of soldiers coming from their right. Tyler saw that they were going to be overtaken if they continued south, so they turned left and headed east. They were both tired from a long night of running, so the soldiers were right on their heels.

They needed to create some separation or the chase would be over in moments. Suddenly, Tyler spotted an alley to the right just ahead of them. When they reached it, he grabbed Layne by the shoulder and pulled him in. Layne gave a small cry of surprise. The soldiers were so close that they didn't have time to stop and turn into the alley, so they passed it by. They had seen where Layne and Tyler went however, and it would be only moments before they would stop and come back. Tyler hoped that would be enough time.

He turned to face the entrance to the alley and concentrated. Once again, the ground started shaking. Almost immediately the street in front of them stared to rise up. Debris tumbled to the ground as the cobblestones and the earth beneath rose up to form a wall in the entrance of the alley. Up and up it rose until it was taller than Tyler. Finally, it stopped when it reached the height of the buildings on either side. Tyler wavered on his feet and slumped to the ground. Layne rushed over and knelt down beside him.

"That should hold them off for a while," the wizard said.

"Are you alright?" Layne asked. "What's wrong? Are you hurt?"

"No. I'm not hurt. Just mentally exhausted. I've used a lot of magic tonight without much rest. Just give me a minute and I should be alright."

"Okay. How long do you think the wall will hold?"

"Oh, the wall will stay there forever," Tyler answered. "At least, until someone breaks it down. But the soldiers will probably climb over it before too long. It's not that high."

Right on cue, Tyler and Layne saw the head of a soldier pop up over the top of the wall. The man swung his legs up over the edge and fell to the ground. He landed on his feet and started towards the two men on the ground. He drew his sword. "Stay where you are," he said.

*　　*　　*

Layne slowly rose to his feet. Tyler stayed on the ground. The soldier slowed. Without even thinking of grabbing the sword at Tyler's hip, Layne walked towards the man. The soldier pointed his sword at the big man. "Stop," he ordered. "Stay right there."

Layne just kept walking. He didn't have a weapon, but he didn't care. He was not going to be captured again. He was not going to be tortured again. He would rather die in this alley right now than spend one more night in a cell.

Once again, Layne reached deep down for strength that he didn't know he had. He was exhausted and in pain, but he couldn't let that stop him. As the soldier swung his sword, Layne caught his arm, stopping the blade fast. The soldier swung at him with his other hand, but Layne caught that as well. Layne kicked the man in the chest, sending him flying backwards. He let go of the man's hand, but grabbed hold of his sword. The man hit the ground hard. He lay there, groaning in pain. Layne was about to finish him off when he saw more heads pop up over the wall.

One man, then another, then a third dropped down from the wall and drew their weapons. Layne backed up to stand protectively in front of Tyler. He glanced at his sword. "I wish this were an ax," he said to himself. Luckily, Tim had trained them in all types of weapons. That was one lesson he could still believe in.

The first man reached him. Layne parried a thrust and counterattacked with a thrust of his own. The man had obviously underestimated

Layne because he was injured. Layne's sword made contact and the soldier grunted in pain, then fell to the street.

Layne faced two more men. Behind them, more men were clambering over the wall. Layne knew he was in trouble. Even if he wasn't injured, he wouldn't have been able to defeat them all. Especially not with a sword.

The two men spread out to let others join them. Layne furiously tried to come up with a plan. Something flew past his head and slammed into one of the soldiers. Layne glanced back to see Tyler on his feet. He could tell the wizard was concentrating. Several chunks of earth broke free from the ground and rose up into the air. They hovered there for a moment, then they flew forward. They missed hitting Layne by mere inches and hit each one of the soldiers. They all went down in heaps and didn't move again. Layne turned to see Tyler collapse once again. He rushed to the fallen wizard and knelt beside him.

"Are you okay?"

"What?

"Are you okay?" Layne repeated.

Tyler didn't answer. He looked around at their surroundings. "Where are we?"

Layne was concerned. "You don't remember?"

"No."

"You must have used too much magic. You have to think. Try to remember. You saved me from my cell and we have been on the run all night. Remember?"

"No…wait! Where were we headed?"

"You said you had a contact. We were headed to your contact's house."

"A contact? Really?"

Layne glanced up and saw more soldiers climbing over the wall. "Please think. Hurry. You had a contact. Where does your contact live?"

"My contact…west. I think he lives west of here."

"Good! Very good. Can you get up?"

"I'll try," Tyler replied. He grabbed Layne's arm and pulled himself up. Layne quickly looked around. The alley opened up behind them. "Come on," he said to Tyler and started for the alley's entrance. He glanced over his shoulder. Two men had dropped to the street and were hurrying after them. Layne saw more men on the wall. He didn't think they were going to get away, but he kept going. He didn't know what else to do.

Suddenly a dozen or so men appeared in the alley's entrance. They all had weapons drawn. They didn't bother to advance on Layne and Tyler. They knew they had them trapped.

Layne stopped. He looked back behind them. The soldiers were almost on top of them. A few more seconds and Layne would have to fight. Layne saw a door to their right and without thinking headed for it, dragging the wizard behind him. There was a window next to the door with light shining out of it. He rushed through the door, which was unlocked, pulled Tyler in after him, and slammed the door closed. He threw the latch to lock it and turned around.

He was facing a family of four. A man, a woman, and two little boys that couldn't have been older than five or six. The family was staring at the two intruders with open mouths.

"Hello," Tyler said to the family with a grin.

"Is there a back door?" Layne demanded. The family didn't answer. Soldiers outside started banging loudly on the door. The family flinched at the sound, and seemed to come out of their daze.

"Is there a back door?" Layne asked again, louder this time.

"Yes," the man said. "Through there." He pointed behind his family to the back of the house.

Layne grabbed Tyler and rushed in the direction the man pointed. They went down a short hallway, past a few small rooms, and found a closed door. Layne tested it and found it unlocked. He could hear more pounding on the front door. Soldiers were shouting for the homeowners to open up. It didn't sound to Layne like they were going to comply.

Layne and Tyler rushed through the back door and shut it behind them. They were in a small, fenced-in yard. The fence was only about waist high to Layne, so they couldn't hide in the yard. They immediately went for the small gate in the fence that opened out onto the street.

Layne looked both ways, but didn't see any soldiers, so he headed west. He hoped that Tyler would recover from his magic use soon. Layne had no idea where the contact's house was. He just knew that he had to go west.

As they made their way down the street, trying to stay in the shadows, Layne glanced over his shoulder. He saw a group of soldiers searching the backyard of the house they were just at. Layne picked up his pace, almost dragging Tyler. He silently willed the soldiers not to look in their direction until they could turn a corner.

He turned the first corner he arrived at, hoping he wasn't moving farther away from their destination. He looked at Tyler and was happy to see that the wizard looked more lucid than before. He just needed to avoid detection until Tyler was fully recovered.

He noticed some movement up ahead, and quickly entered another alley. He waited, crouched down in the shadows until the group of soldiers passed. They took a quick glance in the alley as they passed but didn't notice the two men.

Tyler started groaning.

"Are you alright?" Layne asked.

"Yes." Tyler looked around at their surroundings. "Where are we?"

"I'm not sure. We are in an alley right now. I decided to wait for you to recover before we started out again. I didn't want to take us in the wrong direction."

"Good thinking," the wizard replied. "Let me rest for a minute more, then I will take a look and see if I can recognize where we are." Layne nodded and leaned his head back against the wall. He suddenly felt very tired.

Before Layne knew it, he was being shaken awake by Tyler. The big man hadn't realized he had dozed off. Tyler went to the alley's opening and looked both ways down the street. He motioned for Layne to join him. Layne did so and they crossed the street, making their way west again.

"I know where we are," Tyler told him as they walked. "We are only a few blocks from my contact's house. We are very lucky to have made it this far without knowing exactly where we were going."

They didn't say anything more to each other as they made their way along the streets. They had to hide several more times as patrols came close. They were lucky though and were never caught.

Finally, Tyler stopped Layne and said, "Just around this corner is the door to my contact's house. We are almost there."

The two men crept slowly toward the corner of the building. They looked around the corner and saw dozens of Dark Watch soldiers in the area. There was no way they would be able to reach the door without being seen.

Tyler leaned back against the building and sighed. "Now what are we going to do?"

"What we need," Layne said, "is a distraction."

"A distraction?"

"If we can get the soldiers' attention on something else, we might be able to make it to the door before they see us."

Tyler nodded. "Good idea."

"Can you provide us with one?"

Tyler smiled. "Yes, I can."

Tyler concentrated. Layne waited. Suddenly, he heard a loud noise across the street. Layne looked in that direction and saw the roof of a building coming down. It slid off the building and onto the street below with a loud crash. Several soldiers were standing beneath the roof and were crushed. Every soldier in the area turned toward the noise. Several men rushed over to aid their fallen comrades.

"Okay, now," Tyler said. They rushed around the corner of the building and made for the door. They didn't stop to make sure no one was looking. They just ran. As soon as they reached the door and came to a skidding stop, it opened for them. They both dove in and someone shut the door behind them.

The room they were in was dimly lit with a single candle on a table at the far end of the room. There were two comfortable looking couches facing each other, and a large plant in a pot set up against one wall. One doorway led to a dark hallway. There were two other men in the room. One was sitting on one of the couches, and the other was standing by the door. He was the one who had let them in.

Layne and Tyler slowly got to their feet. Layne was looking at the man who had opened the door for them. He looked familiar. Finally, Layne recognized him. "You!" He stepped forward aggressively. "You sentenced me to death!"

Tyler was there in an instant, as was the other man. "Calm down," the wizard was saying, and the other man jumped in front of Layne, trying to hold him back.

Layne glared at Tyler. "This is your contact? This judge? He sentenced me to death! You know that. You were there."

"Wait," the judge said. "You don't understand." Even injured, Layne was a powerful man. He made it difficult for Tyler and the other man to hold him back.

"Be quiet," Tyler said. "If the Dark Watch hears us talking, we're done for."

That brought the men back to their senses. Layne finally calmed down, but he still didn't look happy. He turned to Tyler. "Tell me what is going on. Why are you on my enemy's side?"

Tyler took a deep breath. "These men are not the enemy, Layne. They are working against Riktor. They helped me free you."

"Then why did they sentence me to death?"

The man who had let them in answered. "It was just a ruse. Riktor has a lot of the townspeople in his pocket. They think he keeps them safe from criminals. When they heard that you had attacked him and almost killed him, they wanted your head. If I hadn't have appeased them and pronounced a death sentence on you, they probably would have taken matters into their own hands and attacked you right there in the courtroom. That's why I pronounced a death sentence on you but postponed the actual beheading to give Tyler time to get you free."

Layne thought about what he had just heard. "Thank you for helping me. I am sorry I tried to attack you just now."

"It's understandable." The man stuck out his hand. "I am Oscar. This man is Kargen. We are judges here in Names. But unlike Riktor, we don't abuse our authority. We want the best for the people. We know you have been arrested unlawfully and are glad that we were able to help you escape." Layne shook his hand, then did the same with Kargen.

"We haven't escaped yet," Tyler said. "We are still in town and surrounded by enemy soldiers. We still need to be careful."

"Tyler is right," Oscar said. Suddenly, there was a knock at the door.

"Judge Oscar?" someone called.

Oscar looked alarmed. "One minute," he called. "It is the soldiers," he whispered to his companions. "They are here to check on us. They feared that you would come and find us and try to kill us since we sentenced you to death. That is why there are so many soldiers here. Tyler, take Layne out the back and hide in the wagon."

Tyler nodded and the two men did as Oscar asked.

When they had left the room, Oscar opened the door. "Yes?"

The soldier at the door was young. He glanced in the room before saying anything. "We have reports that a couple squads have run into the two fugitives but have been unable to capture them. It seems that an Earth Mage is the one helping him escape. Is everything alright here?"

"Yes," Oscar replied. "Everything is fine."

"A man told me he thought he heard shouting."

Kargen stepped forward. "Yes. That was us. We were arguing. Oscar doesn't think I should leave tomorrow. He thinks it is too dangerous with the prisoner on the loose, but I must go. I have no choice. I am sorry that our argument disturbed you soldiers."

"That is alright," the young soldier replied. "I will keep you updated when I hear more reports. Just ask us if you need anything."

"Okay," said Oscar. "We will. Thank you." He shut the door.

The two judges made their way to the back door. Oscar had a small back yard with a small fence. The yard was just big enough to fit a wagon. A gate opened out onto a back street. The plan was to have Kargen leave town with the wagon while Tyler and Layne hid inside. They had filled the wagon with hay so the two men could hide. Hay is easy to hide in, but it is also very itchy. It wasn't going to be a comfortable ride for Layne and Tyler, but it was the only thing they could think of.

After the soldier left, Kargen went out back and found the two men in the hay. They were both already asleep. The judge, deciding to let them rest, went back into the house to prepare to for tomorrow.

21

"Dad," Aiden said. "Do you know that man?" Tim didn't answer. He was staring at the stranger. "Dad?"

Tim turned to him. "What?"

"Do you know that man?"

"Yes. Yes, I do."

"Who is he?"

Since the group had stopped, the man had started walking towards them. He was tall, with a medium build, and short blond hair. He had a blond goatee. He was wearing chain mail over leather armor. He walked with his back straight and head held high. There was confidence in his gait. As he walked, Tim dismounted. The rest of the group did as well.

He stopped in front of Tim. "Did you hear me Timmond? We need to talk."

"David. It's been so long."

"Yes, it has. It has been fifteen years." He looked at Aiden and smiled. "Ah, this must be Aiden. Wow, you have gotten big." He looked over the group. "Is Veronna with you? I bet she looks just like her mother."

Aiden was shocked. "You knew my mother?"

David nodded, his grin widening.

"Dad, who is this?"

David's grin vanished. He turned to Tim. "You didn't tell your kids about me?"

"No," Tim replied. "They know very little of my past."

"But this isn't just your past. I'm a part of their past too."

Aiden asked the question again. "Dad, who is this?"

"Aiden," Tim said, "This is your Uncle David."

"Uncle? You have a brother?"

"No," David said. "I am your mother's brother."

Veronna came up to them in time to hear what David said. "You are our mother's brother? You are our uncle?"

David looked at her. "Wow. You are the spitting image of my sister." A tear was running down his cheek. Veronna rushed into his open arms. Aiden hung back.

"It is so good to see you guys again," David said. He was grinning from ear to ear. He stretched a hand toward Aiden. "Aiden, come here. Let me give you a hug. We're family."

Aiden looked at his father. Tim nodded, and Aiden did as David asked. He gave his uncle a stiff hug, then backed up to stand next to his father again.

David let go of Veronna and addressed Tim once again. "We can catch up on the last fifteen years later. Right now, we have to get out of here."

"Why?" Tim asked.

"Because a large force of Zantan Robbers is headed this way. They know where you are and they are almost here. We have to move quickly."

"How do you know?" asked Brione. "Have you seen them? How many are coming?"

"I have not seen them," David answered, "but I know there are a lot of them."

"I don't understand," said Aiden. "If you haven't seen them, how do you know they are coming?"

"Oh, he knows," Tim told him.

"But…"

"That's enough for now," said Tim. "If David says that we need to go now, then we need to go now. We can talk later. For now, we'll follow David's lead."

The mercenary group was very well trained. Tim gave an order, and they complied without question or complaint. They didn't know the stranger who had approached them, but they all trusted Tim's judgment. They quickly mounted and waited for Tim's command.

"We will head north," David said.

"North?" asked Tim. "But that will take us to…No. I can't go there. I left. I swore I would never go back. We have to go somewhere else."

Aiden was stunned. He had never heard such concern in his father's voice before. If Tim was concerned, it meant the situation was serious.

"Listen Timmond," David said. "I understand your concern. But we have no choice. You know that the Robbers can't go there. If we go anywhere else, they will follow and eventually catch up to us. It is the only safe place. We must go there."

Tim hesitated. He looked north, then east, the direction they had been going. After a moment he turned back to David. "Alright. Let's go. I'll be fine."

They sent the word back to the rest of the group that everyone was to be silent and quick. Then, they were on their way. Luckily, David had his own horse, so they didn't have to double-up. They followed the road for a while, then took a smaller road that branched north. There wasn't much they could do about the sound of the horses' hooves on the road with such short notice. But they went as quietly as they could.

It was a warm day, and the horses were sweating freely before long. Their riders weren't doing much better. The sun was bright and hot as they traveled, and it made the group uncomfortable. Aiden looked longingly at the trees that lined the road and the shade they provided. He longed to rest underneath the branches in the cool shade.

Suddenly David called back. "Hurry! They've caught us!"

Aiden's uncle kicked his horse in the ribs and the beast took off. The others followed suite, trying to keep up with the David. Aiden saw movement in the trees. It looked like flashes of yellow, and those flashes were keeping pace with the horses. Were the Robbers really running as fast as horses? That was impossible.

Aiden heard someone yell "Duck!" He did so. He saw something coming at him fast. He got down as low as he could on his horse and shut his eyes. He felt something rush by just over his head. He watched it as it went past. To his astonishment, it turned around in mid-air and came back at him. Once again, Aiden crouched as low on his horse as possible, and the object barely missed him.

"Watch out!" his father yelled, and Aiden looked back again. He saw several figures on the road behind them. They were running. Suddenly, every figure pulled out a strange curved object and threw them at the group. Aiden watched the weapons flying towards him. He knew he was going to die. There was no way he could escape them.

These weapons were thrown a little lower to the ground than the previous one was. The first one hit Aiden's horse in the legs. It cut right through two of its legs and the horse went down with a scream. As Aiden fell along with the horse, he felt the rest of the weapons fly past his head. When the horse's body hit the ground, Aiden flew forward over the horse's head. He hit the ground hard, the breath was knocked out of him. As he lay there trying to get a breath, he heard the scream of several more horses.

He was finally able to gasp in a breath. He ached all over. He didn't dare move for fear that something was broken. As he lay on his back, looking up at the sky, he saw the blurs of the weapons overhead, going back to the figures who had thrown them.

All he could hear was horses screaming in pain and people shouting. Suddenly, his father was standing over him. "Aiden, are you alright?"

"I don't know," Aiden answered.

Tim glanced back over his shoulder at something. "We have to hurry. Can you stand?"

"I don't think so."

Tim bent down and with a growl, lifted his son into his arms. As he lay in his father's arms, Aiden had a good view of what was happening behind them. He saw the figures who had thrown the strange weapons sprinting towards them. They were very close. They had yellow skin.

"Everybody, run!" Tim shouted to the group as he raced away with Aiden. Every step his father took jostled Aiden painfully, but he didn't complain. The alternative was much worse.

The group took off as fast as they could. Several of the horses were either maimed or killed, so the horseless people had to double up with others. It had taken too long though. The Robbers were almost on top of them.

There was no horse for Tim to ride, so he just ran. Suddenly, David, Zach, and Jaden were in front of him. "We will stall them as the rest of you make your escape," David said.

Tim stopped running. "No," he replied. "There are too many. I will help you."

"Don't be ridiculous," David said. "None of the others know the way. You do though. You need to lead them to Zion. We will catch up."

Tim nodded. "Alright. Be careful."

Tim started running again. The rest of the group was far ahead by that time. There was nothing to be done about it. Tim would catch up eventually.

*　　*　　*

It was only moments before the Robbers reached the three men. David was standing in the middle with Zach to his right and Jaden on his left. There were at least half a dozen yellow-skinned men coming for them. David pulled out a large mace while the other two drew their weapons. They each carried two short swords.

With a clash the two groups met. Zach and Jaden fought with unmatched speed and skill. David fought with the strength of his god.

Up came David's mace to block a sword strike. Then he sent it around to deflect the swing of another Robber. David could see in his mind the attacks of the Robbers before they did them. It was the power that God gave to his champions. His Paladins. David's foresight allowed him to parry every blow with ease, then counterattack when the opportunity presented itself.

His mace collided with the head of a Robber, then David swung it around in front of himself again. The man who he had hit crumpled to the ground, his head a ruined mess. The other Robber gave a yell and attacked. Blow after relentless blow rained down on David, but he was able to block every one. Finally an opening presented itself and David took it. He swung his mace low, sweeping the Robber's legs out from under him. The Robber hit the ground and tried to get up immediately. Before he could though, David was on top of him. His mace came down with lightning speed, hitting the Robber in the chest and crushing his ribs, along with everything they protected.

David looked up and saw that his two companions had dispatched the rest of the group.

Suddenly, David felt something to his left. "Duck," he cried and hit the ground. The two dark-skinned warriors did the same as another one of the weapons flew over their heads. "Stay down," he said. "It will come back."

He looked in the direction the weapon had come from and saw several more Zantan Robbers coming from the trees. He waited for the weapon to pass him by on its way back to its owner, then stood up.

A group of Robbers rushed toward the three men, several of them pulling out more of the throwing weapons. Just as they threw them David put up his hand and the Robbers froze in mid-stride. The weapons also stopped in mid-air. The two dark-skinned men stared in shock.

"How did you do that?" asked Jaden.

David smiled. "God gives me power to defeat evil. All Paladins can do that."

"Let us dispatch them and be on our way," Zach said.

Frozen as they were, it was easy for the three men to kill the Robbers. They couldn't allow them to live and risk them causing trouble down the road. They wouldn't remain frozen forever.

After they had killed the frozen Robbers, Zach and Jaden each took a side of the road and scouted the surrounding area for more enemies. David didn't think that they had seen all that were around.

After a while the two men came back and reported that they had found nothing. David thought it odd that they couldn't find any more when he knew that there were more around. Suddenly the reason came to him. The rest of the Robbers must have followed the rest of the group. Dread rushed through David as he considered the consequences. The others didn't stand a chance. They had to reach the rest of the group quickly.

*   *   *

It was a long time before Tim and Aiden caught up with the rest of the group. The only reason they did catch up was because the group had become concerned about Tim and Aiden and had stopped to wait for them. Tim was relieved to see them.

When the rest of the group saw the father and son, they rushed back to meet them. Tim had tired long before that and had been forced to walk instead of run. His strength had almost given out, but he knew that he had to go on. Brione was the first to reach them and when she did, Tim fell to his knees. She grabbed Aiden from him and helped the young man stand.

Aiden stood precariously on his feet. He had slowly gained strength as they traveled. He felt bad that his father had to carry him; he knew it had been hard on him. But he just didn't have the strength to walk on his own after being thrown from his horse when it had its legs cut out from under it.

He now ran his hands over himself as he stood there, testing for anything broken. He didn't think anything was. He had gotten lucky.

"We are so relieved to see you two," Brione said. "I was about to go back for you. Are you alright?"

"Yeah," Tim said. "Just tired."

"And you?" Brione asked Aiden.

"I think so," the young man replied. "I fell off my horse when its legs were cut out from under it. But I'm alright."

The rest of the group looked relieved.

Tim struggled to his feet. "We have to get going."

Brione put a hand on his arm. "You need to rest. You can barely stand. Where is David? Where are Jaden and Zach?"

"They stayed behind to stall the Robbers," Tim answered.

"By themselves?" Dustin asked. "They need help!"

"No," Tim commanded. "David can handle himself. And with Jaden and Zach to help him, the Robbers don't stand a chance. Believe me, they will be fine. We need to keep moving. They will catch up with us when they can. Let's go."

Not wanting to argue with their leader, they did as he said. They put Tim on one of the few remaining horses. He objected, but the group wouldn't budge on this point. They couldn't travel very quickly because most of the group had to go on foot, but they made steady progress.

Aiden struggled a little at first. He leaned on Dustin as he traveled. Portia offered her shoulder for support, but Dustin insisted he help Aiden. He was afraid that Portia wouldn't be strong enough to support Aiden's weight for a long period of time. So Portia was forced to walk beside the pair, taking quick glances at Aiden as they traveled. When he returned her looks, she would smile encouragingly at him.

The day grew warmer as the afternoon wore on. The exertion of traveling left the group sweating and uncomfortable. No one spoke much, they were too focused on getting away from their enemies. Tim, who knew where they were going, led the group on his horse. Princess Dana, also on a horse, traveled beside him. Veronna, on the last horse, traveled just behind. The rest of the group followed in no particular order. When Dustin tired from helping Aiden walk, Brione took over.

After a while, Aiden was able to walk on his own power, and the traveling became a little easier. Suddenly, Veronna said, "I wish Layne were here. He would be able to lighten the mood." That comment made Aiden smile. He knew it was true.

"Remember the time when he fell into that patch of poison ivy and all he did was joke about it?" Aiden asked. "You would have thought he would have been miserable, like almost anyone else would be, but instead he laughed and made fun of himself."

Veronna laughed. "And then he chased me, threatening to touch me and give me poison ivy too."

"Do you think he is alright?" Brione asked quietly, not looking at anybody.

"Yes," Dustin said immediately. Everyone looked over at him. "I know Layne better than anyone else. He can take care of himself." Dustin chuckled. "That guy can get himself into very serious situations. But then he gets himself back out again. He is amazing. He will be just fine."

Aiden reached over and put a hand on Dustin's shoulder. He gave his friend a smile. "I agree. He will be fine. We will see him again soon."

After that they traveled in silence, everyone lost in their separate thoughts. Their progress was agonizingly slow. They had no idea if David, Zach and Jaden were successful in delaying or stopping the Zantan Robbers. But they could go no faster. Even if they doubled up on the horses, they had too many people to have all of them ride.

Suddenly, Tim saw movement to his right. They were still in the forest, and it was hard to see in the trees. He concentrated harder. He saw something fly out of the trees towards the group. He immediately knew what it was.

"Duck!" he yelled and jumped off his horse, using the big animal as a shield. Everyone immediately did as Tim had commanded. They had learned not to question their leader. Unfortunately, one of them was too slow.

Dorn was not used to taking orders in a life or death situation. He was used to taking orders in a palace situation, when it didn't mean life or death. When it was a matter of life or death, the smallest delay could kill you. Dorn had not learned that yet.

When Tim had yelled "Duck," Dorn, instead of ducking immediately, looked around first. He had seen the blur of movement and tried to get out of the way, but he wasn't quick enough. The flying blade caught him on the top of the head, taking off his scalp. Dorn fell to the ground, the top of his head and his skull missing. Blood and brains started seeping out of the hole. Dorn blacked out.

When the weapon passed by the group again on its way back to its owner, everyone got to their feet to face the attack. Only Veronna noticed Dorn lying on the ground. She gave a cry and rushed to his side. Everyone heard her cry out, but no one else could follow however because five yellow-skinned men stepped out of the trees.

Tim was in the middle. Aiden stood on his right, Brione and Dustin on his left. Suddenly, Dana was standing next to Aiden. She was holding two short swords.

"What do you think you are doing?" Tim asked her. "Get behind us."

"No. I want to help."

"Don't be ridiculous. You'll only get yourself killed."

"I can fight," she replied. "Jaden has been teaching me for the last few months. I'm not as good as Jaden of course, but I can hold my own. Besides, you will need every fighter you can get to defeat these enemies. You need me."

Tim thought as he watched the Robbers coming closer. They didn't seem to be in a hurry. "Okay. But stay close. You have never fought enemies like these before. If you stay close to us, you should be alright."

Portia came running up beside Dana. "I want to help, too."

"Can you fight?" Tim asked her.

She put her head down. "No," she said. "But I want to help."

"I think you should stay back," Tim said. "It's too dangerous for you to be up here. Maybe you should go help Veronna."

Portia shared a look with Aiden. "Alright," she said. "You be careful," she said to Aiden and walked to where Veronna was trying to keep Dorn alive.

Aiden watched her kneel next to the fallen man, then he turned back to the threat. The five Robbers were almost to them. "Attack!" Tim shouted and rushed forward.

Aiden could tell the Zantan Robbers were surprised by the move. They had expected the group to wait for their arrival. The five Robbers gave ground almost immediately. The mercenaries had them retreating, but it didn't last long. The Robbers recovered very quickly, and the tide of the battle began to turn.

Aiden began to give ground. His injuries still ached and they slowed him down. Dana, the least experienced of them, also gave ground, though Aiden was impressed with her swordsmanship. She was a lot quicker than Aiden would have thought. Brione and Dustin also gave ground, but more slowly than Aiden and Dana. Only Tim kept his enemy on the defensive.

Aiden ducked under a slash, then brought up his sword to deflect another slash from his enemies second weapon. It was difficult to fight an enemy with two swords when you only had one. Especially when that enemy was as skilled as a Zantan Robber. He was able to glance over at Dana. She was avoiding the weapons of her enemy, but she was obviously overmatched. He didn't know how much longer she could holdout.

Suddenly, Tim was there at her side. He had dispatched the Robber he was fighting and came to her aid. Together, they had little trouble defeating the man.

Aiden, Dustin, and Brione were having worse luck. The man Dustin was fighting had a gash on his right arm. Dustin had pushed the button on the hilt of his new sword and the blade had grown. The Robber was surprised by it, and the longer blade had slashed across his arm. But Dustin hadn't scored another hit since then.

Brione had tried the same tactic after Dustin had, but her enemy hadn't been surprised. Her enemy showed no marks, while Brione had several cuts and slashes on her arms and torso.

Aiden felt pain in his arm as his enemy's blade finally hit its target. He was starting to wear down while his opponent didn't show any sign of slowing. Finally, Tim was at his side. He arrived just in time because just then Aiden's strength gave out because of his injuries and he fell to the ground. He fell right at his dad's feet. Tim stepped back and tripped over Aiden. He fell hard on his back, his legs draped over his son's body.

Aiden saw the Robber standing over them. His raised his sword. Although he immediately plunged it down toward Aiden and Tim, the movement seemed to be in slow motion. The closer the blade got, the more Aiden knew his life was over. Not able to look at the blade as it descended, Aiden shut his eyes and braced himself for the death blow. It never came. He heard a clash of metal on metal and opened his eyes.

He saw Jaden standing above them. He had deflected the Robber's sword with a blade of his own. Jaden fought the Robber back, away from Tim and Aiden. Before they could get back to their feet, Zach leaped over them and joined the fray.

Once the two dark-skinned warriors joined the battle, the fighting was over quickly. The group ran over to Veronna and Portia, who still had their hands over the top of Dorn's skull holding everything in as best they could. A few minutes later, David came running up to them. He looked relieved to see everyone alive.

"Good," he said. "I see Jaden and Zach reached you guys in time."

"Actually," Tim replied defensively, "we held our own just fine until they got here."

"Dad," Aiden said. Tim turned to his son. Aiden gestured to the man lying on the ground, fighting for his life. "Dorn."

"Oh, yes," his father replied. Tim turned to David. "Dorn was seriously wounded by a boomerang. Will you help him?"

"Let me see him," the Paladin said.

Everyone parted for him except Veronna and Portia. "Please move," he said gently.

"We can't," Veronna replied. "If we move our hands, his brains will spill out. He will die."

"That does sound serious." He gently moved Portia out of the way and placed his big hand over Veronna's small one. "Move your hand child. It will be alright."

Veronna moved her hand from underneath her uncle's. David pressed down hard on the wound, keeping everything inside where it belonged. Veronna stepped back and into the protective arms of her father. She was crying.

David looked at Tim. "His name is Dorn, correct?"

"Yes."

David put his other hand over the one already on Dorn's head and shut his eyes. "Dorn," he said. "By the power of the Almighty God which he has bestowed upon me, his servant, I say unto you be healed."

For a moment David sat unmoving, his hands still covering Dorn's head. Then, ever so slowly, he lifted his hands away. The group looked and saw Dorn's head whole again, just like it was before the attack. The girls gasped at the sight, the men stared in disbelief. Dorn opened his eyes and looked around. A big grin formed on his face. David helped him to his feet and clapped him warmly on the back.

Everyone began talking at once.

"That was amazing!"

"How did you do that?"

"I've never seen anything like that before!"

Tim stood back, staying away from the rest of the group.

22

The dark-skinned man watched Amanda disembark from the ship. It had been a dull two-month trek. The man hated sailing. Nothing ever happened on a ship. All he did, besides keeping an eye on his charge, was stare out at the endless expanse of water. If he ever had to sail again, it would be too soon.

You're here, came a voice in his head. *Good. Bring the girl to the palace.*

Yes, Master. Master, if I may?

Speak, came the reply.

Why did you send me to get this girl? What importance does she hold for you?

My amusement. You wouldn't know this, but it can get boring being as powerful as I am. I am going to use her to cause trouble with a group of people I am watching. It should be enjoyable to see the outcome.

I am sure it will, Master.

The dark-skinned man didn't know what to think. He had gone through a lot of trouble to find and bring the girl here just for his master's amusement. He followed Amanda onto the docks, then took the lead. He led her to the streets beyond where a coach waited to take them to Parkos.

*   *   *

Zach's master was in his head, watching through his eyes as the group came closer to the fabled city of Zion. Everyone knew that this was where the People of God lived. At least, that is what they called themselves. Other people might disagree.

As they reached the edge of the People of God's land, Zach's master was suddenly gone. His presence had just vanished. It wasn't normal. You could feel the master leaving your head, but this time he felt nothing. His master was there one moment then just gone the next. He looked over at Jaden. "We must be very wary in this land," he whispered. "The master cannot come here." Jaden nodded.

*   *   *

Aiden stood with the rest of the group on a hilltop and looked down into the valley below. The city that sprawled out below them was unlike any city he had ever seen. In the center of the large city was a massive building. David had told them that it was a temple. Its base was incredibly wide, and the building narrowed as it got higher. The top was flat with a single, thin spire soaring into the air. Aiden had never seen a building so massive. Or beautiful. It looked to be made of white marble.

The four streets extending away from the temple in each direction were broad roads lined with trees. They ran perfectly straight all the way through the city. They looked wide enough to allow several carriages to travel side-by-side. Other streets intersected the main one at ninety-degree angles. In fact, all the intersections that Aiden could see were ninety-degree angles.

The buildings themselves, while not comparable to the temple, were beautiful and very well kept. Even at this distance he could tell that there was no damage to the walls or doors. The streets were kept clean and litter free. It was the cleanest, most beautiful city Aiden had ever seen.

Besides the beauty, he hoped that this place would offer a respite from the struggles of their journey. Now that he had time to stop and reflect on what had happened to him since Platte had arrived at their fort with fifty hired thugs, he realized that this had been a hair-raising couple of months. He had almost died countless times and had been afraid more times than he ever had in his entire life. He also realized that he was completely exhausted. All he wanted to do was get to wherever it was that they were going to stay and sleep.

He looked at his uncle, glad he had joined them. He knew that without David, the group would probably be dead right now. He thought about their last encounter with the Zantan Robbers and their terrifying weapons. Uncle David had called them boomerangs. He said that they were created by Imbuers. An Imbuer was a wizard who specialized in creating magical items. A boomerang could cut through almost anything, and it always came back to the person who threw it. The only safe way to handle a boomerang was to where special gloves, also made by Imbuers, which could catch the boomerang and not have it cut right through.

Tim thought that it would be useful to have a boomerang, but the group couldn't get the gloves off the dead Robbers. No matter how hard they tugged on the gloves, they wouldn't come off. It must have been part of their magic.

David had said that Zion was where the people of God lived, and that God would not allow Zantan Robbers to enter. They would be safe during their stay. Aiden was relieved.

*   *   *

Tim stood on the hill to the side and a little behind his son. Memories of the night he had left came flooding back to him. He had done as he had told David he was going to do and had stopped at the first town he came to and bought a horse and wagon. He had been carrying Aiden by that time for several miles and the wagon was worth the price.

He hadn't known where he was going, he just followed the road. More than once he second guessed himself. What David had said about the children hit home. Could he take care of his children on his own in a place he didn't know? His doubts were so powerful that he almost turned around more than once. But he stayed strong and kept going.

He had reached Kingston and made his way directly to the docks. It was only then he realized that somewhere deep down he had planned on coming here from the beginning. He wanted to get as far away from his past as he could, and there was nowhere further than across the sea.

Tim shook his head and brought his thoughts back to the present. As he looked down on the city that he had called home for most of his life, he was surprised by the feelings that welled up inside him. His emotions were running wild. He realized that he missed Zion very much. All his memories of the place, except for his last days in the city, were happy ones. This was the place he had met his wife. This was the place that both his kids had been born. He looked over at his son with pride, then glanced back behind him to his daughter. She was chatting with David. Veronna looked so much like her mother. He realized then that he had a grin on his face.

His grin faded when he remembered that this was the place that God had betrayed him. This was the place where his world had come crashing down, where his faith had failed him. Suddenly, he didn't want to go down the hill and enter the city of his birth. He didn't want to be anywhere near here. He knew that he would be recognized.

*   *   *

David stood behind and a little to the side of his old friend. He was watching Timmond while he talked with his niece. It was Tim now. His old friend had informed him that he has shortened his name after he left Zion. Tim was looking down at the city and grinning. That grin gave David hope. No one was happier when Tim had married his sister than David had been. Tim, his oldest friend. They had considered each other brothers even before Tim and Crystal were married.

Tim had been devastated when Crystal had died. David understood. He knew how much Tim loved his sister, and he knew how hard it was for him. But while David turned to God in his grief, Tim had turned away from Him. He had blamed God for the loss of his wife.

Tim's reaction had shocked David. Tim had been the leader of the Paladins. He had been the best of them. David had never known another man with more faith and humility. When David had spoken to Tim after Crystal's death, Tim was filled with anger. He had cursed God for taking away his wife when he had always done whatever God had asked of him. He had turned away from his faith.

David had talked to him, tried to get him to see reason, to help him understand what had happened and why. But it had done no good. Tim was just too bitter about the loss of Crystal.

But seeing the look on Tim's face now as he looked down into the valley gave David new hope. He wanted nothing more than to have his friend find his faith again. Maybe this trip back home would push him towards that.

His hope faded away when Tim's grin did. The look that appeared on his face was one that he had seen many times just before Tim had left. Bitterness. David thought that his presence reminded Tim of his wife's loss. Tim gave David a cold look whenever they made eye contact. It was hard to believe that this was the same man who had been David's best friend for most of his life.

But no. He couldn't be discouraged. He must believe that Tim could find his faith again. There had to be a reason that God had told the prophet where Tim and his group were. There had to be a reason that God wanted them brought to Zion. Tim had been too good of a Paladin to just forget everything he once stood for. He would find his faith again. And David would be there to help him.

*   *   *

Aiden looked around in the early evening light at the buildings he passed. His first assessment from the top of the hill had been correct. There was no sign of disrepair or dirt on any building. Even the paved roads were immaculately clean and well kept. They must have a large maintenance crew to handle such a task.

They were traveling down the main street, heading toward the huge temple in the center of the city. The setting sun was directly behind the building, the light seeming to make the building glow. It was a beautiful sight.

Tall trees ran down the center of the street in a perfectly straight line. Smaller trees with colorful blossoms ran in a straight line down either side of the street. Several people traveled on the street, some riding in horse-drawn carts, but most were on foot. Everyone the group passed called out a greeting and waved to the strangers. The people were laughing joyfully or smiling at the least. Aiden had never seen such happy, friendly people in his life.

"Are the people always like this?" Aiden heard Brione ask David.

David smiled. "Yes, they are. Having God in our lives makes us very joyful indeed. That is why we keep our city clean and in good repair. Being children of God, we have great respect for ourselves. We keep our surroundings clean to reflect how we feel about ourselves."

"What a great place to live," Portia said.

"Yes," David said. "It is."

Veronna came up to Aiden. "Isn't this place wonderful?"

"Yes, it is," Aiden said.

"If I lived here, I would never leave."

Aiden just smiled at that.

"Aiden?"

"Yes?"

"Do you really think we will be safe here?"

He looked at his sister. "Yes, I do. David said we will be, and I believe him."

"Good."

Veronna looked troubled. "Hey. What's wrong?" Aiden asked.

Veronna looked at him. "Aiden, I've been so scared these last few days."

"Really? I thought you have been handling things so well.

Veronna gave him a small smile. "Thanks. But it has been all a show. I've been trying to be tough for you guys, but inside I've been terrified. All I want to do is lie down and cry."

Aiden put his arm around her and pulled her close. "I know. I feel the same way."

"You do?"

"Yes, I do. I mean, we've almost died so many times. If it wasn't for Dad, Zach and Jaden, and David, we would be dead right now. But we're not. We've made it this far and now we'll be safe. I promise."

"Do you think we could just stay here in Zion forever?"

Aiden laughed at that thinking it was a joke, but when he looked at his sister, she wasn't even smiling.

*   *   *

"How does it feel to be back home?" David asked Tim.

"Actually," Tim answered, "it just feels like home. It is almost like I never left."

David was surprised by the answer. He was surprised that Tim had answered at all. He didn't think Tim was going to, but he had tried to get a conversation going anyway.

David offered his old friend a smile. "Good. I'm glad you feel that way. I was hoping that it wasn't going to be uncomfortable for you." Tim didn't look at him. He kept his gaze forward as he walked. "A lot of people miss you, you know. They still talk about you a lot."

"Do they?"

"Yes."

"Who is the prophet now?" Tim asked.

"It is still Turner."

"Oh."

This conversation wasn't going the way that David had wanted. But at least they were talking. "I believe that you will be staying at the temple while you are in Zion."

"What has happened to my old house?"

"Nothing," David replied. "It is still there, empty."

"Then I would prefer to stay there, if possible."

"Yes, I suppose that would be fine."

"And I would like to go there immediately."

"But Turner wants to see you tonight!" David said.

At last, Tim turned to David. "Do you have any idea what we have been through? Do you know how many times we have been attacked since we left our home? Do you know how many people have tried to kill us? Tried to kill my kids? We've fought Goblins and Zantan Robbers! We have lost a member of our family. We have been terrified since we landed on this continent. We are tired and worn out and all we want to do is rest. We will not go see the prophet tonight and I don't care what he thinks. We are going to my old house and going to get some rest. Do you understand?"

David was taken aback. The situation quickly fell out of his control. "Yes, Tim. I understand. I will inform Turner of your decision and come to escort you tomorrow morning. When should I come by?"

"First light should be fine."

"Alright then. I will come for you tomorrow. Get rested up." He went to Veronna and Aiden and smiled. "Well, I was thrilled to finally see you again after all these years. I am proud to see the man and woman my niece and nephew have become. I can tell your dad did a good job in raising you two. We have a lot of catching up to do. But rest for tonight and we will see each other again tomorrow." He gave them each a hug and went on his way. The group watched him go.

"Well," said Tim. "Follow me. My old house is this way."

They followed down a broad street that ran left off the main road. This street, though smaller, was no less clean and tidy. It was starting to get dark, so there were fewer people on the streets now. It suited Tim just fine, though. He wasn't ready yet to talk to people who would recognize him. After a while they turned right onto a smaller street, this one lined with much smaller buildings than the previous two that the group had traveled on. They looked to be small family homes.

Tim stopped four houses down and turned to face a house on his left. This home was a little bigger than the ones surrounding it. The door was in place and looked sturdy, but there was no glass in the windows.

Instead, boards had been placed over the holes to keep people, animals, and the weather out.

Tim searched the bushes to the right of the door, looking for the key. It was probably so rusted that it would fall apart in his hands, despite the box he had put it in.

He couldn't find the key. It wasn't where he left it when he left his home fifteen years before. Someone must have taken it.

He was surprised at how much the thought of someone going into his house upset him. He hadn't lived here for fifteen years. He shouldn't care. But this had been his and Crystal's house. This had been where they had planned to raise their children. It was a violation.

But then he saw the small box sitting on the front porch. He didn't see it before because of the fading light. It was made of heavy wood, and when he opened the top, he found the insides lined with red cloth. Inside was the key to the front door, in perfect condition. He grabbed the key and held it to his heart. He thought of all the times that Crystal had held this exact key. He felt a tear streaming down his face. He had thought that he was finished crying for her and the emotions that came to the surface by just being at the house they had shared together surprised him. He missed her so much!

Normally the iron key would have rusted over the fifteen years of not being used and being out in the elements, but the red cloth inside the box had been blessed. Such blessed cloth could keep anything dry and safe for an eternity, no matter where it was kept.

"Dad, someone put your key in that box, didn't they?"

Tim looked at Aiden, who had asked the question.

"I did. I hid it in the bushes, but apparently someone found it and went inside and boarded up the windows to protect the house. Someone wanted to keep the house safe for me. They must have thought that someday I would return."

"That was nice of them," Aiden said.

"It was probably Uncle David," Veronna said.

"Yes," replied her dad. "It probably was."

Tim stepped to the door and put the key in the lock. He turned it and heard the click of the lock. He gently pushed the door and it opened with a quiet squeak. It was too dark inside to see anything.

Tim remembered where the lamp was, on a shelf beside the door, and lit it. The familiar room came into view and Tim couldn't help but smile.

The room was just as he had left it fifteen years ago. If it was David who had come into the house, he hadn't changed anything. Directly across the expansive room was a large fireplace. On either side of the fireplace, facing each other, stood two comfortable looking chairs. Closer to Tim, facing the cold fireplace, was a couch. There was a small table leaning against each wall, each one held a potted plant. Of course, all the plants were dead.

Hung up on the walls were several finger paintings that were obviously done by a small child. Tim remembered the look on Aiden's little face when Crystal had hung those up for everyone to see. His little son had beamed with pride. Tim's smile grew wider.

There were two doors leading out of the room. One led to the kitchen, the other to a hallway that led to the rest of the rooms in the house.

Dust covered the floor in a thick coat. The only footprints were the ones made by the group when they entered. Tim suddenly felt very sad that his beloved home had been empty for fifteen years. It deserved better than that.

"Is this where we used to live?" asked Veronna. She was grinning from ear to ear.

"Yes," Tim replied. "You were both born here." He turned to Aiden. "Guess who did the paintings on the wall."

"Me," his son said. Aiden was not smiling.

"What's wrong, son?"

"Dad, I am standing in a house that I used to live in, but do not remember at all. I am in a city that I don't remember. I just met a family member that I didn't even know existed. I don't even want to contemplate what I don't know about your past. But I would appreciate it if you would tell us. Veronna and I deserve to know."

Tim looked at his son. Aiden held his gaze. Finally, Tim sighed. "You're right. You guys do deserve to know. About everything. And I will tell you. Please, sit down."

Everyone, not just Tim's kids, took a seat. They had to brush the dust from the furniture with their hands first. Brione, Aiden, Veronna and Portia sat on the couch. Dorn sat on one of the chairs, Dana on the other. Dustin, Jaden and Zach remained standing. While it was obvious that Dustin was listening, the two dark-skinned men seemed not to care at all. They were looking out the open doorway into the night beyond.

Tim lit a fire, but he spoke as he worked. "I was born in this city. I grew up here. David and I became best friends when we were young. That is how I met Aiden and Veronna's mother. David and I were the same age, Crystal was a year younger. David and I did everything together. He was like a brother to me.

"When we were a little older, I developed a small crush on Crystal. She was very beautiful and I began visiting David's house to see her, just as much as him."

Tim finished building the fire, brushed off his hands and stood up to face the group. "David and I had been fascinated with Paladins. Both our parents raised us to go to church and give our lives to God. We would go watch the Paladins train and dream of becoming Paladins ourselves. All we wanted was to become God's champions. We worked at it and trained. It was easier for me because I was born with the gift of fighting. I was a natural. I learned very quickly how to use almost any kind of weapon. David on the other hand wasn't. He had to work a lot harder than I did. But we helped each other and we both became Paladins."

Veronna interrupted him. "You are a Paladin?"

"I was a Paladin. Not anymore."

"You had the power of God?"

"Yes Veronna, I did."

"You were able to heal people like Uncle David healed Dorn?"

"Yes, I did."

"What happened? Why don't you have it anymore?"

"Patience Veronna. I will get to that point."

The young woman blushed. "Sorry."

"It's alright. When I wasn't busy training to become a Paladin, I was spending my time with Crystal. You see, I discovered that she liked me as well. At first, we kept it hidden. I didn't want David to find out and become angry. But Crystal and I finally decided to tell him together. When we told him, he was thrilled. I was relieved. He said that he wouldn't trust anyone except me with his sister. After that, the three of us were inseparable.

"David and I became Paladins when we were nineteen years old. It was the greatest day of my life until a year later when I married Crystal.

"Life was bliss. Crystal and I couldn't be happier together. I moved up quickly in the ranks of the Paladins and within two years I became their leader. I was commander of the greatest fighters in the world. And then Aiden was born. God truly blessed us.

"When Crystal became pregnant again it was almost too much. Life was perfect. We already had a beautiful son, so we were hoping for a little girl. But a few weeks before the baby was due, Crystal became very sick. She was bedridden and could barely eat or drink anything. We were afraid for the health of the baby, but we had faith that God would bless us once again.

"The baby came, and she was healthy and beautiful. It was a girl, just as we had hoped. But our joy soon ended when we realized that Crystal was just getting worse. Giving birth had been hard on her. But she kept her spirits up. That was her way.

"When it became apparent that her life was in danger, I decided to give her a blessing. Remember what David did with Dorn? He placed his hands on his head and prayed to God." The group nodded. "Well, that is the way we give blessings. You see, a Paladin has no real power on his own. The power a Paladin uses is given to him from God. It is God's power. A Paladin must be worthy to use it.

"There is something else you need to know about blessings. When we give blessings, we have no idea beforehand what we are going to say. We open our minds and let God put the words into our mouth. We say whatever comes into our heads. That way it is a true blessing and not just what the Paladin wants.

"Well, when I put my hands on my wife's head and opened my mind, I didn't like the words that came in. I had already started the blessing, so I just stopped mid-sentence. I apologized and started over again. But the same thing happened."

"What words came to your mind?" asked Princess Dana. Everyone was on the edge of their seats, listening intently to the fascinating story.

"Sometimes, not often, but sometimes, we will bless a person to die. It is their time and God will not permit them to be on this earth any longer. It was always sad when we did this, but the family members understand."

"God wanted you to bless her to die," Aiden said.

"Yes," Tim said softly.

"Oh, dad," Veronna said. Tears were streaming down her face. "I am so sorry."

"I couldn't take it. I left the house and fell to my knees outside. I prayed harder than I had ever prayed before. I begged God to let her live. I told Him that I had dedicated my entire life to Him and I had done everything He had ever asked of me. All I wanted was for my wife to live. That wasn't too much to ask, was it?

"After a long time, I returned to the house, certain that God would see reason and give me what I wanted. I returned to my wife's side and started giving her another blessing. But it was the same this time as it had been the last. So, I changed the words. I didn't say what God wanted me to say. I told my wife that she would get better and live a long and happy life. But I didn't believe it. And I could tell that David knew something was wrong.

"A week passed. All Crystal wanted to do was hold Veronna in her arms. She was too weak to feed Veronna, but we found another woman who could do it. The only time Veronna left her mother's arms was to be fed and changed. Aiden spent majority of his time with her, too.

"I did my daily duties, but my mind wasn't on them. All I could think about was my wife, dying slowly in bed. I think she knew it was inevitable too. That is why she spent every moment she could with the kids.

"At the end of a week, she had the kids taken to another room and we had our last conversation. She told me that it would be alright. She knew she was going to a better place. I cried and told her that I couldn't take care of the kids by myself, that I needed her so much. She just smiled and said I would have help until I figured it out. I asked her to stay with me. She said she couldn't. She asked me not to cry, to be strong. But I couldn't help it. My world was ending. She didn't shed a single tear. She told me that she had been the happiest woman in the world during the last few years that she had been married to me. She thanked me and said good-bye."

Tim sniffed and wiped away tears from his cheek. "A few minutes after she said good-bye, she died. I lost it. I had never cried so hard in my life, before or after that. Then I rushed out of the house. David saw me go and followed me, hoping to console me.

"I fell to the ground in almost the exact same spot as before. But this time I didn't pray. This time I was so full of rage that I cursed God at the top of my lungs. I told Him that I had done everything He had ever asked, and yet He betrayed me. I called Him petty and cruel. I said He liked to play with peoples' lives, then destroy them on a whim. I told Him that I would never follow Him again.

"I stood up and turned around and saw David standing there. His mouth was opened in shock. He couldn't believe what he had just heard. I tried to walk past him. but he reached out and grabbed my shoulder, stopping me. Before he could say anything, I told him to shut up and walked back into my house. I made everyone leave. I didn't want any visitors.

"For the next couple of weeks, I didn't leave the house. I forsook my duties and spent all my time with my children. People came by and brought us food, but they never stayed long." Tim smiled sadly. "I don't think they thought I was very good company.

"Even my parents came by and tried to console me, but it was no use. Nothing anyone said or did took my pain and anger away. Finally, people stopped coming over.

"After a couple of weeks, I just decided to leave. I would take my kids and go far away. I couldn't live in Zion anymore, my life here was over. By that time the only person who visited was David. He saw me packing up our things and asked me what I was doing. I told him I was leaving. He asked when I would be coming back. I said never. He tried to talk me out of it, but it didn't work. I grew angry and threw him out of the house. He left, but I feared he would tell my parents. They were the last people I wanted to see. So, I quit packing and took what I had and left with Veronna and Aiden. I locked the house and out of habit hid the key in the bushes. Your Uncle David confronted me again as I left the city. But I couldn't be swayed. I left and never looked back.

"I sailed to Blanderly because I figured that was just about the furthest away from Zion I could get. I never expected to come back here again. I can't believe I am here now."

The room fell silent after Tim finished his story. Finally, Veronna got off the couch and gave her father a hug. "I am so sorry, dad," she said. "I had no idea." Aiden was there as well. "Me neither," he said.

Tim sniffed. "It's alright. I'm alright. I still have you two. You guys are my life now."

"Dad," Aiden said. "Are your parents still alive? How about mom's? Are we going to me our grandparents?"

"When I left here fifteen years ago, yes, they were still alive. Now, I have no idea."

"Do we have other uncles or aunts?" asked Veronna.

Tim took a moment to answer. "You do have one aunt. My younger sister, Deadawn. But she is not here. She is two years younger than me and when she came of age, she left Zion against our parents' wishes. We have no idea where she went. We never heard from her again."

"Why did she leave?" Veronna asked.

"She didn't believe in the faith of the people here. She didn't follow the teachings of our parents. She was rebellious and did her own thing. She was never comfortable here, so she left as soon as she could. It broke my parents' heart."

"Do you think you will ever see her again?" Veronna pressed.

"I don't know." Tim looked at the group. "Now, we've had a long, hard journey, so I think it is time for some rest. Knowing David, he will be here at the crack of dawn to take us to see the prophet."

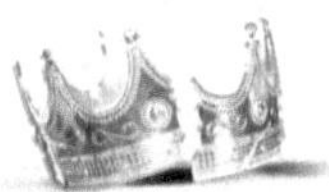

23

Ricardo lost the connection to Zach's mind. He sat there, stunned. That had never happened before. He hadn't thought it *could* happen. He didn't understand it. He thought about what he had seen, replaying it in his mind, trying to discover the reason. Suddenly, it hit him. As soon as the group had entered Zion's borders, his connection had vanished. That must be it. It seemed that these People of God truly did have power.

This was going to be inconvenient, but not a large problem. He would have no idea what the group was doing while they were in Zion, but Zach and Jaden would give him all the details when they came out. He hoped they weren't going to stay there too long.

He stood up from his table and left his personal quarters. He shut the door behind him. His security system reset itself, so he didn't need to worry about his room being safe from intruders.

He strode purposefully through the elegant halls, not noticing the beautiful tapestries or the colorful, fragrant flowers. His mind was focused on his destination, the throne room. He needed to talk to Korlas.

He found the king sitting on his throne, speaking with some of the lesser nobles of the realm. The Prince of Blanderly was standing next to the large throne, looking uncomfortable. He looked up as Ricardo entered the room, then quickly looked away again.

"Your Highness," the noble that was speaking with Korlas said. "Someone must stop these Zantan Robbers. They are terrorizing the countryside. We don't have enough men-at-arms to stop them. Three of the other nobles and I have tried to combine our strength to fight them, but all we have accomplished is to lose half our men. We need your help."

King Korlas drummed the fingers of his right hand on his throne as he thought. His chin was resting in the palm of his left hand. "Yes. I will help you. You are not the first person to come to me with this kind of problem. I know how to deal with these Robbers." He turned to one of his personal guards standing next to the throne. "I want you to handpick fifty soldiers and go with this good man back to his lands. I give you the task of rooting these cowardly Robbers out and destroying them. These Robbers have a reputation as being incredibly dangerous. If you have a hard time finding enough men to go, raise their pay if you have to."

The guard gave a deep bow. "Yes, Your majesty."

The king turned back to the nobleman. "Worry not. No one is more qualified to dispose of the Robbers than my personal guards. They will take care of your problem for you."

The nobleman bowed. "Thank you, Your Grace. Bless you."

The man left and another took his place. And after him, another. A line of people was waiting to see the king. Ricardo was getting impatient. He had asked Korlas once why he didn't employ councilors to see all the people in his place, but the king had replied that he enjoyed meeting with his people. Ricardo thought that Korlas just enjoyed the feeling of power. He liked telling people what to do and being obeyed without question.

After what seemed like hours the petitioners finally quit coming. Korlas turned to Ricardo with a smile on his face. "What is it, wizard?"

Instead of answering Ricardo asked, "You are sending men to kill your own men?"

Korlas barked a laugh. "Of course not. Don't be ridiculous. They have done this many times before. They will find some peasant, kill him, and dip the body in yellow paint."

"Wouldn't it be obvious to people that the yellow color of the dead man's skin is only paint?"

"You would think so," replied Korlas. "But people see what they want to see. They're are always just relieved to have the threat eliminated that they never look close enough at the body to realize anything is wrong. Do not worry, everything will be fine."

Ricardo sneered at the thought of him worrying about anything the king did. "Tim and his mercenaries have escaped your men once again. They now reside in Zion with the People of God."

A look of rage came onto Korlas' face. "Escaped? Again? Fools! They have power given to them by the Dark God himself and they can't apprehend one man!"

Ricardo turned to Prince Easton. "Beware, Prince. We are talking about the man who his coming to kill you. He has repeatedly defeated King Korlas' demonic minions. What do you think of that?"

Easton said nothing, but by the look on his face, Ricardo could tell he was terrified. Ricardo smiled at him, but the prince looked away again.

"You," Korlas said to another of his personal guards. "I want you to take one hundred men, plus a mage, and go to Zion. You cannot enter, but you can wait for Tim and his mercenaries to come out. Kill everyone but the leader, Tim. I want him brought here in chains."

The man bowed. "Yes, Your Majesty."

As the guard turned away, Korlas grabbed his arm to stop him. "And do not fail me."

"I won't, your Majesty."

Korlas released the man and he left.

When the guard was gone Ricardo asked, "Why are you putting so much effort into seizing one man? He is coming here anyway. Why not just wait for him and seize him when he gets here?"

Korlas turned on the wizard. "You do not know this man. I do. You did not grow up with him. I did. You have never seen him fight. I have. He is unbeatable. I have never seen him lose. I will not have him running around free. He would cause too much trouble for me if he were to come here on his own. I won't allow it."

"You fear this man." It was not a question.

"Fear him? No. I have the power of my God. I need not fear him. But I do respect his abilities."

Ricardo didn't believe the king. He could see it in the man's eyes. He was afraid of this Tim.

Korlas didn't know it, but Ricardo had seen Tim fight on numerous occasions. He had watched the mercenary through the eyes of his servant Zach. He knew what kind of an enemy Tim was. And while it was true he was a dangerous man, he would be no match for Zach or Jaden or any one of his warriors. He did not fear Tim.

Easton's curiosity got the better of him. "Why can't your men go into Zion?"

Korlas looked surprised that the prince had spoken. "Because, Little Prince, Zion is the home of the People of God. I am a servant of the Dark God. The two do not mix. Followers of the Dark God cannot go into Zion. It is as if a force pushes against them when they try."

"Can the People of God not come here?" Easton pressed.

The question seemed to anger Korlas. He didn't like to be reminded the limitations of the god who gave him his powers. "Unfortunately, they can. They can go wherever they please."

"So if…" Easton started, but Ricardo silenced him with a sharp gesture.

"That's enough," he said. "You are going down a dangerous road, Prince Easton."

Easton finally seemed to notice the look on the King's face. He thought better of what he was about to say.

"No," said Korlas, a dangerous tone in his voice. "Please, continue. What were you going to say, Little Prince?"

Easton swallowed. "I was only going to ask if your normal soldiers could enter Zion."

Ricardo could tell that Korlas didn't believe Easton, but the king didn't press the issue. "Yes, they can. But the People of God are a powerful people with the best trained fighters in the country. If I sent my soldiers into Zion to apprehend Tim, they would not come back out. No, my way is best. My soldiers will attack them when they are away from the protection of Zion's borders."

"What will you do with Tim when you have him?" Ricardo asked. "If he is such a threat, why bring him here at all? Why not just kill him and be done with it?"

"Because that would be too easy. I do plan on killing him. But I want him to know it was I who beat him. I will finally have bested him. I want to kill him myself."

"I think you plan too much," Ricardo said. "If you truly think this man is a threat to you, just kill him. Sometimes doing things the easy way keeps you out of trouble. Too much planning can backfire."

"I thank you for your concern, Wizard, but once again, do not worry about it. Everything will be fine."

"The only thing I am worried about is losing my job. You pay me very well to be your advisor, and so I advise you. But I have no love for you."

"Nor I for you," Korlas replied. "I have told you before that one day I will kill you, and I meant it. But not today. No, today you are useful to me."

Ricardo turned to leave. "Tell me," said Korlas, and the wizard stopped. "Do you know what Tim's group is doing now? Can your powers penetrate the People of Gods' defenses?" When Ricardo didn't answer, the King continued. "I thought not. You think you are more powerful than me wizard, but you are not. Remember that."

Without looking back, Ricardo left the room.

*   *   *

Easton watched the wizard make his exit. His heart was lifted a little by the information he had just received. For now, Dana was safe from these evil men and their minions. He hoped she would stay in Zion while the rest of the group came after him, but deep down, he knew she wouldn't. He knew she would come for him and do her best to protect him. They had always been very close. In truth, Dana was the only person in the world he cared for.

He also just discovered that King Korlas and his pet wizard were not all powerful. They couldn't see into Zion or send their men in there. There were people more powerful than they were. There were people that they feared. Somehow, they didn't seem quite as intimidating as they had before. But he had to continue to be careful though. He still had to hold his tongue and act meek if he wanted to survive. He had almost made a serious mistake by asking too many questions. Luckily, Ricardo had stopped him. A slip of the tongue could get him killed. He knew that he would still be in danger with Tim, but if what he had heard about the mercenary was true, and with Dana there doing her best to keep him safe, he would probably be in safer hands with Tim than he was with Korlas.

"Take our Little Prince back to his cell," the king commanded, and a very large guard took him by the arm and led him out of the throne room.

*　　*　　*

The secret door opened, and the yellow-skinned man entered the room. The man immediately dropped down to one knee. After a moment he rose and said, "You have orders, Master?"

"Yes," Korlas replied. "I have just sent one of my personal guards with a wizard and one hundred soldiers to capture my old rival, a man named Tim. He is the leader of a mercenary group. I have sent out your brothers on more than one occasion, but they have failed me each time. I want you to take four Robbers with you and trail the group I sent out. Keep hidden, do not let them know you are there. When the battle is engaged and opportunity presents itself, I want you and your men to capture this man and kill the rest of his group. Do you understand?"

"Yes, master."

"Good. Now go."

The Zantan Robber left without another word.

*   *   *

Layne could hear the sounds of the city around them as he and Tyler hid in the hay. He had never been so itchy in his life. The hay itched against the skin of his face and arms, but it also got under his shirt and made his stomach and back itch as well. He had to be as gentle as possible when he scratched though. If he scratched too briskly, he might knock the hay off them and they would be discovered. It was all he could do to lay there and remain still,

Layne tried to whisper something to Tyler once, but hay got into his mouth and he had almost gagged as one long piece went down his throat. After that, they traveled in silence, except for the sounds of the city.

It gave Layne time to think about all that had happened to him the last few months. Life had been good for him and his brother recently. It had taken Layne a long time to get over the murder of his parents, and if truth be told, he wasn't sure he ever did. But the pain was gone when he thought of them now. Now he and his brother had another family, Tim's mercenaries.

The mercenary group was truly a family. Sure, they weren't all related by blood, but they were connected by something even stronger still: love. Tim was like a father to him, and Brione and Dustin and Aiden and Veronna were his siblings. It didn't matter how much he teased the others; he loved them.

Tim had taught him to be good and honest and just. He had also taught him how to fight and defend those who couldn't defend themselves. Tim had taken him and Dustin in when they didn't have anywhere else to go, and he gave them a home with his own family. Yes, life had been good.

Until a few days ago. Either Tim had lied to him or the mercenary leader was very naïve. Life wasn't about being just and good. Life was hard and cruel. Life was about survival and taking care of yourself. While Layne had nothing but good feelings before, now he felt nothing but rage. Rage at the captain of the Dark Watch, rage at Riktor, rage at Veronna for not being able to take care of herself, rage at Tim for leaving him there to be tortured even though he was innocent of any wrong doing. Rage at himself for putting others first. If he hadn't have helped Veronna, he never would have been arrested.

Well, he wasn't going to do that anymore. He was going to live for himself for a change. He knew how good of a fighter he was. He could make a living with his axes. He already did that as a member of Tim's mercenaries, but he didn't need Tim. He could do this on his own. But he would have to find the group and say goodbye to Dustin first. And to Aiden as well.

As he lay there, itchy in the hay, he thought about his escape the night before. He realized that as he was fighting for his life, the rage had gone away. He had almost felt like his old self again. Then when the fighting was over, these feelings came storming back. That was the key. He had to keep fighting or he would lose himself to the rage.

His thoughts were interrupted when the cart came to a stop. He heard Kargen's voice, and then another man's as well. They must be at the city gate. It didn't sound like the guard wanted to let Kargen out of the city.

"No one leaves through the Mouth of the City by order of the captain of the City Watch," the man was saying. "The criminal who attacked the good captain escaped from prison last night and so no one is allowed out of the city until he and the wizard who helped him escape are found."

Next Layne heard Kargen's voice. "You mean someone actually helped that vile criminal escape? How awful!"

"Yes. A wizard." He snorted. "Magic-wielding scum. The city guards should round all the wizards in the city up and kick them out. They don't belong here. We don't want them here. It is too bad that the criminal injured Riktor so bad. He would do something about them."

"Well my good man," said Kargen, "I am also a judge. I work with Riktor. If you let me through so I can go see my sister who is sick, I promise to speak with my fellow judges about the wizard problem in the city."

"Your sick sister, huh?" the soldier asked. "And where does this sick sister of yours live?"

"Where does she live? Uh, just a few miles north of the city. She has a small plot of land and a little cottage where she lives all alone."

"What is the hay on your cart for?"

"She has a couple of horses. Whenever I go see her, I bring a cartload of hay. It makes her life just a little bit easier."

"Why does she live by herself?"

Just our luck, Layne thought. *We had to run into a nosey guard.*

"She used to live with her husband, but he died a couple years ago from an illness. I have tried to get her to move back to the city, but she refuses. She says that her and her husband had put too much work into the house to just leave it. So I visit her as often as I can and always try to at least bring her some hay for her horses."

There was a long pause. Layne guessed that the guard was considering everything he had just heard. "Alright," the guard answered. "But please allow me to escort you to your sister's house. I would feel terrible if anything happened to you on the road after I allowed you to leave the city against orders."

Layne knew that to decline the soldier's offer of an escort would look very suspicious. Apparently, so did Kargen.

"That sounds like a great idea," the old judge answered. "I would feel much safer with you. But don't you have to stay at your post?"

"We have enough men here to guard the gate without me," the guard said. "It would be fine if I escort you."

Kargen agreed and Layne heard the city gates creaking open. After a few minutes, the cart was on the move again.

Layne heard Kargen and the soldier chatting as they traveled, but he didn't pay attention to what they were saying. Instead he was thinking of a way to get rid of the soldier. They couldn't just kill him, someone would come looking for him when he didn't return to his post. He was sure that other guards had seen the man leave with Kargen, so they would be looking for him if the guard didn't return. They couldn't reveal themselves and try to run because the soldier would know that Kargen had helped them. They couldn't stay hidden and let the man continue to travel with them because he would know something was wrong when they never reached Kargen's sister's house.

He wanted to talk to Tyler and see what he thought, but he didn't dare. The guard might overhear and they would be caught. Tyler seemed to have his own idea however, because he quickly made his way out of the hay and onto the ground. With a muffled curse, Layne threw himself out after the wizard.

When he stood back up and brushed the hay from his clothes, he found Tyler standing tall and with a fist-sized stone hovering above his upturned palm. The soldier had noticed and was facing them from his horse, a sword in his hand. Layne drew his own sword. The soldier glanced over at Kargen, obviously confused.

Kargen was speechless. He had a terrified look on his face. Obviously, he thought that they had just been caught in their lie.

"You old fool," Tyler said to the judge. "The two men you were looking for were hidden in your own cart, right under your nose! And now you have helped us escape. Is this what the judicial system has come to in Kingston? Are all the judges as old and blind as you?"

The soldier put himself between Kargen and the wizard. "Get away from here," he said to Kargen. "Ride to your sister's house and I will deal with these criminals."

"But…"

"Just go. If you stay, you might be injured. Do not worry about me. I can handle these two."

Kargen gave an apologetic look to Layne and Tyler, then went on his way. The soldier was looking at Tyler, so he hadn't noticed the look.

"I will give you a chance to surrender right now," the soldier said. "Drop your rock, and you drop your sword and come back with me quietly to the city. We don't need this to get messy."

"I don't think so," Tyler said.

"Yeah," Layne added. "If I go back, I am going to be beheaded, even though I didn't do anything wrong. I am innocent of any wrong doing. I will not go back."

"Well," said the soldier, "then I will have to bring your bodies back with me."

"Listen," said Tyler. "We don't want any trouble. Just let us be on our way and you can be on yours. We don't have to do this."

"What? Are you scared?" The soldier sneered.

"No," Tyler replied and threw out his right hand. The stone went flying towards the soldier but missed. The soldier had expected it and had ducked. He began to laugh but didn't realize that the stone had stopped in midair and was flying back towards him. His laughter was cut short when the stone hit the soldier in the back of the head. The man's helm took the brunt of the impact, but the blow still knocked the man off his horse.

The soldier quickly climbed to his feet, but he couldn't see because the stone had knocked the helm over his eyes. While he tried to pry it off his head, Tyler rushed to the horse. He jumped onto the saddle and motioned for Layne to get on as well. But before the big man reached the horse the soldier had removed his helm and was rushing in for the attack.

Layne blocked blow after blow with his sword. He was just an average swordsman. If he had his axes the soldier wouldn't stand a chance. But as it was, the soldier was better than Layne with a sword and he quickly had Layne retreating.

Layne was desperately trying to defend himself when he saw another rock flying at the soldier. This one hit him in the back of the head and the man slumped to the ground. Layne checked to see if the man was dead or simply unconscious.

The man was only unconscious, which was what Tyler wanted. The two men had no desire to cause any more trouble and killing a soldier out on the road would have done just that. Although they did take his horse.

The two men left the soldier on the side of the road so someone might find him and continued towards the site where they were to meet Tim and the rest of the group. Tyler sat in front and controlled the reigns, Layne was on the back and held onto the back of the saddle. He wasn't going to go into the group's camp holding another man around the waist.

He was planning what he would say to the group when they entered the circle of boulders. Besides the bodies of what could only be Zantan Robbers, the clearing was empty. The group was gone.

"There is no one here," Tyler said.

Layne looked at the wizard. "Now what do we do?"

24

There was panic in the streets. That was the report Queen Laurel got from every messenger that came to see her. The townsfolk were terrified.

The last man on the war council to be murdered was Costuck. After that, the assassin just stopped killing. The questioning of the men who fit the description Syth had given turned up nothing. They all denied the charge of course, and questioning hadn't provided any answers. Reluctantly, Laurel let everyone go. After that, the murders ended. She had been filled with hope that the nightmare was over.

That was, until about a week ago. Someone was found murdered in an alley a few blocks away from the palace. No one worried about it too much. It was a homeless man who didn't have any family. But then the next day more bodies had been discovered. And more on the third day.

These killings had been like the ones in the palace. No one had any idea who was committing them. They had no leads. Everyone looked at everyone else with suspicion. Was it the baker? Was it the boy down the street that played with your son? Was it one of the soldiers in the City Guard? It could be anyone.

The one way it differed from the killings in the palace was that these new murders seemed to be random. There had been a pattern to the palace murders. That was not so with these new murders in the city. Since the killings only happened at night, Queen Laurel enforced a curfew. No one was to be out on the streets after nightfall for their own good. But some people ignored the curfew. Those who did ended up dead.

It would be much harder to find the assassin in the city than it had been in the palace. Tosun was a massive city with innumerable places to hide. Queen Laurel was at a loss of what to do. While she was safe in her palace thinking, her people were being murdered in the streets.

With a great feeling of despair, she fell asleep. Her dreams were of yellow-skinned assassins running rampant through the streets of Tosun and killing everyone in sight.

*   *   *

Syth stood in the shadows and waited for a patrol of soldiers to pass him by. They were patrolling the streets to keep the townsfolk safe, and also to find the murderer if they could. *They had better not find the murderer,* he thought, *for their own sakes.*

After that night when he was supposed to kill Sam and changed his mind, he had begun to think it was getting too dangerous to kill the queen's advisors. Sooner or later, he would be caught. He had told his master of his misgivings and was allowed to change his tactics. When he told his master his plan, the wizard was very pleased.

His master was even more pleased as he watched his most trusted and capable servant work. He relished in the panic that the actions of Syth were creating. It might not do much to detriment the queen's cause, his master had told him once, but it sure was entertaining.

The soldiers moved on and Syth left the shadows. He had laid the bodies of the four people he had killed in the middle of the alley behind him. They were sure to be found in the morning. He didn't know who they were, but he didn't think they were homeless. They were dressed too nicely and didn't smell bad enough to be homeless. He had caught them by surprise. The first two, the man and woman, had died before they knew what was happening. The two children, a boy and a girl, had tried to flee. What the family was doing out in the alley at night with all the killings going on was a mystery to Syth. They were fools. Fools didn't deserve to live.

This family was not the only one he had killed that night. In all he had killed a dozen others and had set up their bodies in a row just like he did with the family. Nobody could mistake these deaths as random killings after he laid the bodies out nicely in a row. It would strike even more fear into the populace.

It was a good night for going about unseen. The sky was full of clouds and there was no sign of moon or stars. It made his journey back much easier.

It was a long walk back to the palace. At first, he had stayed close to the palace, but then he realized that if he never killed anyone far away from the palace that would narrow the search. He wanted the queen to think that the killer could be anywhere, which is why he started traveling farther away from the palace each night.

He made his way onto the palace grounds. A ten-foot high wall surrounded the grounds, with several openings dispensed throughout so people could enter. Each gap in the fence was guarded by two guards. He didn't want the guards to see him, so instead of entering through one of the gaps, he did what he did every night. He scaled the wall. He went to a part of the wall where there was a corner. The corner was a ninety-degree angle and he used both sides of the wall to quickly run up and over.

He hit the ground and crouched low in the shadows. He looked all around to make sure no one had seen him. When he knew the coast was clear, he made his way to the palace. When two patrolling guards came near, he flattened himself on the ground. They didn't notice Syth even though they came within a few feet of him.

I'm surrounded by fools, he thought with disdain. *People are being murdered in the streets and the palace guards aren't paying attention to their surroundings. I could probably kill every person in this palace and never get caught. Fools.*

After the soldiers were out of sight, he got to his feet again and continued on his way. He avoided the main entrance and went around to the back. His quarters were on one of the higher floors, but the climb was easy. There were vines and window sills that provided easy handholds. The climb was made a little slower when he had to skirt around windows that had lights in them to avoid being seen, but he still made it up to his window quickly. He had left it unlocked so he could get back in. He crawled through into his sleeping chamber. He had left a lamp lit by the window so from the palace grounds it looked as if he had never left.

His sleeping chamber was small and sparsely decorated. Nothing adorned the plain white walls except several weapons hanging from hooks; daggers and swords, even a small throwing ax. There was a small bed, a washbasin, a table and chair by the window, and a trunk to hold his clothing. He had chosen this room himself. When the queen offered him a larger one, he had declined. This small room fit his needs.

You are doing well, came the voice in his head.

Thank you, Master.

But we need to do more. Enough of these commoners and homeless people. Tomorrow night I want you to kill someone of high standing.

As you wish, Master.

Syth put out the lamp by the window and went to sleep.

*   *   *

The next morning Queen Laurel called her war council together. The eight men filed in and stood before the queen. Syth was on her right, facing the council members. Laurel had not yet replaced Costuck on the council. They were two men short of a full council, but she dared not add anymore members. The risk to their lives was still great.

"Council members," she started. "I thank you for meeting together on such short notice. I know the hour is early and I apologize for waking you up, but I have something important to tell you all.

"Last night I had a dream. It was not the kind of dream that adults usually have, but more of a child's dream. I dreamt of ten great knights in dark red armor and pure white cloaks. The ten great Sentinels of old. I am sure you are all familiar with the stories?"

"Yes, My Queen," Gyles said. "All the children of the realm are familiar with the Ten Sentinels."

"That is good. If you all recall, the Ten Sentinels were the ten greatest knights in the kingdom. Blanderly was at war then and the king raised these knights to be protectors of the realm and its people. The country rallied around these brave men and peace was brought to the land once again. The people believed in these men. They gave everyone hope.

"After peace was restored, the king asked each one of the men what they would like as a reward. Every single one of them said that they wanted to return home to their families. Thus, the king disbanded the Sentinels and they were never needed again.

"Until now. What we need now is hope. The people of my city live in fear of their lives, and due to my failure to find the assassin, they have lost all hope. My people need to feel safe again. They need to feel like everything will be alright. They need the Ten Sentinels."

"You are going to raise up the Sentinels once again?" asked Jaxon.

"Yes. I plan to have the Ten Sentinels protect my people again."

"I agree with your plan," Sam said, "but how will you choose these men?"

"I will do something else that I believe will lift the hearts of the townsfolk. I will hold a tournament. The Ten Sentinels will be chosen from the winners of this tournament."

"That is a great idea, Your Majesty," said Crew. He didn't seem to be affected by the questioning. He wasn't offended that he had been a suspect in the murders at the palace. He did his job with great enthusiasm.

"Who will be eligible to compete in this tournament?" asked Trigg.

"Why, everyone," answered Laurel. "Anyone who thinks they can be a Sentinel is welcome to compete."

"I like it," said Sam. "You bring back the Sentinels to give your people something to believe in, and you do it in a way that will take their minds off their problems." He gave the queen a big smile. "It's brilliant!"

Laurel smiled back. "Thank you, Sam. Now, we just need to plan this thing. We will need ideas for the events and the rules. I need all your help to put this tournament on."

They all bowed to her. "Yes, Your Majesty."

"I am going to announce the tournament to the people today. Tomorrow morning I will want to hear all your ideas. Now, you are dismissed."

The men bowed again and left. Except Sam and Syth.

"Your Majesty," Sam said. "May I speak to you in private?"

"Of course." She turned to Syth. "Syth, please order the announcement that I will be addressing the people today in King's Square at noon."

"Yes, My Queen." The dark-skinned man bowed and left.

"What did you want to talk about, Sam?"

"Well, it's about Syth."

She looked at him. "What about him?"

He hesitated for a moment, as if he was afraid to say what was on his mind. "I don't trust him, Your Majesty."

"You don't trust him?" Sam shook his head. "And do you have a reason not to trust my personal guard?"

"Well, for one, what do we really know about him?"

"I know that he has been my faithful servant for almost two years now," she replied defensively. "I know he always does as I ask, and I've always felt safe around him, and my daughter has always felt safe around Jaden as well. I do know those things."

"Yeah but do you know where he came from or why he left? Do you know what he did before he arrived here? Do you know anything about him, Your Majesty?"

Laurel paused a moment to think. She didn't know the answer those questions. "No, I don't."

"And yet you have this man heading the investigation of the murders."

"Yes. He is the most capable man I know. And he is having a little bit of success. He has a lead on the one who is helping the assassin."

"Does he really?"

Laurel was taken aback by the question. "Do you mean tell me that you think he is making it up? That he really didn't see a man helping the assassin?"

"I don't have any proof," Sam answered, "but I don't believe he saw the assassin. I think he wants us to believe that there is a yellow-skinned man running rampant through the city on a killing spree. But he might be the spy. He might even be committing the murders."

Laurel couldn't help but grow a little angry at his words. Syth was her friend. "If you have no proof, then why do you think these things?" She wasn't able to keep the anger out of her voice.

"Forgive me, Your Majesty. I meant no offense. I know that Syth is your trusted advisor and guardian."

"He is more than that," Laurel said, more gently this time. "Syth is my friend. I have lost my husband, my son, and my daughter. Syth is all I have left. He has been with my family for almost two years."

"I know, Your Majesty. But I cannot just turn away from my gut instinct. I believe that you are in danger as long as Syth is around."

She barked a laugh. "Syth would never harm me. If he wanted to, he could have a hundred times before now."

"Think about it, Your majesty. The killings didn't happen until Syth came here. Correct?"

"Yes," Laurel had to agree. "But he had been here for a long time before they did."

"True," Sam said. "But he couldn't have started killing people just after he got here, now could he?"

"No."

"And you said that he is the most capable person here, correct?"

"Yes."

"Do you think him capable enough to pull these killings off without getting caught if he wanted to?"

"Definitely."

"Then we can't rule him out, Your Majesty."

Laurel thought about it for a moment. "No, I guess we can't. You're right. But what would you have me do?"

"Well, for starters you can keep him away from our war meetings. If he is a spy, then we definitely don't want him to know what our battle plans are going to be."

"Alright. But how would I keep him away without rousing his suspicions?" They both thought about it for a moment. "I know," said Laurel. "I can have him step up his efforts to find the assassin and his accomplice. That will keep him busy and out of the meetings."

"That's a good idea. Now, are you going to allow Syth to compete in the tournament?"

"I had planned on it. I had a feeling that he would be one of the ten. Do you think that is a bad idea?"

"I don't know. How do the townsfolk feel about him?"

"I don't know."

"Well, everyone knows he is an outsider. I wonder if they would feel comfortable having him as one of the Sentinels. They might not trust him as much as they would men from Blanderly."

"That is true. I will have to think on it."

"I also want to have him watched."

"Watched? Don't you think he would notice?"

"Not if the watchers are subtle. We only need to watch him at night. That is when all the murders have occurred. I will post men in the hall outside his sleeping quarters, and window at night."

"His window?" Laurel asked. "Do you really think that is necessary?"

"If Syth is the killer then I don't think he would leave the palace through the main entrance. He would sneak out, so he wasn't spotted."

"That is true. Alright. Do what you will, but I don't want you to think that I believe you. I will not believe that Syth is the assassin until I find concrete proof. Do you understand?

"Yes, Your Majesty."

"You are in charge of this little investigation of yours. I am not going to command men to watch my friend. All commands will come from you. I will have no part in it until it is necessary. But I give you leave to use whatever means you feel necessary to find out if Syth is the killer short of throwing him in a cell and interrogating him."

"I understand, Your Majesty."

"If you don't find any evidence of your suspicion, then I want this matter dropped. I will not have you hunting Syth because you don't like him. Is that clear?"

"Yes, Your Majesty. And thank you for understanding."

"Is there anything else, Sam?"

"No, Your Majesty."

"Then you may go." She couldn't keep the ice out of her voice. Sam was just trying to protect her, but she couldn't help but be angry at him for accusing her friend of doing such terrible things.

Sam bowed and took his leave. Although Laurel didn't want them to, her thoughts kept returning to what Sam had said about Syth. Could it be true? Could Syth really be the assassin? It would explain why they could learn nothing from the men they had questioned about helping the assassin. Syth could be making the whole thing up.

She hoped it wasn't true, not only because Syth was her friend, but also because if he was the assassin then they were all in grave danger. The yellow-skinned assassin that had murdered her husband had sounded terrifying from the accounts she had heard, but she was positive that Syth was even more dangerous.

Over the hours that followed she tried to think what she would do if they discovered that Syth was committing the murders. She came up with no answer. She counted on Syth. He was all she had left. She truly hoped he was innocent because she didn't know what she would do without her dark-skinned protector and friend.

When noon came and she stood before the townsfolk on a wooden platform they had built for her that morning, she couldn't help but glance over at Syth, who stood on her right. The thoughts and feelings that came to her were not ones that she had expected. She had thought that she would be able to look upon him and see her protector, but instead she saw Syth as a potential threat to her kingdom. She forced herself to not look at him again.

She made her announcement, and the reaction she received from the crowd was the one she had been hoping for. What Gyles had said about all the children in Blanderly knowing the story of the Ten Sentinels was true. It was a story that every Blanderly person was proud of. All young boys dreamed of being a Sentinel while they played. All young girls imagined being rescued by one. The sound of the crowd's cheering was deafening, and it lifted Laurel's heart.

When she announced that they would have a tournament two weeks from that day, the response was almost as good. Everyone enjoyed a celebration. It took peoples' minds off their daily troubles. It would give them something to cheer for and get excited about.

She would have liked to hold the tournament sooner, but something of this magnitude would take time to put together. They needed time for word to be sent all over the country, and time for the participants to arrive. She was sure that hundreds of men would come looking for fame and glory. It would be a child's dream come true to become a Sentinel.

She was pleased with the crowd's reaction, but she had a lot of work to do, so she took her leave and returned to the palace.

Todd leaned against a tree as he watched the lit window. He was the one charged with watching Syth tonight. He was not happy about the job; no one would have been. Everyone was intimidated by the dark-skinned warrior. But if he was lucky, Syth would never appear and he could go back to bed. He had been waiting for hours already and had seen nothing. It was getting difficult to stay awake.

Suddenly, something obscured the light coming from the window. A figure had appeared and to Todd's astonishment began to descend the wall. Fear suddenly overwhelmed the young soldier. *He's climbing down the wall! He's coming!*

The figure dropped to the ground, disappearing from view. Todd drew his sword and stood on his tiptoes, trying to see Syth. He saw nothing.

What should I do now? Should I report to Sam or wait until morning? Finally deciding that there was nothing to see, he stopped looking for Syth and turned to go back to the palace. *I will report this at once,* he decided.

He took two steps and came face-to-face with Syth. Todd stopped dead in his tracks.

"Were you spying on me?" Syth asked.

Todd could only whimper. He knew he was going to die.

"Not very smart of you," Syth said. Todd saw a flash of movement, then saw no more.

25

Aiden rode beside his uncle on their way to the temple. Veronna rode on the other side of David, while everyone else rode behind. David requested that his niece and nephew ride with him so they could get to know each other better. Veronna jumped at the chance while Aiden grudgingly agreed. He saw the attitude that his father had towards his uncle, so Aiden couldn't help but be a little suspicious of his motives. He wished that Portia was riding next to him, but she had stayed behind out of respect for his uncle's wishes.

David was telling them about the Paladins. "We are considered the finest fighters in the country. Possibly the world. The reason for that is we are God's chosen warriors. We have the power of God with us when we go to battle. He protects us. But there is a catch."

"What is it?" Veronna asked, wide-eyed. She was hanging on their uncle's every word.

"We have to be worthy of God's protection. We have to live the way he would have us live. Otherwise, we are on our own, and that is a scary thought."

"David…" Aiden began, but his uncle interrupted him.

"Uncle David," he said.

"What?"

"Please call me, Uncle David."

"Why? What is the difference?"

"Using the title uncle shows respect."

"Well, I will call you uncle when you earn my respect. Until then, I will call you David."

Veronna gasped. "Aiden!"

David seemed to consider a moment. "Alright then. How about I call you Tim's son until you earn mine."

Suddenly Aiden felt very ashamed.

"I'm sorry Uncle. I didn't mean it."

"There is a difference in the way Veronna acts with me and the way you do. Why do you have a problem with me, Aiden?"

Aiden sighed. "I think it is because of my dad. He seems uncomfortable around you. He doesn't seem to want to be around you. I guess it has just rubbed off on me. I'm sorry."

"I understand. You must remember that your dad and I were best friends when we were younger. But we didn't get along very well the last couple weeks he was here. We had several confrontations. That is why he feels uncomfortable around me. But that doesn't mean that I care about you two any less, or him."

Veronna smiled at her uncle, and Aiden said, "Okay, Uncle David."

"Now," said David, "What were you going to say before?"

"Before? Oh yeah. I was going to ask if any Paladins ever die if God is protecting them."

"Yes, they die. It doesn't happen very often, but every once in a while, one will. If it is there time, there is no stopping it. But like I said, it doesn't happen very often."

"Oh."

"But if all of us are living the way we are supposed to and we have God's protection, there is not a force on earth that can stop us."

"So," said Aiden, "what was my dad like when he was younger?"

David smiled. "He was the best."

"He still is," Veronna interrupted.

"I'm sure he is. He was funny, caring, charming, a natural fighter. And most importantly, he was a man of great faith. His faith seemed unshakable, until my sister died. I was shocked that he lost it.

"He was a great leader of the Paladins. Even though God helps us all, none of us could stand against your dad or defeat him in training. He was the best of us." Aiden smiled at that. He could easily picture his dad like that.

They passed the training yard and saw several men training. They had every kind of weapon you could think of. Some used swords, some axes, some maces or flails. About half also had a shield. They were all fully armored and didn't look to be taking it easy on their opponents.

"Uncle David," Aiden said. "If God protects you in battle, why do you train so hard?"

"It is all part of doing our part. We have to do what we can for God to bless us. If we just sit around and expect God to do everything for us, he won't. It is like a partnership. We have to show him that we are willing to keep our end of the bargain."

"That makes sense," Veronna said.

"Can anyone be a Paladin?" Aiden asked.

"Anyone who is worthy can," his uncle replied. "You have to be worthy both as a fighter and spiritually. The spirituality is probably the more important part of it. It takes a special kind of person to be one."

"Are there any women Paladins?" asked Veronna.

"No. All Paladins hold the power of the priesthood. That is the power to act in God's name. Only men can hold it."

"Why?"

"Because women have other privileges and responsibilities that men don't. We each do our part. If one gender has all the responsibilities, that would be unfair. It all works out."

Veronna nodded her understanding.

"Do you have a standing army besides the Paladins?" asked Aiden. As they traveled towards the temple, he had not seen any soldiers walking the streets. They had been everywhere in Kingston and Blanden.

"No. At times of war volunteers enlist into the army and help defend the country. But we are very seldom at war. Most people are afraid to invade our lands, and everyone knows we do not attack other people. We are mostly left alone and we live peaceful lives."

"So why do you need the Paladins?"

"Because there are sometimes people who decide that the world would be a better place without the People of God in it. Or they want our land and try to take it from us. It doesn't happen often, but it happens."

"Has it happened since you became a Paladin?" asked Veronna.

"Yes," their uncle replied softly. "Once."

"What happened?" asked Aiden.

"It was terrible. War and battle are always terrible." Aiden didn't think his uncle was going to say anymore, but after a few moments he did. "The People of Order hate anyone who does not believe the way they do. They think they are God's chosen people and therefore are perfectly within their rights to take whatever piece of land they want in God's name. About ten years ago their king decided that they wanted to take Zion.

"Knights of Order have the reputation of being incredibly well trained. They are haughty and prideful and do not think that a follower of Chaos, which is what they call anyone who is not of their faith, can stand up to them in a fight. That is why they invaded Zion.

"When we go through training our teachers try to explain the horrors of war. The blood, the pain, the sound of men and horses dying. The fear. But nothing can prepare you for a battle. I'm sure you know exactly what I am talking about, Aiden. You have probably experienced the same things in your capacity as a mercenary. And you Veronna. You haven't taken part in any fighting, but you have stood aside in fear and watched your enemies attack your family. You also know what I am talking about." The siblings nodded.

"Well, I experienced all these things that my teachers told me about. We had God with us that day and we turned the Order warriors back.

That was one of the days that a Paladin fell in battle. But we do not mourn for our fallen brothers. We know they are with God. But we do mourn for their loved ones who will not see them again in this life time.

"Anyway, a long story short, we drove them back and they have never attacked us again. Besides that, I have occasionally done battle with the Zantan Robbers, but that feels different. They are an abomination before God, they are not human anymore. It is harder to kill your fellow sons and daughters of God. I hope I never will have to do that again."

"I'm sorry you had to go through that, Uncle David," Veronna said.

David smiled. "You have a good heart, Veronna. Just like your mother." Veronna smiled at that.

David asked them to tell him about themselves and they spent the rest of the trip to the temple talking about their lives. Despite his earlier misgivings, Aiden began to like his uncle. He laughed a lot and his humor seemed genuine. He had kind eyes and didn't treat them like little children. He could tell why he had been best friends with their dad.

Finally, they reached the temple. If it looked huge from a distance, it was enormous up close. It was the biggest thing Aiden had ever seen, besides mountains.

"Wow," Portia said. "It is huge!"

David grinned at everyone's expressions.

"Why does it need to be so big?" Dustin asked. "What is it used for?"

It was Tim who answered. "This is the headquarters of the religion. The prophet and his assistants live here, plus all the important issues of the church are taken care of here. There is no wasted space. Every single room in this building is used. Believe it or not, the building needs to be this big."

"Wow," Veronna said quietly.

David led the group inside. They entered a large room with a huge oak desk on the right of the doorway. Several people were sitting behind the desk. Every one of them smiled at the group as they filed in. The walls were a brilliant white. The floor was white tile with a large colorful rug that covered most of the floor. There were several small tables with potted plants and flowers. Every wall had a door.

The women behind the desk all wore nice dresses. Not fancy or richly decorated, but nice. The men wore white shirts with collars. Aiden couldn't see their pants, but he guessed they were very nice.

"How may we help you, David?" asked a smiling older woman.

"I have brought these good people here to see the prophet," David answered. "He is expecting us."

"He is?"

David nodded.

"Alright. Do you know the way?"

"Yes. I have been there many times."

With that, David led the group through the door directly across from the entrance to the building.

They entered a hallway. Once again, the walls and floor were white. "The white represents purity," David explained. "God is pure and only pure things can be in his presence. We strive to become pure in this life so we can be with God in the next."

Aiden didn't know what to think about the existence of a next life, but he didn't say anything.

The building was beautiful. All the wall and floors in every hallway and every room were white. The only color came from the rugs and paintings on the walls. The rugs were beautiful. They were of every different color and design. The paintings ranged from nature scenes to people. Aiden guessed that the people were important figures among the People of God.

There was a quiet reverence to the place. The people they passed by always spoke softly. Even David spoke softly when he addressed the group. Aiden couldn't imagine anyone speaking loudly in this place. It just seemed like the wrong thing to do.

It took a long time to reach the prophet. His chambers were near the top of the temple. They went through numerous hallways and rooms, up countless staircases, past dozens of people who lived and worked in the building. They even saw a group of three Paladins coming from the opposite direction. Their eyes widened when they saw who David was escorting.

The three men stopped, standing side by side, so the group couldn't pass by. "Good morning David," the one in the center said. "How are you doing on this fine day?"

Aiden's uncle shook the man's hand. "I'm doing quite well, thank you."

Before David could say anything else the other man's attention fell on Tim. "I don't believe my eyes," the man said. "Timmond, is it really you?"

Tim looked uncomfortable. "Yes, Reese. It truly is me."

"It has been so long."

"Yes," Tim agreed. "Fifteen years."

"And these two must be your kids." He looked at Aiden and Portia.

"Yes," said Tim. "No. I mean, yes, this is my son, Aiden. But this," he gently grabbed Veronna by the arm and pulled her forward, "is my daughter Veronna."

Reese smiled warmly. "Ah yes, I see it now. You look just like your mother."

"Thank you," Veronna said.

There was an awkward silence until David said, "Reese is now the commander of the Paladins."

"Well, congratulations," said Tim, shaking his hand again. "Did they replace me with you?"

"No," Reese replied. What was that look in his face? Irritation? "They replaced you with Brandon, but he has since received a new calling."

"Really? He was the perfect man to replace me. What did they call him to be?"

It was David that answered. "First councilor."

"Oh. I see. Well, they made a good choice in making you the new commander, Reese. I am happy for you."

"Thank you."

David spoke up. "We'd best be on our way. Turner is expecting us."

"Oh, by all means." The three Paladins stepped aside to let the group pass.

Aiden looked at his father as they walked. "You two don't really like each other, do you?"

Tim chuckled. "You caught on to that, huh?" Aiden nodded. "Well, we were kind of rivals when we were younger. It was a healthy rivalry, nothing dangerous. But we didn't like each other. I turned out to be better than him at almost everything we did. He grew very bitter. Especially when they called me to be the commander. He wanted to be it." He chuckled again. "I can't believe he finally made it."

They continued on and experienced no more delays. Up and up they went until they finally stood before a pair of double doors. They were well made, but plain. David opened them wide and led the group in.

The room was a lot smaller than Aiden had expected. He thought that a man as important as a prophet would have large, elaborate rooms. This room was barely big enough to fit the prophet, two other men who Aiden assumed were the prophet's councilors, and the mercenary group.

The prophet was sitting beside a small desk, writing in a book. His councilors each had their own desks, smaller than the prophet's, and they were each writing in their own books. They all put down their quills and looked up when the group entered. The prophet smiled and stood up when he saw David. Turner shook his hand and welcomed him. When Turner saw Tim, his smile looked forced. "Timmond."

"Hello Turner. I'm back."

"I see." The prophet was a tall man. Thin with broad shoulders. He was older, probably around sixty, but his white hair was thick and his hands were strong. His face was wrinkled, but there was a strength to it. His brown eyes were young and bright and looked like they belonged to a much younger man. Like all the men Aiden had seen in the temple, the prophet wore a white collared shirt. Since he was standing, Aiden could see the top of his pants. They looked to be of soft fabric, dark and neatly pressed. He was an impressive figure.

Tim introduced everyone in the group and Turner greeted them all warmly. Veronna was told once again that she looked just like her mother, and once again Veronna blushed and said thanks. The prophet introduced his two councilors. The first councilor was Brandon, a man a few years younger than the prophet. The second councilor was a much older man, small and frail looking with a soft voice. His name was Mark. There were not enough chairs for everyone, so the girls were allowed to sit while the men stood.

Turner and his councilors sat back down behind their desks. "Now," said the prophet, "tell me what brings you back here after all these years."

"Well, as you know," Tim began, "David found us and told us about a large group of Zantan Robbers and…"

Turner held up his hand and Tim stopped talking. "I know that," Turner said. "I wanted to know why you came back to Parken. What brought you back across the sea after fifteen years?"

Tim put a hand on Dana's shoulder. "Her father was murdered by a man that her brother hired. That man was a Zantan Robber. Her brother fled here afterwards and is planning to take over Blanderly with King Korlas's help. Dana's mother hired us to come after the prince and retrieve him."

"I see. And how are you going to do that?"

Tim shrugged. "I don't know yet. I have been thinking about it the entire trip, but I haven't come up with a concrete plan yet. But I will."

"Well, you have a very dangerous mission ahead of you. You do realize that Korlas is a Dark Paladin?"

"Yes."

"And do you know that he has a wizard from the east as a counselor?"

"I did not realize that," Tim admitted. "But I have dealt with wizards before. We will be fine."

"If what I hear is true," Turner said, "this wizard is very powerful."

"What kind of wizard is he?"

"A kind you have never encountered before."

"Really?" said Tim. "Can he do some kind of new magic that no one has seen before?"

Turner looked at Tim for a moment without answering. "No. He can do every kind of magic."

The statement surprised Tim. "That is impossible. No one can do that."

"This man can. He can control the elements, he can move objects with his mind, he can create elaborate illusions, and he can raise the dead and control them. He has the ability to see events around him and manipulate them. Yes Timmond, he can do anything. That is what you will be facing if you continue your quest. Not to mention King Korlas himself and his entire army. Do you still want to continue with this job?"

Tim didn't hesitate with his answer. "Yes. I gave my word to Queen Laurel and I will not go back on it. I will continue."

"Well, in that case, maybe we can lend a little help. I will have five Paladins accompany you to Parkos."

"We would be truly thankful, Turner."

David spoke up. "Turner, I would like to be one of the Paladins that go with them, if I may."

"Of course, David," the prophet said. "I was planning on asking you to go anyway. I will pray and choose four others."

Brandon stood up. "Turner, I would also like to go. I was the commander of the Paladins once."

"Yes, you were, and a good one, too," Turner agreed. "But I feel that it would not be right for you to go. You are now my first councilor. That life is no longer yours. I am sorry, but I think it best if you stay here."

"Whatever you say," said Brandon and he sat back down.

Turner turned back to Tim. "Now, when would you like to depart?"

"Actually," said Tim "I would ask something of you."

"And what would that be?"

"We have two friends who are headed this way. We were supposed to meet up with them just north of Kingston, but we were forced to leave early. Now they don't know where we are. If you could send out someone to meet them like you did with us, we would appreciate it."

"I think I can do that. What are their names?"

"There is a large young man named Layne, and another young man who is a wizard. His name is Tyler."

"I will pray about them too and send out someone to find them and bring them here."

"Thank you, Turner. You have been most helpful."

"Before you go," said Turner, "there are a few people who would like to see you. Brandon, if you would show them inside please."

Brandon stood up and walked to the door. He opened it and said, "You may come in now."

Four people walked into the room. Two men and two women, all older. All four looked emotional and rushed toward the group. One couple, the man tall and thin, the woman a little shorter but also thin, went straight to Tim.

"Hello son," the man said. He was grinning from ear to ear. He put his right hand out towards Tim.

"Hi Dad," Tim answered and, ignoring the extended hand, pulled his father into a warm embrace. He also pulled his mother in as well. "It is so good to see you," Tim whispered.

The other couple, both average height and a little on the heavy side, grinned at David as they passed but went straight for Aiden and Veronna. "You must be Timmond's and Crystal's kids," the man said.

"Yes," said Veronna. "I am Veronna and this is Aiden."

"Yes, we know," said the woman. "We knew you both when you were younger. We are your mother's parents…your grandparents." Veronna threw her arms around her grandparents and Aiden followed suite.

It was very overwhelming for Aiden. Suddenly, he was meeting all these family members he never knew. He was swarmed with hugs and kisses and kind words. He found himself struggling vainly to get out from the middle of everything. He finally succeeded and went to stand over by Dustin, who was on the outside of the group by himself.

He didn't look happy. It took a minute for Aiden to realize what was wrong.

"Do not worry, the men who Turner sends to find Layne will succeed."

"I know," the ex-knight replied. "It is just that I see you surrounded by all of your family and I just feel bad that mine isn't here with me."

"I understand," Aiden said.

Veronna ran over to the two men. "Come on," she said, grinning from ear to ear. Aiden could tell she was enjoying herself. "We are going to grandma and grandpa's house to get to know each other better. Let's go!"

"Which one?" Aiden asked, but his sister had already run out towards the door. Aiden and Dustin looked at each other, then followed.

26

Campbell stepped off the last step into the bustling common room of the inn. He was a large man, with fat bulging up over his belt, and the trek down the stairs from his room had winded him. He had to brace one arm against the wall and catch his breath. When he was ready, he made his way to the bar and sat heavily on a stool. It barely held his bulk.

"Innkeeper. A word please."

The innkeeper, who was even fatter than Campbell, made his way over to the merchant. "Yes?"

"I plan on leaving on the morrow and I require men to guard my wagons. I already have five men, but I think I will need at least a few more. Do you have any regular customers who might wish to hire themselves as guardsmen?"

"Not that I know of," said the large innkeeper. "But you are welcome to take a look at the people who come in tonight and offer to hire anyone you wish."

"Thank you."

"Will you be wanting anything?"

"Yes, may I have a pitcher of ale?"

"Of course."

"And a leg of lamb and some bread and cheese wouldn't be amiss either."

"Of course. Anything you want."

The innkeeper hustled off to get the merchant food and drink. Campbell was very wealthy and wasn't stingy with his coin. The innkeeper gave Campbell whatever he wanted as quickly as possible. He knew that Campbell would make it worth his time.

After a serving girl brought him the pitcher of ale and a tall glass, he turned his back to the bar and watched the men in the room.

Most of them he passed over with just a quick glance. They seemed to be farmers and shopkeepers, just gathering with friends for a drink at the local inn before they went home for the night. These were not the kinds of people he was looking for. He would need men who knew their way around a sword or an axe, because the roads were treacherous these days with bandits and goblins and other creatures attacking travelers.

Campbell ate his dinner, finished his ale, and ordered some wine. Then he went back to watching the men in the inn. A few men went upstairs to bed, a few more came into the common room from the street, but none of the newcomers were what Campbell was looking for. Time passed, and Campbell was beginning to think it was hopeless, when two men walked into the inn. One was a large man with a beat-up face. The other was shorter than the first, but still tall, thin, and had a short-trimmed goatee. He had a black eye. They sat down and ordered dinner from a serving girl that went to their table.

Campbell watched them as they ate. Especially the large man. He had a hard look to him that most of the other men in the room didn't. *Now that is the kind of man I need.* He stood up from his stool, about to make his way over to the two men when someone walked by their table and accidentally bumped into it. The table jerked and the pitcher of wine that was on it tipped over, spilling red liquid onto the larger man.

The man shot up out of his chair, knocking it backwards onto the floor. The man who had accidentally bumped into the table put his hands up and backed away. It didn't calm the big man down. The big man grabbed the other man and punched him in the face. Blood spurted from the other man's nose as his head snapped back. The large man's companion jumped to his feet as well and yelled for him to stop, but he didn't listen. He punched the unfortunate fellow again.

The man was a local, and several of the other locals got to their feet. The smaller newcomer looked around and saw what the other men were doing. He grabbed his companion's arm, but the big man shook the hand off and tried to punch the other man a third time.

Before the blow landed however, a local man grabbed the big man's arm. Another man grabbed the injured man and tried to pull him away from the newcomer. When he failed to do so a second man joined him. Together, they succeeded in pulling the injured man away from the grip of the large man.

With his victim now out of reach, the big man turned on the man who was holding his arm. He brought his other arm around and landed a punch on the side of the man's head. The other man punched back and landed a solid blow in the newcomer's stomach. The newcomer simply grunted and kneed his opponent in the groin. The man went down. The large man laughed and went to find another opponent.

Campbell saw a local man grab the smaller newcomer. The newcomer said something and put his hands up. He wanted nothing to do with the fight. Ignoring him, the local man picked him up, held him over his head, and slammed down onto the table. There was a loud crack, but the table held. The man groaned in pain and just laid there. His attacker let him be.

The big man was struggling. He grabbed one man and threw him away, punched another in the gut and then pushed him to the floor, then he was grabbed from behind by two men and held in place. A third man punched him in the face, then in the gut. Before he could punch him a third time, the big man kicked him in the chest, sending him to the floor.

With a roar the man pulled both his arms forward, bringing the two men holding on with them. He head-butted the man holding his left arm, and when that man let go and fell to the ground, he grabbed the other man and threw him away.

The strange thing was, the large man was laughing the entire time. He was enjoying himself.

Four more men came for the newcomer, but before they could attack there was a whistle from the inn's doorway. Everyone stopped in their tracks and looked to the doorway to find the village's constable with a silver whistle to his lips. Behind him were two more men. All three wore armor and carried swords.

"What is the meaning of this?" demanded the constable. "Where is the innkeeper?"

The fat man who ran the inn had been hiding behind the bar during the fight. At the sound of the constable's voice he stood up, smoothed his rumpled apron, and said, "I am the innkeeper."

"What happened here?"

"Well, these two newcomers started a brawl. It is all their fault. Arrest them!"

"Is this true?" the constable asked the newcomers.

"Sort of," the smaller one said. "I didn't do anything. He started it all. I was just minding my own business and he started a fight. Arrest him!"

The big man glared at him.

"What? Don't look at me like that. It was your fault. I'm sick of you getting us in trouble and getting me beat up!"

"Alright," said the constable. "You're both coming with us."

The three men came into the inn and started toward the newcomers. "Wait!" The three men stopped and everyone in the inn looked at Campbell. "Don't arrest those men. Please. I want to hire them."

"Hire us?" asked the smaller newcomer.

"Hire them?" asked the constable.

"Y…yes. I want to hire them as guards for my wagons. I need them. Please don't arrest them."

The constable looked at the innkeeper.

"Well, they can't stay here!" he howled.

"What if I pay you extra for a room for them?" asked Campbell. He had never seen anyone fight like the big man. Outnumbered, he had still held his own. And that was with his bare hands. He was exactly what Campbell was looking for. He didn't want the smaller man, but he guessed that if he hired one, he would have to take both of them.

"I want triple the normal rate," said the innkeeper.

"Triple? That is outrageous!"

"Look what they did to my common room! Look what they did to my customers!"

"Alright, alright," said Campbell. "I will pay you triple if you let them stay here tonight."

"And I want you to give each man that big ox injured ten gold coins for their injuries."

Campbell looked at the big man again before answering. "Alright, I will do all that you ask if you just let them stay here tonight and leave with me tomorrow."

"Wait a minute." said the smaller newcomer. "You should probably ask us first before you start making plans."

"Okay," said the merchant. "Would you like to be guards for my wagons? I will pay you."

The big man walked right up to Campbell and looked him in the eye. "Give me two hand axes and a battle ax, preferably a large one, and we will be your guards."

"Hold on a minute!" said the smaller one. "We don't even know where he is going!"

"I am going to Parkos to deliver to the palace. To King Korlas him-self. That is why I need guards. It is very important."

"See Tyler," said the bigger one. "He is going the same way as we are. We should join him."

"Alright." Tyler sighed and turned to the merchant. "Buy us another dinner, a pitcher of wine, and that room for the night, and we will go with you."

*   *   *

The next day found Layne walking beside one of the four wagons that Campbell was taking to King Korlas. The wagons were overflowing with weapons, rugs, chests, and several other items.

The merchant had hired five other men from the inn besides Layne and Tyler. Two of them were involved in the fight. Whenever they saw Layne and Tyler, they glared at them and fingered their weapons. They made Tyler nervous, but Layne paid them no mind.

Campbell was thrilled when he found out that Tyler was a mage. He had admitted that he didn't want to take Tyler along after he had watched the fight, but now he says it was worth the money he had to spend to keep them from being arrested. Layne told Tyler that now that the men from the inn knew he was a wizard, they wouldn't cause any trouble. But the wizard didn't believe him.

Yesterday was not the first fight they had been in. It wasn't the second either. It was the third. They were thrown out of every inn they visited, because Layne couldn't stop starting fights. He even tried to start one on the road with a pair of travelers passing by, but Tyler stopped him. He said that if you started a fight in an inn, it was just a brawl, but if you started one out on the road, it was considered banditry. That stopped him.

But the mage was unable to stop Layne from fighting in the inns. He started them on purpose. He was looking for a fight each time. It was the only way to control the rage that overtook him when he wasn't fighting.

He glanced over at his companion and saw how bad his face looked. He almost felt guilty. It was his fault that the mage had gotten beat up. He would have felt even guiltier if the wizard had lifted a finger to help out during the fights. But no, he had just stood to the side and watched as Layne had taken on multiple foes at a time. It almost served him right that he had been attacked because he had been in Layne's company. Now, Tyler was furious with him.

Layne ached all over, every step hurt. But it was a good ache. It told him he had been doing what he was meant to do, fighting. And it made him smile to think that he had given much worse than he had received. He only had to glance over at the two guards who had been in the fight yesterday to see the truth of that.

They were a dozen in total, if you didn't count the men driving the horses that were pulling the wagons, and the merchant. The merchant was the only one who was mounted. His bulk was being carried by a large, spirited stallion. The horse they took from the city guard that confronted them when they escaped was tethered to the rear wagon. Tyler had planned on riding, but the merchant discouraged him. He said that if he was the only one riding, the other guards would get angry and there would be trouble. So, Tyler walked with the rest of them.

Layne put his hands on the heads of the two hand axes that were strapped to his waist. It felt good to have axes again. He was too clumsy with a sword, but he was an expert with an axe. He could feel the weight of the battle axe strapped to his back. It was comfortable. It felt right. He had given the sword to one of the other guards.

They stopped at midday for a lunch of bread, apples, and dried meat, and they washed it down with warm water. During lunch, the merchant started to become antsy. Layne asked him what was wrong.

"Rock gnomes," the fat man answered. "This is their territory. They live in a huge rock formation a couple miles off the road. Sightings are rare, but every once in a while they will attack merchants traveling in the area and steal all their goods. I know a man who had this happen to him once. He said it was terrifying. He lost all his goods and half of his guards. That is one of the reasons I wanted more men."

"What are rock gnomes?" Layne asked.

It was Tyler who answered. "Rock gnomes are short creatures who have skin that looks and feels like rock. But it isn't. The only weapons they use are rocks or stone clubs. They also live in rock, on the side of cliffs or in rock formations. They are very strong, and their hard skin is resistant to all but the strongest weapons. Maces and flails work best, but swords are almost useless against them."

"But sightings are rare, right?" asked Layne.

"Yes," answered Campbell.

"We should be okay then."

"Maybe," said the merchant. "But sometimes they attack. So I would like to get out of this area as quickly as possible. And when we do make camp the men on watch must be very alert."

They continued their journey after that and made good time that day. Everyone was footsore and tired when they made camp for the night, but spirits were high because they saw no sign of rock gnomes. Only Layne's spirits were low. He hadn't fought in hours and he could feel the rage creeping back into him again.

They woke up with the sun the next day and Campbell told the group that they should be out of rock gnome territory by late afternoon. It was late morning when a rock hit one of the guards in the head and knocked him out cold.

It had come from behind a steep hill on the right side of the road, so everyone turned in that direction. Suddenly, dozens of rocks filled the air and fell upon the men. Most were the size of Layne's fist, but a few were even bigger. Two more men were hit and injured.

"Rock gnomes!" Campbell cried. He struggled to get under one of the wagons. Several other men were doing the same. Layne quickly realized that there wouldn't be enough room for him and Tyler under the wagons, so he pulled the wizard behind the closest one and crouched down, trying to become as small a target as possible. Rocks were landing all around them. One hit the wagon above them and broke a board with a loud crack. The board came off and hit Layne a glancing blow on the shoulder. It hurt, but it wasn't bad enough to hinder him.

The barrage of rocks finally ended. Men scrambled out from under the wagons and Layne and Tyler got to their feet. Only Campbell stayed where he was.

Suddenly, a dozen small creatures were running down the hill towards the group. Tyler had been right. They were short and their skin was the dull grey of stone. Their faces were flat, and they had two holes where their noses should have been. Their ears were tiny, and they only had wisps of dark hair on their heads. Their legs were short, their arms long and lean, and they all carried crude clubs made of rock. Their only clothing were small loincloths around their wastes.

With a high-pitched shriek, they descended on the men. Layne remembered what Tyler said about swords being worthless against them and he was glad for his axes. The mage had said that only the strongest weapons were of any use, so he took his massive battle axe off his back and stepped out from behind the wagon to face his foes.

The gnomes hit them like a wave. One man broke his sword on a gnome's chest, then the gnome hit him with its stone club. Blood sprayed and the man fell. Layne swung his axe, but the gnome he was aiming for jumped back out of the way. It swung its club but missed. Layne took a chip out of its head with the next swing, but it didn't faze the creature.

"Can't you do anything?" Layne asked Tyler as he dodged another swing. "Can't you throw it around like a doll or something?"

"I told you," Tyler answered from behind the wagon, "they are not really made of rock, they just look like they are. I have no power with them."

Layne's axe took off a finger, then a chunk of elbow. The gnome shrieked and kept coming. "Layne, look out," Tyler said. Layne glanced behind him to see another gnome coming for him. He quickly stepped to the side. The club from the gnome he had been fighting swung past him harmlessly, but it hit the gnome that had come from behind. It crushed the unfortunate gnomes face and it hit the ground and didn't move again. Then Layne was attacking again.

Layne heard Campbell cry out. "My goods! They are taking all my goods! Stop them!"

Suddenly, several of the larger rocks that the gnomes had thrown at the group rose up from the ground. They hovered where they were for a second, then rushed straight for the gnomes who were pilfering the wagons. Several were hit, but only a few went down. The rest shrieked their high-pitched shriek and continued to dig through the wagons.

Layne was finally able to dispatch his foe. He had found a soft spot in the creature's head, just behind its ear. The gnomes were beginning to retreat to the hill. He stepped in front of them to bar their way, but most just ran around him. He swung his axe, his aim true, and he took down one gnome who had stolen several valuable rugs. He got another one who was taking away several large bags. Layne didn't know what the bags contained.

There were no more gnomes by the wagons. They were all either dead or scrambling up the hill with the stolen goods. "Go after them!" Campbell was yelling. He was running around and waving his hands in the air, trying to get his guards' attention. "Don't let them get away! They are taking my goods! Those goods are for the king!"

There were only seven men standing, including Layne and Tyler. Three were dead, their skulls bashed in or their chests crushed by the gnome's weapons, and two more were on the ground, moaning in pain. There were six dead rock gnomes.

Campbell was digging through the remnants of one of the wagons. He didn't notice that no one had moved to go after the creatures. "Where is it? I can't find it! It has to be here!"

"What are you looking for?" asked Tyler.

"A chest. A large wooden chest. It has an item in it that the king wants more than anything else I have. It is very important that I get it to him. If I don't, something very bad will happen to me, I know it." He continued to rummage through the cart. "It's not here. It's not here! They must have taken it!"

"Are you sure you put it in this wagon?" asked Layne. "Could it be in another one?"

"I'm certain I put it in this wagon. But I will check the others."

"We'll help you," Tyler said, and he and Layne looked through a wagon together. They searched every wagon, and Campbell searched the ones that the others searched first, but it was no use. The chest wasn't there.

Campbell dropped to the ground. "They've taken it," he said, and he began to weep.

Layne crouched down beside him. The feeling of rage was gone because of the fight he just had. He was almost back to his old self again. "Don't worry. We can go get the chest back for you."

"What?" asked Tyler.

Layne looked up at Tyler as the wizard stormed over. "We can get it back for him."

"Are you crazy?"

"What do you mean?"

Tyler pulled him up to his feet and started dragging him away. "Did you see those creatures? Did you see what only a dozen did to us? They killed three men and injured two others! There could be hundreds of these things in their lair!" When they were a hundred feet away from the rest of the group Tyler stopped. He lowered his voice. "What are you doing? Why would we go get the chest? That is for King Korlas; our enemy. If he wants what is in the chest so bad, we probably shouldn't help him get it."

"That is true," Layne agreed. "But should we just leave it in the hands of the rock gnomes? If it is some kind of weapon, they could use it to harm innocent travelers on the road."

"But if it is a weapon, then Korlas will use it. He might use it against the people of your homeland."

"What if we get the chest but don't bring it back to Campbell? What if we just take it and go on our way?"

"You would lie to him?"

"Wouldn't you?"

"Well, if you are intent on protecting the innocent, you might think about Campbell. I believe he was right when he said that bad things will happen to him if he doesn't deliver the chest to the king. Do you want that over your head?"

"No." Layne thought for a moment. "So, what do you think we should do?"

"I don't know. Our main goal is to meet up with your group. We will be delayed if we go after the chest."

"But I think that going after the chest is the right thing to do. We will figure out what to do with it after we get it back." They walked back to the rest of the group. "I just hope that the other guards will agree to come too."

About thirty minutes later Layne, Tyler, and the three guards who agreed to accompany them looked over the crest of the hill at the valley floor below. They were lying on their stomachs, trying to stay as low as possible so the rock gnomes patrolling the area wouldn't spot them. The little creatures were everywhere in the valley. There were a dozen or so scrambling around on the side of the huge rock formation they called home.

The rock formation soared hundreds of feet in the air. It was wide at the base and stayed the same width about halfway up, but then it gradually narrowed the higher it went. The top couldn't have been more than a few feet in diameter. There was a small black hole at the bottom that served as an entrance.

"Is there another way in?" Layne wondered aloud. He didn't expect an answer.

Tyler answered anyway. "There looks to be smoke coming out of the top. There must be a hole up there. But since I don't use wind magic, that is of no use. We couldn't get up to the top. And even if we could, it might be a straight drop once we got in the hole. We could fall to our deaths. No, I think the only entrance is that one right there." He pointed at the hole.

Layne gave the wizard a look but didn't say anything. He studied the formation for a few more minutes, then he turned back to Tyler. "Since the formation is rock, what can you do with it that would get us inside?"

"Well, I could do any number of things with it. But I don't know how many of them would get us inside."

"The first problem is all the gnomes that are outside of the formation. There is no way that the five of us can get through all those creatures. We will need you to use your magic to get us through them."

"Okay. There is a lot of stone there, so I should be able to do that. But it might mean killing every one of them. Is that alright with you?"

That was the question. Was Layne alright with killing hundreds of creatures that probably had nothing to do with the theft of Campbell's property? Only a few of the creatures had attacked the caravan. But, if they were left alive, would all these gnomes attack another innocent traveler in the future?

"Yes. We will do what is necessary. I am afraid that if we leave these creatures alive, they will prey off unsuspecting travelers in the future."

"But we don't know that for certain," the wizard argued. Layne could tell that Tyler wasn't keen on the idea of killing so many gnomes.

"That is true. Just kill as many as you need to get us in there."

"Alright. I guess I could blast the rock from the formation and take out the gnomes that way."

"Alright," said Layne. "Will that take a lot of effort?"

"Yes."

"Well, since there are several gnomes right by the door, if the rocks get too close and block the entrance, will you have enough mental energy left to clear them out of the way so we can get in?"

Tyler thought about it. "I might. We will have to see."

"Alright," said Layne. "Do it then."

"I'm afraid I won't be any good in a fight afterwards."

"That's alright. If you can take out the gnomes outside of the formation and get us in, the other three and I will go search for the chest while you hide out here and rest." He turned to the three guards. "Do you guys agree with that plan?" They all nodded. "Alright then. That is what we will do. Just get us in safely Tyler, and we'll do the rest."

"Alright," said the earth mage. He concentrated. Layne glanced over at their three companions again. They had all traded in their swords for axes. One even had a large hammer. Luckily, neither of the men that had been involved in the bar fight had come with them. That could have been a bad situation. Those men had decided to stay and guard the carts.

For a moment nothing happened. Tyler just lay there with a look of concentration on his face. Layne was beginning to wonder if the task was too much for the wizard when the side of the rock formation facing the hill that the group was on exploded outward in a shower of huge boulders and small stones. The sound made Layne and the other three men flinch. Tyler, who had been on his elbows, collapsed in exhaustion.

Boulders rained down on the gnomes below. The handful of gnomes that had been crawling on the formation were thrown off along with the stone. Gnomes everywhere were being crushed. They scrambled around like ants, trying to get away. But there was no safety to be found. After several moments of intense sound and reverberation, the avalanche finally stopped. The men looked up to see the scene below them.

Nothing moved in the valley below. No more rock gnomes were on the formation. Everything was dead. There were little broken bodies all over the place. Layne felt disgusted, but it had had to be done. "It worked," one of the men cried. "It actually worked!"

"But now the opening is blocked," said Layne. It was true. The boulders came too close to the entrance and closed it off. "So now what do we do?"

"Well," Tyler said weakly. "If you make your way down to the formation, I might have enough strength to lift the boulders out of the way by the time you get there."

"Might?" asked another of the men.

"That is all I can say. I can promise you no more than that."

"Well," said Layne, "that seems to be our only option. We will try that." The men started to get to their feet. Layne stopped them with a motion of his hand. "We must be very careful. We have no idea how many of the gnomes remain inside." When the three men nodded their understanding, they all got to their feet and made their way down the hill to the valley below. Only Tyler remained behind.

The hill was large and the slope uneven, so it took a while for the men to reach the bottom. Tyler watched them go. He also scanned the area for any movement. There might be survivors, and they would be very angry.

The men made their way through the scattering of boulders and over dead bodies. Tyler thought he could faintly hear something, but when he tried to listen closer, the sound was gone. He had no idea what it could have been.

Suddenly, a dark wave of squirming forms came out of the hole at the top of the formation. Tyler realized it was the rock gnomes. Hundreds of them. They were shrieking in fury. They poured down the sides of the formation toward the ground.

He looked down at the group and saw that they were at the pile of boulders that blocked the entrance. They had also noticed the rock gnomes and were jumping up and down and waving their arms, trying to get Tyler's attention. Tyler had to hurry and get those boulders out of the way before the rock gnomes reached his companions. They wouldn't stand a chance against that many foes.

Quickly the wizard shut his eyes and concentrated. He couldn't take any more time to build up his mental strength for the task. He hoped he was strong enough.

He tried with all his mental might to lift the heavy boulders. He opened his eyes and saw the boulders slowly rising off the ground. He glanced up and saw that the gnomes were now halfway down the formation. *Hurry!* he thought to himself. *Move faster!* He concentrated harder, trying to move the rocks faster. It worked, a little.

But then, the boulders stopped in midair. He couldn't raise them any further. They weren't high enough. The boulders started to shake in the air. It was all Tyler could do to hold them up. The gnomes were now almost to the ground. This plan wasn't going to work.

He saw the four men get on their bellies and crawl underneath the boulders. That was the only way they could get through. They went one at a time. Tyler could no longer see them. He had no idea if they had gotten in the entrance or if they were still underneath the boulders. He knew he had to keep them in the air a little longer to give the men enough time to get through.

The gnomes reached the ground. About half of them were coming toward the hill where Tyler was hiding. He had to get away. He had to hide somewhere before they caught him. But to do that he would have to drop the boulders. He saw a few of the gnomes start crawling under the boulders as well. That made up his mind. He stopped concentrating and the boulders immediately dropped to the ground with a thud, squashing the gnomes underneath.

The mass of gnomes continued to advance on his position and he quickly looked around for a place to hide.

*   *   *

Layne heard the mass of boulders crash down behind them. Dust flew up from the floor and overwhelmed them, making it difficult to breathe or see. The four men coughed, trying to get the dust out of their lungs. Layne didn't know if it was pitch black in the formation or if the dust prevented them from seeing anything. After a few minutes the dust finally began to settle, and the men could breathe easier. They could also begin to see dim light. It wasn't pitch black after all.

Balls were stuck in the rock periodically throughout the corridor that gave off dim light. Layne had never seen anything like them before. He decided that this must be the work of some kind of wizardry. The big man was glad that the gnomes weren't able to see in the dark. Then they wouldn't have had the light source and the men would have been in trouble.

Layne looked around his immediate surroundings and saw the arm of a rock gnome sticking out from underneath the boulders that blocked the exit. It must have been crawling underneath when the boulders came down.

"How are we supposed to get out?" asked one of the men.

"I don't know," Layne replied, "but right now our first concern is finding the chest for Campbell. Then we can find a way out of here. Is everyone alright?"

All the men nodded and the group started out. The corridor was small. Layne's shoulders barely missed brushing the wall as he walked, and his head only came a few inches short of the ceiling. All the dust that flew up when the boulders hit the ground must have come from outside, because there wasn't any in the corridor.

The formation seemed to be empty. They saw no trace of gnomes as they walked. They all must have left out of the top. Layne wondered if the men would be able to escape the same way. But how would they get down to the ground? Well, he would think of that when the time came. Right now, they had to find that chest.

Layne had been sure that they were going to die when he saw the swarm of gnomes coming down the side of the formation. Despite the sheer drop, the gnomes stuck to the side and came swiftly down. When Layne saw how slowly the boulders began to rise, he had thought that they would be overwhelmed. But Tyler had saved the day once again. He had raised the boulders just high enough for the men to crawl under. It looked like he had dropped them just in time too. The gnomes had been trying to crawl under and get to the intruders. Suddenly, Layne wondered if the gnomes would simply crawl back up the wall and come back into the formation through the opening in the top. And if they didn't, would they search the area for any enemies and discover Tyler on the hill? Either way, they were in trouble. Layne realized that he hadn't thought this plan through carefully enough. But the only thing to do now was to press on.

So, they walked. The path twisted and turned so much that Layne no longer knew which direction they were going. The path never forked though. It was just this one long corridor.

Finally, they came to a large, round room with three other passages leading out. This was where the gnomes kept their pilfered treasure.

The room was piled high with chests and weapons and coins. Expensive looking carpets and tapestries were thrown in amongst golden goblets and silver mugs. Jewels encrusted platters and knife hilts sparkled in the dim light. Layne wondered what use the gnomes had for so much treasure. Several gnomes were roaming around the pile and inspecting its contents. One caught sight of the four men and let out a warning cry to its comrades.

Half a dozen of them rushed the men. "They are coming!" one of the men shouted. The four men raised their weapons and waited.

One man went down when a gnome leapt onto him. Man and gnome rolled around in a tangle of arms and legs. The three other men could do nothing to help the man because more gnomes were attacking them. Layne faced one.

He was holding his duel hand axes. He slashed at his opponent with one, then the other, but the gnome was able to dodge both. The rock gnome wasn't holding a weapon, but it swung at Layne with its fists. The big man knew that even a bare-fisted blow by these creatures would injure you.

Layne dodged the swing and counter attacked. He hit the gnome in the chest with one ax, pieces of hard skin chipping off the creature, but missed with the other ax that was aimed at the creature's head. "Remember, their soft spot is behind their ears," he said to his companions.

Out of the corner of his eye, Layne saw another gnome jumping for him. He ducked and the airborne creature flew right over him. It hit the wall hard, but immediately got to his feet. Now Layne had to face two of the creatures at once.

He heard grunting and his companions breathing hard, but he couldn't see how they fared. He had to concentrate only on the two gnomes before him. Without waiting for them to overwhelm him, he went on the offensive. He slashed down at the first gnome, then put up his ax to block the punch of the second gnome. He spun around, swinging at the newcomer's head. The gnome ducked, but Layne brought up his second ax in a vertical swing, hitting the creature underneath its jaw.

The blow didn't do serious damage to the gnome, but did send it flying backwards and away from the fight for the moment. It gave Layne a short respite, because now he was only fighting one enemy.

He knew the other gnome wouldn't be gone for long, so he immediately attacked the remaining creature. He threw blow after blow down on the gnome. His swings were quick and precise, so much so that the gnome had no chance to dodge. The creature had to throw up his arms to block the blows. Chips of hard skin flew away from the creature and Layne saw a trail of blood forming on its arm.

The creature shrieked in rage and pain and rushed in for the attack. It bowled into Layne, threw its arms around him, and took him to the ground. Layne and the creature rolled around on the pile of treasure, each trying to get the advantage. Layne ended up on top, but the creature threw its head up and hit Layne in the face. Layne rolled off the creature and lay there, dazed. The creature pounced on Layne and wrapped its powerful hands around his neck. Layne couldn't breathe.

His axes had fallen out of his grip when he was rolling around with the gnome and he frantically moved his eyes from side to side, searching for them. He caught a glimpse of one lying on the mound to his right. He stretched out as far as he could with one hand, while prying at the gnome's hands with his other. Finally, he was able to grip the handle. His lungs were burning, struggling for a breath that wouldn't come.

He swung the ax with all his remaining strength. His aim was true. The ax sunk deep into the gnome's head, just behind its left ear. The creature immediately fell limp and rolled off Layne.

Layne gasped as soon as the creature's grip was gone. Because he was concentrating on breathing, he forgot about the second creature that he had been fighting. Suddenly the gnome came into view. It stood over Layne, a large, heavy chest in its upraised hands. It was going to crush Layne with it. Before the creature could make a move, Layne saw an ax hit it in the head, just behind the ear. The rock gnome dropped the chest and fell dead onto the pile of treasure.

One of his companions came into view and held his hand down to help Layne up. He waved the hand away. "Give me a moment," he said. The man turned away to go check on the others.

After a few minutes, Layne was able to get to his feet. His neck hurt, and he was sure it was red. But other than that, he was fine. "Thank you," he said to the man who had saved his life. The other man just grunted. He was examining another man's arm. The injured man winced.

"What's wrong?" Layne asked as he walked up to the man.

"My shoulder hurts," the man replied. "I injured it during the battle. I think it might be broken." Layne glanced around. There were six dead rock gnomes, and all four men were standing. They had done well.

He turned back to his injured comrade. "Let me take a look at it."

Layne gently moved the other man away to survey the injured man's shoulder and arm. The shoulder didn't look right. He grabbed the man's arm and moved it up a little. "Ouch!" the man hollered. Layne put the arm back down.

"Well, I don't think it's broken," Layne said. "It seems to me that it is dislocated. What did the creature do to you?"

"It grabbed my arm and started pulling. I think it was trying to rip it off."

"Did you feel a pop?"

"Yeah."

"Then I am certain. It is dislocated. I need to pop it back into place."

"Do you know how to do it?" the injured man asked.

"Yes," Layne said. "But it is going to hurt."

The man swallowed. "Do it. I can take it. Besides, it already hurts. What's a little more pain?"

"Oh, this will be a lot more pain, unfortunately. But it will only last a moment and you will have full use of your arm again afterwards."

The man nodded. "Alright. I'm ready."

Layne gripped the man's shoulder with his left arm and grabbed the man's forearm with his right. The man shut his eyes and tensed up. Without warning Layne yanked the arm down and away from the man's body. Everyone heard a loud pop, and the man cried out in pain. Layne let go and the man grabbed his arm and swore. He turned his back to the others and swore some more. Layne thought he heard a sniff.

Finally, the man turned around and faced the group again, a small grin on his face. He gingerly moved his shoulder around. "Well, that wasn't so bad," he joked, rubbing his arm. "It feels much better."

"It will be sore for a while, but the worst is over."

"We should get moving," another man said. "Let's find that chest and get out of here."

"Good idea," said Layne. "Remember, it is a large wooden chest, with red writing on the lid. Campbell said it is in a language that he doesn't recognize." They scoured the pile of treasure. Layne was sure it would be easy to find because the gnomes had just returned with it not too long ago. It would probably be right on top of the pile.

But there was still a lot of treasure to look through. After over half an hour of searching, they finally found a chest, but it was the wrong one. There was no writing on the lid. So the men had to continue their search.

It was another quarter hour before they finally found the correct chest. Layne kept looking at the four entrances to the chamber, expecting to see rock gnomes enter and discover the four men, but none came. They seemed to be alone in the rock formation.

"Well," said the man whose shoulder Layne had fixed, "now that we found it, how do we get out of here."

"I don't know," Layne said. "We have three choices, since the way we came in is blocked. I think one choice is as good as the next. Let's just choose."

They followed Layne into the corridor that was directly across from the one they had entered from. Layne thought it was funny that even though he was the youngest of the four men, the others seem to accept him as their leader. One by one, they left the room and entered the dark corridor, hoping that it led to a way out.

Tyler watched as the writhing mass of small figures made its way up the hill. There was no place to hide on top of the hill, and in his weak condition, there was no way he could outrun the rock gnomes. He did the only thing he could think of. He climbed a tree. He tried to get up high where the branches were thicker and would provide more cover. He was about halfway up the tall tree when his strength gave out and he couldn't progress any further. He hoped he was high enough. He clutched a large branch and waited.

The gnomes had scoured the area underneath the huge rock formation for a long time before they made their way up the hill. There had to be hundreds of them. Tyler hoped that all of them had come out of the formation. If any were still in there, the four men might be in trouble. He had no idea how they were going to get back out.

Tyler tried not to breath as the first gnomes made their way under his tree. They were looking at the ground, probably searching for tracks. Tyler had no idea if he had left any when he was searching for a place to hide. If he had, then the rock gnomes would have no trouble finding him. He stayed as motionless as possible, praying that the gnomes would continue on. They didn't. They lingered underneath the tree, and more joined them.

Tyler stared down at them. There was nothing else he could do. He dared not move. He was afraid that even the slightest movement would move a branch and make a noise that the gnomes would hear. He hoped that the branches beneath him were thick enough to hide him.

To his horror, the gnomes looked up. Tyler was sure he would be seen, but their eyes passed right over him. They were not looking up at his tree in particular, they were scanning all the trees.

A bird just over Tyler's head chirped loudly. Every single gnome beneath the tree jerked their heads toward the sound. Once again they were looking right at the wizard. None were looking away.

The tension was starting to make Tyler sweat. He could feel a drop running down his forehead and onto his nose. It hung from the tip, threatening to drop and possibly hit a gnome below.

The bird gave another chirp and took flight. All eyes followed the bird as it disappeared from view. They were no longer looking in his direction. Tyler wanted to let out a sigh of relief, but he held it in.

The rock gnomes began to move away from Tyler's tree. After a few minutes he dared move again. He lifted his head to look at the huge rock formation. About half way up there was a large depression where Tyler had ripped the stone away from the formation. The depression went almost all the way to the top. He felt a pang of regret. It was a pity to damage such a beautiful natural structure.

Tyler saw several rock gnomes crawling back up the formation. They couldn't get back in through the entrance, so they were going to go through the hole in the top. *Oh no,* Tyler thought. *Layne and the others will be trapped!*

*   *   *

This corridor was just like the first. It was narrow, windy, and long, with no other corridors branching off from it. But this one was also going up. Maybe this would lead to a way out.

Layne walked in front, leading the way. Two men, including the one who had been injured, followed, carrying the chest between them. The last man served as rear guard in case any rock gnomes came at them from behind.

The corridor opened into a massive chamber. It was bigger than the treasure room, with nooks and holes all the along the walls. The holes covered the entire room. It looked like this was where the rock gnomes slept. In the far wall was a massive fireplace. There was a fire burning in it now, the smoke leaving the room through a corridor at the far end of the room. That was the only other exit from the chamber. The fire made the room uncomfortably hot, and the men quickly made their way to the exit.

The smoke made it hard to see and breathe in the corridor. The men coughed as the smoke got into their lungs, and they crouched as they walked, trying to stay underneath the smoke.

Because the smoke was so thick, Layne didn't see the rock gnomes until he was right on top of them.

Luckily, he was holding his two hand axes. At the first sign of movement, he swung one of them horizontally, hitting a gnome just behind its left ear. Layne knew he had gotten lucky. He hadn't even aimed, he just swung. The gnome went down in a heap. It hadn't even had time to let out a cry. But there was another gnome just behind it.

Layne swung his other ax, but this time his foe had time to dodge. "Rock gnomes!" Layne called to his companions. The gnome lunged at Layne, but it had to stop short when it found Layne's ax waiting for it.

Layne was able to drive it backwards. He continued forward, not wanting to be pushed back into the large room. This corridor was too narrow for two gnomes to stand side by side, so Layne only had to face one at a time. Plus, he wanted to get out of this rock formation as soon as possible.

He heard the chattering of other gnomes behind the one he was fighting. Suddenly, the gnome quit moving backwards. Maybe it didn't have any more room because of the ones behind it. The corridor was narrow, but it had a high ceiling. The gnome took a great leap and soared over Layne's head. It landed on top of the chest. The weight of the creature made the men drop the chest and they cried out in surprise. Layne couldn't turn around to help his companions because another gnome came at him.

While he was fighting this gnome, he could sense the other gnomes jumping over his head and landing behind him. He heard the sounds of battle. More than one man was grunting and breathing hard, so Layne knew that the men who had dropped the chest had drawn their weapons.

This gnome in front of Layne had a crude club in its hand and he traded blow for blow with the creature, then dropped it when one of his axes hit home. He had no respite though, because another rock gnome took its place, and this one also had a club.

He heard the cry of one of his companions behind him, but there was nothing he could do to help the man.

Layne knew that he needed to end this battle quickly or the men would be overwhelmed. He pushed his attack harder. His axes were a whirl of movement that would be difficult to see even without the smoke in the corridor. His foe backed up slowly at first, but after Layne had disarmed it and had given it several wounds, it turned and ran the other way. Suddenly, there was empty corridor in front of him. Layne turned to see if he could help the other men.

All he could see in the smoke was blurs of movement. He had no idea what was going on. He crouched down as low as he could so he could see better. There was a gnome right in front of him, and he swung at its legs as hard as he could.

His ax didn't break the gnome's skin, but the blow was hard enough to buckle the creature's knees and send it to the ground. The man the gnome was fighting finished him off with an ax to the head.

Layne heard more sounds of fighting on the other side of the man he had just helped, but he couldn't get to it because of the narrowness of the corridor. The other man could though. Together, Layne's two companions defeated the remaining gnome.

After the battle, Layne saw one of his comrades lying dead on the ground. It must have been the man who had cried out. His skull had been bashed in by a club. Now their group was down to three.

"What should we do with his body?" one of the men asked.

"We must leave him here," Layne replied. "It will be difficult enough to escape this place with just the chest. I don't think we'll be able to make it if we have to carry his body out as well."

"But he was my friend."

"I understand."

"I will not leave him."

"Then you probably won't be leaving at all!" Layne shouted. All he wanted to do was get out of there, but this man wanted to slow them down. Layne and the other man stared at each other until the third man stepped in.

"I will help him," he said. "You can lead, and we will carry the chest with his friend's body draped over it."

Layne gave in. "Alright. But if you slow me down too much, I will not wait for you." The two men nodded.

They draped the dead man's body over the chest. It took them a few tries to get the weight distributed correctly. It slid off one side or the other the first few tries. Finally they got the body up and they started out again.

The farther along they went, the steeper the corridor became. Layne was certain now that this passageway led to the top of the formation. Although how they were going to get down once they got there, he had no idea. But it was better than being in here.

To Layne it seemed they had been walking for hours. It didn't help that they had to stop once when the body slid off the chest again. Despite Layne's threat to leave them behind if there were any delays, he did stop to wait as they put the body back onto the chest. But finally, they emerged into daylight.

The scene below the three men was breathtaking. They could see for miles and miles in each direction. But their gaze was drawn west to the hill where they had left Tyler. The great swarm of gnomes covered the hill. Layne couldn't think of how Tyler could possibly still be alive. Even though he hadn't known the wizard for very long, he still felt a pang of regret.

Since Tyler had torn the side off of the formation, the men could now make their way downward. They made their way gingerly, not wanting to slip on the loose rocks that littered the formation. The lead man who was carrying the chest slipped and fell. He kept his grip on the chest, as did the other man carrying it. Layne quickly grabbed onto the chest and together they were able to stop his fall. But the body of the dead man was not so lucky. When the man slipped, the body slid off the chest, hit the formation, and began rolling. There was nothing any of the men could do. The body's momentum took it to the edge and over the side, where it fell the final two hundred feet or so to the ground.

When the body had slipped off the chest and began to roll, the dead man's friend cried out, his echo carried all the way to the hill. Layne could see the writhing mass freeze as the gnomes immediately stopped what they were doing when they heard the sound. As one all the gnomes turned to look back at the formation. They saw the three men standing on their home. With a great cry the gnome force rushed back down the hill to destroy the intruders.

*   *   *

Tyler was clinging to a branch, still trying not to move. He heard someone shout "No!" and saw the gnomes freeze. Tyler slowly looked toward the formation and saw three small figures standing about halfway down. *Layne!* he thought. *He is alive!*

In a manner of moments, the gnomes had all left the hill and were rushing toward the formation. They would swarm over the men with no trouble at all. He had to do something. He didn't know if he had the strength, but he had to try. But what could he do?

Tyler quickly scrambled down the tree. When he reached the ground, he shut his eyes and concentrated.

*   *   *

Layne and the three men stared down at the mass of rock gnomes coming toward them. They had just reached the base of the formation and had begun climbing up. In a few short minutes it would all be over. Layne didn't want to die just yet, but it seemed inevitable.

Suddenly, the rocks beneath them began to shake. Small rocks were knocked loose and fell down the cliff, and the men found it hard to keep their footing. The rock the men were on was dislodged and began to slide toward the cliff.

"What's happening?" cried one of the men. He had fallen to his knees and had put his hands on the rock to brace himself.

"We're going over the edge!" said the other man. The two men, sure they were doomed, started screaming.

Layne wasn't so sure. He was no expert at magic, but he had been around it long enough now to be able to tell when it might be in use.

There was no natural reason for the rock formation to just start shaking like it did. Despite the speed with which the slab of rock was moving, Layne kept his eyes on the hill. Yes, there he was. There was Tyler, standing on the hill. *This is his work,* Layne thought.

The rock slab slid off the edge of the cliff, but instead of falling, it continued to move in the air away from the formation. Layne looked down and saw that the gnomes were almost to the point where the men had just been. A few gnomes tried leaping onto the floating slab, but none came close. Every gnome that tried fell to their deaths.

The rock slab slowly made its way toward the hill.

Tyler strained with the effort of keeping the rock slab aloft. He had been exhausted when he had first tried it, and his strength was quickly dwindling. He had opened his eyes and was now watching the slab coming toward him. Once the slab faltered for a moment, and it dipped sharply, but the wizard was able to right it again.

Tyler quickly glanced down into the valley and saw that the gnomes were not coming after them. That was a relief.

After what seemed like an eternity, the rock reached the hill. Tyler thought it was safe to let it down and he stopped concentrating. The rock roughly hit the ground and the wizard collapsed. The three men had all been knocked off their feet when they hit the ground, but Layne was quickly up again. He rushed over to the fallen wizard.

"Tyler, are you alright?"

All the wizard could do was moan.

The other two men had joined them, the chest held between them. "We need to get out of here," one of them said. "The gnomes are not following yet, but they might if we stick around much longer."

"You're right," Layne said. "Hopefully, they are frightened of wizards." Layne knelt down and lifted the wizard into his arms. Tyler's weight was easy for Layne to carry. "Let's go."

The group left the ruined rock formation and the furious rock gnomes behind, King Korlas' chest safely in their possession.

28

Queen Laurel winced at the sound of clashing steel. The melee portion of the tournament had just begun, and the sound of one hundred men coming together with blunted weapons was so loud that it hurt her ears. There was such a flurry of movement that at first it was hard to tell what was happening. She knew this battle would take a long time to complete, and there were one hundred more men waiting to go after each other when this one was done; only those men would be on horseback. She was not looking forward to it.

Truth be told, she had no love for battle. She had no desire to sit here underneath a canopy on a balcony overlooking the battle grounds. She could think of a thousand other things she would rather be doing, but she knew she had to be there. The men fighting for the honor of becoming a Sentinel expected her to observe. And this tournament had been her idea after all. She was stuck there.

After a while her eyes found her protector. Syth slashed through men like they were standing still. The way he moved was beautiful to behold. Beautiful to her, yet terrifying to his foes.

She had let Syth join the tournament against the wishes of Sam. If she was being honest, it was against her own better judgment as well. The man that Sam had assigned to watch Syth that first night had disappeared. No one had heard from him since. And what was worse, a high-standing noble in the city was murdered that night, along with his wife and three teenage kids. It had been a brutal killing, and even the announcement she had made about the tournament was not enough to keep the people from panicking.

Every night after that an important family was murdered. A merchant one night, a nobleman the next. A well-known and beloved shopkeeper another night. The assassin had decided to leave the small folk alone and go for bigger prey. That was the most terrifying thing about the killer. He was unpredictable.

This tournament couldn't have come at a better time. The townsfolk needed this. They needed this distraction, and they also needed the feeling of safety they would get when the Sentinels were chosen. She hoped her plan worked. She hoped the power of the Sentinels would be enough to stop the assassin.

Sam was furious at her when he found out that Syth would be participating. He said that the fact that Todd had disappeared while watching Syth's room, and that another murder occurred that night, was proof that Syth was the assassin. She also thought it was suspicious, but she needed more proof before she could do anything about it. And she reminded him that no one else who had been set to watch Syth's chambers had disappeared or seen anything suspicious since that first night, but he would not be swayed. The exchange became so bad that she had had to remind Sam of who he was talking to. He apologized and took his leave, but she could still see the rage on his face when he turned away from her. She was surprised to discover how much that look had pained her. He hadn't spoken a word to her since.

Men had come from all over the country; at least the ones who lived close enough to reach the city in time for the tournament. Every kind of person you could think of was there; farmers, the sons of noblemen, shopkeepers, merchant guards, royal knights, miners, people from every walk of life, all looking for fame and glory.

There was one man who was missing that she wished was here though. A man she herself had sent across the sea on a mission to bring justice to her son. Tim. It would be great for the country if a man like

Tim, who was well known all over, would have become a Sentinel. There was not a doubt in her mind that if he were here, he would do well enough in the tournament to become a Sentinel.

All the men on the war council had joined the tournament. Seven of them were in the fight going on right now. Only the newcomers Trigg and Jaxon would fight in the next battle on horseback. She found Gyles. The big blonde man was holding his own against two smaller men who had formed an alliance. She saw Crew walking away from the battle, holding his arm close to his body. Of her other councilors, there was no sign. She searched for Sam but couldn't find him.

She continued to scan the combatants. There! There he was! Sam was striding purposefully toward something, slashing at anyone who got in his way. She looked in the direction where he was heading and saw who he was going toward. Syth. *No! You can't beat him!*

Syth was surrounded by men. It looked like the combatants didn't want him there, so they decided to gang up on him. No one even touched him. One of her councilors was sent reeling, then a large young man who looked like a farmer and wielded a quarterstaff went down. Syth was a dark streak of movement. Men fell back from him quicker than she could count.

She looked back at Sam. He was almost to Syth. Gyles was walking beside him now. It looked like they planned on taking Syth on together. Queen Laurel knew it would be futile.

Syth had cleared a large space around him. Everyone who he had been fighting was either fleeing or unconscious on the ground. He turned and saw the two men approaching. The dark-skinned man didn't move. He just waited for them to reach him. Suddenly, the queen was very interested in the fight. There were other men still in the battle, but she only had eyes for the three men facing each other below her.

Sam and Gyles spread out, going to either side of Syth. Her protector didn't seem concerned. He spread his arms wide, a sword in each hand, one pointing at each man.

Sam and Gyles attacked at the same time. Syth had no problem parrying their strokes. He blocked, then swung, making his foes jump back, then blocked when they came back at him again. None of the two men's blows came close to touching him.

Suddenly, he turned his back to Gyles and attacked Sam with both of his swords. He reigned blows in succession down on Sam, the knight barely blocking them as he quickly retreated. But block them he did. Laurel was impressed. She hadn't seen anyone else able to last this long against Syth.

Syth stopped, spun around, and blocked Gyles' swing. The big man had chased the two combatants, trying to get at Syth from behind. Syth swung at Gyles' midsection, making him jump back, then spun around again and slashed at Sam. The ex- knight was quickly on the retreat again and Syth once again ignored Gyles.

Gyles was set upon by two men, so he was unable to help Sam anymore. These men were skilled. Laurel thought they both were knights. Gyles was good with a sword, but the two men were too much for him and he was beaten down, finally giving up. The two men stepped over Gyles and searched for someone else to fight.

Sam was still losing ground quickly. He was unable to put up a counterattack. He had to put all his effort into defense. Syth started spinning, and blows began to land. Sam was hit in the arm, then the leg, then the shoulder. He barely dodged a blow aimed at his head, then he had to throw up his sword to block a sideways swing.

There were now only four men left in the fight. Syth, Sam, and the two knights that had defeated Gyles. The two knights carefully crept up behind Syth, not daring to get too close. It looked like they were going to let the other two men finish their battle, but then, apparently deciding that it would be easier to take out Syth with three men than with two, they rushed in for the attack.

Just as they reached Syth, he spun around, sending one man lurching backwards and knocking the other man on the side of the head with one of his swords. The man hit the ground, unconscious. Sam took advantage of the distraction and went on the attack. At the last moment Syth spun around again and swept a sword low. Sam wasn't expecting the attack and his feet were taken out from under him. He hit the ground hard. Syth swung down at him. Sam rolled out of the way and Syth's sword hit nothing but dirt. Sam continued to roll, but Syth followed. The dark-skinned warrior was too quick for Sam and when the ex- knight stopped rolling, Syth was there. He hit Sam over the head with one of his swords and the ex- knight was out cold.

Now there were only two fighters left. Syth showed no mercy and the fight was quickly over. Syth stood alone among the fallen warriors. He would be recognized as the winner of the tournament, but he and the runner up would both be chosen for Sentinels. Laurel had hoped that Sam would be one, but he had just missed out. If only he hadn't fought Syth so quickly.

The battle ground was cleared of the wounded. Luckily, no one had been killed. Soon, the grounds were ready for the fighters on horseback to battle. The rules were a little different in this fight. If a man falls off his horse, he is out. Both Trigg and Jaxon were going to fight in this battle. Laurel didn't think they would do very well. Trigg was just a small man, and Jaxon had to be in his fifties.

Syth arrived on the balcony and took his place just behind her chair as the fight began. He didn't say a word. He just watched the battle below.

"What did you think of the fighting men?" Laurel asked Syth.

"One or two were mildly skilled," he answered. "Most of them would be worthless in a real battle."

Laurel didn't like that answer. "And what did you think of Sam?"

"He was the best of them, though that is not saying much. He is no match for me. Although he did last a lot longer than I thought he was going to."

"Well, congratulations," Laurel said. "You will be named a Sentinel." Syth didn't say anything. He just continued to watch the battle.

Laurel didn't think that Syth's analysis of the country's fighting men boded well for the war to come.

She watched her two councilors. They were holding their own. Trigg's small stature didn't seem to be a disadvantage for him. In fact, it looked like it was helping him. He was a smaller target. Laurel watched him knock four men off their horses before he was finally unhorsed. He made it about halfway through the battle.

Jaxon did even better. Though he was older, he had been a knight in the army. There hadn't been a war in all the years he was in the knighthood, but knights of the realm are trained very well. His movements were still smooth and fluid, and he was unhorsing fighters half his age.

This battle took longer than the previous one did. That was probably because Syth was not in there cutting people down left and right.

There was one man though who was clearly the finest warrior out there. He was a big man, and his weapon of choice was a large war hammer with a spike on the other side. The spike was blunted of course, but the hammer still did some damage. Jaxon was unfortunate to find himself facing the man. He fought valiantly, but in the end, Jaxon was knocked from his horse. Jaxon ducked the first swing, then countered with a jab. The sword hit the man square in the chest, but the man was wearing heavy armor and he didn't move even an inch. The hammer came down again and this time Jaxon blocked it with his sword. The heavy blow sent the sword flying from the older man's hand. The next swing hit Jaxon in the shoulder and sent him to the dirt. The fallen man immediately grabbed his injured shoulder and cried out. Laurel expected it was broken.

When the battle was finally over, the big man with the war hammer was the victor. Another knight had taken second place. *Four,* the queen thought. *We now have four Sentinels. Just six more to go.*

The tournament had started just after dawn, and it wasn't quite mid-day yet, but they took a break from the fighting to let the townsfolk get involved.

Carts on wheels were brought onto the battle grounds and it turned into a large market. Food vendors were everywhere, selling any type of food you could think of. Farmers had loaded up their wagons with produce to sell. There were souvenir shops that sold dolls made to look like knights or the queen. There were wooden swords and shields that were popular amongst the young boys. There were bows and arrows, saddles and bridles, people selling horseshoes and people selling people shoes, dress makers and hat salesmen. And of course, tumblers and jugglers and singers, and games for the family.

Laurel watched the people rush by with a smile on her face. Everyone was laughing or grinning. Children were chasing each other around. People were genuinely happy. Not one looked afraid or worried. This was just what the people needed. This was just what she needed.

When the fighting had ended, Queen Laurel had left her balcony overlooking the battle grounds and moved to a pavilion at ground level so she could be closer to the festivities. A few of the people who ran by Laurel stopped and waved or shouted a greeting. The queen would always smile and wave back. The people couldn't get too close to her because her guards wouldn't allow it…

Laurel stood up and said she wanted to go have some fun. She walked out amongst the people, Syth and four other guards surrounding her. Groups of people moved out of the way to let them pass.

When Laurel was a young girl, she had been an adequate archer, so she approached the archery stand. There was a row of targets set up about fifty paces away. She paid the man behind the counter and smiled at the look of shock on his face when he realized who she was. He tried to give the money back to her, but she refused it. "I am just a customer today," she told him. "I will pay like everyone else."

The bow felt good in her hands. She hadn't shot a bow in years and the first arrow she loosed didn't even hit the target. The man behind the counter gave her encouraging words. She just laughed at herself and shot again. Each shot was better than the last and by the time she had shot all ten arrows, eight had hit the target and the last one even hit the bulls-eye.

She laughed and clapped her hands in delight as the man handed her a hand-stitched doll. The doll was wearing a green dress. It had red hair and freckles. Laurel loved it. She thanked the man and, doll in hand, left to find other entertainment.

She bought fried pork on a stick and ate as she walked. She also bought one for each of her guards. She offered one to Syth, but he refused.

A group of children ran up to her and thanked her for such a wonderful day. She chatted with them for a while until their parents discovered what they were doing. They rushed over and grabbed their kids, bowing to her.

"We're sorry, Your Majesty," said one mother. "These kids won't bother you again."

"Oh no," Laurel replied. "They are no bother. I have enjoyed chatting with them."

The parents ushered their children away and Laurel looked around for something else to do, and she saw Sam striding toward her. He had a large lump on his forehead, but other than that he looked fine. He stopped in front of her and gave her a bow. "You're Majesty."

Laurel smiled. "How are you feeling Sam?"

"My head hurts. But other than that, I am alright. I am disappointed that I missed out on becoming a Sentinel."

"As am I. You were very close though."

"You're Majesty, I have bad news."

"What is it?"

"Not here. Can we go someplace more private?"

"Of course." She turned to her four guards. "You may leave me. Go and enjoy yourselves. I will meet you back at the balcony when the archery contest begins. Syth, please come with us."

She turned back to Sam just in time to see him grimace at her last remark. His dislike and mistrust of Syth ran deep. "Let's go over to the gardens," she said. "I doubt very many people will be there."

They walked in silence. Laurel was anxious to know what bad news Sam was talking about, but she would wait until they reached their destination to press him about it. She wasn't sure she wanted to hear it anyway. She had had enough of bad news over the last couple of weeks. *Why can't there ever be any good news?* she thought.

They reached one of the several gardens in the city and found that she had been correct. There was no one else amongst the beautiful flowers and white marble benches. No children chased each other around the large, thick bushes carved into the shapes of people and animals. Everyone was attending the festivities.

Sam sat on a bench and asked the queen to sit by him. Syth remained standing. "There was another murder this morning."

The queen couldn't help but glance at Syth. *But he was here all day,* she thought. She turned back to Sam. "Tell me what happened."

Sam also glanced at Syth before he began. "A shop owner didn't attend the festivities today. He opened his shop for business. A would-be customer entered and saw him and his entire family dead on the floor. The woman ran and found the nearest soldier and brought him back to the scene. The soldier reported to me that the bodies were lined up in a row just like all the others. It looks to be the work of the same killer."

Laurel sat there for a moment without speaking, taking in everything she had just heard. It would have been terrible to find out that Syth was the killer, but at least they had had a lead. Now, with Syth seemingly out of the picture, they were back to square one.

"Where is the soldier who reported the murder to you?" she asked Sam.

"He is waiting next to the battle grounds."

She turned to her dark-skinned protector. "Syth, I would like you to accompany the soldier back to the shop and investigate. Please take a squad of the city watch with you. Track the killer if you can. Please report back to me with anything you find at the scene."

Syth bowed. "Yes, My Queen." Then he turned and left.

When Syth had disappeared from sight, Sam moved closer to Laurel on the bench. "Do you really think that is wise?"

"Yes." Sam looked like he was about to say something else, but Laurel put up her hand and he shut his mouth. "Syth was in my sight all day. He couldn't have murdered the poor shopkeeper and his family. It was not him, Sam."

"Maybe this killer copied the other ones to make it look like it is the other guy. Just because Syth didn't kill these people doesn't mean that he didn't kill the other ones."

"But this killer set up the bodies just like the rest."

"Like I just said," replied Sam, "it could be a person who copied the other murders. I have heard of that happening before."

"Or, maybe," said the queen, "it isn't Syth at all. Maybe it is someone else."

"I need to go to that shop," Sam said.

"Why?"

"To look around. I need to see if the scene is exactly like the other ones, or if there are some differences. If it is a copy of the previous murders, something will probably be different about this one."

"I see."

"Do I have your leave to go investigate?"

"Yes, if you must."

"Thank you, Your Majesty."

He got up from the bench and began to walk away.

"Sam!" The man stopped and turned back to Laurel. "Do not make this a monster hunt. Do not try to manipulate what you find just to make it look like Syth is guilty. I want an honest investigation, and if you don't find anything that could be proof that Syth murdered these people, end it there."

Her tone was stern. She was done with Sam and his games. She now truly believed that Syth was innocent. Sam bowed and walked away without a word.

*   *   *

Queen Laurel returned to the battlegrounds just as men were finishing setting up the targets for the archery competition. She had lingered in the garden for a long time after her talk with Sam, enjoying the solitude. As a queen without a king, she never had any free time anymore. When her husband was alive, he had taken care of most of the affairs of the kingdom and she was free to do as she pleased. She made appearances at important functions and often sat in attendance at court, but other than that she didn't have many responsibilities. Now, the ruling of the kingdom was on her shoulders alone, and she was beginning to feel the weight of that responsibility. So it was good to be able to sit and relax in the beautiful gardens for a while, forgetting her cares.

She watched the first group of men line up fifty paces from the targets. She noticed the absence of Crew. He had planned to compete in the archery contest if things went badly in the melee, but since his arm had been broken, he wasn't able to. She felt bad for him.

The first group had twenty men in it. Each man shot three arrows at the target directly opposite him. Once everyone had shot, they added up the points of all three arrows to get a final score. If a man hit the bulls-eye, he got twenty points. If he hit the middle ring, he got ten points. And if he hit the outer ring, he got five points. If the arrow missed all three rings, he didn't get any points. The five men with the highest point total moved on to the next round.

The soldier in charge called for the competitors to lose their first arrow. About half the men hit the bulls-eye. These men were cheered heartily by the crowd. A few totally missed the target altogether. These men were laughed at by the people watching. The men sent off their second and then their third arrows. Two men had a perfect score of sixty. Three men had twenty-five, and all the rest had less. The five men who were moving on to the next round raised their arms into the air and shouted in triumph. The other fifteen men walked away disappointed.

There were three more group of archers, each supposed to be holding twenty men. The last group only had nineteen because Crew was unable to compete. Laurel found her mind wandering. Instead of paying attention, she was thinking about the murder that was committed that day and wondered what Sam and Syth were discovering. She didn't have much hope of Syth being able to track the killer down because they had been unable to do that so far, but she knew that if anyone could do it, he could.

The second round started. This time there were only two groups, with ten men in each group. The targets were moved back to one hundred paces. Only very skilled archers would be able to hit the bulls-eye at that range. The men fired their three arrows. The two men who had gotten perfect scores in the first round of the competition got perfect scores again. The top five moved onto the final round, which would take place after the next group of men had their turn.

Once again, Queen Laurel found it hard to pay attention to the competition. This time her thoughts moved to her daughter. She wondered if Dana had found Tim and his group. She wondered if Tim and Jaden were keeping her daughter safe. She felt a tear running down her cheek. She missed her daughter so! She thought that the tear was also for her lost son, Easton. She couldn't help but miss him, too. Not for the first time she wondered if she had made the right decision in asking Tim to kill her son. It seemed like the right thing to do at the time, but now she almost regretted it. She regretted that she would never see her son again. Another tear ran down her cheek and she quickly brushed it away. It wouldn't do to have her subjects see her cry.

The final round began. The ten men with the top scores lined up. This time, the targets were one hundred fifty paces away. Only the most skilled archers could hit the bulls-eye from that range. Now Laurel couldn't help but be interested. She wondered if anyone would be able to make that shot.

Crew sat down next to her. She looked over and gave him a smile. "How is your arm?"

Crew looked at the bandaged arm. It was being held tightly against his body by a sling. "It doesn't hurt anymore, thanks to the healers. But it is still useless." He looked out at the competitors. "If my arm wasn't injured, I could make that shot."

"I'm sure you could," Laurel replied.

The ten men shot their three arrows and to the crowd's delight and astonishment, the two men from the first round hit the bulls-eye all three times again. The crowd roared and clapped in appreciation of the men's talents. These two men would be named to the Sentinels. *Six down. Four more to go,* Laurel thought. *We are over half-way there.*

29

Syth turned from the blood smeared on the floor when he heard the door to the shop open. Sam walked in and looked around. *Why is he here?* Syth thought. Sam spotted Syth and walked right up to him.

"The queen gave me leave to conduct my own investigation," he stated. "What have you discovered so far?"

"The men Her Majesty sent with me have been looking for anything suspicious in the shop. They are trying to find out if anything is missing."

"Where are the bodies?"

Syth motioned to the counter with his head. "Behind there."

Sam walked around the counter and looked down. Syth knew what he was seeing. The bodies of the shopkeeper, his wife, and his two children, a boy and a younger girl, were lying side-by-side. Their legs were perfectly straight, their arms were at their sides. Their eyes and mouths were closed. They would look like they were sleeping if not for the long slash across each one of their necks. There was a pool of blood underneath each victim. The scene looked exactly like every killing that Syth had committed. This was without a doubt the work of a copy-cat.

Sam crouched down for a closer look and Syth lost sight of him. Syth walked around the counter and stood above the ex-knight. Sam was looking in the shopkeeper's pockets.

"Are you stealing from the dead now, Sam?"

Sam glanced up at him. "No. I am looking to see if anything is in their pockets. If there is, then the killer didn't rob them. The victims of the previous murders all had their possessions still in their pockets. Nothing was taken."

Syth saw Sam pull out a coin from the dead man's pocket. He held it up for Syth to see. "The murderer didn't steal anything from the bodies."

"So that means that it was the same guy," said Syth. He didn't pose it as question. He wanted Sam to come to that conclusion.

"Not necessarily," Sam replied. "If anything is missing from the shop, it could still be someone else who wanted it to look like it is the same killer."

Sam got up and brushed off the knees of his pants. They had gotten dirt and blood on them when he had knelt down. He tried to walk past Syth, but the dark-skinned man grabbed his arm and stopped him.

"What are you doing?" demanded Sam.

"You think it is me, don't you?"

"What?"

"You think I'm the killer. You are trying to convince the queen that I am the assassin. Don't deny it. I see the look in your eyes when you look at me. I see the mistrust and hatred. Before you do anything stupid, just remember the fight we had today. Remember how badly I beat you."

Sam pulled his arm away and stalked past him. Syth couldn't help but grin at the man's discomfort. He turned and watched Sam make his way to one of the soldiers and start up a conversation with him.

Syth stepped out onto the porch of the shop and looked around. He saw some scuff marks on the wood. He crouched down and when he got closer he could tell that several men had been in a hurry to get away from the shop. These must have been the killers. But where did they go?

He looked around again, trying to find more signs of the men's passing. He saw an overturned stone down the street a little bit. The street was paved, so there were no footprints to be seen, but the stone had most likely been knocked over by someone in a hurry. He went to examine it.

Syth heard someone call his name and he turned to see a soldier watching him from the doorway. "What are you doing?" the man called. Syth just waved him away with his hand and turned back to the stone. He knew which way the men had gone when they left the shop, so he looked in that direction. There was something on the corner of the building just ahead. When he reached the spot, he saw that it was a bloody handprint. It looked like the man had been running very quickly, turned the corner, but had to grab onto the corner of the building to make the turn. Slitting someone's throat is messy business and you are bound to get some blood on your hands when you do it. This handprint came from the killer.

Syth went around the corner of the building and examined the area. The street was paved like all the others, with buildings lining it on either side. He turned his head from side to side as he slowly walked down the street, looking for anything out of place.

There were trees placed periodically on either side of the street. Dirt surrounded each tree and Syth examined these areas, looking for footprints. About one hundred paces down the street, he saw some.

There were several footprints in the dirt; it looked as if at least half a dozen people had passed over this spot. By the distance between each print, it looked to Syth as if the people who had left the prints had been running. They were going somewhere in a hurry. Could these be the same people who had been at the shop? Syth thought it was likely. It seemed to Syth that the people had run down the street then turned here at the tree and headed down a side street. Syth made his way to that street.

It was more of an alley than a proper street. The shops to either side were very close together, and the sun found it hard to penetrate the almost-touching roofs over his head. The shadows were deep, and Syth stopped for a second to let his eyes adjust to the darkness.

He heard voices, but he couldn't tell what they were saying. He saw a light about halfway down the alley. He moved toward the light and discovered a door. The door was closed, but it didn't fit the doorway correctly and there were gaps that let light and sound through.

As he reached the doorway, he discovered that the men inside were arguing.

"I think you guys are stupid!" said one voice. "Why did you kill them? Couldn't you just rob them and leave?"

"And leave witnesses?" said a second voice. "I don't think so! They could have watched us run away and told the city watch where we went. Then, they could have provided a positive identification when the watch caught us and brought us back to them. No, it was better this way."

"But the penalty for murder is much harsher than the penalty for robbery," said the first man.

"It's alright," said a third voice. "They will never find out that it was us. We laid the bodies out side by side just like the yellow-skinned assassin does. The authorities will believe that he did it, and we are in no danger."

"You don't even know if the assassin has yellow skin!"

"Well, that's what the rumors say."

The first man seemed even angrier now. "Rumors! You are risking our lives on rumors! Just you wait. Any moment now the queen's dark-skinned protector will have tracked you here and he will burst through that door and arrest us all. Just you wait!"

Syth couldn't help himself and chose that moment to do just as the man had said. He drew his swords and kicked in the door. All five men in the room turned to him with shocked expressions on their faces. The first man Syth heard speak was still pointing at the doorway.

"It's him!" a man cried and drew his sword. "No!" cried the first man, but it was too late. The fool attacked Syth. He thrust his sword forward, but Syth easily stepped out of the way and brought one of his own swords down onto the man's outstretched arm, severing it just above the elbow. The man's arm and sword hit the ground and he grabbed the bloody stump and cried out. He hit the floor and curled up, weeping. "My arm! My arm!"

No one else had made a move.

"Well, well, well," said Syth. "What do we have here?"

The man who had been pointing to the door when Syth came in dropped to his knees. "It wasn't me! It was them!" He gestured to the other four men in the room. "I told them to just rob the shopkeeper, but they killed him against my wishes!" Syth knew that this was the first voice he heard. This man hadn't wanted them to kill anyone.

"You are the leader if this band?"

"Yes. I am the leader." The voice was quiet now. He was a big man, more fat than muscle, but he had the look of a fighter to him. "My name is Parson. But I never wanted anyone to die."

"Yeah, he's the leader," one of the men said. "He makes us do things to people. Arrest him!"

"No!" the leader exclaimed and turned to the man who had spoken. "You always go too far! It was never my attention to hurt anyone!"

An argument broke out between the two men and soon all the thieves were yelling. "Silence!" Everyone immediately went quiet and looked at Syth. "That's better. I am not going to arrest anyone. I have a proposition for you that will be beneficial to all of us."

"What kind of proposition?" the leader asked.

"I propose that you guys work for me."

There was a pause and then everyone laughed. Syth waited patiently for the laughter to subside.

"Work for you?" one of the men asked. "And what would we be doing? Protecting the queen?" He laughed again.

"I think you misunderstand," Syth said. "You would not be doing anything different than what you are doing right now."

Everyone looked confused.

"I am the one who has been killing all the people," Syth said.

"You?" asked the leader. Syth nodded. "But why? You are the queen's protector? Why would you kill her subjects?"

"I serve Queen Laurel, yes, but she is not my true master. I do the will of my true master, not the queen's. What is your answer?"

"If we join you, what is to stop us from turning you in? I am sure that the queen will offer a hefty reward for turning in the assassin."

"Because if you turn me in, I will kill you. Slowly. No, you will not turn me in. What is your answer?"

The leader wanted to know more. "Why do you need us? You seem to be doing a good job on your own."

"My movements are being watched. The queen's advisors are getting suspicious. I need people to work for me so I can do my job of protecting the queen."

"And we would be doing the same thing as before?" asked another man.

"Yes. You would be robbing and murdering to your heart's content. But you will be following my orders from now on. You will be richer and more feared than you have ever imagined."

"It sounds good to me!" one man exclaimed. The others shouted their agreement. The leader didn't seem inclined to accept Syth's offer though.

"I don't know about this," he said.

"We will join you," said a man, and Syth could tell that it was the second man who had spoken when he had been listening outside the door.

"Good," said Syth. His master had told him about King Korlas and the Zantan Robbers. While Syth hated Korlas as much as his master did, he had to admit the organization of a secret society of thieves and murders was a good idea. While he was tracking the men to this building, he had come up with the idea to form his own secret society to take over the work he had begun. "The first thing I want you to do is recruit everyone you know who might be interested in joining us. But be inconspicuous about it. We don't want the city watch to hear about us." The men agreed.

"Now, I must be getting back. I am trusting you to do as I have asked. I will contact you again in a few days. Wait for me here." He looked down at the injured man on the floor. He was still moaning about his lost arm. "But I will need a body to bring back to the city watch." He took his sword and stabbed the man in the heart. The moaning stopped.

He picked up the body, tossed it over his shoulder, and left the building.

*   *   *

The sound of the riders coming together was loud in Laurel's ears. It was the first match of the joust, and already Laurel didn't like it.

Jousting was a brutal sport. Two horsemen charged at each other full speed, a long lance aimed at the opposite rider. True, the lances were made of wood and the riders wore heavy armor, but it was rare that anyone came out of a joust uninjured. She had even heard of riders dying in a joust. But the crowd loved it. They cheered louder for the joust than they had for any of the other three competitions.

One man went down as his opponent's lance hit him square in the chest. The lance broke and the man fell hard. The horse kept running around until a groom rushed out and grabbed the reigns. The crowd roared even louder.

The man's squire ran out and helped the fallen rider to his feet. He slowly moved away as the winner of the match led his own horse around the yard and waved to the crowd. He would move on to the next round while the loser was out of the tournament, his hopes of becoming a Sentinel dashed.

On and on it went throughout the morning. Rider after rider fell to the lance, and rider after rider led their horse triumphantly around the yard. A few men were not able to leave the yard on their own. One man was hit in the head with a lance and he didn't move again when he hit the ground. The crowd gasped as the lance struck the rider's helmet, and everyone got to their feet and leaned in for a closer look.

The medical team ran out to the man and checked him. They told the crowd that the man was alive, just unconscious. They picked him up and carried him off and the tournament continued.

Laurel found her thoughts wandering to the previous day. She thought about how Sam came to her, the fury plain on his face. *What is wrong?* she had asked. *Syth has disappeared!* he had answered. The guard who had seen

Syth leave told her that it looked like he was trying to track the murderer. Sam had scoffed at that and said that it would be impossible for anyone to track the assassin in the city. *He is up to something* Sam had proclaimed. Queen Laurel was getting tired of Sam's suspicions.

Syth had arrived about an hour later with the body of a dead man. He said that he had tracked the man to his hideout, and after the man had confessed to killing the shopkeeper and his family, he had fought him and killed him.

Convenient that you killed the man instead of bringing him to the Queen to confess, Sam had said.

The man would not be taken alive, Syth had retorted.

Laurel interrupted their argument. *Do you think this is the man who has been committing all the murders?* she had asked.

I doubt it, her dark-skinned protector had answered. *He didn't seem capable enough to have killed all those people and gotten away with it.*

That meant the killer was still out there. The man that Syth had brought back had just been a copy-cat. According to Sam, the poor shopkeeper and his family had been murdered and then the shop had been looted. Although the victims' possessions had not been taken from their bodies. Laurel felt like crying again. Oh, how she missed her husband! Oh, how she needed his strength right then!

She looked back to the tournament just as another man was brutally knocked off his horse. The victor led his horse around the area, just like all the rest had done, but this one stopped in front of Queen Laurel. She was surprised. She was on a balcony, but it was fairly low and within the man's reach. He held out his hand to her and she saw a rose held gently in his gauntlet. She took the rose from his hand and held it to her breast. "Thank you," she said. The man didn't say a word. He just turned his horse around and rode away. His visor was down, so she hadn't been able to see his face.

She looked down at the rose and felt tears streaming down her face. Suddenly she felt much better. This man's small act of kindness had lifted her heart out of the depths of despair. She felt her smile grow wider. She realized that the entire crowd was watching her now. She gave them a wave and the crowd let out a roar louder than any other they had done so far. She closed her eyes and let the sound wash over her. She truly felt loved by her people. She felt closer to them now than she ever had before.

Finally, mercifully, the joust ended. The winner of the joust was the man who had given her the rose. She was glad. The two champions of the joust stood on the raised platform and waved to the ecstatic crowd. Four events were down. The joust had taken all day to complete, it had the biggest group of participants out of any of the events, and the final event would take place the next day: the large scale battle.

*   *   *

There were only eight contestants in the large battle. Each contestant was a general in charge of two hundred men. They could choose what kind of soldiers they wanted in their army and how many of each. The soldiers had blunted weapons, and the arrows had no points on them.

This was a challenge of battle tactics. A general had to plan his strategy beforehand, and then make any needed changes during the battle. They had to be able to think quickly and react to difficult situations. This was the contest that Laurel was most interested in. Out of her advisors, only Gyles had signed up for this contest. He had been a squad leader when he was a knight, so he had some experience. Sam had wanted to sign up for it as well, but he hadn't thought he would need to. He had been confident in his ability to win the melee competition, and now it was too late to sign up. He was not happy about it.

The first battle of the day was starting. It pitted Gyles against another knight who never had any experience leading men in battle. The other knight had chosen two hundred members of the cavalry. Gyles had a mixture of archers, cavalry, pike men, and swordsmen. When the battle had begun, the less experienced knight sent his entire force right at Gyles' army. The man wanted to finish this battle quickly and he thought that he could easily over power Gyles. He was wrong.

Archers loosed their arrows, but they had little effect on the charging soldiers. They wore heavy armor and the arrows, without heads, simply bounced off. Just before they reached Gyles' army, he brought his pike men out front. The long pikes knocked the soldiers off their horses, and then it was easy for the swordsmen to finish them off.

Not all the horsemen had fallen, however. There weren't enough pike men to take down all the cavalry, and they made quick work of the archers. But there weren't very many of them left and the combined might of the pike men, cavalry, and swordsmen took care of them. Gyles was victorious, and he was moving on.

The next battle for Gyles wasn't so easy. He faced an opponent that had a good mixture of troop types as well. Gyles tried to send his cavalry around a hill to come upon the other army unawares. The problem was that the other general had the same idea. The two cavalries met up in the middle and had a great battle. The other knight had a larger force of cavalry than Gyles did, and his cavalry lost the battle. The other cavalry, however was now too small to make a flanking maneuver, and they retreated back to their commander.

Gyles had not been idle however and he had sent the rest of his force forward to attack his opponent. His archers shot arrows at their foe, and while the other army hid behind their shields, the pike men and swordsmen attacked. The enemy archers' arrows were nullified by the pike men and their large shields. Plus, the enemy archers were few in number, and soon no more arrows flew from the enemy camp. By the time Gyles' archers' arrows had stopped falling and the enemy's men had come out from behind their shields, Gyles' force was on them. The fight was almost over when the cavalry returned, and they almost turned the tide against Gyles, but there were too few to win against Gyles' men. Once again, Gyles was victorious. He was going to move onto the finals. But, being in the final two, he had already won a spot as a Sentinel. Laurel was thrilled.

Gyles ended up losing the final battle. His opponent's tactics were straightforward and not very skillful, but they were effective. The general was a high-ranking member of the city watch, and he had handpicked all his men from the ranks of the watch. They were well-trained and they proved it on the battlefield.

The man sent his force straight at Gyles. No flanking maneuvers, no trickery at all. His pike men were in front for defense, his archers in the middle, his swordsmen at the rear, and is cavalry on either side of the formation. He lost a few men to arrows, but not many. By the time the two forces met, the watchman had only lost a dozen or so soldiers. They proved they were the better trained of the two forces and quickly overran Gyles' army.

We have all ten, Laurel thought when the battle was over. *Finally, it is done.*

*   *   *

That evening, after celebrating and feasting, they had the ceremony to make the ten victors into Sentinels. The ten men stood on a raised platform in the center of the arena that they had used for all the challenges except the final battle. The crowd was cheering wildly for the men that would do their best to protect their country. Queen Laurel stood in front of them along with a servant. The servant held ten snow white cloaks over his arm.

Syth was closest to her. Next to him stood Kyler, the knight that had taken second place in the first melee. Then came Marlen, the knight who had taken second place in the second melee. After him came the huge mercenary Bruce, the hammer wielding fighter who had won the second melee. After Bruce was Ned, an older farmer and his son, Garland. They had won the archery contest. Then came Martin, a knight and the second-place finisher of the joust. After Martin was Earl, the winner of the joust and the man who had given her the rose. He was a large man, with a face most women would swoon over. Then came Gyles, her advisor, and last was Francis, the city watchman and winner of the final battle.

She looked at each of them in turn. These were the men that were going to infuse the country with hope once more. These were the men who would be the protectors of her people, who would be talked about for years to come. She hoped they were up to the task.

Laurel stepped in front of Syth. She spoke loudly for all to hear. "Syth, from the distant land of Abberdon, you have been found worthy to take up the title of Sentinel. Do you accept this position of honor and responsibility, and do you swear to guard the realm and everyone in it from their enemies?"

Syth didn't answer immediately. "I cannot accept," he said finally. The crowd gasped, and Laurel could hear whispering all around her.

She didn't know what to do. She hadn't expected this. She didn't know what to say. Syth saved her the trouble from saying anything when he continued to speak.

"I am not from this land. I am a stranger here. And while I have been accepted by the good people of Blanderly with open arms, the fact remains that I have another home where my heart lies. I am not fit to be a protector of this realm, just a protector of my queen. I must respectfully decline this honored position and ask that you give it to the runner up of the melee, Sam."

The queen looked over at Sam who was standing off to the side. He didn't look happy with Syth's proclamation. Laurel knew that he didn't want the title of Sentinel to be handed to him, he wanted to earn it. She was afraid that for that reason he might decline as well.

"Sam, please come forward," Laurel said.

As Sam walked up, Syth moved by him on his way off the platform. He grinned at Sam, and the queen's advisor shot him a look full of venom. Laurel saw the look and knew that Sam was terribly embarrassed.

Sam stood where Syth had just a few moments before, and Laurel asked him the same question. Sam didn't answer right away, and Laurel was afraid he would decline just like Syth did, but finally Sam accepted. Laurel took one of the white cloaks from the servant and swung it around his shoulders. Then, she pinned it closed. The crowd roared in approval, but Sam's visage didn't soften.

The rest of the ceremony went smoothly. Everyone else eagerly accepted the title of Sentinel, and they all swore their oaths to protect Blanderly and its people. Everyone was beaming with pride when the queen pinned their cloaks on. Laurel let out a sigh of relief when it was finished.

30

"Teach me to fight."

The remark surprised Aiden. He looked over at Portia to see if she was smirking. She wasn't. Her face was stern and serious.

They were watching a group of Paladins train. Aiden was impressed with their fluid and precise movements. With or without their god's protection, these warriors would be formidable indeed.

This was the first time in a couple days that Aiden and Portia had been alone together. They didn't say much to each other, but they didn't have to. Just being close to one another was good enough for Aiden. They were constantly being herded from one relative's house to another. Aiden was thrilled to be meeting so many relatives that he never knew existed, but it was tiring. While he loved them dearly, he was glad to have a little time away from them. Veronna, on the other hand, was just the opposite. She couldn't get enough of the family. All the attention was on her. Everyone was telling her how she looked just like her mother. One of their grandparents, their mother's mother, gave her a hand painting of their mother. She truly had been beautiful.

"What?" he asked.

"Teach me to fight," Portia said again.

"Why?" Aiden didn't know what else to say.

Portia threw up her hands. "Because I am sick of being helpless when we are attacked! I am sick of hiding behind everyone else and hoping everyone will be safe. I want to make a difference."

"That is not what I meant," said Aiden. "Why me?"

"What do you mean, 'why you?'"

"Why do you want me to teach you? Look around you. Every person you see would be better at teaching you how to fight than me."

Portia grinned. "Like who?"

"Well, my dad for one. He is the best fighter I have ever seen. Dustin, Brione, my uncle, every single one of those Paladins training down there. Jaden, Zach."

Portia made a sour face at the last two names. She was not fond of the two black-skinned fighters. She didn't trust them.

"Yeah, but I doubt any of them would be willing to train me. Plus, you just said that your dad is the best fighter you have ever seen, right?" Aiden nodded. "Well, he trained you. I believe you will be just as good someday. You will do just fine training me. Please?"

She made a face that Aiden hadn't seen before. It was pouty, and yet excited at the same time. Aiden couldn't resist. He smiled at her. "Alright."

She gave a squeal of delight and threw her arms around Aiden. She squeezed him so hard he couldn't breathe. "Okay!" he tried to say. Finally, she let go and said, "Let's go!"

They started walking together and then stopped when they realized something. They didn't know where the training equipment was! They had to interrupt the Paladins in their training sessions and ask directions. Not surprisingly, the lead Paladin didn't get angry at the couple for interrupting them. He seemed eager to help and even offered to take them there himself. Aiden declined, not wanting to bother the man more than he already had. He told him that with the directions the man had given them, they would have no trouble finding the building that had the equipment.

As they walked Portia surprised Aiden by grabbing his hand and holding it in her own. When she didn't let go, he was even more surprised.

She glanced at him and smiled, then looked forward again. She was acting like this was a normal thing! Aiden didn't dislike it though.

They took their time and enjoyed their walk together. People they had met in the last few days waved to them as they passed by. Luckily, no one stopped to chat. The two youngsters wanted to be left alone.

Finally, they found the building they were looking for and went inside. It was a large, one room building. All four walls were covered with weapons and armor. There were also several large tables covered with weapons and armor. Every kind of weapon you could think of was on display. Two men were looking at one section of wall covered with swords. They both looked at Aiden and Portia when they stepped inside.

One smiled and came over to them. "May I help you?"

"Yes," replied Aiden. "We want to train."

"Well, there are quite a few instructors here that I'm sure would be willing to help you. Would you like me to take you to one?"

"No," said Aiden. "You don't understand. I am going to train her. We don't need an instructor. We just need weapons."

"Oh. I see."

Just then the second man came up to them. "Don't you know who this is?" he asked his companion. "This is the son of Timmond."

"Oh," said the man. "I guess in that case you probably don't need an instructor." Aiden smiled. "What kind of weapons do you need?"

"Well, we need training weapons."

"Wood?"

"Yes."

"Follow me."

They followed the two men to a section of the wall in the far corner of the enormous room. There they found the training weapons. They were made of wood, but weighted so they felt like a real weapon in the user's hands.

"What kind of weapons will you be using?" one of the men asked.

"Well, I like swords," said Aiden. "I'm not sure what kind of weapon Portia will use."

Portia walked down the line of weapons, inspecting each one. She shook her head at the axes and moved on. She glanced at Aiden. "Which one do you suggest?"

"Well, if you are set on having me teach you, I would suggest you choose a sword, since that is my weapon of choice."

"Okay. That makes sense." She walked to the swords and studied them. "You choose the one you are going to use."

Aiden stepped forward and looked at the swords. He saw one that looked to be about the same size as his sword, which he had left at his dad's house, and took it off the wall. He gripped the hilt in both hands and held it out straight in front of him. The weight and balance seemed right. The he took a couple of swings. He smiled in satisfaction and said, "This one is perfect."

Portia studied the swords again and picked one. The tip immediately dropped to the floor. "It's too heavy," she said and hung it back on the wall. She found another one, a smaller one, and grabbed it. She held it up and smiled. She copied Aiden and held it out straight in front of her, a serious look on her face. Then she took a couple of swings. She smiled at Aiden and said, "This one is perfect." Aiden laughed.

"Come on," Aiden said and turned to leave the building. Portia followed.

"Wait!" came a cry from behind them. They both stopped and turned to see one of the men running toward them. He reached them and said, "May I watch you two train? I remember Timmond from when he lived here before and I would love to see his son in action."

Aiden, not looking pleased, turned to Portia.

"No," she said. "I would rather you didn't. You see, it will be my first time using a sword, and I'm afraid I would be terribly embarrassed if someone was watching me. Sorry."

The man looked disappointed but said that he understood.

Aiden and Portia left the building and searched for a secluded area to train in. Portia was telling the truth when she told the man that she would be embarrassed if someone saw her practicing with a sword.

They found a large grove of trees and entered. In the center of the grove was an opening. It was large and quiet. They stood in the opening and looked around. The trail that led here through the trees twisted and turned, and they could see no opening in the trees in any direction. This would be a good place to teach Portia.

"Stand here," he told her, and then he went and stood a few paces away. She held her sword down with the point touching the ground. "Lift your sword up in front of you." She did so. "Not straight up. Hold it at an angle."

She did so. "Like this?" she asked.

"Yes, that's better," Aiden replied. "That way you can swing the sword for an attack or bring it into position to block."

Aiden searched his memories for the training methods his dad had used for him when he was just starting out. Portia didn't say anything. She was patiently letting Aiden sort through his thoughts.

Finally, Aiden was ready. "First, I'm going to teach you how to block." Portia nodded. "Now, blocking is very difficult. You have to anticipate where your opponent is going to attack. Inexperienced fighters tell you where they are attacking with their eyes. Pay attention to where they are looking, and you can easily block. But more experienced fighters look you in the eyes, not where they plan to attack, so it can be harder to tell where to put your sword."

"Why can't I just look at my enemy's sword and block it that way?"

Aiden smiled. "Let me show you." He swung his sword slowly at her. He swung very wide, then very high. Portia easily put her sword up to block all his swings. Suddenly, Aiden tapped her shoulder with his other hand. Not very hard, but hard enough to make her take a step back.

"Whoa," she said. "I didn't even see your hand move!"

"That is why you shouldn't look at your opponent's weapon all the time. He could hit you or kick you or stab you with a weapon in his other hand."

"What do you do?"

"A lot of it is instinct. You need to make a very quick study of your opponent and be able to predict what he will do. That is very hard, but with enough practice, you can become good at it." Aiden smiled again. "You can also glance at his weapon or at his eyes from time to time."

"Sounds complicated."

"It is very complicated. But it is important to learn. Now, let's begin. I am going to tell you where I am swinging, and you will block. Sound good?"

Portia nodded. "Yes." She was smiling.

"Up," Aiden said, and took an overhead swing at her. She put her sword up and blocked the strike. "Left." Again, she easily blocked Aiden's sword. "Up," he said again. This went on for a few minutes, then he started going faster. "Up. Down. Left. Up. Down. Right." Faster and faster he went, and Portia found it harder to block his strikes.

Finally, she missed his sword, and it hit her in the arm. "Ouch!" she said and moved back. She stood there, glaring at Aiden and rubbing her arm. "That hurt."

"Sorry," Aiden said and shrugged.

Portia walked back to Aiden and held her sword up in front of her. "Again."

Aiden started slowly again. Up. Down. Down. Right. Up. Left. His swings came faster and faster until he hit her again, this time on the leg. Again, she fell back, this time limping a little.

"It gets too hard when you go fast. I get my directions mixed up."

Aiden had an idea. "Let's try it again." Portia frowned at him. "Come on. It will be easier this time, I promise." She reluctantly came back to him. "Ready?" Aiden asked. Portia nodded. "Think of a map," Aiden said. Portia gave him a confused look, but had no chance to respond, because Aiden had started the drill again.

"North!"

Aiden swung quickly, but Portia had her sword up in time. It took her a moment to realize what Aiden had done, but when she did, she smiled. "Again," she said.

"North. South. East. West." Aiden called out directions, and Portia blocked each strike. Aiden went faster and faster, but Portia easily blocked each swing. He could not hit her. At first, she had a look of concentration on her face, but after a while she was smiling. Aiden was, too.

"North," he yelled, and Portia had her sword up. But Aiden didn't swing down, he took a slice from left to right, hitting her in the leg. "Ouch!" she cried and backed away again.

She looked at him, glaring once again. "You cheated!"

"Me?" Aiden said. "How did I cheat?"

"You said north, but you actually came east! You lied!"

"Do you think your opponent will tell you where they are going to swing? Well, they won't. They will try to trick you, do things that will surprise you. That is the way my dad taught us how to fight. Always keep your enemy off guard."

"Well, it hurt," Portia said.

Aiden felt bad. But he was just trying to teach her. "I'm sorry. Let me see your leg."

"No." She backed away further.

"Come on," said Aiden. Let me see it."

He was close enough to touch her now, but she turned away from him. He turned with her, his body leaning over her back. Suddenly, she turned into him, and they were face to face.

"Let me see it," Aiden said.

Portia smiled. "No."

Then they were kissing.

Aiden froze. He hadn't expected this to happen and he didn't know what to do. Portia's eyes were closed, but Aiden's were opened wide. Finally, sensing Aiden's hesitation, Portia opened her eyes, and quickly backed away.

She stepped away from him, a look of embarrassment on her face. "I'm sorry. I thought you wanted…"

"No!" said Aiden. "You don't understand. I did…I do…it's just that you surprised me and I've never…" He stopped talking, suddenly embarrassed as well. His face turned crimson.

"Oh," said Portia. "I see. You have never kissed a girl before. Is that it?"

Suddenly Aiden was too embarrassed to look her in the eye. Instead, he looked at his feet and nodded.

"I'm sorry. I didn't mean to make you feel bad. I just find it hard to believe. I mean, you're the greatest guy I have ever met. I thought that the girls would have been lining up to kiss you."

Aiden looked up again. "I haven't really had the chance to kiss anyone. The only girls I have been exposed to for any amount of time are my sister and Brione, and I'm not going to kiss them."

"I see." Portia walked back to Aiden. "So? Do you want a second kiss?"

He thought about it for as long as it took to nod his head. Then they were kissing again. This time, Aiden kissed back.

After a while, Portia broke away, a grin on her face. "Eh. It wasn't that great. But we can work on it. You will get better with practice."

"What!" Aiden said and grabbed for her, but she quickly skipped away. He chased her, both of them laughing. She reached her sword and picked it up. He stopped.

"You have distracted me for too long," she said, still smiling. "We have to get back to work. Now, teach me how to strike someone with this thing."

And so, he did. He taught her the difference between swings and thrusts, and when to use each one. He taught her when it was beneficial to spin and when not to. He also had her practice defending more. He had her watch his eyes to tell where he would swing. And then he came after her hard. He didn't call out any directions, he didn't give away his attacks with his eyes. She had to use everything he taught her to keep his sword at bay.

She was a quick learner and did well. He hit her a dozen times, trying his best to make the blows light and as painless as possible, but she blocked many more. They trained for several hours, neither wanting to stop, and at the end he was very impressed.

Finally, when it was difficult for both of them just to stand up, they decided to stop. Despite their exhaustion, they were both happy and smiling. That was the longest amount of time they had spent completely alone with each other, and they didn't want it to end. So, they sat together, talking.

"I think I should try another kind of weapon," Portia said.

"Why? You are doing really well with the sword."

"It's just so scary being that close to my enemy. I mean, I was scared today when we were sparing, and it was with you. I can't imagine what I will feel like when the fight is real."

"What did you have in mind?"

"I don't know. Something I could throw or shoot from a distance."

Aiden thought for a moment. "A bow might be too difficult. You have to pull the string back and hold it steady. Some of those bow strings are really hard to pull back. You could use a crossbow. You don't have to pull back the string, you just have to reset it. Then you can aim and pull a lever and the quarrel goes. It might be easier than a bow."

"But what if someone gets close to me. Would it be good for hand-to-hand combat if I needed it?"

"I guess you could hit an enemy with the crossbow, but it wouldn't be very effective."

"So, is there a weapon I could use for both up close and far away?" Portia asked.

"Yes." He turned to her and squeezed her arm. "I don't know if you are strong enough though." She smacked him in the arm. He laughed. "A javelin is like a throwing spear. It is a little shorter, so it's easier and more accurate to throw. But you can also use it in hand-to-hand combat as well. You can use it like a quarterstaff with a blade on one end. How does that sound?"

"I think I would like to use that."

"Okay. But I am not an expert with those. Would you be willing to be trained by someone else who is?"

"Sure." Portia stood up. "I'm hungry. Let's go find something to eat."

Aiden got to his feet as well. As they started back to the building to return their practice weapons, Aiden said, "If you do decide to use javelins, I would also suggest that you keep a sword in your possession as well. You did well with it today."

Hand-in-hand they made their way to the weapons building. On their way there they ran into Tim. He smiled when he saw them walking hand-in-hand. Aiden and Portia smiled back at him.

Tim noticed the weapons in their hands. "What's going on?" he asked them.

"Portia asked me to teach her swordplay."

"Really? And how did she do?"

Aiden smiled at Portia. "Very well. I think she might be good enough to defeat a small child now." Portia smacked him in the arm, and Aiden laughed. "But seriously, she did well. I was impressed."

"Good," Tim said.

"But I find that it is scary to have to be that close to my opponent," Portia said. "I was wondering if you would be willing to teach me how to use a javelin."

"A javelin, huh? I think I could do that. I would be a better teacher at that than Aiden." He turned to his son. "Where are you two headed?"

"We are going to return these weapons and then find something to eat."

"I'm also hungry. Do you mind if I join you?"

"Of course not," Aiden and Portia said together.

The three of them walked together to return the weapons, then walked towards the temple to the eating hall. Aiden's uncle David found them and came up to them. He looked excited.

"God has finally revealed to Turner Layne's location. He is sending me and three other Paladins to go get him. We leave in the morning."

"That's great!" exclaimed Aiden. He couldn't keep the grin off his face. He couldn't have received better news. Portia squeezed his hand and put her head on his shoulder.

"Would it be alright if I accompanied you?" Tim asked David. The Paladin looked surprised. "I am very concerned about him." Tim continued. "And I think it would be easier for him to come with you if someone he knows is there. What do you say?"

"We'll have to talk to Turner about it."

"No, we don't. I am not a part of his religion anymore. I don't need his permission to do anything. The choice is yours. I would really like to go with you."

David thought it over for a moment. "Alright. You can come. I think you're right about Layne needing to have someone he knows there. It might be best if you stayed at the temple tonight. All the rest of us are, and we're leaving at first light."

"Alright," Tim said. "Sounds good."

*   *   *

The dark-skinned man led Amanda up to the large stone steps to the front gates of the palace. She was very nervous now, and she wished she could spend more time in the beautiful gardens to think. She had never seen such a beautiful place before, or such a large building as the palace.

As she and her escort approached the two guards, she began to get even more nervous. The men were very intimidating in their armor with the devilish figure on their chests. They both had large swords strapped at their waists and held pikes in their hands, the butts of the weapons resting on the ground. Her escort stopped in front of them.

The two men looked at her. "What do we have here?" asked one of the guards.

"I am bringing this girl to my master. Please let us through," said the black-skinned man.

"I don't think so," said the guard. "I think you should take her to the king. He does rule here, after all. I think he will enjoy her. Hand her over."

"No. Let us through."

"Hand her over!" The guard reached for Amanda, but the dark man stepped in front of her.

"I wouldn't do that if I were you," he said. He put his hand on the hilt of his sword.

"If you won't hand her over, then we will just take her by force." He started to draw his own sword, but the dark man's sword was at his neck quicker than he would have believed possible. He didn't even see the dark-skinned man move. Amanda's mouth gaped open. She hadn't seen the man move either.

"Let us through," Amanda's escort said again.

The other guard brought down his pike and pointed it at the dark man. "Put your sword down and back away," he said.

"No."

The man stabbed at the dark man, but he kicked out and knocked the pike aside with his foot, then he had a sword in his other hand, pointing it at the man's chest. "Let us pass. My master is expecting us. You don't want to get on his bad side."

The guards hesitated, but finally both men stepped aside to let Amanda and her escort through.

The inside of the palace was almost as beautiful as the outside, but Amanda had a hard time enjoying her surroundings. She was becoming aware of just how dangerous her captor really was. His master must be even more dangerous. Suddenly, she was very frightened.

She followed her escort through the elaborate corridors, not noticing the sites around her. She was very worried now, wondering what she had gotten herself into. She was regretting agreeing to come with this man. Although she didn't think she really had had a choice in the matter. If she had refused, Amanda had the feeling that the man would have forced her to come with him anyway.

After a little while, the man left the main corridors of the palace and entered smaller, less elaborate hallways. *These must be hallways that servants use*, she thought. *Strange.*

Finally, after what seemed like hours to Amanda, they stopped in front of an unremarkable doorway. *Is this his master's chambers?* she thought. *It looks so normal.*

Her escort knocked loudly on the door and waited. After a moment, the door opened. Amanda didn't see anyone who could have opened it. The doorway was empty.

Her escort walked into the room, Amanda having no choice but to follow him. They entered a square chamber that had a couch and a couple chairs. A man was sitting on the couch, watching her enter the room. He stood up.

He had dark skin just like her escort, but he was dressed in dark purple robes that had gold running down the sleeves and around the neckline. The man looked young. *Is this his master? He looks no older than my companion.*

"Ah, Amanda," the man greeted with a smile. "It is so good to finally meet you. I hope you had a pleasant journey."

Amanda was taken aback by the greeting. The man's kindness was obviously feigned, but what was the point? There was only one way to find out.

"My journey was fine. Thank you. May I ask why you brought me here?"

"Straight to the point, huh? I like that. Serving as the king's councilor I am bombarded with empty words and pleasantries every day. I do tire of it. It is nice to speak with someone who is above all that." Again, Amanda was confused.

"I brought you here," the man continued, "to give you what you want."

"How do you know what I want?"

The man laughed. "Oh, I know. I have my ways. I know of your desire to kill your former lover, Dustin."

"He was not my lover." Amanda looked down. "Our relationship never got that far."

"Lover or not, I want to give you the chance for revenge. Are you interested?"

"Why would you want to help me? What do you gain out of this?"

"Helping people is what I do, Amanda. I have possession of great power, and I have chosen to use this power to help other people. Please don't laugh. A lot of people do when I tell them this. But I have a soft spot in my heart for those less fortunate than I. I learned of your situation and my heart went out to you. I decided that I had to help you.

I know where Dustin is. I know he is coming to Parkos. He will be here soon. Do you want revenge on him?"

Amanda didn't know what she wanted, but she didn't think it was very wise to tell the man that. He brought her all the way here for this. He would probably get angry at her if he realized that he did that for nothing. She didn't trust this man at all and she knew that his story about wanting to help other people was a lie, but she thought it best to play along for now.

"Yes. I would like that very much."

The man smiled at her. "Great! It makes me happy to hear that. Now, Dustin is on his way here, so I will need to find you rooms to stay in while we wait for him." He turned to her escort. "Please take her to the guest tower and watch over her while she is there. See to any need she might have."

The man nodded. "Yes Master." He turned to Amanda. "Please come with me."

"I will send for you when Dustin arrives," the dark man in purple robes said as Amanda and her escort reached the doorway.

As she walked down the hallway beside her escort, Amanda glanced back over her shoulder. She saw the man standing in front of the couch, watching her leave. Then the door to his chambers closed by themselves.

Ricardo watched Amanda leave until the door closed. He chuckled to himself. *Too easy,* he thought. *She believed every word I said. Her desire for revenge clouded her judgment.* The wizard was in a good mood. He loved nothing more than to manipulate other people who had much less power than he did. He enjoyed controlling other peoples' lives. He was the most powerful man in the world, he deserved to have absolute control. He laughed again. This was going to be fun.

31

Layne felt the rage storming through him as he walked. His assault on the rock formation had been a couple days ago and he hadn't fought since. He tried to spar with the other men in the caravan, but after the first man agreed and Layne had accidentally injured him, all the others refused his offers.

He didn't know why, but fighting was the only thing that kept the rage at bay. If he didn't fight, the rage consumed him. He would think about everything that had been done to him, about all the lies that Tim had taught him, about how he was innocent and yet punished severely. He would think about how his group, his family, had just left him to his fate and had a stranger who they had just met break him out of his cell. His loved ones had abandoned him. He would never forget that.

They were traveling northeast, with only one other road that could actually be called a road, branching off to the north. They had passed that two days ago, and this road had gone on straight ever since.

They had not been bothered by anything since the rock gnomes, and they had been making good time. They had seen a few other travelers heading in the opposite direction, but nothing that he would call an enemy.

Before the rage had enveloped him, he had been thinking about the item that they had stormed the formation to recover. He wondered if it was worth the lives that had been lost. He wondered what kind of item an evil king would want to possess so badly. It must be an object of great power. If that was the case, then he needed to keep the king from getting it. But how was he going to do that?

But now, all thoughts of the king and the item had disappeared from his mind. There was only the rage. Tyler saw the look on Layne's face and asked if he was alright, but Layne just glared at him and didn't answer. Tyler quickly looked away. He knew what was going on. He didn't say anything else to Layne.

It was late afternoon when Campbell stopped the caravan and called for the guards to come forward. Layne walked to the front of the caravan and saw what had made Campbell stop. Standing in the road, about fifty yards in front of them, were five men. Five armed men.

"Who do you think they are?" asked one guard.

"Probably highwaymen," said another.

"What should we do?" asked the first.

"We will continue forward," said Campbell. "I want all of you to stay up front. Layne, you lead. The rest of you, follow behind. The wagons and I will bring up the rear."

They did as the merchant had said and started forward again. It was strange, but Layne thought that one of the men looked like Tim. As he got closer, he realized it was Tim. Layne was surprised. *Why is he with these men? Where are the others?*

"Layne!" Tim called out. "Is that you?"

Layne walked faster, right toward Tim. Tim spread his arms, expecting Layne to hug him. Instead, the big man shoved Tim with both arms, almost sending the mercenary leader to the ground.

"What..." said Tim, stunned.

"You!" cried Layne. "You lied to me!" He shoved Tim again. This time, Tim was ready for it and he didn't go as far back. "You abandoned me!" Another shove. This time, Tim didn't budge. But he also didn't do anything to stop the younger man. He let Layne play out his rage. "You left me in a cell!" This time, instead of pushing Tim, he fell against him, sobbing. Tim put his arms around Layne and held him, not saying anything. "Do you know what they did to me?" Layne asked into Tim's chest. "Do you?"

"No," Tim said quietly. "I don't. But I'm sure it was hard to endure."

Layne pushed away from Tim and looked at his mentor and teacher. "Why?" he asked. "Why was I punished for something I didn't do? Why did you leave me there? I was innocent!"

"I know you were innocent. We had to leave. We could do nothing for you. If we would have stayed in the city, we would have all been put to death. Then we couldn't have helped you. But we had Tyler get you out. And it worked. You are safe now."

"You had a stranger get me out! I needed you and you had someone I didn't even know help me!" As the words came out, Layne knew they were true. That was one reason he was so angry. He had needed his family. Dustin, his brother. Brione, who he thought of as an older sister. Aiden, his best friend. And Tim, his father figure. The man he looked up to. The man he idolized. They had all left him when he had needed them the most. "I needed you," he said, quieter this time.

"I am so sorry."

"Sorry? You're sorry? You have no idea what they did to me. They tortured me after a bogus trial. They hurt me for days. I wanted to die. Then I almost got my wish. They sentenced me to death! I did nothing wrong and they sentenced me to death! You! You taught me that there was good in the world. That most people were good and wanted only justice. Was that justice? Tell me! Was it?"

"No."

"It wasn't! You lied to me! You lied!"

Tim could only shake his head. He looked heart broken. "No. I didn't lie to you."

"You did!"

"No. People are good. Justice does exist. Don't let one horrible person make you give up on your beliefs."

"Not my beliefs," said Layne. "Your beliefs. That is what you taught us. And we believed you. Like fools, we believed you!"

"Layne, I know what was done to you was very terrible, but can we discuss this later? I came to take you to a place where we are safe for the time being. I have come to take you back to your family. Come with me."

Layne looked at Tim for a long time, not saying anything. This decision was pivotal. He had told himself he was not going to go back to the group. He was not going to let Tim lie to him anymore. But he did want to see everyone again before he left the group for good.

"Okay. I'll go with you."

Tim smiled and sighed in relief. "Good,"

"But you have to do something for me first," Layne continued.

"Of course!" Tim said without thinking. "Anything you need."

"Fight me."

The remark surprised Tim. "What?"

"Fight me!"

"Why?"

Tyler spoke up. "Please do it. Trust me, he needs it."

Tim still looked confused, but he agreed. "Alright. I will do it if you need me to."

Without another word Layne had his battle ax in hand and swung it at Tim. The strike was quicker than Tim had thought it would be, and he barely got his sword out of its scabbard and up in time to block. Layne swung again, this strike even quicker. Everyone else, merchant, guard and Paladin alike, watched the confrontation wordlessly.

"Are you trying to kill me?" Tim asked as Layne attacked again. Layne said nothing, instead letting his ax speak for him as he kept up the attack.

Tim had taught Layne to fight with an ax for the past two years, and he knew what to expect. That is the only reason Layne didn't cut him in half with his huge ax. Instead, Tim blocked every blow, but didn't swing back at Layne.

"Fight me!" Layne cried. "Don't just stand there, attack me!"

"No," said Tim.

"Do it!" yelled Tyler from the side. "Please!"

Tim was very confused, but he did as he was asked. He started attacking.

He did easy swings at first, not even trying to make it difficult for Layne to know where he was going. But the other man sneered at him. "Come on! You can do better than that! Challenge me!" So, Tim did.

Tim's attacks started coming faster and faster. At first Layne was able to stand his ground, but then he started falling back. Finally, Layne was steadily giving ground. Suddenly, Layne's foot kicked out and caught Tim in the stomach, halting his attacks. Layne didn't give his opponent any reprieve. He immediately started attacking.

Tim had to duck under a high swing, then jump back out of the way from a swing aimed at his belly. On came Layne, swinging wildly. The look on Layne's face had changed. Where before it was full of rage, now Layne was grinning. That look scared Tim more than Layne's fury had.

On and on went the battle. First Tim retreated, then Layne, then Tim again. Back and forth they went for what seemed to Layne like hours. But at last his rage subsided and exhaustion hit him. He stopped his attacks and went to one knee, dropping his ax to the ground. Okay," he said. "I'm done."

Tim, relieved, dropped to the ground beside him. "What was that all about?"

Layne didn't answer him. Tyler came up to them and did though.

"He needs to fight to keep his anger away."

"What?"

"Ever since being tortured, he's felt an overwhelming rage. The only thing that makes it better is fighting. When he fights, he goes back to his old self again. That is why I asked you to do that. He needed it."

"Is that why you were so aggressive?" Tim asked Layne. Layne nodded.

"I am sure you can imagine the kinds of problems his condition caused us after we left the city," said Tyler.

"Yes," said Tim. "I can."

Tim turned back to Layne. "Would you have killed me if I missed a block?"

This time Layne answered. "I don't know. When the rage hits me I am not myself. I don't know how far I would have gone. I'm sorry. But if I don't keep fighting, it will happen again."

"Why are you like this?"

"I don't know. It is probably the result of the torture I had to endure."

"I am so sorry, Layne," Tim said. "If I could trade places with you, I would."

"I know."

"Did you really mean everything you said before we fought?"

"I don't know that either. I meant them when I said them. But now?" He shrugged.

"Well," said Tim, "we can't have you like this. Something is wrong and we need to figure out a way to help you. I think I know someone who can help. Will you come with me?"

Layne looked at the four men who were conversing with the merchant. "Who are those men?"

Tim got to his feet, Layne following, and then they heard clapping. They looked around and saw all the guards of the caravan applauding.

"That was amazing!" said one.

"I have never seen a display like that before!" said another.

"That's the mercenary, Tim!" said a third.

"He's amazing!"

"So is Layne!"

Tim just shook his head and walked to the four men, Layne following close behind.

The Paladins were smiling, David widest of all. "It was good to see you fight again," he said to Tim.

He didn't answer. Instead he said, "Layne, these men are Paladins. We have been staying in Zion, their home, while we waited for their prophet to tell us where we could find you. Guys, this is Layne, our lost family member and brother of Dustin."

David put his hand out for Layne to shake. "It is a pleasure to meet you Layne. I have heard a lot about you. You're all the group seems to talk about. I am Aiden and Veronna's uncle, David." The other three introduced themselves and shook Layne's hand. Then Layne turned to Tim.

"What happened to you guys?" he asked. "Why weren't you at the meeting place?"

"A group of Zantan Robbers attacked us. They knew we were there, so we had to leave before more came. I'm sorry we weren't there. I think we have a lot to tell each other on the way back to Zion."

"We must be on our way back," said David. "But first." He turned to Campbell. "I understand that you have an item that King Korlas wants very badly."

Campbell's jaw dropped. "How do you know about that?" he asked.

"How did he know about that?" Layne asked Tim.

"Trust me, he knows," was all the mercenary leader said.

"Our prophet gets revelation from God," David was saying. "God told us where we could find Layne. God told the prophet that you have this item. He also said that we cannot allow the king to have it. You must give it to us."

"Why, you are no more than common thieves!" Campbell roared.

"You misunderstand me," said David. "We are not going to take it from you by force. We will give you gold for it. We want to buy it."

"I'm sorry, I can't do that. King Korlas himself sent me to acquire this item. If I don't give it to him, he will kill me."

"How much did he pay you?"

"Two hundred pieces of gold."

"We will give you five hundred. We have it right here." He walked to his horse. They dismounted from their horses, leaving them on the side of the road.

Layne could see the desire in the merchant's eyes when David pulled out two large bags of gold from his saddlebags. The Paladin walked back to the group, a bag of gold in each hand.

"I will give you this gold if you give me the item. Are we agreed?"

Campbell looked torn. He obviously wanted the gold, but his fear of the king kept him from accepting immediately. "But what if the king finds out what I have done? No amount of gold will save me then."

"Go into hiding then," David said. "Buy passage on a ship and sail to Blanderly. The king cannot find you there. You will be safe."

"But this is my home," the merchant complained.

"Then stay here," David said. "It is your choice. But whatever you choose, I cannot let the king take possession of this item."

Campbell still hesitated. "You can come back to Zion with us if you would like," said David. "You will be protected there from the king. You can stay there as long as you like. In fact, all of you can. Anyone who would like to come to Zion is welcome to."

That settled it for the merchant. "Alright," he said. "I will give you the item for five hundred gold pieces and I will come with you to Zion. The item is in that wagon over there. It is all yours."

After David gave the two bags of gold to Campbell, one of the guards led him to the cart that held the chest. David lifted it up out of the cart and put it on the ground. It was large, but lighter than David had expected, and he was able to manage it by himself. The other Paladins gathered around as David crouched down, examining it.

He looked up at Campbell. "How do you open it?"

Campbell looked at David like he was an idiot. "I don't know," the merchant replied. "It never occurred to me to try and open the king's chest!"

David didn't reply. He went back to examining the chest. There was no way to open it. No key hole.

"Didn't you think it odd that the man who made this chest and gave it to you didn't give you a key as well?"

"No, not at all. Magical chests are quite common. I see them all the time in my work. I just thought that the king would already know the magic word to open the chest. I don't worry about things like that. My job is to deliver the goods and collect the money, nothing more."

David stood up. "Alright, we'll figure out how to open it when we get home." He turned to the merchant again. "Since you are coming with us, I'll just put this back in the wagon and we'll be on our way. Is everyone else coming too?"

A couple of the guards agreed to come to Zion with them. But most of them, the ones with families, turned down the offer and went on their way.

The group turned back the way they had come and started for Zion. Tim walked beside Layne. He was thrilled to have Layne back with the group where he belonged, but at the same time he was very concerned about the young man's mental state. He needed help, and Tim hoped that Turner could provide it.

32

The group was gathered together in front of Tim's house, waiting for their leader to return with Layne. Everyone was excited that Layne had finally been found, and they were all eager to see their friend again. Dustin's huge grin wouldn't leave his face, and even Brione had a small bounce in her step.

They were laughing and joking. Then Aiden remembered something and turned to Brione. "Hey. We never finished our conversation."

"What conversation?" Brione asked.

"You were telling Portia and I about how you met my dad."

"I thought we finished that conversation," she said. "I worked as a bouncer at a tavern and met him there. That was it."

"But you never finished the story," Portia put in. The three friends were sitting on the ground, their backs up against the house. Portia and Brione were sitting on either side of Aiden. Portia leaned forward so she could see around him. "You got to the part where you were asked to leave by the owner, but then we got interrupted and we didn't get to hear the rest of the story."

"Oh." Brione seemed uncomfortable for some reason. "There isn't much more to tell."

Aiden, knowing Brione well enough to tell she didn't want to talk about it anymore, dropped the subject. But Portia didn't know Brione very well yet, so she kept on.

"But we want to hear the rest. You can't just begin a story and not end it."

"Portia," Aiden said. "Don't push her. Apparently, she doesn't want to tell the rest of the story. And that's fine."

"But…"

"Shh."

"It's alright," Brione said. "She is right, I shouldn't start a story and not finish it. And besides, she probably won't relax until I give in. So, I will tell the rest of the story. But it is a difficult thing to tell."

She lowered her voice, so only they could hear. The rest of the group stood apart from them, talking with Dustin, who was obviously relieved that they had finally located his brother.

"Well, after I was fired by the owner of the tavern, I left feeling very depressed. I had no idea what I was going to do for work after that. I had my head down as I walked, not paying any attention to where I was going. I almost bumped into Tim, and I would have if he hadn't said something to me and stopped me. I looked up and was startled to see Tim standing before me. He was smiling at me. I was embarrassed. I said, 'Excuse me,' and tried to walk by him.

"He told me to stop, so I did. I didn't look at him though. He asked me if I was fired, and I nodded. He said he was serious when he told me that he would be a lucky man if I worked for him. I looked at him then. He asked me to join his mercenary band.

"I couldn't believe what I was hearing. I couldn't believe that the famous Tim was asking me to work for him. I didn't feel worthy of such an honor, and I told him so. But he told me I was being ridiculous and that he thought I was very worthy to be in his group. I hesitated, but finally accepted. I think I hesitated because I was nervous. The greatest fighter in the land would be watching me every day. It terrified me. But at the same time, I was excited as well. Any young fighter dreams of fighting with Tim's group.

"I told him that I needed to go home and get the rest of my stuff. He and his partner, a man named Parson, the second-in-command of the group, escorted me. Parson was a huge man, much taller and wider than your dad. While your dad was kind, Parson was gruff and vulgar, and I was intimidated by him from the first. Not many people can intimidate me, but he did."

"I remember him." Aiden said. "He was so big and I was so little. I was scared of him, too, although I don't think he tried to scare me on purpose."

"On the way to my house," Brione continued, "I told your dad about my relationship with my brothers. I didn't tell him why they disliked me so much, just that they did. They let me live there, but they ignored me, pretended that I didn't even exist.

"When we reached my house, my brothers were home." Brione smiled. "They were shocked when they saw Tim come in behind me. They fell over each other trying to shake Tim's hand and welcoming him into their home. To their surprise, his greeting was not friendly. They asked what was wrong and he told them what I had said about them. They glared at me, but at least they had the decency to look ashamed.

"They were even more shocked when Tim told them that I had been invited to join his group and that I wasn't going to live in their house anymore. One of my brothers laughed and told Tim that it was ridiculous for him to hire me on. Tim didn't say anything. He just looked at my brother and his mirth melted away under your dad's stare.

"I went to my room and packed up all my stuff. I didn't own much. I had a few sets of clothes, a blanket and pillow, a small doll my mom made for me before she died. That was about it. I already had everything else on me. I left my room, never to return, and found that I was happy and excited to be leaving that house. I had nothing but bad memories there and I was glad to start my life anew.

"When we were about to head out the door Tim turned around and scolded my brothers for the way they treated me. I said good-bye to them, but none of them spoke or looked at me as I left. I never saw them again." Brione gave a little laugh. "It is weird, but part of me misses them."

"Really?" asked Portia, not understanding why she would miss such cruel people.

"Yes. They were my family after all. Even though they had no love for me, they were my brothers and the only family I had after my parents died."

"Now you have us," Aiden said.

"Yes," Brione replied with a smile and patted Aiden's knee. "Now I have you."

She continued with her story. "After we left the house Tim apologized about speaking to my brothers that way. He said it was none of his business and he had no right to talk to them the way he did. I told him that I was glad he did it because I never had the courage to stand up for myself around them. I could stand up to an armed man twice my size without blinking, but not to my own brothers.

"Your dad's camp was about a day away from my house and our journey was filled with conversation. Tim and Parson told me about some of their adventures and their backgrounds. I in turn told them a little about myself. I immediately had a connection with your dad. I felt comfortable around him, more comfortable than I had felt since my parents died. And, I must admit, I was immediately attracted to him.

"The first few months of being in the mercenary group went by very quickly. I spent most of that time training. It was true that I was a good sword fighter, but I found out very quickly that I was the least skilled in the group. There were five other men in the group beside Tim and Parson, and they had all been trained by your dad. I had a lot of catching up to do, and I found myself getting very frustrated. Your dad was very supportive though and he was continually encouraging me. After a while, I did see an improvement in my fighting ability.

"All the men treated me with respect, on Tim's orders. They never had a woman in the group before and some of the men didn't know how to act. They were used to having little kids around because you and your sister were there. Tim asked me to be patient with them. He said they needed a little time to get used to having a woman in the camp.

All of them treated me well, even Parson. Although he would give me lewd looks sometimes when our paths crossed. Never around your dad though.

"After a few months of training, your dad decided I was ready to start doing jobs with the rest of the group. My first job was with Tim and Parson, and we easily completed it. The place where we had to go was a few days away from the camp, so we had to stop for the night a couple times.

"One night I was laying in my tent, thinking about how much my life had improved since I met Tim and joined his mercenary band. I owed so much to your dad, and I thought that I was falling in love with him. I made a very rash decision and went to his tent. I stood outside the front and whispered his name. He told me to come in and I did.

"We chatted for a while and I told him how grateful I was to him and how much I enjoyed being in his group. He told me that he was happy to have me and that he thought I had made huge improvements in my swordplay. After a while I got the courage up to tell him how I felt about him. I told him that I was falling on love with him and then I…" she paused.

"Then you what?" asked Portia.

Brione swallowed and continued. "Then I…offered…myself…to him."

Portia gasped and Aiden was shocked. None of them said a word for a moment.

Finally, Aiden asked, "What did he do?"

Brione smiled again. "He very gently turned me down. He told me that I deserved to be with a man who loved me the way I loved him. He told me that he did love me, but more like a friend or even a daughter than a lover. I was devastated. I told him that I understood, and I immediately left his tent to go back to mine. When I stepped out of your dad's tent, I found myself face to face with Parson. I asked him if he heard what your dad and I were talking about and he just grinned at me.

"I ran past him to my tent, but he followed me there. I tried to close the front flap before he reached it but I was too slow. He said that if I needed company for the night and Tim was not interested, he would gladly join me. I told him no, but he came in anyway.

"He got angry with me when I told him no. He asked me if I thought Tim was better than him. I said no. He became very aggressive and I screamed at him to get off me. He told me to be quiet, but I kept on screaming. Suddenly, he was yanked off me and out of the tent. I looked out the open tent flap to see him sprawled on the ground. Your dad was standing over him, demanding to know what he thought he was doing.

"Parson explained that since Tim had turned me down, I might want someone else. Tim said that it was obvious that I didn't want him, and he should have stopped. Then Parson got angry with Tim and said that it was his fault. Tim had brought temptation into camp when he brought me into the group and it was only a matter of time before the other men took advantage of me.

"I immediately felt ashamed. I thought he was right. Once again, my mere presence was bringing trouble to someone who was just trying to help me. I interrupted their conversation and told them that I would leave immediately, but your dad told me that I was being ridiculous and that I had done nothing wrong. He said that Parson was going to have to leave. Parson went red in the face and swore at me and told me it was my fault.

"He came at me with a roar, trying to attack me. Tim stood in his way and didn't let him get me. Although Parson was much bigger than your dad, he couldn't get around him. Finally, Parson had had enough, and he punched your dad in the face, sending him to the ground. He charged me but I hit him with the palm of my hand right between the eyes, just like I did to the man in the tavern. The blow stunned Parson, but he didn't go down. Instead he drew his sword and came at me again.

"Your dad was on his feet quickly and he put himself between me and Parson. He asked Parson what he was doing, and he replied that he was going to kill me. Your dad said that he wasn't going to allow that.

Parson laughed at him and asked how he was going to stop him. Parson had a sword, your dad didn't. Your dad said that didn't matter. He wasn't going to allow him to kill me.

"I was shocked when Parson actually swung his sword at your dad. I didn't think he would really do it. By the look on your dad's face, I could tell he didn't think so either. But he was able to duck under the swing, then come up and grab Parson's arm. He spun around behind Parson's back, still holding his arm, and lifted. Parson struggled, but Tim did not relent and after a few moments I heard Parson's arm snap. He cried out in pain and dropped the sword.

"Your dad let go of him and he fell to his knees, cradling his broken arm. Tim picked up the sword and held it to Parson's throat. 'I think it is time for us to part ways,' he said. 'Get your gear and leave immediately. I never want to see your face again.' Then he threw the sword down and came to me.

"'Are you alright?' he asked. I nodded, but he saw the look on my face. He pulled me into a hug and I cried. Suddenly, we heard a roar and turned to see Parson on his feet, holding his sword in his good hand. He roared again and rushed us.

"This time I was the one who stopped him. I kicked him in the groin when he got within reach, he doubled over and dropped his sword again. He lay there on the ground, groaning in pain. 'Gather your things,' Tim said to me. 'It doesn't look like he is going to leave, so we will leave him.'

"We gathered our things as quickly as we could and left. Parson was sitting up against a tree, and as we walked past him, he called out. 'I will get you Brione!' Full of anger, your dad stopped and abruptly turned back to him. 'If you come for her,' he said, 'I will kill you.' Without another word, he turned away from him and we left.

Brione went silent after that. "What happened then?" asked Portia.

"We never saw him again. But I think Tim really would have killed him if he had come for me. He has always been very protective of me, even though I'm pretty good at taking care of myself."

"What happened with you and my dad after that night?" Aiden asked. "Were things uncomfortable between you two?"

"Surprisingly no," Brione answered. "We never spoke of it again, and he acted as if it had never happened. Things stayed comfortable between us and I am glad for that.

"After that Tim gathered the group together and had a meeting. He said that we needed to have a new second-in-command. He said that over the next few weeks he was going to evaluate everyone and choose the best person for the job. I didn't think I had a chance. I went about my daily routine just like always. Tim watched us train and fight. He had us take turns leading a job. I was shocked, as was everyone else, when Tim announced that he had chosen me. A few men grumbled a little too loudly about it, and Tim heard them. He said that his decision was final and if anyone didn't like it, they knew where the door was."

"Tim was sterner back then," Portia said. "He seems more kind now."

"He has changed," Brione said. "He has lightened up a little since then. But the group seems a lot closer now than they did back then. We seem more like a family now. It didn't feel like a family back then."

They heard a commotion down the street. The entire group quickly made their way to the main street that ran through the center of the city. They saw the group that had gone to get Layne making their way towards them. There were more people than before, and they had several wagons with them. Veronna caught sight of Layne first and cried out. She ran full speed and slammed into Layne, who was grinning widely. The young girl's momentum pushed Layne back a few steps, but he kept his balance and hugged Veronna tightly.

The rest of the group caught up and there were smiles all around. Dustin stood before Layne and put out his hand. Layne knocked his hand away and stepped in for a hug. The two brothers held each other for a long moment, talking too softly for the others in the group to hear.

The brothers separated and Layne turned to Aiden. The first thing big man noticed was Aiden and Portia holding hands. The smile disappeared from his face. "So you two are together now, huh?"

Aiden quickly dropped Portia's hand. Portia turned red. "Uh, yeah," Aiden said. "Things have changed since we saw each other last."

"I can see that." There was no warmth in the big man's voice.

Brione was next and Layne smiled at her and hugged her. He said something and Brione laughed. Aiden was hurt by Layne's reaction. But he also understood. He hadn't even thought of how Layne might feel when he saw Portia and him together. After everything that had happened, he had almost forgotten how much Layne had liked Portia.

Dana stepped up to Layne and spread her arms for a hug. Instead of hugging her, Layne stepped in and kissed her long and hard. Everyone was shocked, Dana most of all. When they broke their kiss, Dana was smiling broadly.

After that, the group started moving again toward the temple. Aiden and Portia walked a few paces behind Layne. Aiden was very disappointed. He had imagined his reunion with his best friend much differently. Portia was holding his hand again and she stroked his arm as they walked. "I'm sorry," she whispered. "This is all my fault."

"No," Aiden replied. "It is not your fault. It is no one's fault. Layne is just going to have to learn to deal with the fact that we are together. It will be hard, but he will do it. He cares for me too much for something like this to come between us. Don't worry, he'll be alright."

Portia didn't say anything, but she wasn't so sure.

*　　*　　*

"That is very interesting," Turner said.

Turner and Layne were alone in the prophet's private chambers. Layne had told Turner his story in full. He was hesitant at first, but Tim had asked him to do so, had told him that he was sure Turner could help him if he was honest, and he decided to trust in his commander.

Layne decided that he was sick of letting his anger control him. He wanted help.

"I have never heard of anything like this happening before," the prophet continued. "True, you have been through a terrible ordeal, but it is curious that it would change you so profoundly. It is hard to say what God has in mind for you."

"God? What does God have to do with this?"

"Everything. God lets us makes our own choices. We have to suffer the consequences. Normally, when you make a good choice, God blesses you. But every once in a while, even when you make a good choice, which yours obviously was, God lets bad things happen. In the end, the person usually finds that the bad experience makes them stronger. It turns out to be a blessing. I can only assume that is what is happening with you."

"You think that this is some kind of trial devised by God to make me stronger?"

"Partly. I think you getting arrested and being tortured was your trial. Now we have to decide how you will deal with it. I don't think your mind is dealing with it very well, do you?"

"No."

"Now, what to do about it?"

Layne didn't say anything as he watched the prophet behind his desk, but truth be told, he was getting impatient. Turner just sat there with his eyes closed for a long time. After a few minutes, Layne started to think that the prophet had fallen asleep.

Finally, the prophet opened his eyes and regarded Layne.

"What were you doing?" asked Layne.

"I was praying," Turner replied.

"Praying?"

"Yes. You would be surprised at the power of prayer. God loves us and wants to help us. He asks that we have faith in him and ask him for the things we need. I was just asking him to help me discover the best way to help you."

"And what did God say?"

"I got the impression that God thinks you are strong enough to overcome this problem, but I cannot help you. No, the people who can help you are your friends and family. Your loved ones. They care deeply for you and want to help you. Use their strength to bolster your own."

"My coming to you for help was pointless," Layne said harshly, his patience almost gone.

"No, it wasn't." the prophet replied calmly. "Before, I had no idea how to help you. But now we know where help lies. The strength to overcome this lies within you, and in your loved ones."

The prophet didn't say anything after that. The two men stared at each other for a moment, then Layne asked, "Can I go now?"

"Yes. We are done here. You may go. But remember what I said."

Without another word, Layne got to his feet and left the room.

33

Syth could hear several men in the shack speaking to each other before he reached the door. At first, he was angry at how loud the men were speaking. A passer-by could easily overhear their conversation and turn them in to the city watch. But then he realized what all the loud speaking meant.

It meant that the men had recruited a lot of people. It meant that Syth would have a small army at his disposal.

He paused at the door for a moment, trying to hear exactly what they were saying. With all the separate conversations going on at once it was hard to distinguish one from another. But he did hear bits and pieces that he understood.

Most of what he heard was concern from the men in the room. They didn't trust Syth. They believed him to be working for the queen. Yet the promise of wealth had brought them here, nonetheless. Their greed overcame their fears.

Syth walked into the building and softly shut the door behind him. Immediately the conversations ended, and everyone turned their attention to Syth. He didn't say anything for a moment. He looked at all the men in the room, silently studying each one. There were around twenty men.

"I am glad you all have come," Syth said. "You all have shown me the kind of men you are by being here today. You are the kind of men who would rather take what you want instead of working for it." There were a few grumbles in the room from men who didn't know if they were being insulted or not. "You are men who take the easy way instead of the honest way. You are men with no morals or conscience. You are exactly the kind of men that I need."

The previous leader of the group, Parson, stepped forward. "We have done as you've asked. We have recruited as many people as we could safely. Now, what are your plans for us?"

Syth could tell why this man had been the leader of the group. He didn't think that anyone else in the room would have had the courage to step forward and ask that question. By the look in the men's eyes, he could tell they feared him. This man showed no fear. "I want you guys to do what you do best. Rob, steal, murder, rape. Just continue to do what you have been doing. Only this time, you will be organized. Your attacks will be planned instead of random. You will have the ability to fight back if you are caught by the City Watch. This way you will be more successful than you ever have before."

A man to Parson's left started to raise a cheer, but Syth was quick to silence him. He kicked the man in the gut, doubling him over and sending him to the floor. "Fool!" Syth said. "You have to be quiet! Do you want to get caught? Do you want to bring the entire City Watch down on us?"

The man groaned but was able to shake his head.

Syth addressed the room. "If you want to be successful you will have to be smarter than this man." He pointed at the man on the floor. "If he had cheered like he had wanted to, someone passing by might have heard him. No one can know about us. No one can know that this many men have gathered in this little shack. It would look very suspicious."

Parson helped the man get back to his feet. "Sorry," the injured man mumbled.

"What is our first task?" asked Parson.

Syth smiled and told them.

*   *   *

Over the next two days Layne was allowed to rest and recover from the trying journey he had just been through. He spent a lot of time with Princess Dana, and almost no time at all with Aiden. The only times that he did anything strenuous was when he sparred with anyone willing to do so.

One time, Aiden volunteered to be Layne's sparring partner. Layne didn't say a word. He led Aiden to the practice grounds and immediately drew his massive battle ax and attacked. Aiden was surprised that he hadn't gone to get practice weapons and he barely drew his sword in time to block the blow.

It was a massacre. Layne didn't hold back, and Aiden didn't stand a chance against the larger man's fury. The big man finally stopped when his rage was played out and he left Aiden on the ground without a word. Aiden ached all over and had a shallow cut over his left eye. He wanted to believe that Layne had cut his face on accident, but he couldn't make himself do so. Aiden didn't spar with Layne again after that.

Tim spent a lot of time teaching Portia how to use a javelin. Javelins are shorter and lighter than spears, which was perfect for Portia. He taught her the correct way to throw a javelin and how to defend and attack with one in hand-to-hand combat. Once again, Portia was a quick learner. Tim's only concern was that she didn't have sufficient strength to throw the javelin with any affect against an armored opponent.

So now Portia walked around with a short sword strapped to her belt and half a dozen javelins strapped to her back and sticking up over her shoulder. It took Aiden a long time to get used to seeing her like that.

When they weren't training, Tim was speaking with David about their journey to Parkos. Dustin and Brione were in charge of getting all the supplies that they would need together. Zach and Jaden did their own thing; no one bothered them. Aiden, Portia, Veronna and Dorn had a lot of spare time. Veronna spent most of her time with her grandparents. Aiden spent some time with them too, though not as much as his little sister. Aiden and Portia had gotten closer to Dorn during their stay in Zion and they spent a lot of time together swapping stories.

Dorn would tell of some of his experiences as a servant in the palace. He had nothing but love for the late king and his family. Portia seemed to be fascinated by the way things work in a palace. It didn't interest Aiden as much, but he listened politely. Portia would tell stories of her years on the sea with her father. These stories did interest Aiden. Not only was he interested to learn more about this girl he had come to care deeply for, but the stories were exciting. She told of harrowing storms that had almost sunk her father's ship. She told of the few times that their ship had been attacked by pirates. Apparently, not only was her father a great ship captain and hunter, but he was also a master swordsman. Aiden thought it odd how he had never seen Gunfer wear a sword. He asked Porta about it and she said that her father kept his sword in his cabin unless he needed it. Why would he need to wear a sword on his own ship?

Aiden told them stories about growing up in a mercenary company and about having such a famous man as a father. The truth was, he had no idea just how famous his father was until they went on this journey. To Aiden, he always seemed like a regular guy who just happened to be almost unbeatable in a fight. His dad never talked about his past at all. His stories weren't as exciting as Portia's were. He had only just begun to go out on jobs recently. In fact, this was only his second job. Most of his stories were about the mischief he and Layne would get into. Or about the times when Layne would make other people angry with him because of his pranks. Telling these stories made Aiden sadder about the wall that had come up between him and his best friend. He wondered if things between them would ever go back to way they used to be.

The group was beginning to get excited about leaving Zion and continuing their journey. They had appreciated their days in the city and the safety they had found. It was good to rest and recover their strength and restock their supplies. But they were itching to get out on the road and get this job over with. Tim especially. This job had been a lot of trouble for the group, and the hard part hadn't even started yet. He wanted to finish it as quickly as possible and go home. He had to admit though, that he did enjoy his stay in Zion. It was good to see family and friends again, to be around people that felt nothing but love towards him and his family. He had dreaded coming here, but now he was glad that he did.

On the day before they planned on leaving Zion, Tim walked up to his daughter. She was at his parents' house, visiting with them one last time.

"Veronna, can I talk to you?" he asked.

"Of course," she replied.

"Sit down please." She did so. "Veronna, I have been thinking. The journey so far has been terrifying and dangerous, more so than I had thought it would be. We could have died many times, and I feared for you and Aiden most of all. I do not think that the journey will be any less dangerous as we go forward, and I have decided that it would be best if you stayed in Zion with your grandparents. If they agree to it, that is."

"Of course, she can stay here," her grandmother said. "She is welcome here for as long as she likes."

"No!" Veronna said. "I don't want to stay here." She turned to her grandma. "No offense Grandma. I love being here with you, but I want to go with my dad. I need to go with my dad." She turned back to Tim. "If I stay here, I will just be worried about you guys all the time. I wouldn't be able to eat or sleep because of worry. I need to go with you. I need to be close to you."

"But then I won't be able eat or sleep because of worry over you," Tim said.

"I know. But what safer place is there for me to be than with you and Layne and Zach and the rest. No one can beat you guys in a fight!"

"Here, Veronna. A safer place for you to be would be here."

"I know dad. But please don't ask me to leave you. I don't think I could take it. If you did, I would follow you like Princess Dana and Portia did. My place is with you."

Tim studied his daughter for a long time. He couldn't bear the thought of putting her in danger again. But he knew his daughter spoke the truth. Her place was with him. She would follow them if they left her here. He wanted her to be safe, but he couldn't bring himself to leave her here. He smiled. "Alright. You can come with us."

"Thank you!" she cried and threw her arms around Tim. As he hugged Veronna he looked over at his mother. She had a concerned expression on her face.

"I don't think it is a very good idea to bring her with you, Timmond. I think she should stay here with us."

"She is right, Mom. Her place is with me. I cannot leave her. Besides, we will have five Paladins with us. One of them is their leader, and another one is Veronna's uncle. We will be safe with them. She will be fine."

Finally, his mother reluctantly relented and Tim left his daughter with her and went to finish his preparations. Veronna was practically hopping up and down with excitement.

*   *   *

Aiden and Portia were sparing when Layne appeared at the far end of the field they were in. Aiden had his sword and Portia had her javelins. Once again, Aiden was surprised at the progress Portia had made in such a small amount of time.

Portia saw Layne first and called for Aiden to stop.

"What's wrong?" Aiden asked, breathing heavily.

"Look," she replied and pointed over to the side.

Aiden looked and saw Layne watching them. He was alone. Aiden wondered where Princess Dana was. They had been together almost constantly since Layne had returned to them.

Layne started walking towards them. Aiden decided to meet him halfway. "Wait here," he said and walked to his best friend.

They stopped about five feet away from each other.

"Hi," said Layne.

"Hi," Aiden replied.

"So, how are you?"

"I'm okay, I guess. You?"

Layne nodded. "Good. I'm good."

There was an uncomfortable pause.

"Listen," Layne said. "I want to apologize. I was too hard on you when we were sparing."

"It's okay."

"No, it's not. I was angry and I was taking my rage out on you, even though it wasn't your fault. You don't know what I have been through, and when I saw you and Portia together the other day it was too much." Aiden tried to say something, but Layne put his hand up, silencing him." No, let me talk."

Layne looked around his friend to Portia, who had slowly been coming closer. "Could you come here please?" he said. She looked happy to have been asked and she hurried to Aiden's side.

"I want to apologize to both of you. The way I acted was uncalled for. Portia, you know I like you a lot. I have since the first time I saw you. And Aiden had never been interested in you before. When I saw you two together I just snapped. All I could think about was my feelings. I had just gone through hell and now I see my best friend with the girl that I like. That was just too much.

"I feel bad because I have been using Princess Dana these last few days. I know that you liked her before, so I did what I did to make you mad. I feel terrible about that and I need to tell her what I did, but I really don't want to. But maybe I don't have to, because I am starting to like her. She is a lot different than I had thought." He grinned. "That's funny isn't it? We both end up with girls that we didn't like but the other one did.

"Anyway, I'm rambling. I just wanted to say that I am sorry and that I am happy for you two. And I also wanted to thank you, Portia."

"Thank me?"

"Yeah. You were there for Aiden when he needed you. Because we all know that otherwise there was no way he could have functioned without me." He gave Aiden a friendly slap on the back. Then he turned serious again.

"I didn't have anyone there for me. I had lost all hope. I would like to say that the things Tim taught us kept me going, but that would be a lie. I didn't even believe those things anymore. No, what kept me going was my anger. My rage at what was happening to me." He swallowed and looked down. "I almost lost myself. I feel guilty for the way I acted. I need your patience. I will be a difficult person to be with in the coming days. But I need everyone to be with me and support me. Can you two do that?"

"Of course," said Portia and she threw her arms around Layne and hugged him tight. When they let go Layne put his arms around Aiden.

"I'm glad you're back," Aiden said into his friend's shoulder.

"Me too," Layne replied.

They broke their embrace and started walking back to where Aiden and Portia had left their weapons. "So. You want to try sparing with me again?" Layne asked.

"Actually, no. I don't," Aiden said. They both laughed.

"I will," said Portia.

Layne looked at her. "Really?"

"Yeah. I mean, isn't it important for me to learn how to fight enemies that use different weapons? Wouldn't I fight someone with an ax differently than I would fight someone with a sword?"

"Good point," Layne said. "Alright. But I won't go easy on you. I will push you. I know you're used to Aiden not going easy on you, and yet you still dominate him."

"Hey!" Aiden said.

Layne ignored him. "But don't expect that from me. I am much better than him, so don't think it will be so easy anymore."

Portia grinned. "Good. That's the way I like it." She shot Aiden a grin.

Aiden couldn't help but grin himself. It was good to have Layne back.

Even though Layne had been joking, it was obvious to see that he was a better fighter than Aiden. He had his huge battle ax out and was pressing Portia hard. He had instructed her to dodge his strikes instead of parrying them. His weapon was too heavy for her lighter javelin to affectively block. It would either get knocked from her hand, or worse, break. So, she did as she was instructed and ducked, stepped aside, and jumped back to avoid his swings.

Despite what Layne had said earlier, he could tell that he was in fact going easy on Portia. Not too easy though. You can't learn and become better if you are not challenged. That is what his father said, anyway.

After the battle, with both fighters sweating freely and breathing hard, the three friends went looking for something to drink. They found a small stream not far from where they sparred and they dunked their heads in, drank their fill, and sat down together on a large rock and watched the water rush by.

After a few moments of silence Layne said, "I want to tell you what happened to me."

The other two were surprised. "Look Layne," Aiden said. "You really don't have to if you don't feel comfortable talking about it. We would understand."

"I know," Layne said. "But I want to. I told your dad about it and I felt much better afterwards. I think it helps to talk about it, and I can't think of anyone I would rather tell than you two."

"Alright," said Aiden. "We would love to hear it."

Layne told his story. The entire story. He didn't hold anything back. Aiden and Portia were shocked at the things Layne had had to go through. At one point, Aiden glanced over at Portia and he saw tears running down her cheeks.

To Layne's credit, he told his tale with very little emotion. The only emotion that Aiden could detect in his large friend was anger. When Layne was finished, Portia once again threw her arms around him and held him close. She was crying freely now.

"Wow," was all Aiden could say.

"See?" Layne asked. "This is what I could have used when I was being tortured. A beautiful woman with her arms around me." All three laughed at that.

*   *   *

There was a knock at the door. "Come in," Turner called from behind his desk. The door opened and Tim stepped into the room. He nodded at Mark and Brandon, who were sitting behind their own desks on either side of the room. Then he went to stand before Turner's desk.

"You asked me to come see you?" Tim said.

"Yes, I did. Pull a chair over here and have a seat. I have something important to tell you." Tim did so. "God has given me some information that will be critical to you and your mission." the Prophet continued. "There is a large force of men sent by King Korlas waiting for you outside of Zion's borders. I do not know how they discovered you had come here, but I do know that they are being led by one of Korlas' personal guards. You know what that means, right?"

"Yes. That means that the leader is a Dark Paladin."

"Correct. There are also a few Zantan Robbers with them. Their goal is to apprehend you."

"I know of Korlas' desire to capture me," said Tim. "I have already run into a group of Robbers that told me that."

"Do you know why?"

"Let's just say that Reese wasn't the first Paladin that I had a rivalry with. Korlas and I never liked each other much. We always were in competition, and I always won. He took it a lot more seriously than I ever did."

"Probably because you were the one who won, and he was the one who lost all the time."

"Perhaps," Tim said.

"So, given this new information, do you still want to continue with this journey?"

"Of course. Nothing will keep me from completing a job once I have taken it."

"Alright then. It is a good thing that you will have some Paladins accompanying you. They will be great help against the Dark Paladin and the Robbers."

"Yes, they will," Tim said. "And thank you for having them come with us. I really appreciate it. We will need all the help we can get."

"I am glad to help. I still think of you as a citizen of Zion, Timmond. Everyone does."

"Is there anything else? I have a lot to do before we leave tomorrow."

Turner looked at Tim for a long moment. "No," he said finally. "There is nothing else. You may go."

Tim got to his feet and left.

34

The companions were up before dawn the next day. Tim's mercenaries met the five Paladins at the armory. Tim's group upgraded their weapons and each one who was good with a bow received one and a quiver of arrows. Tim had wanted the group to travel light when they had started out on their journey, so they had left their bows and arrows at the fort and had brought more essential items instead.

They ate a quick meal right there in the armory and went over their plan. They were going to leave Zion on the road that Tim and the Paladins took when they went to get Layne. They would get on the King's road from there and follow that all the way to Parkos. Before they went to the palace to get Easton, they would find an Imbuer. No one was able to get the chest with the item that Korlas had wanted open, so they decided to find an Imbuer to tell them how to open it and what the item inside did.

Just before they left, Tim and the Paladins told the rest of the group about the enemies that were waiting for them just outside of Zion. The companions were nervous, but they set their jaws firmly and were determined to see this through.

"Do you still want to come with us?" Tim asked Veronna. She nodded and Tim smiled at her strength. "If anyone wants to stay, they can. This will be very difficult. We have come through a lot, but the most dangerous part of our journey is yet to come. I will not think any less of anyone who decides to stay here."

"Don't be ridiculous," said Brione. "None of us are going to abandon you now."

"I know you guys won't," said Tim. "But I was talking to the others. Princess Dana, are you sure you want to continue on with us? Turner said that anyone who wishes to stay here is welcome to. How about you Dorn? Portia? Would you rather go back to your father? I'm sure he is very worried about you."

"I know he is," said Portia. "I am worried about him too. But my place is with you. With Aiden. I want to continue on."

Both Princess Dana and Dorn also wanted to continue with them. With that decided, they shouldered their gear and started out.

With the chest strapped to the back of one of the horses, they mounted up and rode out of Zion. Tim and David had decided to take this less used road instead of the main road out of Zion in the hopes that they could avoid their enemies. They guessed that the enemy force was camped on the main road. They guessed right.

They met no resistance when they left the city. They made their way quickly but quietly as possible. Everything seemed to be alright. The forest around them teamed with life. Music from countless birds filled their ears. They turned their heads at the sound of squirrels scurrying in the trees. The world didn't seem to know the danger that lurked in the forest. Even though everything seemed normal, the group was wary.

They sent out Zach and Jaden to scout out the area ahead and to either side of them, but when they returned, they reported that they had seen nothing. The group began to breathe a little easier. Maybe they had avoided their enemies altogether.

*   *   *

As soon as Zach left Zion's borders, he felt his master enter his mind.

Zach!

Yes, master.

Finally! Report!

Zach told his master what had transpired during the time they had spent in Zion and told Ricardo that they had taken the less traveled route out of the city to avoid King Korlas' troops.

Go to his troops and lead them to the group.

Yes, Master.

*   *   *

Ricardo smiled. Finally! He had hated not being able to see through his men's eyes. He hated not being in control.

Truthfully, he didn't care about Tim's group. He didn't care if they were killed by Korlas' men or not. But he would watch the conflict through Zach's eyes. It would be enjoyable no matter the outcome!

He saw Zach make contact with Korlas' force. He saw him flee from them, but not too fast. He wanted them to be able to follow him. Then he heard Zach tell the group that he had seen nothing. Oh, how surprised the group would be when over one hundred men burst through the trees and attacked them! Ricardo laughed out loud.

*   *   *

Tim saw the two dark-skinned warriors mount their horses. They brought them close together and Zach said something to Jaden. Jaden nodded and then they separated. Then Tim heard a commotion to the right. He looked that way and saw movement in the trees.

Suddenly a force of soldiers broke out of the tree line and charged the group. "Run!" cried Tim, and he kicked his horse in the ribs to set it moving faster. Everyone else did the same and the chase was on.

The men on the far end of the line tried to cut off the group's escape, but they weren't quick enough. The group rushed past them before they could close in on them. But their enemies were also mounted, and they were right on the group's heels.

Suddenly, a great wind came up and blasted the group. The horses reared to the side and everyone had to have a white-knuckle grip on the reigns and an iron-like clasp of their legs to keep themselves from falling off their horses.

Before long, Veronna's strength gave out and she toppled from her horse. She cried out as she did, and the entire group stopped their horses and turned around to help her. They reached her just as their enemies did and there was a great clash of weapons. All Veronna could do was curl up in a ball and cover her head with her arms and hope she didn't get trampled by a horse.

Suddenly, her uncle was there. He had dismounted. He picked her up and, ignoring the fighting all around them, took her to the safety of the trees on the left side of the road, the side that the enemy force hadn't come out of. He gently put her on the ground. "Stay out of sight," he told her, then rushed back to the battle. Veronna saw him take down a foe with a swing of his mace, then he was lost in the confusion of men and weapons and horses. It was overwhelming to watch, and she couldn't take it anymore. She hid behind a tree and shut her eyes. But she couldn't shut out the noise.

*   *   *

Not all the enemies were mounted, and Tim preferred to fight on foot, so he jumped off his horse. Two men faced him, grinning, confident that their greater numbers would overwhelm their foe. They had no idea who they were dealing with.

The first one came in fast, thrusting a sword straight out at Tim. Tim easily knocked the blade aside with his own, then took a mighty swing. The man jumped back out of the way of the sword, but was surprised when Tim, ignoring the other man, came right at him. The mercenary leader gave no quarter as he reigned down blows on the poor man. Tim swung at the man's head, but his opponent ducked. He swung his sword horizontally, and the man barely put his own weapon up to block, the heavy blow almost taking the sword from his opponent's grasp. The blow made the man stagger backwards. When the other man came too close, Tim spun around and easily fought him off with a brutal attack, then turned back to his overwhelmed opponent.

The soldier tripped over a root sticking up from the ground and went down. Tim was on him immediately and the soldier never rose again.

Tim quickly turned to the remaining soldier and had him backing away immediately. Tim went high then low, his movements getting quicker and quicker. Finally, despite the large sword he wielded, he proved too quick for his foe and he changed the direction of his sword in mid-swing and his sword bit into flesh. The soldier dropped dead and Tim looked for more men to fight.

*   *   *

The Paladins proved too much for the men they faced as well. Almost every strike dropped an enemy. No weapons searching for them found their mark. It was like they knew exactly what their opponents were going to do before their opponents did. Soon, all enemies in the vicinity fled as quickly as possible. All but one.

A single man wearing black armor with a red demon emblazoned on the chest rode his horse toward them. He carried a large hammer in one hand. The five Paladins fanned their own horses out so that they were in a line facing the Dark Paladin. All five knew what this man was immediately. Yet they had no fear. They knew that their god was more powerful than his.

A foul darkness shot out from the man, engulfing the five Paladins. They held their weapons up to the sky, and they started glowing. The light from their weapons pushed the darkness away, until it finally dissipated completely.

The Dark Paladin was shocked, but recognition came quickly as to who these men were. With a cry he kicked his horse and charged, realizing that the power his god gave him could be matched by these men. He thought the only way to take them down was in close combat. He reached Reese first and reigned heavy blows down on him. Reese blocked each one with his long-handled ax, then countered with a mighty swing.

The Dark Paladin blocked and tried to attack again, but he was thrown off his horse by a heavy blow from David's mace. The Dark Paladin hit the ground hard but was back on his feet immediately. He was one of King Korlas's elite soldiers and he wouldn't be defeated that easily.

He sent forth the darkness again, just to distract his foes. They immediately raised their weapons skyward to repel it. That was when the Dark Paladin struck. His hammer knocked one of the Paladins off his horse before the man had time to react to the attack. The Dark Paladin rushed in for the killing blow, but the man rolled out of the way.

Once again, the Dark Paladin was shocked. No man had ever been able to move like that after they had been hit a solid blow by his hammer. He had expected the Paladin to be dazed at the least, possibly dead already.

The Paladin was on one knee when the hammer smashed in again, once again too quickly for him to react. The man flew ten feet through the air, then landed hard on his back. This time when the Dark Paladin approached, the man was unable to move. He was unconscious.

Before the killing blow could fall however, the injured Paladin's brothers came to his aid.

The heavy blow of David's mace sent the man sprawling on the ground, his hammer flying away into the trees. Then a sword cut into the man's leg where there was a crease in his armor, then an ax took the man's head. The leader of the enemy force was dead.

*   *   *

Aiden had seen his uncle take Veronna to safety and had told Portia to follow them.

"No!" she said. "I can fight! I will fight with you!"

"I know you can fight," Aiden replied. "But my sister can't, and I need you to protect her. Please!"

Portia knew that he was just trying to get her to safety, but he did have a point. "Okay," she said. She kissed him quickly and led her horse to the trees.

Aiden found himself side by side with Tyler. Several men were coming at them, but they didn't get very close. A dozen large rocks rose up from the ground and flew at the men. Everyone of them went down. One or two tried to get back on their feet, but Aiden dismounted and rushed over to make sure none of them did.

Suddenly, a second great wind rose up and hit them like a hammer. The wind knocked Tyler and Aiden off their mounts. As they were sprawled on the ground, the sound of their horses fleeing in their ears, they saw a man walking toward them. He obviously wasn't a soldier, for he wore no armor. Instead he wore loose fitting grey robes over his skinny frame.

"A wind mage!" Tyler cried, though it was hard for Aiden to hear him over the roar of the wind.

A moment later the ground in front of them churned and rose up, creating a barrier between them and the wind.

"Ah!" came a voice from the other side of the barrier. "An earth mage! Let's see which is more powerful, wind or earth!"

Tyler leaped out from behind the shelter. As soon as the wind mage saw him, he brought the wind up again. Tyler was knocked from his feet once more. He crawled back behind the shelter beside Aiden.

"He has us trapped," the wizard said.

"What should we do?" Aiden asked.

"I have an idea."

Suddenly the barrier and the ground around it exploded in front of Aiden, large chunks of earth rising to form a huge, vaguely human shape with boulders for hands and feet and smaller rocks that served as eyes. Up and up the earth rose, until the creature was a good twenty feet tall. Towering over the two men on the ground, it turned its attention to their foe. The enemy mage concentrated, and Aiden could see the air in front of the wizard solidify. It was also in the shape of a human and stood as tall as the creature Tyler had summoned. Tyler looked stunned.

The two creatures rushed at each other with startling speed. When they collided, Aiden could feel the impact. Chunks of earth dropped to the ground at the feet of the beasts. The earth creature flew backwards, rolling head over heels when it hit the ground. When it finally stopped and got to its feet, the air monster was already there.

Tyler ran up to Aiden. "We've got to get out of here. If he can control an elemental more powerful than mine, he is much stronger than I thought!"

Aiden watched the titanic battle before him. It was true, the air creature was winning the battle. It had the earth creature on the ground and was mercilessly raining down blows on it. Suddenly, the earth creature gave a great heave and the air elemental flew over its head. No damaged was done though, for the elemental floated gently to the ground. The earth beast jumped to its feet and charged. It punched its enemy in the face. The air elemental staggered backwards, obviously injured. The earth elemental gave no quarter. It was on it in a flash. Punch after punch landed. Face, torso, face, torso. On and on it went. The air elemental tried to take to the sky, but the great earth beast grabbed it and pulled it back to the ground.

Aiden felt another great wind come up, and the earth elemental began to slide backwards, away from its foe. It placed its feet firmly on the ground it was created from, but it was no use. The wind was too great, the elemental continued to slide. Aiden was a good hundred feet away from the battle by now, but he still had to brace himself to keep from being blown over. Then he noticed the enemy mage.

"Why is he just standing there?"

Tyler also noticed the mage. He stood still, staring at the combatants, concentration painted on his face. "He's not strong enough to control the monster without concentrating," Tyler said. "This is our chance, Aiden. Distract him! If his concentration is broken, his elemental will attack him!"

Aiden ran for the enemy mage. It was slow going because of the wind the air elemental was producing. He stopped, picked up a rock and threw it, but it didn't go far. "The wind is too strong!"

"Maybe I can help," said the mage. He concentrated for a moment and another large wall of earth burst up, this one right in front of the air beast. The rush of wind died down immediately. The great earth beast didn't hesitate, it rushed past the barrier and was on its enemy immediately.

Aiden didn't hesitate either.

Not wanting the mage to counter, he rushed full speed for him. The mage, having all his concentration on the battle, didn't see Aiden coming at him. Aiden hit the mage at full speed and they both hit the ground. Aiden was bigger and stronger than his enemy, plus he landed on top of the mage, so he immediately got to his feet while the mage stayed on the ground, the breath knocked out of his lungs.

Movement to the side caught his attention. He glanced that way and saw a terrifying sight. The massive air elemental was rushing straight for him! He flung himself out of the way, afraid that he hadn't gone far enough. But the elemental wasn't coming after Aiden. It wanted the one who had called him here. It wanted the air mage.

The poor man's screams made Aiden turn away in horror. Luckily, the screams didn't last very long. When Aiden looked again, the beast was gone. All that remained was the shredded body of the dead mage.

Aiden searched for Tyler. He found him just in time to see the wizard dismiss the earth elemental. Tyler looked over at him and nodded.

*　　*　　*

The two dark-skinned warriors fought side by side. All who came at them fell immediately. Princess Dana was with them as well, swords in hand. But she never got a chance to use them. Zach and Jaden disposed of their enemies too quickly for her to join in. She looked around and spotted Dorn several feet away. He looked frightened and confused. "Dorn!" she called. He looked over at her. "Come over here!"

He rushed to her side. "Stay by me," she ordered. "You will be safe with us." Dorn nodded, then let out a small cry as a man rushed up to them, sword in hand. Princess Dana was on him before Jaden or Zach could react. Her quickness proved too much for the man and he soon fell to her blades.

"Princess," said Jaden when there was a break in the fighting. "It is too dangerous for you out here. Please go hide with Portia and Veronna. You as well, Dorn."

"No," said Dana. "I want to fight with you."

"It is too dangerous for you," the dark-skinned warrior replied. "Please go. Zach and I will be fine. But if you stay here, I will worry about you."

"Alright," she agreed. "Come Dorn. Let's go find the others. They may need our protection."

*   *   *

Dustin, Layne, and Brione held their own. Layne, not being used to fighting on a horse, had dismounted and was swinging his duel axes with deadly affect. Brione and Dustin had stayed on their horses, both fighters experienced fighting on horseback.

A group of men came at them in a tight formation. Layne met them first, axes a blur. He held the group back long enough for Dustin and Brione to charge in and attack them on their flank. The group of enemies fell quickly.

"Didn't Tim say something about seeing Zantan Robbers with these men?" Brione asked.

"Yeah," said Layne. "Where are they?"

All three scanned the battlefield until Dustin saw them. He pointed. "There they are! Five of them. And they are heading… No!"

Dustin kicked his horse and it bolted forward, to the spot where Dorn and the women were hiding. Brione and Layne followed.

Another group of men converged on them before they got far however, and the way was blocked. Layne was on foot, so he wasn't as fast as the other two and their enemies surrounded Dustin and Brione before Layne got there.

Dustin looked back over his shoulder at his brother. "Don't worry about us. Go protect the others!"

Layne skirted the battle as quickly as he could and spotted the women and Dorn. They all stood back to back, whatever weapons they carried held out defensively before them. They were surrounded by the five yellow-skinned warriors. Layne had heard the stories that the group had told him about the Zantan Robbers, but it still surprised him to see men with yellow skin. Layne wasn't close when the five men started closing the circle around his friends. "No!" He cried and threw one of his axes with all his might, running as fast as he could behind it.

Layne's shout had alerted the five Robbers and they all turned to see the ax flying at them. They easily dodged out of the way, the ax imbedding into a tree behind them. Princess Dana took advantage of the distraction and rushed one of the Robbers. She sliced him in the arm and the man turned abruptly to her. He looked at his bleeding arm, grinned, and raised his weapon. Dana immediately started backing away from him, her swords held out before her defensively.

Portia hurled one of her javelins at the man, but he knocked it aside with his sword. Never taking his eyes off Dana, he kept advancing on her. Then Layne was there.

He jumped in front of the Robber and swung at him with his remaining hand ax. The Robber dodged easily and counter attacked, but Layne also dodged. Layne attacked again, pushing the Robber back. Layne, not getting even close to hitting his foe with his ax, rushed at him and tackled him to the ground. The Robber hit the ground and threw his legs up, using Layne's momentum to send him over his body. Layne hit the ground and was immediately on his feet. Fortunately, the Robber had tossed him next to the tree that his ax was in. Layne pulled the ax out of the tree trunk and grinned. He rushed at the Robber again.

Layne was more potent with two axes. Relentless, he attacked the Zantan Robber, keeping him on the defensive. The remaining four Robbers realized that the newcomer was much bigger threat than the rest of the group, so just before Layne had overwhelmed their companion, they joined the fray.

Layne expected that though, and he was ready for them. He turned to the first one and blocked his attack, then kicked him, knocking him back. Another one came up from behind and Layne spun to block his attack. Layne went low to duck under another man's weapon, then spun on his knees, axes extended, and took the feet out from under the two men. Layne was immediately back up and rushed one of the men on the ground. The Robber rolled out of the way of Layne's axes and got to his feet in time to take Dana's sword in his back. The man looked at the several inches of steel sticking out of his chest, then fell to the ground, dead.

Layne smiled and nodded his thanks to her, then turned to face another Robber.

*   *   *

Brione and Dustin were hard pressed on all sides. Both of them could do nothing but defend as attacks came from the front, behind and the sides. Only their training and their quickness kept them alive. Dustin blocked one swing with his sword, then another attack with his gauntlet. Brione didn't have a shield or gauntlets, so she had to wave her sword from side to side to deflect her enemies' blows.

A sword got behind Brione's defenses and sunk into her leg. She cried out in pain and stabbed down, her sword going into the man's neck. The man slipped to the ground, but the sword stayed in her leg. She grabbed the hilt, grimaced, and pulled the sword out. Now, she had two weapons with which to defend herself.

Now that Brione had two weapons, men started falling around her. Dustin, however, had a man latched onto his leg, trying to pull him from his horse. He stabbed the hand holding his leg and the man released and backed away. Before Dustin could pursue, Tim stepped up behind the man and stabbed him in the back, dropping him to the ground. With three fighters now instead of two, they routed the rest of the soldiers. They heard fighting off to the side and saw Layne and Dana engaged with four Zantan Robbers. They went to help.

*   *   *

Layne was facing two Robbers, Dana the other two. Out of the corner of his eye Layne saw Dana trip and fall. Immediately the two Robbers went in for the kill. "No!" Layne yelled, and, forgetting the two men he was fighting, went to her aid.

The Robbers turned to face him when he got close, but his powerful blows knocked them back. One went down, and Layne was able to chop off his leg at the knee before he could get away.

The other man attacked Layne, but the big man deflected the blows and swept his leg out, tripping the Robber. Layne sunk one ax into the fallen man's chest, then turned to face another man who had come up from behind.

Instead of going for a killing blow like the other Robbers had done, this man aimed for Layne's hands. His blade connected with Layne's left hand and the ax fell to the ground. Layne now held one ax in two hands. The Robber tried the same tactic once again, but Layne was ready for it and was able to avoid the sword strike. He counter attacked with a high swipe and the Robber ducked. Suddenly Layne felt a tugging on his leg and glanced down. The man whose leg Layne had chopped off had crawled over and was now trying to pull Layne to the ground.

Layne finished the job and killed the man on the ground, then turned back to his other foe. Layne could see Dana fighting the last remaining Robber a few feet away. She was holding her own, but he could tell she was overmatched. He would have to finish the foe off quickly.

*   *   *

Before Tim, Brione and Dustin could get to the group, another group of soldiers barred their way. The three would have to fight their way through to get to their friends. They hoped they could do so in time.

*   *   *

Layne went on the offense again. The Robber expertly blocked every blow, but he was forced to give up ground. Suddenly one of Layne's blows connected and the Robber's sword went flying. Unarmed, the Robber turned to flee. Layne, not having time to pursue, threw his ax and it struck the fleeing man in the back. He heard a scream and turned. Princess Dana was down, her sword was lying on the ground several feet away and she was holding her arm. The Robber advanced on her, but then, Veronna threw herself on top of the Zantan Robber, trying to save Dana's life. The Robber shook Veronna off, then had to contend with Portia and Dorn, who stood protectively over Dana, their weapons in front of them. Layne rushed to their aid.

Dorn rushed in on the attack, but the Robber knocked him aside. Portia thrust at him with her javelin, but the man caught it and tore it from her hands. He swung the javelin horizontally at her and struck her across the face. She went down in a heap. The Robber tossed the weapon aside and lunged toward Veronna, who had gotten back up to her feet.

Before the Robber reached her, Layne pulled his massive ax from his back and rushed in. With a yell he bowled the Robber over, each of them going to the ground. They both got to their feet immediately and the Robber charged in. His swings were lightning quick, and Layne had a hard time deflected the blows with his heavy weapon. Several cuts appeared on his arms and torso. He tried to counterattack, but the blows were too slow and the Robber easily dodged out of the way.

The Robber went on the attack again and soon Layne's ax went flying away. Layne stood before his enemy, unarmed. The Robber started walking forward, but was held up by Princess Dana, who had grabbed his legs. The Robber shook one of his legs free and kicked Dana in the head. Dana went limp and the Robber turned his attention back to Layne.

Layne saw Dana's unconscious form and screamed. He attacked the Robber with his fists, connecting solidly with his face. The Robber staggered backwards but caught his balance quickly. Layne rushed in and the Robber thrust his sword straight out. Layne caught his arm by the wrist, the sword poised a mere few inches from his throat.

The Robber smiled at Layne and pushed something on the bottom of his sword's hilt. Suddenly, the blade extended and punctured Layne's neck. Layne's eyes went wide and blood streamed out of the wound. The Robber pushed the button again and the blade shrunk back to its normal size. Layne fell to the earth.

<h1 style="text-align:center">35</h1>

"No!" Dustin yelled. He saw his brother catch the Zantan Robber's arm, and he knew what was going to happen. He was too far away to do anything about it though. All he could do was watch in horror as the blade went into his brother's throat, as his brother's body slid to the ground.

"No!" he cried again and spurred his horse on faster. He tried to run the Robber over with his horse, but he jumped out of the way. Dustin jumped off his horse, sword in hand, and went after the Robber. The Robber turned to face him and there was a loud clash of steel.

The Robber was the better fighter, but Dustin's rage made up the difference. His sword had never moved so fast, his attacks had never hit so hard. At first the Robber was standing his ground, but eventually he began to lose ground to his tireless enemy.

Getting desperate, the Robber tried a bold move. He dropped to the ground and kicked his leg out. Dustin's feet weren't set, and the move tripped him up. He hit the ground face first. The Robber was back on his feet immediately and went in for the kill, his blade aimed for the back of Dustin's neck.

Suddenly Tim was there. He blocked the killing blow with his broadsword and jumped defensively in front of Dustin. The Zantan Robber didn't hesitate and attacked the newcomer, but Tim was a much better fighter than Dustin and he quickly had the Robber furiously backing up. Tim didn't waiver in his attack. Soon the Robber's weapon went flying to the side, but Tim still didn't let up until the Robber's head had rejoined his weapon, and his body fell to the ground.

Tim just stood there for a moment, leaning on his sword. He turned back to the group when he heard a girl cry out. He saw the group gathered around their fallen friend. Dustin was kneeling next to Layne's body, his dead brother's head cradled in his lap. He was sobbing. Princess Dana and Veronna were screaming. Aiden just stood there, staring, with Portia holding onto his arm, her head buried in his shoulder. Her body was shaking with sobs. Brione had her hand in front of her mouth. "No, no," she repeated over and over. Dorn averted his eyes. Jaden and Zach stood to the side, blank expressions on their faces. Tyler was also kneeling next to Layne's body, tears glistening in his eyes. The five Paladins approached.

A tremendous feeling of rage boiled up inside Tim. He dropped his sword, fell to his knees, threw his head back and screamed at the top of his lungs. "Curse you! Curse you God! He was young! He had so much life ahead of him! Why? Why did you take him? Why not take me? I am older! I have turned away from you! Why?" He was racked by sobs. His voice was quieter now. "You are no god of mine. You are cruel and heartless." His voice got louder again. "Do you hear me? You are cruel and heartless and no god of mine!"

He glanced at the five Paladins as they dismounted and walked up to the group. David's face showed shock and hurt. Tim got to his feet and walked up to him. "Do you see?" he demanded. "Do you see what your god has done? You call him kind and loving." He gestured to the group of people grieving over their fallen friend. "Do you call that kind and loving? Do you? I call it cruel. I call it heartless. He was young. He was good. It was not his time." Tim spat to the side and went to Zach.

"You said you never saw anyone! You said there was no one there!"

"I didn't see anyone," Zach said calmly.

"I find it hard to believe that you would miss a large force like that!"

"Their scouts must have spotted me and avoided me. They had a Dark Paladin with them. Maybe he used dark magic to hide their army. I do not know."

Tim had nothing to say to that. He turned away from the dark-skinned warrior and headed for the group.

David hesitated, then followed. When he reached the group, Aiden came up to him.

"Can you heal him?" the young man asked. "Can you do what you did for Dorn and heal him?"

David put a hand on his nephew's shoulder. "I'm afraid not. Your friend is already dead. God has seen fit to take him from this world and I do not have the power to contradict him. We cannot raise the dead. I am truly sorry."

Aiden nodded his understanding, his disappointment plain on his face.

Dustin looked up from his brother, his face red from crying. "We have to bury him."

"Bury him?" asked Brione. "Don't you want to burn his body?"

"No," Dustin replied. "It doesn't seem right to burn his body. Both Captain Gunfer and David told me that they bury their dead here on Parken. I think that will be more appropriate. I want to bury him."

*   *   *

There was a grin on his face as Ricardo left his chambers. The battle had gone very well. Not only had all of King Korlas's men been killed, including the Zantan Robbers, but someone in Tim's group had died as well. It couldn't have gone better. He couldn't wait to tell the king the news.

He quickly made his way to the king's audience chamber where he knew the king would be. He got to the chamber and the king was holding audience, so he stayed at the side of the room and waited.

The game that King Korlas played disgusted Ricardo. He couldn't understand why the people that came before him couldn't see right through Korlas' façade. Korlas was an evil man, and the kind exterior that he had was fake. Ricardo would never stoop so low as to pretend he was something he is not.

While he waited, he studied Prince Easton, who was standing behind and to the side of the throne. He studied the young man every time he waited for Korlas to finish. The king said that he brought the prisoner up every day to teach him how to rule. Ricardo thought it was a waste of time. If it were up to him, he would kill the weakling prince and just take Blanderly by force.

When the prince had first been captured, he had looked hopeless and beaten. Slowly the look changed to one of acceptance, and then finally to one of determination. The king didn't seem to have noticed the change in Easton, but Ricardo did. The prince was up to something, and while Ricardo didn't think that Easton could accomplish whatever it was that he was planning, the wizard still wanted to know what it was. He would have to pay the prince a visit in his cell very soon.

After an hour or so the flow of petitioners finally ended, and the king turned to the wizard. "Well, Wizard. What do you have for me today?"

Ricardo couldn't keep the smile from his face. "The force you sent after Tim have been killed. Every single one of them."

"Killed? Everyone? How could this have happened? I sent one hundred men!"

"They had five Paladins with them."

The king roared in anger. "Paladins!" Then he noticed that Ricardo was grinning. "Why are you grinning? Do you think this is funny?"

Ricardo laughed out loud. "Yes. Actually, I do think it's funny. I told you to just let Tim come to you. I am your advisor. I advised you and you ignored it and this is what happened."

Korlas roared again and suddenly Ricardo felt searing pain in his abdomen. He clutched at his midsection and hit the floor. He couldn't breathe. All he could see was red. All he could hear was Korlas screaming in rage. Ricardo tried to put up defenses against the pain, but he couldn't. When he thought that he would pass out because of the pain, it suddenly stopped. He gasped in a breath and sighed in relief. Then the anger came.

He struggled to his feet. "I will kill you for that someday."

Korlas laughed. "Kill me? I just proved to you that I am stronger than you. My god will not let you kill me."

"I will kill you," Ricardo repeated.

"You were helpless before me just now. Could you defend yourself against me? No. You are weak, and I am strong. You will never kill me."

"You are wrong."

"Then kill me now! Do it! I am right here. Kill me right now if you can. Come on. I'm waiting." Korlas laughed at him again. "See? You can't. So, stop wasting my time with empty threats and do your job and advise me."

Ricardo didn't say anything, but he decided that he would kill Korlas someday. He felt more loathing for Korlas right then than he had for anyone ever before. He couldn't keep the loathing out of his eyes. If Korlas noticed it, he didn't say anything about it.

"Now," said Korlas, much calmer this time. "I hired you to be my advisor. So perhaps you should advise me."

Ricardo had to take a deep breath before answering. "Let him come to you. Do not send any more men to go after him. All you are doing is thinning out your forces. Let him attack you here where you have your full strength. Then you will be strong enough to capture him."

"You are right," the king agreed. He chuckled. "You were right. I should have listened to you in the first place. Oh well. My mistake. But I think I will follow your advice this time. I pay you well for it. I might as well make it worth my money."

The king was overflowing with arrogance. His display of power had given him courage. But one day he would regret that display, Ricardo vowed. One day, he would die for it.

*   *   *

They buried Layne on top of a hill that was a few hundred feet away from the sight of the battle. While Tim, Dorn and Dustin dug the hole with small shovels the Paladins carried in their packs and the rest of the men kept an eye on the surrounding area, the women of the group made a marker. They found two long, narrow logs and lashed one piece crosswise to the other piece. They carved Layne's name on the horizontal piece and each left a short, loving message to their fallen friend.

When the hole was dug and the marker was ready, they gently laid the body in the hole. There wasn't a dry eye in the group, except for the two dark-skinned warriors, as they covered the grave with dirt. Even the five Paladins, who didn't know Layne very well, were saddened at the grief the mercenaries felt over their fallen friend.

When the job was finished, they stuck the marker in the ground. Portia and Veronna had found a few small flowers in the immediate area and they laid them on top of the grave. The group stood silently around the grave for a long time, remembering their friend and loved one. Finally, Tim spoke.

"I guess I should say something."

He moved to stand beside the marker. He studied it. "This marker is beautiful. You ladies did a wonderful job on it." He stood there for a moment and read what the girls had written. A single tear streamed down his cheek. Then he turned back to the group.

"In the past, sometimes people would come up to me and ask me who the best fighter I knew was. I have had different answers throughout the years. But if someone were to come up to me today and ask me that question, without hesitation I would answer Layne. And I am including everyone present here today. I mean, he killed three Zantan Robbers all by himself. There are not very many people who could do that.

"He was quick and strong and a fast learner. I taught him something once and he picked it up immediately. He was a pleasure to watch in action.

"But even though he was an amazing fighter, he was an even better man." He looked at Dustin. "I know the kind of people your parents were just by knowing you and Layne. They did an amazing job raising him. And so did you, Dustin." Brione put a hand on Dustin's shoulder and he put his own hand over hers.

Tim continued. "Layne would have done anything for anyone in this group. Even the newcomers. He was a fierce friend who loved his family more than anything else. He was quick to laugh and slow to anger." Tim couldn't help but smile. "He could lighten the mood in almost any situation. His smile could melt anyone's heart. The twinkle in his eyes showed a man who was excited about life and loved to try new things. He was one of the most likeable people I have ever known.

"Layne gave his life for his loved ones." He looked at the girls in the group. "I have heard your whispers. I know you each blame yourself for Layne's death. But don't. He put himself in danger in Kingston for Veronna, and even though something terrible happened to him because of it, he put himself in danger again today. That is how much he loved you. Given the chance, I know he would do it again. Any one of us men would do that for you girls. So please, don't feel guilty. Layne wouldn't want you to.

"Now we have to say good-bye to a man we each loved very much. But I know he will be with us. When you love someone so much, and they love you just as much, a part of their spirit stays with you. They give you strength when you need it. They give you courage when you need it. He is still with us. So, don't be sad. Be happy that we can keep him in our hearts forever. We love you Layne."

He stepped away from the grave and stood by his daughter. She threw her arms around his waist and hugged him tight. No one said a word for a moment until Brione walked to the front of the group.

"Layne was one of the most annoying people I have ever known. But he did it on purpose." She couldn't help but laugh. "He teased everyone all the time, especially me. He was always joking around, he was never serious. Even when the situation called for seriousness, he wasn't. He was always smiling and laughing. And these things used to really get on my nerves.

"Then, when we were traveling without him, I found myself missing him terribly. What I wouldn't have given to have him there teasing me! I then realized that the group needed him." She smiled. "We all know that I am serious enough for the entire group. Then when you add in the personalities of everyone else in the group, we need Layne's personality. We need him to remind us that life is enjoyable. If life is just serious all the time, what is the point? We need to enjoy ourselves as much as we can. Layne taught me that. I will always be grateful that I knew him. I will always be grateful that I had that wonderful boy in my life. I will miss him terribly. I don't know what we will do without him."

She stepped back to her original place beside Dustin. He didn't look at her, but he put his hand on her shoulder and gave it an appreciative squeeze.

Aiden stepped up front. He didn't say anything for a while, he just stood there, looking at his friend's grave. He sniffed and finally looked up. "He was my best friend," he said simply. Then he stepped away and stood beside Portia again.

After a while Dustin walked to the front of the group. He sniffed, wiped the tears from his face, looked down at the hastily dug grave, and then looked up at the group.

"He deserves better than this," he began. "Layne was one of the best men I have ever known. He deserves to leave this life with much more celebration than this. This small burial doesn't do him justice. But this is all we can give him right now.

"He is all I had left. My parents were taken from me too soon, and now my brother is dead. I am alone." He lifted his hand to silence everyone's comments. "I know that I still have all of you, and I am grateful for that. I really am. But Layne was the last of my family. It is different. I consider you guys my family, but you are not. Not really. Only Layne was. And now he is gone, and I am all that's left. I don't know how I will go on." He lowered his head again. He took in a deep breath then looked once again at the group. "I will need you now more than ever. Every one of you. I am finding it difficult right now to think of a reason to keep going. A reason to keep living. I need you guys to give me one. I need your help to continue to go on. Will you help me?"

"Yes" said Brione.

"Of course," Portia chimed in.

Tim stepped up to Dustin. "We are your family Dustin. We will always be here for you. If you ever need anything, just ask us. Every single one of us would do anything for you. Never forget that."

The two men went back to join the group. David suddenly stepped forward and faced everyone. "I didn't know Layne very well," he began. "But I heard a lot about him and I have been listening to the words that you guys have said. I know that he was a good man who had a lot of love in his heart. God teaches us that we should love all men, that we should love everyone around us. Layne gave his life for someone else. He died so that someone else would live. That is the epitome of love. That is the greatest act of love that someone can do. Since Layne did that he will be taken to God's side and live in happiness and peace for eternity. Try not to be sad. He is in a good place and he is happy. I know that."

As David stepped away, he walked by Tim. "Thank you," Tim whispered to his old friends as he passed. David nodded.

The group stood at the grave for a while after that. No one wanted to leave. No one wanted to move on because when they left the grave site behind it would be like they were leaving Layne behind. No one was ready for that. Finally, Tim decided that they needed to journey on.

"Well, let's go" Tim said. "We have done all we can do here. We need to get going." He turned and walked away. One by one, with Dustin being the last, they turned and left the grave site of their friend and loved one.

36

Wyst sat straight up in his bed as the door to his room burst open and he saw a tall silhouette standing in the doorway. The torchlight in the hallway of the inn behind the person made it impossible to see any features. Wyst was naked from the waist up, his torso pale and thin. His long, white hair covered his bare shoulders. His hair was white, but he was only in his twenties. He pulled the covers up to help keep off the late night chill. "Who are you?" he asked the stranger.

He was surprised to hear a female voice answer. "I am a bounty hunter hired by the mayor. You are a necromancer, are you not?"

"How dare you burst into my room in the middle of the night!" Wyst was furious. "I paid good money for this room and I don't appreciate getting disturbed!"

"Answer the question," the woman said again. If the man's outburst had affected her, she didn't show it. "Are you or are you not a necromancer?"

"Look at me," he said. "You can tell that I am. Why waste my time with pointless questions? What do you want? Why did the mayor hire you?"

"The town has been having some problems with undead recently, which is obviously the work of a necromancer. Three people have been killed and the townsfolk are in an uproar. I was hired to capture the necromancer responsible. That would be you."

"Are you serious? I didn't do anything! I just got into town today. I am only passing through! I did not raise any undead!"

"I don't see any other necromancers around," came the reply. She turned her head from side to side. "Do you?"

"Listen," Wyst tried to reason with her. He got out of bed and stood up before her. She was as tall as he was. "I am not the man you are looking for. I am sick of being hassled just because I am a necromancer. I don't want to fight you, but I will if you try to take me in. I am innocent and I will defend myself."

"I hoped you would say that," the woman smiled as she spoke. "It makes it more fun when the people I track down put up a fight."

Wyst was about to put a curse on the woman, but she was too quick. Faster than he could think of the curse she brought a hand up with a spear that he hadn't noticed before. The butt end of the weapon came around and smacked Wyst across the face. Dazed, the curse left his mind. He couldn't think straight. He couldn't see straight. He felt the floor beneath his head and wondered how he had ended up on his back. He saw the silhouette of the woman standing over him.

"That wasn't much of a fight," she said, mockingly. Then he saw the shadow of the spear coming at him and everything went black.

*　　*　　*

Two days after the group buried Layne they rode into a small town. The streets were empty. Not a soul was in sight. But it wasn't like the town that they had passed through that had been sacked by goblins. They could tell that people lived in this town. Clothes were drying on lines strung out between two trees, children's toys were strewn all over the ground. There was even a pie cooling in a window, its aroma enticing to the group.

"This is Trimadore, if I remember correctly," Tim said.

"Yes, it is," replied David.

"Where is everyone?" Brione asked.

"I don't know," replied Tim. "Let's find out."

They continued through the town. Finally, they passed a side street and glanced down it. At the far end of the street they saw a large crowd gathered around a platform. They could see a few figures on top of the platform, but they were too far away to see exactly what was going on.

"Let's go see what everyone is doing," said Tim, and he led them down the street. When they got closer, they could see that one of the men on the platform had a noose around his neck. Another man was addressing the crowd. There was a third person on the platform as well, a tall woman holding a spear in front of her, its butt on the ground, its point in the air.

Tim stopped in his tracks. "You have got to be kidding me," he said for the second time this journey. His eyes were locked on the woman.

"What is it, dad?" asked Aiden. "Do you know the man who is about to be hanged?"

"No," the mercenary leader replied. "Not him. But I do know the woman with the spear. I can't believe she is here."

"Who is she?"

It took a moment for Tim to answer. "She is my sister, Deadawn. I haven't seen her since I was twenty and she was eighteen. How long ago was that? Eighteen years?"

The man who was addressing the crowd brought Tim out of his thoughts. "This man has been found guilty of being a necromancer. He is the one who has been raising the dead and having them attack the town. He will be hanged for his crimes!" The group started forward again.

"It wasn't me!" the man with the noose around his neck yelled. "It is true that I am a necromancer, but I did not have any undead attack your peaceful town. I am just a traveler passing through. I am innocent!"

"You are a necromancer and all necromancers are evil. Therefore, you must be punished!"

"This is not right," one of the Paladins said. "That man is not guilty."

"Who cares?" asked Reese. "The man is correct. He is a necromancer and therefore evil. One less necromancer is a blessing to the world. Let the man be hanged. It is none of our concern."

"Are you saying that he didn't have any undead attack the town?" Brione asked the Paladin who had spoken up first.

"Yes. God is telling me that he is innocent of the charges they are putting upon him."

"Dad, we have to stop this," Veronna said. "We can't let an innocent man die."

"I agree," Tim said and started his horse forward.

"Wait," said Reese and grabbed Tim by the arm as he went by. "What are you doing? We can't meddle in the affairs of this town. It is none of our business. Besides, what about your quest?"

Tim glared at Reese and jerked his arm out of the other man's grasp. "Two innocent men have already died on this journey. I will not stand aside and let a third die as well. I am going to stop this."

He spurred his horse forward again. "Make way!" he called out when he reached the crowd of onlookers. Most of the people grumbled or cursed at him, but everyone moved out of the way to allow the rider through. The rest of the group hurried after Tim, trying to get through the throng before the crowd closed the gap.

"Do you have any last words?" the speaker asked the doomed man. The necromancer didn't reply. Instead, he spit in the speaker's face.

The speaker turned red with rage. "Do it!" he yelled and the woman with the spear stepped forward to push the prisoner off the platform.

"Stop!" Tim cried and the woman, seeing Tim for the first time, stopped dead in her tracks. The look on her face told the group that she was as surprised to see Tim as he was to see her.

The speaker turned to the newcomers. The look of rage on his face hadn't diminished. "What is the meaning of this?" he demanded. "Who are you? What gives you the right to stop what I have begun? Do you know who I am?"

Tim got down from his horse and stepped up onto the platform. He stopped a few feet from the enraged man.

"Well, answer me!"

"Which question should I answer?"

"All of them!"

"I am Tim. I am a traveler passing through, just like your prisoner there. I happened to hear what you were talking about as I was walking by and I came to investigate. I am glad that I did." He pointed to the prisoner. "That man there is innocent of any wrong doing. You need to let him go and send some men to find the one who is actually responsible."

"Are you crazy?" the man yelled. "I have already passed sentence! My word is law in this town. This man is going to die for his crimes!"

"Your word is law, huh?" Tim asked. "Then you must be the mayor."

"Yes! I am the mayor! Now get off this platform and let me do my job!"

"I can't do that. I will not let you kill an innocent man."

"Oh? And how are you going to stop me?"

Tim drew his sword. "I will stop you by force if I must. I promise you this. You will not kill this man."

The mayor turned to the woman on the platform. "Don't just stand there," he said. "Get rid of this man."

The woman didn't move. She just stared at her older brother.

"Hello Deadawn," Tim said.

"Hello Timmond," she replied.

"What?" the mayor demanded. "You two know each other? How?"

"He is my brother," she replied, not taking her eyes from Tim.

"Your brother!"

"Yes. I haven't seen him in almost twenty years."

"Bah!" the mayor said and walked away from the siblings, cursing loudly.

Tim gently took Deadawn's arm and led her to the far side of the platform. "Did you capture this man?" Tim asked his sister.

"Yes. That is what I do. I am a bounty hunter. I am not so different from you. You left Zion just as I did, and I have heard that you are a mercenary. What is the difference?"

"Did you know for certain that this man is guilty?"

"No. It was a job. I find who they want me to find and bring them in, and they give me money. That is how it works. If the person is guilty or not is none of my concern."

"That is the difference between us," Tim replied. "But I have no desire to judge you right now. It is good to see you, sis. It looks like you have done well for yourself. How are you?"

"I can't complain. I have become one of the most sought-after bounty hunters in the region, and because of that I get paid very well."

"When was the last time you went back to see mom and dad?"

"I have never gone back to Zion after I left. I can't stand it there. You know that. And apparently neither could you. Why did you leave anyway?"

"You don't know, huh?" She shook her head. "Crystal died soon after giving birth to our daughter. I was angry at God for taking my wife away when she had done nothing wrong. I took my children and I sailed across the sea to start a new life."

"Oh Timmond. I am so sorry about Crystal." She gave him a quick hug. "But your children," Deadawn said with a smile and looked around at the crowd. "Are they here with you?"

"Yes, they are." He turned and called to his kids. They were standing on the ground, watching the encounter between the two siblings with the rest of the group, although they couldn't hear what was being said. They ran up the stairs and stood before their aunt. The rest of the group followed more slowly.

"Is this Aiden?" she asked. "You are so big! You were just born when I left Zion. And who is this little girl? I don't know her."

Veronna blushed. "My name is Veronna."

"You look just like your mom," Deadawn said, beaming. "I loved your mother very much. She never judged me when so many other people did." She turned to her nephew. "And you look a lot like my brother. The family resemblance is strong."

Aiden didn't know what to say. "Thanks."

The mayor came storming back over. "Can we get back on track please?" he asked. "Sorry to interrupt this little family reunion, but there is a very important matter we need to deal with." He pointed to the prisoner. "What are we going to do about him? I can't just let him go. If I start letting prisoners go that I have sentenced to death it will create anarchy!"

Deadawn turned to her brother. "He is a little dramatic," she said with a laugh.

"You will let him go," Tim said. "Then you will find the real man responsible." When the mayor started to argue Tim put his hand up to silence the man. "I am not giving you a choice in the matter. You will release him."

"But what if he is guilty?" the mayor exclaimed.

"He is not."

"But how do you know? Did you witness the killings? Did you see who it was that called the dead back from their graves and ordered them to attack my town? Did you?"

"No," Tim admitted. "But I know he is innocent."

"Okay," said the mayor. "This is what we are going to do. I will not kill this man, but I also will not let him go. I will put him back in prison, and if you want another necromancer found, you will go and find him yourselves. I will give you three days. If you don't come back with the real criminal by then, I will hang this man for the crimes he has committed. Deal?"

Tim looked hard at the mayor. "Yes. We have a deal. Do not kill this man for three days. I will be back before then." He turned to Deadawn. "Would you like to join us? We could use you."

Before she could answer the mayor interrupted. "I was hoping Deadawn would keep an eye on the prisoner to make sure he doesn't try to escape."

"It will cost you more money," she said.

The mayor sighed but said, "Alright."

"But..." Tim started but Deadawn interrupted him.

"Are you going to pay me?" she asked. Tim shook his head. "Then we have nothing more to talk about. I agree to watch the prisoner for double my usual fee."

Tim watched her walk over to the necromancer and cut him down. Then she pulled him roughly to his feet and hauled him away. Tim was disappointed in his sister, but in truth, he was not surprised that she chose money over him. She had never been big on the idea of family, which she proved when she left Zion and never returned. He shook his head sadly and turned back to the group. "It looks like we have work to do. Let's go find ourselves a necromancer."

They left immediately. Not only were they concerned about finding the necromancer quickly, but they also wanted to get back on the road as soon as possible. Reese had been angry with Tim for taking the job of finding the necromancer, but Tim didn't care. The others agreed with Tim's decision though, so they happily followed him. Reese reluctantly came as well.

Everyone happily followed him but one. Dustin didn't care. All he cared about was the hole in his heart where his family used to be. The others tried to talk to him, but all they got in return was a grunt or a nod, so they finally stopped trying. Dustin appreciated their concern for him, but he had no desire to speak with anyone at the moment. He couldn't care less about either of the necromancers. But he followed Tim and the rest of the group anyway.

Tim had sent Jaden and Zach out as scouts in the hopes that they might find some sign of the necromancer or his undead minions. Jaden came back quickly and said he found some odd tracks. He led them off the path they were on and to the strange tracks.

They looked human, but the things that had made the tracks had constantly dragged their feet as they walked. "They look like the tracks of the undead to me," one of the Paladins said. "I have fought undead before and that is how they walk. It looks like there were at least a dozen of them."

"Well then," said Tim. "If we follow these tracks back to where they originate, they should lead us right to the one who raised them." He gestured for Jaden to lead the way. The dark-skinned man took off with the rest of the group following.

"We shouldn't have to go very far," the Paladin explained to Tim. "An undead cannot go very far from the one who raised it. If it ventures too far away, the magic goes away and the body falls to the ground, lifeless."

The Paladin was proven right when just ten minutes later the tracks ended. "It looks like a lot of bodies once laid in this spot," Jaden said.

"I'll bet that the necromancer dug up the bodies, placed them here, and then raised them all at once," Tim said.

From there it was easy to find and follow the tracks that could only belong to the necromancer. They led to a small wooden building with a pond in front of it and a cliff rising high behind it. The group could see a large cave opening in the cliff.

Tim gathered everyone around him. "Zach, Jaden, and I will go investigate the cottage. I want the Paladins to make their way to the entrance of the cave and secure it."

Before Tim could continue, Reese interrupted him. "I don't take orders from you, and neither do my men. I am in charge of the Paladins, not you. Not anymore."

"It's alright, Reese," David said. "Tim is the leader of the company who was contracted for this journey. He is the leader of the group who is going after the necromancer, and we were ordered by the Prophet to accompany him."

Reese just stared at Tim for a long time. "Fine," he reluctantly gave in. Tim could tell that the rivalry between them, at least in Reese's point of view, was still going strong. Tim felt differently.

"Alright," Tim continued. "I want the Paladins to secure the cave entrance, but don't go in just yet. Wait for the rest of us. The rest of the group will stay here and watch the area. Brione will be in charge. Make sure nothing comes at us from behind." He looked around. "Does everyone understand?" They all nodded. "Okay. Let's go."

The Paladins made their way to the cave entrance. They could see torch light a long way into the cave, but nothing else.

Tim and the two dark-skinned fighters went toward the hut. Tim headed straight for the door, while the other two swung around wide on either side. Tim reached the door and tried the handle. It was unlocked. The other two checked the windows on the sides of the hut, then went and joined Tim in front.

"The building is only one room and I could see two figures inside," Zach reported.

Jaden nodded. "I saw the same thing."

"What were the figures doing?" Tim asked.

"Just standing there," said Zach.

"Odd. Male or female?"

"They were both male," Jaden said.

"Where are they exactly?"

"They are standing in the middle of the room, on either side of the door. They are both facing the door."

"And they didn't notice you looking at them?"

"No," both men said in unison.

"Alright. Let's go in. I'll go first, then Jaden, then Zach. I will go right, Jaden left, Zach stays in between."

Both men nodded their confirmation and Tim threw open the door and quickly rushed into the room. He went right and confronted the man standing there. He had to quickly duck under the fist coming at his face. He struck out with his sword, stabbing the man in the stomach, then retracting it. If the man felt the stab at all, he didn't show it. Another fist flew at Tim and he had to duck again. When he straightened up, Tim finally got a good look at his enemy.

His clothes were tattered and hanging loosely from his body. His arms were bone thin, and the skin on his face was stretched thinly over his skull. He only had a few clumps of hair on his head, and his eyes had no life in them. A second look at another punch coming at him showed Tim that the man's arms weren't just bone thin, they were actually bones. This man's body had been raised from the dead.

"How do we kill them?" asked Jaden from behind Tim. Tim quickly glanced over his shoulder to see Jaden and Zach battling the other undead creature side by side. The two warriors stabbed the creature repeatedly, but to no effect.

"I don't know," Tim admitted. "Try to cut off everything. Arms, legs, head. Everything." Taking his own advice, instead of ducking under the next punch, Tim stepped to the side of it and brought his sword down on the arm, cutting it off just below the shoulder. The creature didn't react in any way. It just attacked again with its other arm, which Tim promptly cut off. Armless, the creature continued to walk towards Tim. Tim took a horizontal swing and the thing's head went flying. The rest of the body stopped where it was and crumpled to the floor.

"Cut off its head!" Tim yelled to his companions.

Zach did just that, and the body of the creature they were fighting hit the ground as well.

They searched the shack but found nothing of interest. They left the building, motioned for the rest of the group to follow, and then headed for the cave entrance. Tim waited for the others to arrive before he told them what they had found in the shack.

Veronna gasped at the description of the undead creatures they had fought. Everyone else looked either frightened or disgusted.

"That is the way to kill them," the Paladin who had experience fighting the undead said. "You need to cut off their heads. I don't know why that works because they are not alive, but it does."

"Okay," said Tim. "Now that we know how to kill them, that will make things a lot easier. Don't waste time and energy attacking them any other way. It doesn't do anything." Everyone nodded. "Now, we don't know what we will find in there, but I am guessing that if the necromancer is in there, there will probably be a lot more undead creatures. So be prepared for that.

"I want Zach, three Paladins, and I to go in first. Then the rest of the group, with Jaden and the other two Paladins bringing up the rear. Understood?" Everyone nodded again. "Alright. Let's go."

37

As the group walked in, they saw a light in the distance. They couldn't tell how far away the light was because the passage turned to the right at a slow angle about a hundred feet down. Everything before the light was dark. It was hard to see anything unless they were very close to it.

They walked in silence. About halfway to the light Tim bumped into something. "Everyone stop," he said in a loud whisper.

He reached out and felt at the thing he bumped into. It was another standing corpse. "Here is another one," he said. "I wonder why this one isn't moving." He poked at the body, but it still didn't move. "If anyone bumps into one, just chop off its head. We don't want them coming to life and attacking us from behind." Taking his own advice, he cut off the creature's head with a great swing of his sword. The body fell to the ground. "Let's go," he said and started walking again.

Before they turned the corner, they encountered four more undead creatures. These just stood there as well, unmoving. They cut off their heads and continued on their way.

They turned the corner and saw a room. This was where the light was coming from. They were still a long way down the corridor from the room, but from where they were standing, it looked to be huge. They finally came up to the entrance of the room and discovered that it was indeed cavernous. The ceiling had to be at least a hundred feet high and the far wall was at least that far away from where they stood. The floor in the center of the cavern was lower than where they stood, and a wide shelf about five feet higher than the floor in the center circled the entire room. The floor directly in front of them led down to the center. Dozens of undead creatures stood unmoving on the shelf. In the middle of the cave was a desk covered with papers. Behind the desk stood a man. This man reminded them of the necromancer they were here to save. He was dressed all in black and had pale skin and snow white hair. He was staring at the group as they entered.

"How did you like my guards?" the necromancer asked.

"We didn't," Tim simply said. "Are you the necromancer that has been raising the dead and having them attack the townsfolk?"

"You get right to the point I see. Yes, that was me. What are you going to do about it?"

"There is another necromancer that has been falsely accused and arrested for your crimes. We are here to take you in and prove his innocence. If you come with us willingly, it will be easier for you."

The necromancer laughed. "Do you really think you can take me in? Look around you! Do you not see my soldiers? They will do anything I want them to. They do not talk back. They do not ask questions. They do not disobey. The perfect soldiers, don't you think? If you try to arrest me, I will wake them up and have them destroy you all."

"We know how to kill them," Tim replied. "They pose no threat to us."

"You have never fought a necromancer before, have you?" the man asked.

Suddenly, several of the undead sentries started moving. They climbed off the shelf and headed for the group.

"Brione, Dustin and I will take the necromancer," Tim ordered. "The rest of you take care of the undead creatures."

The three that Tim named slowly headed toward the necromancer. If he was nervous about being outnumbered three to one, he didn't show it. He looked at Brione and suddenly she cried out and dropped her weapon. She crouched down on the floor and started sobbing. Tim, confused, ran to her but was hit with a feeling of such terror that he almost dropped his sword and fled. On the other side of him, Dustin did turn and flee, screaming in fear.

Tim heard the necromancer laugh and he did his best to fight the terror that threatened to overwhelm him. He gritted his teeth and growled in frustration. He tried to replace the feeling of terror with rage. Slowly, the rage took over and the feeling of terror passed.

Tim straightened and started towards the necromancer again.

"A strong one I see," said the necromancer. "This should be fun."

When Tim was still a few steps away from the necromancer, all his strength left him. His arms dropped, his weapon hit the floor, and his legs gave out. His body followed his sword to the ground and all he could do was lay on the floor and listen to the sounds of battle all around him and the laughter of the necromancer. "Not so strong anymore, are you?" the necromancer said. Tim saw the necromancer walk toward him, a dagger in his hand.

*   *   *

Aiden ducked under a heavy blow from an undead creature then cut off its head with his sword. But as soon as the dead thing hit the floor, another one was there to take its place. The group had formed a protective circle around Veronna, Tyler and Dorn. Tyler was almost useless in hand-to-hand combat and would be in trouble if he had to face one of the undead things directly.

Aiden quickly glanced to his left and saw that the Paladins were holding their own. He turned his attention back to his enemy just in time to chop off an arm that was coming at him. No blood flew from the wound and spilled to the floor. No shriek of pain came from the monster's mouth. The undead thing was silent as it fought.

Another swing took the things head off and Aiden found a short reprieve. He looked to his right and saw the two black-skinned fighters working as a team and quickly dispatching any creature that came at them.

Something flew past Aiden's head so quickly that he barely got a glance at it. He couldn't look and see where it went because another creature was coming at him. This one was much larger than the others. It came at him on all fours, its great mouth open in a silent roar, its teeth long and still sharp. Aiden had only seen two of these creatures in his life, but he knew it to be the carcass of a bear. A big one.

*   *   *

Tyler was frustrated. He had to be protected by the stronger fighters, and it was too chaotic around him to fire stones at his enemies without hitting one of his companions. The stones likely wouldn't do much damage to these undead things anyway. Blunt weapons were not the best for these creatures. He watched helplessly with Veronna inside the circle as the fighting raged all around them. At least they seemed to be winning. Although there were many more creatures that they hadn't encountered yet.

Finally, sick of feeling helpless, Tyler prepared to help, in case the opportunity arose. At that moment, several rocks were hovering in the air and Tyler surveyed the area to see what help he could be. It was a good thing he did. Suddenly, he saw an opportunity and one of the rocks flew away, barely missing Aiden's head.

*   *   *

As Tim watched the necromancer slowly walking towards him, the wizard suddenly stopped in his tracks, a stone striking him in the head. The necromancer stumbled a bit to the side, then shook away his dizziness and started forward again. Tim could see a line of blood running down the wizard's face.

The necromancer spotted another rock soaring his way and was able to duck under it, but the rock distracted him from another threat. He didn't see Dustin rushing towards him. The ex-knight had gotten far enough away from the necromancer to shake off the effects of the curse and had immediately rushed back to help his friends. With a roar he swung his sword at the evil wizard. The roar alerted the necromancer to the attack and although the blow connected, the wizard had enough time to dodge just enough so the sword cut into his side, but not enough to do much damage. It had hurt the wizard though.

The necromancer stumbled back, falling into his large desk and moving it backwards several inches. Before Dustin could move in for the kill though, a handful of the undead creatures changed direction and went for him. He had to give up ground as the creatures pressed in, and the necromancer had time to scramble to safety behind the desk.

But since the necromancer had to use his powers to change the orders for the creatures, the effects of his curses wore off and Tim and Brione got back to their feet.

*   *   *

Aiden fell back in fear. The massive creature was faster than the other ones and much bigger. A shower of stones pelted the bear, but they had no effect. The creature swept one great paw across, and Aiden's sword swung automatically to block the creature. Unfortunately, the powerful swipe merely knocked the weapon aside and the paw hit Aiden and sent him flying away. The bear pursued and tried to crush the fallen man, but Aiden was able to roll out of the way…right into the legs of another undead creature.

The creature punched down at Aiden and hit him in the shoulder. His shoulder immediately went numb and he couldn't maintain his grip on the sword. That would have been the end for Aiden had not Portia been watching him. As soon as the bear had knocked him aside, she screamed and ran toward him. She was small and quick and easily swerved and dodged her way through the fighting, javelin in hand.

She reached Aiden right when the creature was about to punch him again swinging her javelin horizontally and severing the creature's arm. Seizing her opportunity, she sliced the head off the monster with her backswing and watched as the creature tumbled to the earth, dead. It wasn't until she was pulling Aiden to his feet that she remembered the bear. She turned just in time to see the creature's paw coming at her.

Her impulse to duck was automatic and she quickly thrust her javelin towards the bear, but it had no effect. The next paw swipe knocked the weapon from her hand. She tried to reach for one of the extra javelins strapped to her back, but she had to roll out of the way to prevent another strike.

Aiden stepped protectively in front of her, not knowing what he could do against this monstrosity. He didn't think twice about it, he just reacted. The bear stood up on its hind legs, its head over ten feet from the floor. It gave another silent roar and went back to all fours. It charged Aiden and the man barely was able to dive out of the way. Aiden had not been far from the wall, and the creature's momentum took it crashing into it. The collision didn't really hurt the undead bear, but as it turned to face Aiden and Portia again, they saw that the impact had taken half its jaw off. The bear didn't seem to notice as it rushed at them again.

Aiden and Portia dodged the bear once more, wondering what they could possibly do to defeat the monster.

*   *   *

Tim, Brione, and Dustin defeated the undead creatures in their way and then they surrounded the necromancer. The fallen man scooted away from them, but he had nowhere to go. Every so often, another creature would rise and lunge at them, but the necromancer was in too much pain to completely control the undead.

"You are beaten," Tim said. The necromancer didn't say anything. He just sneered at them and continued to scoot backwards.

"Give up and we shall go easy on you."

"Give up so I can get hung in a public square? I don't think so."

"Why did you do it?" asked Brione. "Why did you have your creatures attack the townsfolk?"

"Revenge!" he answered with a smile. "You have no idea the way people treat necromancers. If they see us walking down a street, they will call us names and throw things, or worse. They deserved what I did to them. And it was worth it."

"Worth your life?" Tim asked.

"Yes," the necromancer answered.

Tim quickly moved in and before the necromancer could react, he hit him across the head with the hilt of his sword. The necromancer immediately went limp. All the undead that had been moving suddenly fell to the ground, lifeless.

*   *   *

As Aiden and Portia tired, they shot each other distressed looks, knowing their time was running out. They didn't think they were going to get out of this battle alive, when suddenly the creature dropped to the floor, unmoving.

Aiden and Portia watched, eyes wide, waiting a few moments to confirm the creature truly was down. When they realized it was, and understood that the necromancer must have been defeated, they fell into each other, holding each other in relief. A few minutes later, David approached them and knelt beside them.

"I am so sorry," he apologized. "I saw the bear go after you and tried to come to your aid, but there were too many undead creatures and I couldn't get to you. I am sorry."

"It's alright," Aiden said. "We are okay."

Everyone regrouped around Tim.

"What if he wakes up on our way back to town?" Aiden asked.

"Leave him to us," Reese said. "We will make sure that he doesn't cause any trouble if he wakes up."

"Alright," said Tim. "Let's get him back to town and free the innocent man."

*   *   *

The necromancer woke up on their way back to the town, but the Paladins were true to their word and the necromancer did nothing to harm the group. Tim wasn't sure if the necromancer had given up or if the Paladins were able to prevent him from using his powers. Either way, they made it back to the town without incident.

Dusk was approaching when they arrived, and the streets were almost empty of people. It seemed that all the townsfolk who had been gathered in the square before had gotten tired of waiting and went about their business.

The group made their way to the square and found a few town guards lounging around the platform that the prisoner was on before. They asked for directions to the jail, then made their way over to the building. Tim asked most of the group to stay outside, bringing Reese, David, Brione and Dustin inside with him.

A man was seated behind a large desk. Deadawn leaned against the wall holding her spear upright in front of her, a bored expression on her face. Past the desk were a handful of cells with one solid wall and bars on the other three sides. The only prisoner was the necromancer. He turned his head and quickly got to his feet and went to the bars when he saw who it was.

"You found him?" he asked. "Am I to be freed?"

"I should have known you would be fast," Deadawn said. She turned to the man behind the desk. "Go get the mayor and tell him that Tim is back with another necromancer."

"I don't take orders from you," the seated man complained.

"Go!" Deadawn yelled, and the man was on his feet so fast that the chair fell all the way over backwards and crashed to the ground. The man rushed through the door, the sound of Deadawn's laughter chasing him out.

"Did you have any problems with the necromancer?" Deadawn asked her brother.

"A little."

"Ha! I had no trouble at all with mine!" she boasted.

"That's because you took me by surprise!" the necromancer behind the bars exclaimed.

"Alright then," Deadawn said. "Attack me now. Do something to harm me when you are not surprised."

The necromancer stared at her for a long time. Finally, he shook his head. "No. I will do nothing to hinder my freedom, now."

Deadawn laughed at him. "Coward."

"You have changed, Deadawn," Tim said quietly.

She turned to her brother. "Oh? Does the new me not please you?"

"Not at all," Tim replied without hesitation. "I remember a kind girl. True, you never accepted God or the church's teachings, and you were always a little hard-headed and stubborn, but you were never cruel."

"Life will do that to a person."

"Yeah, I know all about what life can do to you."

There was an awkward silence for a moment. Finally, Deadawn said, "Timmond, I am truly sorry about Crystal. She was a good woman."

"Thanks," Tim said.

They were saved from further conversation when the door opened and the mayor walked in, followed by the man who had been sitting behind the desk and several armed guards.

"You are back sooner than I had thought you would be," the mayor began. Then he noticed the new necromancer standing between the two Paladins. His eyes widened. "You brought him here? How dare you! Don't you know the harm he could cause?"

"Do not worry," David said, trying to calm the man down. "He will cause no harm with us around."

"Are you sure?"

"Yes. You have no reason to fear."

The mayor took a deep breath and visibly calmed down. "Alright then. What did you find out?"

"We discovered that this man is the one who sent the undead creatures to attack your town," Tim said. "The other necromancer that Deadawn brought in is innocent of any wrong doing."

"I wouldn't say that," Deadawn said.

"What is that supposed to mean?" asked Tim.

"He is a necromancer," she replied. "He is far from innocent."

"You know nothing about me!" the necromancer behind the bars shouted.

"And are you innocent, Deadawn?" Tim asked quietly.

"What are you talking about?" Deadawn demanded.

"How many innocent people have you hurt simply for money? You don't care if the people you hunt down are guilty or not."

She was silent for a while. "I don't ask questions, because I don't want to know," she finally replied. "It is easier not knowing."

"Join us," Tim offered again. "We do our best to make a difference. You could be using your skills for good, not just for money."

"I already told you, I'm not interested."

"But Deadawn…"

"No!" She yelled and Tim went quiet. "I don't want your life, Timmond. Don't ask again."

With that, she rushed out of the building. Tim started to go after her, but David's hand on his shoulder stopped him. "Let her go," the Paladin said.

The group turned back to the mayor and his prisoner.

"Now that the family drama is over," the mayor said with a smirk, "Let's get back to business." He turned to the necromancer that Tim's group had brought in. "Now what should we do with you? Do you confess?"

The necromancer just stared at him.

"If he does not confess to you," David said, "know that he has already confessed to us. He told us that he is guilty; he is the one who sent the undead creatures to attack the town. The other necromancer is innocent. Let him go and do with this one whatever you feel necessary."

"Oh, I don't think so," said the mayor. "The bounty hunter was right. They are both guilty because they are necromancers. I think I will string them both up side-by-side tomorrow."

"We can't allow you to do that," said David.

"You would defy my wishes? I am the mayor of this town. My word is law."

"Nevertheless, we won't allow you to harm the innocent necromancer."

The mayor thought about it for a moment. If he had been planning on defying a Paladin, he apparently thought better of it. "Fine," he said. "But you have to take him with you. You are the one who wants him, so you are now responsible for him. If anyone of my soldiers sees him alone in the future, they will arrest him again and hang him for his crimes."

David looked to Tim. Tim nodded. "Agreed. Let him out and we will leave your town with him."

"What about the other one?" asked the mayor.

"What about him?"

"If you guys leave, who is going to make sure the other necromancer doesn't harm us?"

One of the Paladins stepped forward. "I will stay and make sure he does nothing to harm anyone."

"Are you sure?" asked Reese.

"Yes. After justice is served, I will try to find you again."

"No," Reese said. "After you are done here, go back to Zion. You have done your part to aid us in our cause. Go home and be with your family."

"Thank you. I will. And good luck to you."

The mayor unlocked the door to the innocent man's cell and let him out. He stepped out of the cell and breathed a deep sigh of relief. "Thank you," he said to the group. "I owe you my life."

"Now get him out of my town!" the mayor said, and the group left the building with the necromancer. They quickly explained to the rest of the group what had happened inside and left the town.

"I saw Aunt Deadawn run out of the building," Veronna told Tim as they made their way out of town. "I called to her, but she ignored me. Is she alright? Should we go find her and make sure?"

"No," Tim replied. "She doesn't want us to find her. She made that perfectly clear in the building. Let's just be on our way."

38

As Easton lifted his face out of the mud, he could hear people around him laughing. He coughed and mud came flying out of his mouth. He glanced up at the soldiers watching him and his older brother, the crowned prince, spar. He was a prince of the realm, and they were laughing at him! Rage boiled up inside and Easton struggled to get up, but the mud was slick, and he slipped and fell back down again, mud filling his mouth and nostrils. At that, the crowd laughed even harder. Even Jordan joined in the laughter.

He felt a hand on his shoulder and immediately knew it was his sister, Dana. She helped him to his feet. She was always helping him. Part of him resented her for that; princes shouldn't need help from their sisters. But another part of him loved her for it. She was the only person who didn't laugh at him or tell him that he should be more like his older brother, Jordan. Jordan was perfect. He did everything well. Easton was a disappointment.

"Stop laughing at him!" Dana yelled at the onlookers, letting go of her brother and taking a step toward the crowd. "He is your prince! Show some respect!"

"Sorry," Jordan said as the laughter died down. "We didn't mean anything by it."

"Even so," Dana said, "you shouldn't be so mean to him." She turned back to Easton. "Come on, let's go." She grabbed him by the arm and led

him away. Easton glanced over his shoulder at his brother and the rest of the people. He glared at them and they started laughing again.

They left the training grounds and Dana led him to a small pond on the palace grounds. "Clean yourself up," Dana said gently. Easton got down to his hands and knees and washed his hands and face. The water immediately before him turned from a clear blue to a dark brown as the mud came off.

"I'll kill him," Easton said under his breath.

"What did you say?" his sister asked.

"Nothing," he said.

"Yes, you did. I heard you. What did you say?"

"I said I'll kill him!" Easton yelled.

"Easton!"

"Well you asked. That is what I said." Easton saw the look of disappointment on his sister's face. "That is why I said it too quietly for you to hear. Sorry."

"Easton, don't talk like that. You're better than that."

Easton looked at his feet. "No, I am not."

"Yes, you are!"

"You are the only one who thinks so. Everyone else thinks I'm worthless."

"No, they don't. Don't be silly, Easton."

Easton looked back up at his sister. "Yes, they do. Haven't you ever heard father tell me that I need to be more like Jordan?" She shook her head. "Well he has. Several times. 'Just follow Jordan's example' he says. 'You need to be more like Jordan.' 'Why can't you be more like your older brother?' You don't know what it's like being told that. You are the only girl in the family. You are not compared to anyone else. Even if you were, it wouldn't matter. Everyone loves you just like everyone loves Jordan. Both of you are perfect. I'm hopeless."

"Don't talk like that," Dana said again. "I don't think you're worthless. And you just have to prove to everyone else that you're not."

"You really think so?" Easton asks.

"Yes. I really do. You are a very special person, Easton. And if other people can't see that, well then you'll just have to show them."

Easton smiled. Dana could always make him feel better.

* * *

It was hard to live under Jordan's shadow. He was better than Easton at everything. He was bigger, stronger, and faster…he was better at history and math. Even his skills as a horseman and swordsman outweighed Easton's. Jordan's speech was more eloquent and he was easily more charming -- he was the model of a crowned prince. One day, his brother would be king, and Easton would be nothing.

"I bet that if I were the crowned prince no one would laugh at me," he would often say to himself. He could imagine himself as the crowned prince. Everyone would bow to him and do exactly as he ordered. No one would laugh at him because he could have them beheaded.

These day dreams were the only happy memories of his childhood. When he was forced to face reality, life was miserable. The only good thing he had was Dana. Even his parents preferred Jordan to him, but not Dana. Dana spent most of her time with Easton. She would listen to his complaints without judgment. She was the only person he could trust not to laugh at him, the only person he cared for besides himself.

* * *

One day Easton's father forced him to take a hunting trip with Jordan and an escort of soldiers. Jordan and the soldiers were better riders than Easton was, so he quickly fell behind. The entire party had to take breaks so Easton could catch up, and he could sense Jordan's frustration. Finally, Jordan decided to leave Easton behind and he charged off after a fleeing deer. All the soldiers followed the crowned prince and Easton was left behind.

He was furious. He didn't like his brother or the soldiers, but he didn't enjoy being left behind. It was their job to protect him from harm and they just left him. They didn't care. Easton felt the tears starting to flow. The worst part was that Dana wasn't there to help him. His tears quickly changed to tears of rage and he decided then and there that he would stand up for himself. He didn't need his sister to stand up for him. He was a prince and he would do it himself.

He spurred his horse forward and immediately almost fell off. After a short struggle, he was able to hang on and regain his balance. His horse was running full speed and he caught up to the rest of the group quickly. When he found them, Jordan was in the process of skinning a deer. He was an expert marksman, of course.

"You're late, Brother," Jordan said as Easton dismounted from his horse. "I'm almost finished skinning my catch. Would you like to cut it up so we can take it back to the palace?"

"I don't think so, Jordan. That was your kill. You take care of it. I think I will go find my own deer to kill and take home."

Jordan laughed at that. "You? Kill a deer? Don't be ridiculous, Easton. If you chased a deer on horseback, you would immediately fall off. And you would never be able to hit one with an arrow. I'll tell you what. If you finish up here with my deer, I will go kill another one and you can tell everyone that you killed it. What do you say?"

All the guards laughed at that and Easton turned red.

"No. I can do this myself." He walked back to his horse and remounted. He was able to get up with only a little struggle.

Jordan snickered. "You are serious, aren't you?"

"I have never been more serious. Now, if you will excuse me."

He turned his mount around and started off the way he had come. Jordan ordered one of the guards to finish with the deer and he jumped onto his own horse and started off after his brother. He didn't even take the time to wash the deer's blood off his hands.

Jordan urged his horse faster and a few minutes later, he had caught up to Easton. He pulled up beside his brother's horse and looked at him. A look of determination was painted across Easton's face.

"Tell you what, brother," Jordan said. "If you can beat me in a race to that hill in the distance, I will help you hunt your first deer. Sound good?"

"Seriously?" Easton asked.

"Yes."

"Alright. It's a deal." In his excitement Easton almost fell off his horse. Jordan laughed at him and kicked his horse, making the animal leap forward.

Jordan's laughter brought Easton's anger back and he kicked his horse forward too. They followed a wide trail that twisted and turned, and Easton struggled to stay in his saddle. He was determined though, and ready to prove to his brother and to everyone else that he was not worthless.

Jordan would reign his horse in just a little to give Easton a chance to catch up, then, when Easton was close, he would go faster again. The fact that Jordan was toying with him made Easton even more furious. He decided he was done playing by his brother's rules. He left the trail and cut across through the trees.

Jordan glanced back and when he didn't see his brother behind him, he pulled his horse to a stop. "Easton!" he called. He heard a holler and turned back around to see his brother up ahead of him, charging through the trees.

"You're not as dumb as I thought," Jordan said as he got his horse going again.

Easton had to duck under several low hanging branches, then glanced over his shoulder and saw his brother gaining on him. He turned back around just in time to duck under another branch. Leaving the trail might not have been the best idea. He had to maneuver his horse around trees as the forest began to get thicker.

He glanced over his shoulder again and saw that his brother was even closer. He urged his horse to run faster, but the animal had reached its limit. Easton could see the hill just ahead. He hoped his horse could last just a little longer.

Up ahead, Easton saw that he was about to have a problem. Directly in front of his charging horse was a large log, over which was a thick, low-hanging branch that would knock Easton off his horse if he hit it. When the horse leaped over the log Easton ducked as low as he could, his head barely missing the branch. His brother wasn't so lucky.

Behind him Easton heard a loud crack and a cry of pain. He stopped his horse and looked back to see Jordan's horse running at him. When the horse passed by, he noticed Jordan lying on the ground. Easton dismounted *and walked back to his injured brother. When he got closer, he saw that blood was running freely from a gash in Jordan's head. Jordan was moaning in pain. To the side, a branch lay on the ground. Jordan's head had hit it so hard that it broke off the tree.*

Easton knelt next to Jordan. "Jordan?" The only answer he received was a moan. "Are you alright?" More moaning. "Jordan?"

Easton didn't know what to do. Should he help him? Should he go for help? His eyes found the branch lying on the ground, a large portion of it stained red from Jordan's blood. Should he…

No! He couldn't do that. He hated his older brother, but he could never do that. Could he? If he did, he would be the crowned prince, and everyone would respect him and do what he told them to. No one would ever laugh at him again. No! How could he even think that? This was his brother. His family.

"Easton? Jordan said weakly. "What happened?"

"You hit a branch with your head and fell off your horse."

"Where is my horse?"

"I don't know. He ran off."

"Go find him," Jordan demanded.

"I can't find him. I don't know where he went. He could be anywhere."

"I don't care," said Jordan. "It is your fault this happened to me and you have to find my horse."

Easton was angry that Jordan blamed him. "Go find it yourself!" he yelled.

"I can't, you idiot. Look at me, I can barely even move. Are you stupid or something?"

That was it. Easton couldn't take his brother calling him names anymore. He got up and walked over to the branch.

"Where are you going?" asked Jordan, craning his head to see his brother. "Are you going to find my horse?"

Easton stood above the branch, not moving, just staring down at it. What if he got caught? What if someone found out what he did? Then he would be put to death. But how would anyone find out? He could just say that the original hit on the head had killed his brother.

"Easton! Answer me! Are you going to go find my horse? Easton!"

Easton bent down and grabbed the branch. It was heavier than he had thought, and he had to grab it with both hands. "Easton!" his brother called. Slowly he walked back to stand over his injured brother. "No," he said quietly.

"No?" asked Jordan, confused. "No, what?"

"No, I will not get your horse."

Jordan's eyes widened when he saw Easton raise the branch over his head. "What are you doing?"

"I will not get your horse!" Easton yelled, shut his eyes, and brought the branch down on his brother's head.

*   *   *

With a gasp Easton awoke. He was breathing hard and sweat was streaming down his face. It took him a few moments to compose himself. The dream was so vivid it felt more like a memory. He had killed his brother that day with the branch that Jordan had broken off with his head. When the guards had finally caught up to them, Easton alerted them of Jordan's accident. The guards were distraught to find him dead on the scene, but luckily for Easton, he had hit his brother in the exact spot where the branch had first hit him, leaving only one wound.

Dana immediately believed Easton's story, but his parents seemed skeptical. Their strange looks told him that they didn't believe him. They knew that Easton and Jordan hated each other and had hoped the hunting trip might bring them closer together.

They confronted Easton about their doubts and he assured them that what he told was the truth. Still, Easton knew they didn't believe him, and eventually they came to resent him for Jordan's death. His sister had never forgiven her parents for thinking the worst of Easton. Easton prayed she would never discover the truth.

Dana had always stood behind him. She had always protected him. Now it was his turn to protect her. He wouldn't let King Korlas hurt her in any way. He would stop him.

39

Syth led his squad of two Sentinels and ten city watchmen toward the burning building. He was accompanied by Ned, the older man who had won the archery contest, and Bruce, the large man who had won the mounted melee. There were five such squads, each with two Sentinels and ten watchmen handpicked by Francis. The destruction and killing had escaladed soon after the tournament and the Sentinels and City Watch had their hands full.

Syth was impressed at the effectiveness of his little band of bandits. They had swelled to about eighty members now, and his master had given him a gift. Another warrior from Abberdon had appeared before Syth one day saying that he had been in Tosun looking for someone to join up with and their master had ordered him to come aid Syth. The warrior's name was Karch, and Syth had immediately put him to work training the bandits. Karch had been successful in doing so and the chaos that had followed was enormous.

Syth discovered that he enjoyed playing both roles of bandit leader and queen's protector. It was a challenge, of course, but one he embraced.

A squad of firefighters were hard at work throwing buckets of water on the building. They were trained to fight fires, but they were losing. Syth could immediately see that they had no chance of saving the building. He made his way toward a man who was directing everyone else.

"Is anyone still in the building?" Syth asked when the man noticed him.

"I don't think so," he replied. "We sent a team in to search for people when we first got here, but they didn't find anyone."

"Well, that's good. Do you have any witnesses? Did anyone see anything?"

"No. Whoever did this was long gone before we got here. We have no idea who did this."

"Okay. We will leave you to it. We will see if we can find any clues."

As Syth and his group passed the leader by, he dared to grab the dark-skinned warrior by the arm. Syth stopped and looked at him. "Find out who did this," he pleaded. "Find them and stop them." Syth simply nodded and the man let him go.

The irony of it all made him smile. He would find the people who did this, because he already knew exactly where they were. He had planned this fire, and all the other attacks throughout the city. Each of the other groups of watchmen would run into trouble. If they were lucky, his bandits would kill a few of the Sentinels and send the city into even more chaos. But he had to be careful and put on a show of trying his very best to stop the criminals. A few of his bandits would have to be sacrificed to keep up appearances.

He led his team down a back alley, pretending to search for signs of people passing by. At one point he called Ned to his side to ask if he could see anything. Luckily, his bandits had left signs of their passing in their rush to get away from the fire. The old farmer easily found their tracks.

The current group they were tracking consisted of ten men. They were some of the most promising in his band. He was positive that they would do some damage to Ned's group before they were able to get away. They might even kill one or both of the Sentinels.

He led them on a round-a-bout route to the building that Syth had chosen beforehand. It was a warehouse with one large room and a back door. The room was big enough for the bandits to efficiently move around in during an attack and it provided an escape route. Syth would have to kill or capture one or two bandits, but the rest should be able to escape.

He led the group right up to the building's front door, where the trail ended. He was about to force the door open and rush inside when Bruce stopped him.

"Wait," he said. "Shouldn't some of us go around back and cut off any possible escape route?"

Syth had to think quickly. "We don't know how many are in there. It is probably best to stick together so they don't overwhelm us."

"I don't think anyone will be overwhelming you, Syth." the big man replied. "Let me take half our force around the back and you can lead the rest through the front."

Syth was worried that if he resisted, he might look suspicious. Reluctantly, he nodded his agreement and hoped that the band was skilled enough to adjust their original plan.

"Wait for sixty seconds to give us time to get around the back then rush in," Bruce said. "We will come in and cut off their retreat. If we're lucky, we will be able to catch one or two and question them." Again, Syth nodded and Bruce and five others rushed around the corner of the building.

Syth wanted to rush in immediately, but knew he couldn't. Even though the plan was slightly off script, he was still enjoying himself immensely. This is the life he was made for, overcoming adversity. If things always went as planned, life would be boring.

On the count of sixty he kicked the unlocked door in, and rushed into the room. The other six men ran in behind him. With Syth in the center, the other six fanned out to either side of him, weapons ready. From across the room, Syth saw the other group burst in through the far door. The group of bandits did a poor job of acting surprised to see the Sentinels and City Watch, and Syth hoped that they were better fighters than they were actors.

While a few of the bandits yelled and raised their weapons, several others noticed the group coming in from the back door, worried.

They didn't have much time to dwell on their lost escape route however, because Bruce raised his huge hammer and charged.

A clash of weapons rang out as the two forces met. A man swung lazily at Syth, not really trying to make contact. Syth returned the blow, also not trying to score a hit. Suddenly, the man Syth was facing clutched at an arrow sticking out of his chest and then fell dead to the ground. Syth swore under his breath and turned to see Ned stringing another arrow to his bow. If Syth didn't act quickly, every person in his band would fall dead to the old man's arrows. He took a step toward Ned, then stopped as a member of his band stepped in front of him.

"Syth! What is going on?" he asked. Syth swore again and immediately cut the man down. He couldn't allow anyone to see him talking to any of the bandits. He turned back around to see his men falling fast. The bandits were trying to run around the city watch members, without much luck. They were being cut down as they fled.

"Make sure to leave at least one alive," Bruce ordered.

Syth couldn't do that. If anyone else was like the fool who had tried to speak to him a few moments ago, they would reveal everything. Syth would be exposed and his plan would fall to ruins. To save his reputation, he ran after all the bandits still standing. One fell, then another as Syth moved swiftly through the men, ignoring Bruce's request. He couldn't risk leaving any in the group alive.

Within moments, all the bandits were dead and not a single city watchman was injured. Bruce walked up to Syth, and the black-skinned warrior could tell that the large man was not happy.

"What was that all about?" he demanded. "I thought we were going to capture some alive so we could question them. Why did you kill them all?"

"I got carried away. These men were terrorizing the city and killing innocent people. I was so angry, I wasn't thinking clearly."

"I will check and see if any of them might still be alive," Ned said and moved to check the bodies.

"I don't know about you," Bruce dared to say. "There's something suspicious about your behavior. Sam told me that he was wary of you, and I can see why. The queen might disagree, but I am starting to see Sam's point."

"Why are you telling me this?"

"I just want you to know that I will be keeping an eye on you."

Syth took a step closer to Bruce. "That is very brave of you to say that to my face. Most wouldn't dare."

"I am not afraid of you, Syth," the big man replied.

Syth grinned. "Someday you will realize your mistake." He turned away from Bruce, but then stopped and turned back. "I am the queen's man, Bruce. I am closer to her than anyone else. I don't answer to you and I don't have to explain my actions."

"Hey!" Ned called. "I found one that is alive."

That alarmed Syth, but he didn't let it show. "See Bruce," he remarked. "I didn't kill all of them. One survived."

*   *   *

Early the next morning Syth was waiting outside the medical room when the healer emerged. "Is he going to survive?" Syth asked.

"I don't know," the healer replied. "He has already lost a lot of blood and is very weak. We were able to close his wound, but I am afraid we might have been too late. He is beyond our help now. There is nothing more that we can do."

"Nothing? That man might have important information. I need him alive."

"I am sorry, Master Syth. But we really can do nothing more."

"It's alright," Syth said soothingly. "I know you did your best. Send for me at once if anything changes."

The healer gave a bow. "Yes, Master Syth."

Syth left the medical wing of the palace and headed for his chambers. In truth, he hoped the bandit would die. It would make Syth's job a lot easier. And his job had gotten a lot harder that day. Not only did he lose every bandit in the group he had fought, but the city watch had killed every single bandit they had encountered. Every single one! Fifty of his band were gone. Over half of them!

But the worst part was that they didn't have anything to show for their efforts. True, they managed to kill about a dozen city watchmen, but every Sentinel had survived. One or two of them had minor injuries, but nothing serious. Syth's bandits couldn't take another hit like that. He had to come up with another plan.

When he arrived at his quarters, he found a man in palace livery knocking on his door. The man noticed him coming and he turned to Syth and bowed.

"What is it?" Syth asked.

"The queen requires your presence in her chambers."

"Now?"

"Yes, Master Syth. At once."

"Alright. Thank you." He immediately turned and went to see Queen Laurel.

When he arrived at the queen's personal chambers, he found her standing at the window, looking at the overcast sky. He called to her, but she didn't turn. He called again, louder this time and she jerked, startled, and finally turned to face him.

"Sorry, Syth," she said. "I didn't realize you were there."

"Are you alright?"

"I am sorry my friend. But I am not alright. I am very troubled this morning."

"What is troubling you, My Queen?"

"Well, yesterday Bruce came to me after your squad had returned to the palace and he told me something very troubling."

"And what was that, My Queen?"

"He told me that instead of taking prisoners, which was the original plan, you killed everyone. Bruce said that you were acting suspiciously, as if you didn't want to take prisoners. Can you explain yourself??"

"I explained this to Bruce, yesterday," Syth said, "and now I must admit it to you as well, although it shames me to do so. I was so enraged at the torment the bandits had caused our city and I lost control."

"Why would that shame you?" Laurel asked.

"Warriors in Abberdon are trained from a very early age to always remain in control. We do not let emotion rule our actions. I have been successful in doing that my entire life. Until now.

"My Queen, you have taken Jaden and I in, even though we were strangers from a distant land. You have not questioned our motives since we became your family's personal guards. You have given us our privacy and your respect. No one has ever done that before and we truly appreciate it. I have come to think of this country as more of a home than I ever considered Abberdon. Abberdon is a harsh, uncaring land, and I have found this place to be just the opposite.

"It surprises me to feel this way, but I can't help it. Although Jaden is not here, I am sure he would agree. That is why I did what I did. That is why I lost control. I am sorry, My Queen. It will not happen again, I promise."

Queen Laurel paused to consider his response. "You're right Syth. It will not happen again. I am not going to send you out with the Sentinels anymore."

"What? But My Queen…"

She put her hand up to silence him. "You are right. I have trusted you without question. Others called me a fool for doing so, but I believe you do not mean this country harm. That is why I need you now. My advisors have informed me about the situation on my streets. They have held nothing back. I believe these bandits may want to murder me. That is why I want you by side at all times. I will need your protection in the coming days, I am sure."

Syth wanted to protest but could not think of a good reason to disagree. Still, this would complicate his plans. He needed to be out on the streets to successfully succeed. But what could he do? Lost for words, he simply bowed. "Yes, My Queen."

"Thank you, Syth. You look tired. Did you sleep at all last night?"

"No, My Queen. After the fight in the warehouse, my mind was too worked up to get any sleep."

"Then go get some rest. I think I will be alright for a few hours while you sleep."

"Thank you, My Queen." He gave her another bow and left.

*   *   *

After Syth shut the door behind him, Queen Laurel let out a sigh. That was difficult. Despite what she said about trusting Syth, what Bruce had told her yesterday had alarmed her. She found herself not completely trusting her dark-skinned protector, though she might want to.

She didn't want Syth to learn that she didn't fully trust him, so she made up the assassination theory to keep him close to her and off the streets. And, she had to admit, she truly did feel much safer with Syth around. She only hoped that her dark-skinned friend didn't find out about her deceit.

*   *   *

Syth did not return to his room. Instead, he made his way to the servant's corridors. These were passages hidden from the general palace that allowed the servants to move about the palace unseen. The servants he passed would never question his presence here. He had used them many times on his various errands he ran for the queen. There were several small doors that led outside the palace. He headed for one of these now.

He had to get to Karch without being seen and tell him of what had happened. They would have to quickly make new plans that didn't include Syth. Although he was sure that Karch could handle leading the band without him, he still longed to be involved. His life had become much more enjoyable since he had stumbled on the band. The challenge of living two different lives excited him in a way he thought was no longer possible.

When he stepped outside of the palace he went directly to the bandit's hideout. He didn't have time to take a non-direct route. This needed to be done quickly, so he could get back to his room. He truly did need some sleep.

Instead of dealing with the thugs guarding the door, he slipped in through a high window that was a little too easy to climb through. He would have Karch address that problem.

The window led directly into Karch's room, where the dark-skinned man was standing.

"What are you doing here?" Karch asked. "We're not supposed to meet today. It's dangerous to come here too often."

"Things have changed, Karch. Our plan needs to change as well."

"Changed in what way?"

"The queen has asked me to stay by her side at all times. These attacks have made her fear an assassination attempt, and she wants me to protect her."

"Are you sure she isn't doing this because she doesn't trust you?"

"I am sure. She trusts me. She always has. I have never given her a reason not to. But it doesn't matter if she trusts me or not. Either way, I can't come here anymore. I can't lead the men. You will have to take over."

"Well, this is a good thing," Karch replied.

"How?"

"I am quite capable of leading the bandits. We will continue to grow in numbers and cause chaos, but you will be beyond suspicion since you will be with Queen Laurel. In a way, she is helping us."

"You are right," Syth said. "The situation is perfect. How are the men coping with our catastrophic losses?"

"See for yourself."

Karch led Syth out of the room and down the hall to a balcony overlooking the large, main room of the hideout. There were dozens of men mulling about the room. Their numbers had to be well over one hundred. That was more than they had yesterday!

"How is this possible?" Syth asked.

"Thieves and robbers have been coming in waves. This city is full of the filth of the earth and they are all wanting more. Word on the street is that this band will bring them power and wealth that they would never have dreamed of attaining by themselves. So, while yesterday was truly a setback, it is easily overcome. Before long, we will have more men than the City Watch does, and with me leading and training them, the city will easily fall into our hands."

"Hey, Syth!"

Syth saw a large man making his way through the crowded room to a stairway that led up to the balcony. He recognized the big man as the one who had been leading the bandits when Syth had discovered them.

"That is Parson," Karch explained. "He is a leader among the men."

"I know him," Syth said.

Parson reached them. By the look on his face the two warriors from Abberdon could tell that he was not happy.

"This isn't working," the big man said. "We lost a lot of our men yesterday. You told us that this wouldn't happen!"

"I never said that men would not die," Syth told him. "I told you that we would take over this city. Look out there." Parson did. "Look at all the men that have joined us. You don't call this success? Our numbers have swollen to many times the amount of men we had when I discovered you."

"But so many of us have died!"

"You whine too much," Karch said. "You are still alive."

Parson was about to say something to Karch when Syth interrupted. "You are deluding yourself if you think that we will not lose any men. We are facing the City Watch and the Sentinels. These men have been trained by professionals. That is their life. Our men have just started to come together as one. So yes, of course we will lose some men. Perhaps a lot. But we will win. And just think; the more men we lose, the more spoils there will be for the rest of us."

"I still don't like it," Parson said.

"Well," said Syth. "If you don't like it, then you can leave."

"Will you let me just leave?"

Syth smiled. "No."

"Then I guess I have no choice." Parson turned and walked back down the stairs.

"Keep an eye on him. I don't trust him," said Syth.

"I will," Karch replied.

"I must go," said Syth. "I need to return to the palace. I will stop in whenever I can." He started to turn away but stopped and turned back to Karch. "It is too easy to get in the building by the window to your room. You need to fix it."

"I often use that window to go in and out when I don't want the men to know that I am gone. I don't think anyone other than you and I could get up there anyway."

"Just be careful," Syth said. He used the window to leave and headed back to the palace, feeling much better about the situation.

40

"Why were the undead creatures just standing there in the dark?" Aiden asked Wyst.

They were traveling side-by-side and the young man had been asking questions for the last hour.

"Because some of the more powerful necromancers can see through the eyes of the undead creatures they raise. They are used to watch intruders coming."

"Can you do that?"

Wyst sighed. "No. I am not powerful enough for that."

"How does it work?" Aiden asked.

"How does what work?"

"How do you raise something that is dead? How do they move and think?"

"You see," the pale man replied, "when we raise a creature from the dead, a spark comes back to the brain. Living beings cannot function without their brain, so necromancy restores just enough brain function for them to move. They don't really think, they just obey."

"Oh. I see. Is that why chopping off their head kills them?"

"Yes. They don't feel any pain, so nothing hurts them. The only way to stop them is to cut off their brain function again."

"Interesting."

"I don't find it interesting at all," Dorn, who was riding on the other side of Wyst, said. "I find it revolting that someone would do that to a dead body."

"Dorn!" Aiden reprimanded.

Wyst put his hand up. "No. It's alright. I agree. I also find it very revolting."

"You do?" Aiden asked. Wyst nodded. "If you find it revolting, why do you do it? I just thought you liked it."

"I don't like it," the necromancer replied. "I actually can't stand the undead creatures or the curses that we put on people. My father was a necromancer. He also was a very scary man and I was intimidated by him as a child. He urged me to become a necromancer, even though I told him that I didn't want to be one."

"That is awful." Aiden said.

"If you hate it, then why do you still do it?" Dorn asked.

"Because it is the only thing that I know how to do. I can't do anything else."

Aiden decided to not ask Wyst anymore questions about necromancy after that.

*   *   *

The first thing Aiden noticed about Parkos was how big it was. His father had told him that Parkos was the largest city in the known world. That made sense to Aiden since he was also told that Parken was the largest country in the known world.

According to Dustin, the city dwarfed Tosun, and Aiden thought that it was probably bigger than Blanden and Kingston combined. The party gazed down at the city from the top of a hill a half mile or so away, and it stretched out as far as Aiden could see. He could only make out one distinct building from his vantage point. It was huge. It towered over every other buildings in the city. The palace.

"Whoa," whispered Veronna, who had come up beside him and taken his hand in hers. "Look how big it is!"

"How are we supposed to find an Imbuer in there?" asked Dustin. "How are we supposed to find anything in there?"

"I am sure that someone will know where an imbuer is and can give us directions," Tim said.

"Will that make people suspicious of us?" Brione asked.

"No. People are always wanting magical items that only an imbuer can provide. We won't look suspicious at all. Let's go."

Tim started toward his horse but stopped short and turned to the necromancer. "What we are about to do is going to be very dangerous. Maybe this is where we should part ways."

"Actually," Wyst said, "I was hoping to stay with you if I could. I might be able to help you and I don't think that going with you will be any more dangerous for me than being on my own. Please let me stay with you."

Tim thought about it, then nodded his assent.

They remounted and led their horses back to the road and down the hill toward the city. The city was surrounded by a massive wall with watch towers evenly spaced throughout. Aiden could see odd contraptions here and there that his father told him were called catapults.

"Are they expecting an attack?" Brione asked.

"No," Tim answered. "Those are on the wall at all times. Maybe the king thinks it will help deter would-be attackers. It is a show of power."

They stopped talking as they neared the gate. It was a huge opening that would allow their entire group to enter side-by-side. From up close they could see that the wall was at least fifty feet high and about a dozen feet thick. There were a dozen soldiers dressed in blue armor with red creatures that had tails and horns on the chest. They didn't impede the group's progress though, they just silently watched people enter and exit the city.

They passed under the wall and entered a large square that had a large fountain in the center. The square was surrounded by businesses and the mid-morning crowd was bustling about the shops while children chased each other by the fountain. Aiden found the square to be very clean, without a hint of trash or debris on the ground. It reminded him a lot of Zion in that regard. He mentioned that to his uncle.

"King Korlas is from Zion," David said. "It appears that he has brought some of what he was taught there with him here. I remember he always liked beautiful things."

"This square certainly is beautiful," Aiden said.

"I'm sure that every square in the city will be just as beautiful as this one."

Tim asked a passerby for directions to an imbuer's shop, but the man didn't know. He asked a woman but received the same answer. Another man didn't know but he pointed to a shop and said that the owner might know.

"Everyone wait here by the fountain," Tim said. "I will go talk to the shop owner and find out what he knows."

"I will go with you," Veronna offered. Tim smiled at her and hand-in-hand they walked to the building. Aiden smiled at the bounce in his little sister's step as they left.

Aiden sat down on a bench and Portia sat next to him.

"Our adventure is almost over," she said. "Isn't it?"

"Yeah, it is."

"What happens when we are finished, and it is time for you to go back home?"

Aiden looked at her. "I hadn't really thought about that. This task we have seems so huge that I never really thought it would ever end."

"What I meant was, what is going to happen to us when all this is over?"

"I don't know."

"Really?" Portia's voice was high. "That's all you have to say? You don't know?" Her voice was getting higher and higher with each word. "Well, this little journey is going to be over soon, and you need to figure out what is going to happen next!"

"Portia," Aiden said, trying to calm her down. "Everyone is looking at us."

Portia looked around and saw that not only was the entire group looking at them, but also all the people passing by were looking as well. "Oh," she said quietly. "Sorry," she said.

She started to turn away from Aiden. He grabbed for her hand, but she pushed him away and ran off.

"Portia!" he called after her. He started to follow but Brione grabbed his arm and stopped him.

"Let her go," she said. "She needs to be alone right now."

"What did I do?"

"Nothing. She is young and afraid."

"Afraid of what?"

"Listen," Brione sat down and pulled Aiden down on the bench next to her. "I am sorry, but I overheard your conversation. Now, you didn't do anything wrong, but she is afraid that when this is over, she will go back to her father's boat and you will go back to Blanderly. And then what? Will she ever see you again? Will you forget about her? She needs to know these things."

"Oh. I didn't realize. I was telling the truth when I told her that I haven't thought about it."

"Well, girls her age need to know things like that. She is scared that she is never going to see you again."

"What do I do?"

"I think you should talk to her. If she will let you."

Aiden started walking toward Portia, who was standing to the side of the group. She saw him coming and immediately moved away from him. He looked questioningly at Brione. She just smiled and shrugged her shoulders. Aiden sighed and walked back to the group, his eyes never leaving Portia.

"Now what do I do?" he asked Brione when he reached her. "She won't talk to me."

"Just give her some time," she replied. "A girl her age might hold a grudge for a while, but she will come around. Don't worry. Just give her some space for now."

"Alright."

Just then Tim and Veronna came out of the shop and walked to the group.

"That is a weapon shop," Tim told them. "The owner sells what you would expect to find in any weapon shop, but he also sells the occasional magic weapon. He told me where to find the imbuer that provides his magical weapons. He says he is the best in the city."

"He tried to make us to buy one of his magic weapons," Veronna said. "He didn't want to tell us who provided him with the magic weapons if we didn't, but dad persuaded him."

"What did you do?" Dustin asked.

"Nothing. I was very nice about it. Let's go find that imbuer."

They walked through the crowded streets of the city, occasionally noticing a patrol of soldiers dressed in the same armor as the guards outside the gate, but they never paid any attention to the group.

At last, they came upon another large square almost identical to the first one.

"King Korlas is evil, right?" Veronna asked her father.

"Yes, he is."

"Then why does he like such beautiful things? I thought that evil people only liked ugly things."

"Every person is different, Veronna. Some evil people like ugly things, but some like beautiful things. Just like some good people like beautiful things, while some like uglier things. You can't judge everything about a person if you don't know them.

"And, you need to remember that Korlas wasn't always evil. He used to be a Paladin like your uncle. I remember he loved beautiful things. He was a very good gardener and could produce the most beautiful flowers."

"Why did he turn bad?" Veronna asked.

"I don't know," Tim admitted. "I have my own opinions about that, but I am not sure."

"And what is your opinion?"

He smiled at her. "It doesn't matter. Like I said, it is only an opinion. I don't know the real reason why."

Veronna though for a moment. "Do you know any good person who likes ugly things?"

Tim laughed. "Yes. Your mom."

Veronna made a face. "Really? She liked ugly things?"

"She liked one ugly thing. Sometimes merchants come to Zion to trade. One time your mom saw a statue of an ugly little gargoyle. She immediately fell in love with it. She thought it was beautiful, but I promise you, it was hideous. I didn't want to buy it, but she insisted, so I did. We kept it on the mantle by the fireplace. I hated looking at that thing."

Veronna giggled. "Where is it now?"

"We buried her with it. She loved it so much, I buried it with her so she could enjoy it forever."

Veronna went silent after that.

The day wore on and the streets only became more crowded. "I can't believe all these people live in one city," Veronna said. "It is huge, but the streets are so crowded."

"Believe it or not," David said, "the city is starting to suffer from overcrowding."

"Really? How many people live here?"

"I don't know the exact count, but there are millions."

"There is the imbuer's shop," Tim said, pointing to a small building up ahead. "Everyone but Zach, Jaden, Wyst, and the Paladins will go in with the chest and talk to the imbuer. David, you come too. The rest of you will stay out here and keep watch. Our enemy has known where we were this entire journey and they might know where we are now. Keep your eyes open."

The Paladins set down the chest and Tim, Dustin, Aiden and David each took a corner and carried it into the shop.

The shop was tiny and dominated by a long counter opposite the door. A small man stood behind the counter with a closed door behind him. There were no shelves on the walls or items on the counter. Besides the imbuer, the shop was completely empty.

"How may I help you?" the little man asked with a hopeful smile.

Before anyone could answer Veronna asked, "Where is all the merchandise?"

"Excuse me?"

"Don't you sell magic items? Where are they? There is nothing here."

The imbuer laughed. "You are mistaken, little girl. I do not sell magic items. People bring their items to me and I imbue them with magical properties."

"Oh."

"We have a chest here," Tim said. "We believe it holds a magical item, but we don't know what is in it, because we can't open the chest. We were hoping that you would be able to open it and tell us what is inside."

"It is common for magical items to be placed in such chests for protection," The imbuer said. "Bring it here and I'll see what I can do."

The men brought the chest forward and set it on the floor in front of the counter. The little man walked around the counter and leaned over the chest, studying it. Suddenly he stood up straight and looked at Tim. "Where did you get this?"

"That is our business," Tim answered. "Can you help us?"

"Oh dear," the little man said and started pacing the room, wringing his hands. "Oh dear," he repeated.

"What is wrong?" asked David.

The little man stopped pacing. "I need to know how you acquired this chest."

"Why?" asked Tim. "Is there something wrong?"

"I know what this chest is. I know who this was created for."

"You do?"

"Yes. He came to me first and asked me to create it for him. I told him that it was beyond my abilities. I cannot create magical items. I can only imbue items with magical properties. He was very angry and

I thought that he would kill me until I told him about an imbuer in Kingston who might be able to help. So yes, I know what this is, and I know who it is intended for. Now you can understand my desire to know how it came to be in your possession."

"The truth is," David said, "that we intercepted this item on the road and we are trying to keep it out of King Korlas' hands."

"David!" Tim said. "Are you sure we can trust him?"

"Yes," the Paladin replied. "He has no love for the king."

"He is correct," the imbuer said. "I do not. The king pretends to be kind and to care about his people. But I know the real man. He is cruel and evil." The imbuer went silent for a moment as he thought. "If I help you, no one can know about it. I could get in a lot of trouble if someone found out."

"Of course," said Tim. "We never came here. And do not worry, we will pay you enough to make it worth your while."

An obvious change came over the imbuer. Now that he felt the danger was over, he got to work. He rubbed his hands together and smiled. "Now, let's get down to business. This chest is quite amazing." He placed his hands on the chest and ran them lovingly over the object.

"Can you open it?" Tim asked.

"Open it? Ha! You don't understand, my good man. There is nothing in the chest." The imbuer was obviously excited. He saw the confusion on Tim's face. "The chest is the magical item!"

"I don't understand."

"This chest is not just a chest. This chest is the item the king wanted. You see, the item can become anything you want it to be."

"Wow!" Veronna exclaimed.

"Really?" asked Tim. The imbuer nodded. "You're sure?"

The imbuer nodded again. "Try it for yourself."

"Alright. How does it work?"

"All you have to do is put your hand on the item and think of what you want it to become."

"It's that easy, huh?" Tim asked.

"It's that easy."

Tim stepped up to the chest and put his hand on top of it. Suddenly, the chest shrank and became much longer. There were amazed exclamations from the group. Tim was holding a broadsword in his hands.

"Wow!" Veronna exclaimed again. "That was amazing! Can I try?"

Tim gave the broadsword a few practice swings. "The sword is the perfect weight and balance for me. It is much lighter now than it was when it was in chest form."

"Can I try it?" asked Veronna again.

"The item takes on all the properties of what it becomes," said the imbuer. "When it was in chest form, it was as heavy as a chest that size full of items would normally be. When you changed it into a sword it became as heavy as a sword that size is."

"Amazing," Tim said.

"Can I try it now?" Veronna asked once again. She was getting impatient.

"Yes," Tim replied. "Here you go." He handed the sword to her, hilt first.

"What should I turn it into?" she asked her brother.

"Whatever you want," was all he said.

She thought about it for a moment and then the sword started changing. Instead of a hilt she held a paw. A massive black bear stood in the room where the sword used to be. It gave a great bellow and Veronna screamed. The bear turned toward her and she let go of its paw, scrambling away from it as fast as she could.

Before the bear could take a step toward his sister, Aiden dove at the creature. As soon as his hand touched fur he thought of an object and the bear immediately shrank and turned into a pair of boots.

Veronna was crying in terror when her dad rushed to her and wrapped her in his arms. "It's alright," he said soothingly. "It's gone."

"Why would you think of something like that?" Brione demanded. "Why would you do something so stupid?"

"Calm down, Brione," Tim said. "Nothing bad happened."

"Calm down?" She shrieked. "Veronna could have been killed! We all could have!"

"I'm sorry," Veronna was saying.

"We all could have been," Tim agreed, "but thanks to Aiden's quick thinking, we weren't. It's okay. We're safe."

"Why did you lash out at her like that?" Dustin asked Brione.

"I don't know," Brione said, breathing hard. "Maybe it's because we just lost Layne and I thought we were going to lose her too. I was so scared."

Dustin put his arms around her and pulled her into a consoling hug. "It's alright. She is fine. Everyone is fine."

After a few minutes Veronna calmed down. Tim turned her so she was facing him. "Why did you think of the bear?" he asked.

"When I saw the bear on the road I thought it was so pretty. I just wanted to see it again. I didn't know it would be alive and attack me."

"That is the power of the item," the imbuer said. "If you think of a living thing, it will appear and be alive and act just like it normally would."

"I told you that bears are extremely dangerous," Tim told Veronna. "I hope you believe me now."

"I do. I'm sorry." Veronna stood up and went to Brione. "I am sorry Brione. I didn't mean to make you angry."

Brione hugged the younger girl. "It's alright. I was scared for you, that's all. I hope this makes you realize how dangerous magical items can be."

"It does."

Aiden had picked up the pair of boots and was examining them.

"Try it out son," said Tim.

Suddenly Aiden was holding a flaming long sword.

"Whoa!" cried the imbuer. "Be careful!"

"It's alright," Tim said. "Aiden knows how to handle a sword."

Aiden did what his father did and gave the sword a few practice swings. The fire gave a whooshing sound as it cut through the air. Then, the flames went out and Aiden was holding a normal looking sword.

Aiden looked at the rest of the group and grinned. "Do you know how much fun Layne would have with this thing?" Aiden saw a pained look come over Dustin's face. "I'm sorry Dustin. I didn't mean…"

"It's okay," Dustin replied. "We can talk about him. It still hurts, but we can't just forget about him, can we? It's good to talk about him." He turned to Brione and suddenly he grinned. "Can you imagine what Layne would do with this to pester you?"

Brione laughed. "Actually, I can. He could turn it into a huge spider or a bowl of honey and put it in my hair. He did that once. I had to cut it, remember?" Everyone laughed. "Or, he could use it when we were sparing and turn it into a giant ax with a ten-foot handle in mid-swing."

"That is definitely something he would do!" said Aiden, and they all shared a laugh again. Dustin laughed loudest of all.

"Thank you," Dustin said. "It helps to talk about him."

"I take it you lost someone recently?" the imbuer asked.

"Yes," Tim said. "Dustin's brother, just a little while ago."

"I am so sorry for your loss."

"Thank you. With your help today, we may be able to stop other people from feeling this same loss."

"I am glad to help. I must warn you though. I am sure that the king's personal guards have magic weapons. Someone from the palace came to me several months ago and had me imbue several weapons with magical properties."

"What kind of magical properties?"

"Some have the ability to cut through any shield or armor. Some are able to be thrown and return back to your grasp. Others can create a wave of darkness that only the bearer of the weapon can see through. A few more are able to burst into flame at the bearers will."

"Alright," said Tim. "Thanks for telling us. We will be ready."

A few moments later the group left shop.

"So," said Reese. "What was in the chest? What does it do?"

"Nothing was in the chest," Tim replied. "The chest is the item. It can be whatever you want it to be."

"That's pretty impressive," said Reese.

"Yeah, it is. Now, it is time to go to the palace and do what we came here to do. But I don't want all of us going in. This is going to be the most dangerous part of the journey, so I want Dorn and all the girls except Brione to wait at the north city gates."

"Absolutely not," Dana said. "I have come way too far to sit back and allow you to just kill my brother. I told you from the beginning that I won't let you kill him and nothing has changed."

"What if we go in there and we fail, and then you get caught?"

"I don't care. I can't allow you to kill my brother. Besides, I will have Jaden with me. I will be just fine."

"I won't allow you to come into the palace with us. It is too risky. I promise that I will not kill your brother when I find him. I will bring him out to you unharmed."

"Is that a good idea?" asked Brione. "Queen Laurel paid us to kill Prince Easton. Can we disobey her?"

"I have to keep Princess Dana out of that palace. What would the queen think if her daughter was captured under my care? It is too risky. If the queen is angry because of this, I will return the money she gave me."

"If I stay out here, do you truly promise not to kill my brother?" Dana asked.

"I promise to bring him to you unharmed. I will have to think about what to do after that. But you have my word that I will not kill him before I bring him to you."

"Alright. I agree. But only if you take Dorn with you."

Dorn looked at Dana as if she had gone crazy.

"Why do you want me to take Dorn?" Tim asked.

"No offense, but I want someone in there with you who is on my side."

Dorn was about to speak up, but Tim put up a hand to silence him. "Very well."

"But…" Dorn started, but once again Tim silenced him.

"It is settled. If I have to take you in with us to keep Princess Dana safe, then I will. Now let's go."

"Wait," David said as Tim started to turn away.

Tim turned back to his old friend.

"This is where our journey ends. The Paladins can go no further with you."

"What? Why?"

"God wills it so."

"You would abandon us now?" Tim was angry.

"We are not abandoning you," Reese said. "I feel it too. God is telling us that we must turn back. You must do the rest of this on your own."

Tim was about to say something else when David interrupted him. "You know how this feels, Tim. As leader of the Paladins you have felt this many times before. You also know that it is not a good idea to go against God's wishes."

Tim had nothing else to say. What David said was true. He could talk until he was out of breath, but he would never change the Paladins' minds.

"I don't like it, but I know I cannot change your mind. Thank you for helping us get here. We couldn't have done it without you."

David shook Tim's hand then pulled him into an embrace. "You be careful. I think you will be just fine. I don't think that God would forbid us to continue with you otherwise. Come by Zion on the way back. Okay?"

"I will," Tim said, although he didn't have any intention of doing so.

Everyone said their good-byes and they watched the Paladins leave.

"Well," said Wyst. "Our job just got a lot harder."

"There is nothing we can do about it now. We have to continue. Let's go."

Instead of going straight toward the palace, they headed north. As the day grew later, the streets became more and more crowded. The group kept glancing toward the palace in silence. They trusted that Tim knew what he was doing.

After about an hour of walking, they reached the northern gate of the city. Looking through the gates the group could see a forest a few hundred feet away from the city. Tim had them all gather close.

"I want the girls to wait here by this gate because if things go badly, we will need to make a quick escape and we don't want to leave the same way we came in. Plus, we might be able to lose any pursuers in the forest. Now, I want Princess Dana, Portia, and Veronna to wait out here for us. I want you to wait until night fall. If you do not hear from us by then, I want you to head into the forest until morning. Come wait at this gate again for a full day. If we still don't come for you, head back to Zion.

"Now, since our enemies always seem to know where we are, I don't want to leave the girls unprotected. I want Jaden to stay here with them and keep them safe."

"You will need Jaden with you," Dana said.

"Jaden, I will be better able to do what I have to if I know the girls are safe. Will you stay out here with them and keep them safe?"

"Yes," Jaden replied.

"Good. It is settled then. Try not to be conspicuous while you wait. You don't want to bring attention to yourselves. Is everyone ready?" They all nodded. "Alright. Let's go."

"Wait," Veronna said before the group could leave. She rushed to Tim and threw her arms around him. "Be careful."

Tim held her tight. "Don't worry. We will. We will come back for you. You'll see."

Then she went to hug Brione and Dustin. She even hugged Wyst and Dorn. While she was doing that Tim went over to Aiden and whispered in his ear.

"I don't think we should take the weapon in the palace with us. King Korlas might get a hold of it. We can't let that happen. When Veronna comes to hug you, discreetly give it to her and tell her not to tell anyone that she has it. Alright?"

Aiden nodded and waited for his sister. When she finally came over to him, she had tears in her eyes. "Oh Aiden," she cried and threw her arms around his neck. "Be safe!"

"Don't worry. I will be with dad. I will be fine." Still holding her close he said, "I want you to do something for me." She nodded. "I want you to hold on to the magic weapon while we are in the palace. We cannot take it in with us."

"But what if you need it?"

"It is too dangerous. We cannot let the king get it. Will you keep it safe for me?"

She nodded. "Yes."

"Thank you. I know I can trust you to keep it safe. You can't let anyone know you have it, alright?"

"Okay."

He pushed her out to arm's length and reached into his belt. He pulled out a small dagger, but by the time it was clear of his belt, it was a small hairpin. "Keep this in your hair. Don't let it fall out."

"Okay. You can count on me, Aiden." She took the hairpin, kissed her brother on the cheek, and then went to stand next to Portia and Dana. She waved as the group left, watching them until they were out of sight.

41

The group made their way to the palace, trying to look like normal people out on personal business. It was hard to fit in though, with a man as white as snow and another with dark skin. Groups of soldiers eyed them as they passed, but no one tried to stop them. Just before they reached the palace grounds Tim huddled everyone together.

"No one has tried to stop us so far," he said. "But I think that will change when we get on the palace grounds. We need to find a way in where we won't be seen."

"The palace in Tosun has several small side doors so servants can enter and exit the palace unseen," Dorn said.

"Alright," said Tim. "We must look for one of those doors."

Dorn shook his head. "They are well hidden and hard to notice. But I am sure that I can find them. I will lead you into the palace."

"Are you sure?" Tim asked.

Dorn nodded. "I have tried to find a way to be useful to the group from the beginning. Now I finally can be."

Tim put a hand on Dorn's shoulder. "Thank you. We are all glad you came with us."

"We shouldn't all enter the palace grounds at once," Dorn said. "I will go first and search for a door, while the rest of you go in groups of one or two and follow me at a distance."

"Sounds good," Tim said. "Let's go."

Dorn immediately started out. No one gave him a second glance as he went through the large archway in the wall and onto the palace grounds. The group watched him turn right, then disappear.

Tim counted to ten after Dorn disappeared and then sent Brione and Dustin toward the palace. Brione put her arm in Dustin's and they walked like a young couple onto the grounds. They turned right and Tim sent Tyler and Wyst. The guards paid more attention to Wyst as he walked toward them, but they didn't stop him. As they turned right and disappeared from Tim's view, the guards were still watching them.

Tim sent Zach next. After what happened with Wyst, he was worried what the guards might do when they noticed the dark-skinned warrior. One of the guards said something to Zach as he approached, but he ignored him. Without saying a word or glancing the guards' way, Zach followed the others. The guards laughed at the one who had spoken and one of them even playfully slapped the speaker on the back of the head.

That's strange, Tim thought. He and Aiden were the only two left. "I want you to gawk at the palace," Tim told his son. "I want us to look like a father who is bringing his son to see the royal palace for the first time. That will be our cover. No one will be suspicious of us." Aiden nodded.

As they set out toward the palace, Tim couldn't help but feel nervous. It all had come down to this. The last couple months of travel and hardships, of loss and heartache, all came down to this. He had no idea how he was going to find Prince Easton and get him out of the palace. Part of him regretted taking the job. No amount of money would compensate for the loss of Layne. His death hit him harder than any death his mercenary band had previously suffered. A lot of people had come and gone during his career as a mercenary, but he had never felt closer to any group than he did to his present one. They truly were a family.

The sound of Aiden gasping brought Tim out of his thoughts. He looked over at his son and could tell that Aiden didn't need to pretend to be awed by the palace. "It is massive!" Aiden exclaimed.

They had already passed under the archway and the guards were laughing at Aiden. "I have never seen so many beautiful flowers before," Aiden remarked, and the guards laughed even harder.

"It's his first time here," Tim explained to the guards. He ignored the unkind remark one of the guards made about "country bumpkins" and ushered Aiden away.

"Good job," Tim said. "They think we are simple country folk and should pay us no more mind."

"This is the biggest building I have ever seen," Aiden said. "And the most beautiful."

"I agree," Tim said.

"How are we going to find Princess Dana's brother in there?"

"I don't know son. But we have to try."

They saw the group ahead of them and Brione waved them over.

"Dorn found a door," she told them as Tim and Aiden came up to the group.

"Good," Tim replied.

Dorn looked back at the group. "It will be best if we stay in the servant's corridors for as long as possible. As the name suggests, only the servants use those. Now, a palace this size will probably have hundreds of servants, but I am sure we would rather run in to servants than have to deal with armed guards."

"What do we do if we do come across some servants?" Aiden asked his father.

"We don't want to harm anyone we don't have to. We should detain them any way we need to without hurting them, if possible. Knock them out or bind and gag them. We're not here to harm them, but we also can't let anyone find out we're here either." He turned to Dorn. "What does the immediate hallway look like?"

"It goes right to left in front of us. The hallway turns on both sides. I can't tell where either side goes."

"Okay," said Tim. "I think we should split up here. We can cover more ground that way. We try to find Easton as fast as we can. We don't know if he is a prisoner or not, so one group should find the dungeons, and the other group should find the throne room. Zach and I will go to the throne room, everyone else will search for the dungeons."

"Just you two?" Aiden asked.

"Yes. Zach and I should be able to overcome any situation we need to. And you guys should be just fine because of your numbers. If you find Easton, don't try to find us. Just get out and find the girls. If you reach the cells and he is not there, get out and find the girls. We will do the same. Is everyone ready?" Everyone nodded. "Okay. Let's go. Be careful everyone."

Aiden gave his father a quick hug, then followed the rest of the group to the right. Tim and Zach went left.

*   *   *

Ricardo came out of his trance. "They are in the palace."

"What were you doing?" Korlas demanded. Ricardo was in the throne room. He didn't usually get into his spies' minds anywhere but his personal chambers, but the king demanded his presence after Ricardo informed him that Tim and his group were in the city. It required concentration to enter someone else's mind, and so it was harder to do to here in the throne room, but he would have to make due.

Ricardo ignored the king's question. "They are in the palace," he said, louder this time.

"They are? Where?"

"In the servants' corridors. They just got here."

King Korlas turned to a guard. "Get some men into the corridors and apprehend them. Take them alive if you can."

"They have split up. They are in two groups," Ricardo told them.

"Understood," the guard said, bowed to the king, and took his leave.

"You had better be right about this," Korlas threatened.

"Right about what?" the wizard asked.

"About letting them in the palace before we apprehend them."

"Don't worry," Ricardo soothed. "It was the right choice. You'll see." Concentrating again, Ricardo sent his mind out to another of his spies.

*   *   *

Veronna couldn't help but worry. Her father and brother had left her behind before, but this was different. This was the most dangerous mission the group had ever done. She had always known that her father would come back to her safely whenever he was on a job. But this was different. They might not come back, and there was nothing she could do about it.

Suddenly Jaden stiffened. After a moment, he reached out and grabbed Princess Dana by the arm. "Come with me," he said.

Princess Dana held her ground. "What are you doing? Tim told us to stay here."

Jaden kept pulling her. "You must come with me." Dana struggled mightily until she was able to wrench free of Jaden's grasp. Suddenly one of Jaden's swords was in his hand.

All the girls gasped. "What are you doing?" Dana asked again.

"My master wishes to see you, Princess. I must take you to him."

"Your master? Who is your master?"

"The great wizard Ricardo is my master. He commands, I must obey. You must come with me."

"Ricardo? King Korlas' advisor?"

"Yes."

"You were an enemy this whole time?"

"Zach and I have been spying on you, yes. Syth as well."

Dana put her hand up to her mouth. "Oh no. Syth. Mother!"

Jaden grabbed her again. "No more delays. Come!"

"How could you?" Dana cried. "How could you betray my family? We have done nothing to you."

"It is nothing personal. I am only following orders."

"I thought you were my friend."

That made Jaden freeze. "I am your friend," he said.

"No," Dana said. "You are not. A friend would not have done what you did. A friend would not do what you are trying to do to me right now."

Jaden let go of Dana's arm. "You are right. A friend would not do that. And I am your friend. You have been nothing but good to me." Then he dropped his sword and fell to his knees. He started moaning and threw his hands up to his head.

"What's wrong?" Dana asked.

"My…master. He is…trying to make…me bring…you…to him."

"Fight it Jaden! Fight him! Don't let him control you!"

Jaden's moaning grew louder as he fell to the ground and started to roll around. People who were passing by stopped to watch. A pair of city watchmen started coming toward them. Suddenly, Jaden stopped moaning and rolling. He laid on the ground so motionless that the girls feared he had died. Then he opened his eyes and slowly climbed to his feet.

"He is gone."

*   *   *

Ricardo opened his eyes and almost stumbled to the floor. *How did he do that?* he wondered. Rage filled him. No one had ever been able to force him out of their mind before.

"What is wrong with you?" Korlas demanded. "What is going on?"

Ignoring the king, Ricardo once again sent his mind out, searching for other spies in the city.

*   *   *

"Is everything alright here?" one of the guards asked in concern.

"Yes," Princess Dana answered. "Everything is fine now. Thank you."

"What was just happening?" the other guard asked. "We saw that man rolling on the ground and moaning. You were shouting at him."

Jaden spoke up. "I have what you might call episodes sometimes. They look bad but they are not. They always pass fairly quickly. I am fine now."

"Why were you yelling at him?" the first guard asked Dana.

"Sometimes it helps him if I encourage him to fight it."

The guards looked skeptical.

"I know it sounds silly, but it does work."

"Alright. But if you need us, we'll be right over there keeping an eye on things."

"Thank you for your concern." When the guards moved away Dana moved closer to Jaden. "Are you okay?" she whispered.

"Yes, I am fine now. But we are in danger here."

"What do you mean?"

"My master will be furious that I was able to push him out of my head. I didn't even know that was possible. He will send men after us. Men like me. They will be ordered to kill me and take all of you to my master. We must get out of here."

"Okay," Dana said. "Let's go to the woods and wait for Tim and the others there. I don't want to go somewhere that they won't be able to find us."

"Good idea," Jaden said, and the group started heading toward the city gate.

Veronna glanced behind her. "Uh-oh."

"What is wrong?" Portia asked.

"Look behind us. I think we're too late."

Everyone stopped and turned around to see two dark-skinned men walking quickly toward them, swords in hand.

"You keep going," Jaden said. "I will delay them here." He drew his two swords.

"I will stay and help you." Dana said.

"No."

"But you taught me how to fight. You will need my help."

"No," Jaden said again. "They will only kill me and take you. You must escape. Go, run and hide in the forest. I should be able to hold them off long enough for you to escape. Go!"

The three girls ran toward the city gates as fast as they could. But instead of entering the forest, they stopped at the gates and turned to watch. They saw the two city watchmen from before hurry to confront the newcomers. In a flash the dark-skinned warriors both slashed each guard's throat without even slowing down. The guards fell into a heap.

The two men split up, so they were on either side of Jaden. Jaden didn't wait for them to attack, he immediately went on the offensive, attacking one of the men in a blur. Jaden had the early advantage, but his second foe wasted no time in aiding his comrade. Jaden had to halt his furious attack to fend off the second man. Even though Jaden was more skilled, he couldn't defeat the two dark-skinned fighters at once. He held his ground for a few minutes but then a slash across his chest and a stab to his gut sent him to the ground, unmoving.

"No!" Dana cried.

Without pausing, the two dark-skinned men approached the girls.

"Run," Portia said and all three rushed through the gate and toward the forest. Veronna glanced over her shoulder and saw the two warriors being confronted by the guards at the city gate. Veronna looked forward again and ran on.

When they reached the edge of the forest the girls stopped and looked back. The two men continued after them, the guards at the gate lying on the ground in heaps. The girls dashed into the forest.

It was hard to keep up a good pace while dodging trees and jumping over rocks and exposed roots. Veronna looked back again to see that their pursuers had gained a lot of ground on them. They were entering the forest now. Panic set in as Veronna realized that they were not going to escape.

She heard a strange sound behind her, like the ground exploding. She heard the sound several more times and couldn't help but glance back over her shoulder again. Roots were erupting from the ground and attacking the men. Veronna tripped over a stone she didn't see and fell hard to the ground. She turned over on her back and watched.

The men were leaping and dodging the roots that came at them. When they couldn't dodge, they cut the roots with their swords. One even leapt and spun in the air to avoid a root. Finally, a root caught one of the men and wrapped him up and pulled him under the ground. He entered in an explosion of earth and rocks and didn't come back up.

The other man had been slowed by the roots, but he kept coming. Veronna jumped back to her feet and ran again. There was no sign of the other two girls. They didn't realize she had tripped. She was alone.

There were more explosions behind her. She knew that meant that the roots hadn't caught the other man yet, but she didn't dare look back to see how close he was. She put her head down and willed herself to go faster.

Suddenly, there were no more trees around her. She was in a large, grassy clearing with the other two girls up ahead of her. They had stopped running. When she approached them, she understood why.

A tall man stood before them. He was wearing boots, trousers, and animal skins. He looked to be in his middle years, his long dark hair and trimmed beard had sprinkles of gray. But it was not the man the girls were looking at. Beside him a creature stood. A creature that could only be a wolf, a creature that had been hunted to extinction in Blanderly. It looked like a huge gray dog, but the girls could tell it was wilder and more dangerous than any normal dog could be. A low growl came from the wolf.

The man and wolf walked around the three girls toward the forest where they had emerged into the clearing. The girls turned to see that their dark-skinned pursuer had entered the clearing. He didn't pause when he saw the man and the wolf.

"Stop there!" the tall man said in a commanding voice. The dark-skinned man didn't stop or even slow. He kept coming.

Suddenly several wolves emerged from the trees all around the clearing. There were easily a dozen of them, although none were as large as the gray one. The wolves surrounded the intruder and he finally did stop. Without warning, the wolves attacked.

The first few to reach him were the unfortunate ones. He cut down the first wolf that leaped at him, then spun to avoid the jaws of a second. The man was so quick that he stabbed the wolf in the back just as the creature landed. He spun and cut another wolf down just as it was about to reach him. But then there were too many and they finally brought the man down. The three girls had to look away from the grisly scene.

When they looked again, the tall man and the huge wolf were standing right in front of them.

*   *   *

As his spy died, Ricardo was thrust out of the man's head. He knew it was coming this time, so he was able to keep upright when his mind reentered his body. He was furious. This was not going as planned! One of his men had turned against him and two more had been killed.

The king was speaking again, but he continued to ignore him. Once again, he sought out one of his spies.

*   *   *

The fighting was furious. Not long after their group had separated from Tim and Zach, they had encountered enemies. It seemed to Dustin as if the enemies had been searching for them. The group thought they had entered the palace undetected, but they hadn't.

They would have been overrun by the first group of guards if it hadn't been for Wyst. Despite trying to be prepared for anything, the guards had taken them by surprise. Luckily, Wyst had been warier than anyone else and he had immediately thrown out a curse. Their enemies' weapons suddenly seemed to be too heavy for them, and their legs seemed to give out. All of the guards fell to the ground.

"How long will this last?" Brione had asked the necromancer.

"Not long. Like I said before, I am not very powerful. Maybe a few minutes."

"What should we do with them?" Aiden asked.

"We cannot just leave them here," Tyler said. "They will regain their strength and come after us. We must dispose of them."

"I don't like killing helpless people," Brione said. "But I agree with Tyler. They will not be helpless for long. Then we will be in real trouble."

Unhappily, the group went about their grisly work. The deed left a foul taste in everyone's mouth, but at least they didn't have to worry about this group of guards coming after them. It had to be done.

They continued on and almost immediately came across another group of guards. The servants' corridors were narrow, and they only allowed two or three men to stand side-by-side. Dustin and Brione were in front of the group, so they did most of the fighting. Aiden was just behind them, and he tried to help out whenever he could. Tyler and Wyst were in the back of the group. Tyler couldn't do much because he couldn't detect much in this corridor that was not part of the structure. True, he could rip chunks out of the walls or floors because they were made of stone, but that could harm the integrity of the corridor and put the group in danger. It would also be very noisy, and the sound might even attract even more enemies.

Wyst also helped when he could. Dustin had killed one enemy and was facing another one. This one had different colored armor on that had a slightly different symbol than the rest of the guards they had fought. This man was a better fighter than Dustin and he was barely holding him off. A solid punch to Dustin's head sent the ex-knight sprawling on the floor. The man stood above Dustin, sword ready to strike, but before he could, a sword tip exploded out of his chest. The dead man's body slid off the sword and Dustin saw who had killed him. It was the man that Dustin had just killed. Wyst had raised him and had rescued Dustin. The corpse turned and started attacking his old companions.

With the help of the undead guard, they fought off the rest of the enemies, but they immediately heard more boots hurrying in their direction.

"I don't know how much more of this I can take," Brione said. "I am already getting exhausted."

Another group of guards came into sight and Wyst sent his minion straight at them. He killed three of them before they realized that stabbing him in the heart would do no good. They finally cut off his head and then advanced on Dustin and the others.

Tyler found matching clay pots and sent them flying at their enemies. It took them by surprise. One man was hit in the head and he dropped to the floor unconscious. The other pot just grazed a man who was able to throw himself to the floor to avoid taking serious harm.

"Rush them!" Brione ordered and the group did so. This corridor was a little wider than the previous ones and Aiden joined Dustin and Brione at the front of the group. There was a loud clash of metal as the two groups collided.

Dustin parried a strike from the man in front of him, then countered, but his sword deflected harmlessly off the man's armor. He had to duck under the next swing, then stabbed straight out. But once again his blow was deflected by the man's armor. Only then did Dustin notice that this foe's armor was a different color, and the creature on the front was also different. It must mean it was a captain or something.

Dustin was quickly on the defensive as his opponent rained blows down on him. The man forced Dustin to his knees with the heavy blows. His sword fell from his hands, and he braced himself for the killing blow.

It never fell though, and Dustin looked up to see a dagger sticking out of the man's neck. He fell to the ground, dead. The man Dustin had been fighting stood up. If the corpse even knew about the dagger sticking out of his neck, he didn't show it. He just attacked their enemies, killing or chasing every one of them off.

"I need to get that dagger back," Dorn said forlornly. "It has come in handy twice now."

"Thank you," Dustin said.

"That is twice now that you have saved one of our group," Brione said. "It is good that you came with us."

Dorn looked embarrassed. He simply nodded.

"That guy was strong," Dustin said.

"He is wearing the same kind of armor as the leader of the group that attacked us in the forest was wearing," Aiden said.

"That means that he was a Dark Paladin," Brione said.

"If that is the case then we are lucky to be alive," Tyler said.

"Yes, we are," Brione said. "Let's keep going and hope we don't run into any more Dark Paladins."

The group continued on. Dorn was able to pull the dagger out of the corpse's neck. Then the corpse fell lifelessly to the floor.

"Shouldn't we use it?" Brione asked Wyst.

"I am sorry. I hate those things. I don't like to control them for very long. Especially not that one. He felt different than any other I have ever raised. I could still feel his evilness even after he was dead." Wyst shivered.

They turned a corner and Dustin stopped dead in his tracks. Standing in the hallway before him was a dark-skinned man. And Amanda.

Amanda! What was she doing here?

"Dustin," she said simply.

"What are you doing here?" Dustin asked.

"I followed you here," she replied. "We have some unfinished business."

"I will not let you hurt Dustin," Brione said. She stepped in front of him. Aiden did the same.

The dark-skinned man beside Amanda drew his swords.

Dustin put a hand on Brione and Aiden's shoulder. "It is alright." He moved past his two friends and stood before the woman he used to love. "You have traveled a very long way just to kill me. Do you truly hate me that much?"

"Yes," she replied, looking into his eyes.

"Why? Was what I did truly that horrible. I saved your life."

"Then left me to die!" She drew a dagger from a sheath on her belt that he hadn't noticed before.

"You were in no danger," Dustin explained. "I left you very close to a village where you could get help."

"You spurned me. I loved you and you spurned me."

"Because you lied to me." Dustin put his hands to his face in frustration. "Look, we have already been over this. Nothing I can say will change your mind. Come on then. Let's get this over with."

"Dustin!" Brione said.

"What are you doing?" Amanda asked suspiciously.

"You said you came all this way to kill me. So, do it." Dustin opened his shirt a little more so she could see his chest."

"You want me to kill you?" He nodded. "Why?"

"I have nothing left. I lost my parents years ago. Now I have lost my brother. I have no one left. So just kill me. I don't care anymore."

She gasped. "Layne is dead?"

"Do it," he said quietly. "Please."

Amanda just stood there with a shocked expression on her face.

"You heard him." the dark-skinned man said. "Do it. This is why my master brought you here. Kill him."

Dustin shut his eyes as Amanda raised her dagger.

*   *   *

Someone shoved Ricardo and his mind was jolted out of his servant and back into his own head. King Korlas had his hands on him and he was shaking him.

"What is going on?" Korlas demanded. "Why are you just standing there? Have my men captured Tim yet?"

The look Ricardo gave the king made Korlas take an involuntary step back. "Never do that to me again," Ricardo said softly.

"What were you doing?" the king asked again, this time more meekly.

"I was checking on the situation. But you interrupted me. Now leave me be so I can find out what is going on." Ricardo looked at the king until Korlas finally moved away from him, demanding answers from his guards.

Ricardo sent his mind out again, but this time he found nothing.

*   *   *

"No!" Brione yelled and rushed forward, knowing she would be too late to save Dustin.

With a yell Amanda thrust her knife down. At the last moment she turned and plunged it into the unsuspecting dark-skinned man's chest. Surprise and pain showed briefly on his face before he fell to the ground, dead.

Sobbing uncontrollably, she threw herself into Dustin and clung to him. "I am so sorry. I am so sorry," she repeated.

Surprised, Dustin looked back at his companions, but they stood there, dumbfounded. They were as confused as he was.

"I thought you were going to kill me," he said.

"I was, but then I saw you again and you looked so sad. I just couldn't do it. I realize now that I love you more than I hate you. And now when I look at you, all I feel is love. Can you ever forgive me?"

"Forgive you?" Brione said. She was furious. "You were going to kill him! Of course, he will never forgive you!"

"Be quiet Brione," Dustin said. He was looking at Amanda now. He had a small grin on his face.

"What are you doing?" Brione demanded. "Why are you smiling like that?"

Dustin kissed Amanda long and hard. "No!" said Brione. "You can't possibly forgive her!"

Amanda pulled away from Dustin and turned to the rest of the group. "I am so sorry for everything. I let my anger get the best of me. But I know now that I love Dustin and I don't want to lose him again. I did some pretty terrible things to you guys, so I will understand if you cannot forgive me for what I did."

"If Dustin can forgive you," said Aiden, "then so can I."

"Why, Dustin?" Brione asked.

"Because I never stopped loving her. I tried to, but I couldn't. And because now that my family is gone, she can be my new family. I can start all over with her."

"Well I don't forgive you," Brione told Amanda. "Not yet. And if you ever hurt him again, I will kill you." She turned away from Amanda, not wanting to even look at the woman.

"So, what do we do with Amanda now?" asked Tyler.

"What do to you mean?" Dustin asked.

"Well I doubt you want her storming the palace with us."

"That is right," Dustin said. He turned to Amanda. "You must leave the palace. What we are doing is very dangerous."

"No. I want to stay with you."

Dorn spoke up. "Dustin is right. Amanda could get killed. I don't know how useful I can be from now on. Why don't I take Amanda out of the palace to safety? We can wait for you guys with the rest of the girls by the north city gate."

"Okay," Dustin said. "That is a good idea." He looked at Amanda. "Go with Dorn. He will get you to safety and then I will come for you when we are finished. I promise I will not leave you again."

"Alright," she said. "I don't like it, but I will do it." She kissed Dustin again and started off with Dorn. "Wait!" she said and turned back to the group. "I was brought here by the dark-skinned man you found me with. His master, the King's advisor, is also dark-skinned. I know you have a man like them in your group. He is not your friend. Beware of him." Then Amanda and Dorn turned a corner and were out of sight.

"I can't believe you forgave her," Brione said.

"We have more important things to worry about," Dustin said. "If Zach and Jaden are working for our enemies, then that explains how they always seemed to know where we were. It also means that Tim and the girls are in danger."

"We have to go back," Aiden said. "Portia and my sister need our help. We have to protect them."

Aiden was around the corner before he realized no one was following him. He came back. "What are you waiting for? Let's go!"

"We can't just leave," Brione said. "What about your father? He is in danger as well and he needs us to do our part. We can't just leave him in the palace alone. He needs us."

"What do you think we should do?" Aiden asked.

"We should keep going," Brione replied. "We need to find the prince, get him out of the palace, and then we can help the girls. If Jaden doesn't know that we know he is a traitor, then maybe he won't hurt the girls. He hasn't tried to hurt any of us yet."

Aiden reluctantly agreed, and the group went deeper into the palace.

*   *   *

Ricardo was furious. What happened? When he tried to get back into his spy's head, he couldn't find him. Either he had also found the strength to block Ricardo out of his mind, or, more likely, he had been killed. Thanks to Korlas he had no idea what had happened.

He rounded on the king. It took all he had not to blast the king with a fireball and obliterate him then and there. But no. He had to be patient. He would destroy the king, but he had to wait for the right time. There was still one more spy in the palace. He sent his mind out to find Zach.

42

Tim and Zach had not run into any resistance since they separated from the rest of the group. Tim hoped the others were having the same luck. They moved through endless empty corridors without ever stumbling upon a single servant, which Tim thought was very odd.

Finally, they left the servants' passages and found themselves in a large, open room. There were doorways on either side of the room. Small tables lined the walls, each one holding an elaborate decoration. A huge red carpet with intricate designs covered most of the floor. Tapestries hung on the walls. Some were solid colors, some had scenes, but all looked to be well made and expensive.

The two companions walked further into the room. When they reached the center, soldiers began pouring out of both doorways. At least twenty men were in front and in back of them. They were surrounded.

"Forty men is a lot," Tim said to Zach. "But we need to get through them."

Zach stepped in front of Tim and turned to face him. "No. This is where your journey ends."

"What are you doing?" Tim asked in surprise.

"My master bids me to stop you here."

"Your master?" Understanding registered. "You are the spy! You told Korlas where we were! That is how they always found us!"

"Korlas?" Zach laughed. "I do not work for Korlas. My master is greater than the king. No, my master is the great wizard Ricardo. And he bids me to stop you here."

"It is your fault that Layne is dead. You told our enemies where we were, and they killed Layne."

"I guess you are right."

"I am going to kill you for that."

Zach laughed again. "I have longed for this since the beginning. You are the only opponent worthy to face me in your pathetic little mercenary band. But I have studied you and watched you fight. You have no chance of defeating me."

"I disagree. I will kill you. Even if I win, these men will probably kill me. But that is alright. I will have given Layne justice."

Zach drew his swords. Despite what he said, Tim knew that he had little chance in winning this fight. He would have to be at his very best to have a chance. Anger assaulted his senses. He knew it was a mistake to fight angry, but he couldn't help it. Rage filled him at what Zach had done. His betrayal was horrific, because it had cost Layne his life.

Tim went at Zach with a furry he had never known. The dark-skinned fighter was taken by surprise and was immediately losing ground. Even though Tim only had one sword, it was all Zach could do to parry his attacks. Tim had never fought with such speed before, and he knew he would tire eventually. He needed to end this battle quickly.

Zach's smaller swords deftly blocked Tim's larger one. Despite the speed and furry of Tim's attacks, he found no opening. His opponent was too skilled. In a flash Tim dropped into a crouch, then swung his leg around into Zach's ankles. Zach was taken completely by surprise, and he fell to the ground. Tim was up instantly, and he stabbed down at Zach. But Zach was too fast. He rolled out of the way and was on his feet immediately.

"You are full of surprises, Tim. Perhaps this will be a better fight than I had thought."

Zach went on the offensive now. His swords were a blur. But rage and adrenaline filled Tim, and he blocked every swing, dodged every thrust. At first Tim held his ground, but slowly he started to tire, taking one step back and then another.

Zach's attacks were still not getting through Tim's defenses. Tim could see the frustration on his enemy's face. Zach swept his leg out, trying to trip Tim, but Tim's training saved him. Even though he had been giving ground, every step was deliberate and solid. Zach's foot hit Tim's ankle, but the mercenary didn't budge. His feet were planted too firmly. Suddenly, he kicked out and his foot connected with Zach's gut. With a grunt, the dark-skinned man stepped back a few paces.

"You might have more speed and natural skill than me," Tim said. "But I am better trained and more experienced. You will die today for what you have done."

With a frustrated cry Zach came on again. Zach's attacks came even faster this time. Tim hadn't thought that was possible. He quickly gave ground this time, and he was barely blocking Zach's blows. The frustration on Zach's face changed to determination. He could feel his victory was close. It was Tim's turn to cry out in frustration.

He tried to trip Zach up again, but this time his enemy was expecting it. He deftly hopped over Tim's leg. Then, as he landed, he swung down with his sword, slashing Tim's leg before he could complete his sweep.

Tim was upright immediately, but his leg ached, and he couldn't put his full weight on it. *That was stupid,* he thought. *I should have known that wouldn't work twice.*

"You are finished, Tim. Yield to me now and it will be easier for you."

"Never." Tim took a step forward, and although pain shot up his leg, he stayed upright. He refused to let his leg cause his defeat.

He attacked Zach again, but this time he could see that Zach had no trouble blocking his attacks.

"Are you getting tired, Tim?"

With a grunt Tim kept up his attack. His body was tiring, but he could not afford to let up. Normally he would still feel strong, but his furry at the beginning of the fight had quickly drained his strength. He couldn't beat Zach this way. He had to fight smarter.

Tim continued swinging his sword, but he stopped going for Zach's body. He now aimed for his hands, confusing Zach. He didn't understand what Tim was doing.

Tim's sword sliced one of Zach's hands. Zach cried out in pain and dropped his sword. Quickly, Tim kicked it out of the way.

"Very smart," Zach said. "Although you must be getting desperate to try such a move."

"You talk too much." Tim attacked again. Zach was not used to fighting with just one sword, and so Tim quickly gained the advantage. Somewhere deep down Tim found an extra surge of strength and his attacks quickened. Zach missed a block and Tim sliced his arm. Unfortunately, it was not his sword arm. Tim's blows were powerful and he knocked Zach's sword wide. Tim stabbed forward, but Zach was able to spin out of the way. Zach countered with a horizontal swing at Tim's midsection, and he was barely able to lunge backward out of the sword's reach.

Unbeknownst to Tim, one of the soldiers behind him kicked Zach's fallen sword. It skidded across the ground toward the combatants and entangled itself in Tim's legs. Tim couldn't keep his balance and he fell.

He was able to quickly get to his knees before Zach came in. It was all he could do to block Zach's furious attacks. Zach slashed Tim's hand, causing him to let go of the hilt with his left hand. Now, one handed, Tim found it harder to parry Zach's attacks. Suddenly his sword went flying out of his right hand and Zach's boot connected with his head. He went down and he felt Zach's sword pressed up against his neck.

"What are you waiting for?" Tim asked. "Just kill me."

Zach took the sword away. "No. My master does not want me to kill you. I am to take you into custody and bring you before the king."

He motioned for the guards to grab Tim. They hoisted him up and they started escorting him away.

"I have more respect for you now than I did before," Zach told him. "Maybe we will get a chance to fight again one day. Hopefully, it will be to the death.

*   *   *

Aiden was distracted. He couldn't help but worry about Veronna and Portia. Then he thought about his dad being alone with Zach. *Could dad beat Zach in a fight?* he wondered. He didn't know. Now he was worried about his dad too.

They entered a long chamber that was slightly wider than the corridors they had been traveling through. The ceiling was very high. At the far end of the corridor a dozen soldiers stood, barring their way forward. In front of the soldiers stood a woman.

"Stop right there," the woman said.

"Be careful," Tyler said. "A lone woman standing in front of armed men can only be a wizard."

"You can go no further," the woman said. "Surrender yourselves now and come peacefully."

"I don't think so," said Brione. She charged, the others right behind her. Suddenly a great wind came and held them in place. Then they were all picked up off the ground. They twirled around in the air like they were in a tornado.

"Drop your weapons and surrender," the wizard said again.

"Maybe we should do what she says," Tyler said. "There is air everywhere, so she can do her magic anywhere, unlike me. We don't stand a chance."

"Alright," Brione said. "We surrender!"

Suddenly the wind stopped and the group fell heavily to the ground. They stood up and threw their weapons to the floor.

"Pick up their weapons," the woman said. Several men moved to do so. "The pale one is a necromancer," the woman continued. "If any of you start feeling anything odd, say something. We will immediately kill him. Now, bind their hands and bring them."

*   *   *

Tim's capturers threw him roughly to the ground. Defiantly, he immediately stood up. He looked up at the throne and saw King Korlas glaring at him. "Hello Jeff."

"Don't call me that!"

"That is your name, isn't it?"

"That was my name," Korlas said. "But not anymore. I threw it away when I became my Dark God's chosen one. Now I am Korlas, prophet of the Dark God and instrument of his will. Welcome to my palace, Timmond. What do you think of it?"

"Your presence here ruins its beauty."

Korlas ignored the remark. "You have been a thorn in my side ever since you accepted this job from the queen."

"Good. Then the journey has been worth it."

"Enough!" Korlas shouted. "Enough of your insolence. You are in a dire predicament my old friend. I would watch your tongue if I were you."

"Why should I? You are going to kill me anyway, aren't you?"

"I haven't decided what I am going to do to you yet. Perhaps I will kill you. Or perhaps I will make you watch me kill your children first. I know where they are, and I can get them anytime I want."

"Why?" asked Tim. "Why do you hate me so? I never did anything to you."

It took a while for the king to answer. "Because you were always better than me."

"So?"

"You beat me at everything! Everyone knew! You humiliated me too many times, Timmond!"

"Humiliated? I never humiliated you."

"You humiliated me every day! You humiliated me just by being you!"

"I had no idea you felt that way," Tim said honestly.

"I knew I would never be better than you. I prayed and prayed that God would make me better than you. But he never answered that prayer. So, one day I left and found a god that did answer my prayer. And now look at us, Timmond. Here I am, a king, and here you are, a prisoner. Oh, how the tables have turned! I am finally better than you. Now I have power. True power. Allow me to demonstrate."

Suddenly, terrible pain enveloped Tim. He fell to the ground, but the pain was too great to allow him to cry out. He thought every bone in his body would break. He felt like he was about to be ripped in two. Just before consciousness left him, the pain stopped.

"Can you do that, Tim?"

"I would not want to," Tim said. He struggled back to his feet. And it was a struggle. "You have become powerful. But it has come with a price. You have become evil. Is it worth it?"

"Of course! Power is what I have always craved. I am now the best, and everyone knows it."

"Pride?" Tim asked. "You sold your soul for pride? No one ever cared if I was better than you. It was not a competition, Jeff."

"Don't call me that!" The pain retuned. This time it was worse. Consciousness quickly left him.

*   *   *

Aiden and the others were herded into the throne room. The first thing Aiden noticed was his father's body lying motionless on the ground. He rushed to his father's body. No one stopped him.

"What did you do to him?" he demanded. "Is he dead?"

"No," Korlas answered. "He is not dead. But I bet he wishes he were."

Aiden jumped to his feet and rushed King Korlas, but the soldiers who had escorted him were quicker. They seized him before he had taken two steps and bullied him to the ground. He struggled for a moment but quickly realized it was futile.

Tim moaned and opened his eyes. When he saw Aiden being held down by three men his eyes widened. "Aiden!"

Then a man with skin as black as Zach's and Jaden's stepped forward. He was wearing robes. "What happened to Faekus!" he demanded of Dustin.

"I don't know who you are talking about," Dustin said.

"The man who was with Amanda. Where is he?"

"Amanda killed him," Brione said with a forced smile. "One of your mighty warriors was killed by a slip of a girl with no fighting experience."

With a cry Ricardo extended his hand and Brione was lifted off her feet and flung back into the wall. She fell to the floor in a heap.

"That is enough, Ricardo," the king said. "I don't want her killed. I have plans for her. For all of them."

Just then Aiden noticed Zach standing near the far wall. "You!" he yelled, struggling to free himself again. "You did this to him!"

"No," explained the king. "I did this to him. Your father, the famous Timmond, greatest of all Paladins when he was one, was defeated by Zach and brought to me. I did that to him. It was my power that left the mighty Timmond unconscious on the floor. It was me!"

"And what are you going to do now?" asked Tim. Once again, he struggled to his feet, although he stumbled once before he made it up. "Are you going to kill us all?"

"No," said Korlas with a grin. "I am going to do something worse. You Timmond, I will put in a dungeon for the rest of your life. It will be up to your son as to how long that life will be."

"What do you mean?" asked Aiden.

"You will work for me," Korlas said.

"Never!" cried Aiden. "I will never work for you!"

"Oh, I think you will change your mind after you hear what I have to say. You see, if you don't work for me, I will kill your father and then your entire group."

"Aiden don't!" said Tim. "It's not worth it!"

Aiden turned to his father. "It's not worth your life?" he asked.

"Think of all the evil things he will make you do. I would rather die than know that you are being forced to do those things. Please, don't."

"I don't know what to do," Aiden said.

Brione groaned and used the wall to get to her feet. Wyst hurried to steady her.

"As added insurance," Korlas said, "I will have Zach accompany you. If you or anyone in your group decide to rebel, he has orders to kill you. He will report to me everything that happens. Don't even try to betray me. And, if by some miracle you manage to kill Zach, I will kill your father."

"Aiden, don't," Tim pleaded.

"I already lost my mother," Aiden said. "I could not bear to lose you, too."

"Excellent!" Korlas said happily. "It is settled then. Now, you will want to acquire accommodations for your group. But don't go too far. I will send for you shortly."

The guards cut their bonds. With one last look at his dad and without another word, Aiden turned and left the throne room, the rest of the group and Zach following quickly behind.

EPILOGUE

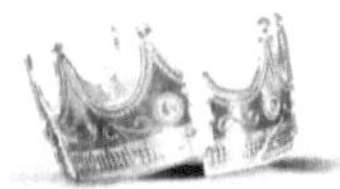

Veronna held her breath as she watched the huge wolf sniff each of them. She felt fear, yet excitement at the same time. Portia gasped when the wolf came to her. Princess Dana inhaled loudly and moved her head back. The wolf didn't spend very much time with either of them, before moving towards Veronna.

The wolf sniffed her repeatedly, lingering on her much longer than with the other two. It was so close that she could feel its breath on her face. Then it circled her once and looked at the tall man.

"He says that you have an affinity with the forest and all living creatures," he said to Veronna. His voice was low and gruff. "He thinks you would make a good Druid. Our numbers are dwindling. Would you like to become one?"

Veronna was shocked. That was the last thing had expected to hear. "Me?"

"Yes. You."

Veronna thought about Layne, and how he had died defending her. She thought about how helpless she had been when the sword punctured her friend's throat. She thought about that same thing happening to the other members of the group, and it made her sick to her stomach. She would not be helpless anymore. She would protect her family! She couldn't help but smile. "Yes."